"IS THE DOOR LOCKED?"

asked Cord. Jaime nodded.

The spark so easily ignited erupted into raging, hot, licking flames of passion that would not, could not be denied. He stretched out beside her to pull her almost roughly into his arms. "Tonight," he avowed raggedly, "I'll be a savage, my dearest, because I want you as I've never wanted a woman before."

But Jaime longed not for a moment, not for a night, but for always and ever.

Unable to speak the longing of her heart, she could only show him with her body how much she cared.

Orchids in Moonlight

 PATRICIA HAGAN

HarperPaperbacks
A Division of HarperCollinsPublishers

This is a work of fiction. The characters, incidents, and dialogues are products of the author's imagination and are not to be construed as real. Any resemblance to actual events or persons, living or dead, is entirely coincidental.

HarperPaperbacks   *A Division of* HarperCollins*Publishers*
10 East 53rd Street, New York, N.Y. 10022

Cover illustration by Roger Kastel

First printing: November 1993

Printed in the United States of America

HarperPaperbacks, HarperMonogram, and colophon are trademarks of HarperCollins*Publishers*

❖ 10 9 8 7 6 5 4 3 2 1

"I'll come to thee by moonlight,
though hell should bar the way."

The Highwayman
Alfred Noyes
(1880–1958)

1

Jaime moved as fast as she dared, trying not to make any noise as she tiptoed from her room in the basement and climbed the stairs.

A glance at the case clock in the hall reminded her that she had drastically overslept, but it had been nearly two in the morning when she had finally completed her chores. Last night, her aunt had suddenly announced she wanted the best table linens freshly washed and pressed and all the good silver polished.

Between her early morning and late-night chores at the boardinghouse, and every day except Sunday spent toiling at Frank Casey's laundry, Jaime was always tired. And last night's ordeal had truly taken its toll.

She went to the back porch for the milk and eggs left by the dairyman, and the sight of overcast skies provoked a frown. Another day of heavy spring showers was in store, which meant a long walk to work in the rain.

Still sleepy, she was straining to focus her eyes to mea-sure coffee into the pot when her aunt's sharp cry startled her, causing her to spill ground beans all over the floor.

"Oh, Jaime, you're late again. They'll be coming down soon, and you haven't even got the coffee boiling. What am I going to do with you? And look at the mess you've made."

"I'm sorry. I'll clean it up later." Jaime rushed to the stove to start the fire. "I was so tired I overslept. But don't worry. I'll hurry. I have to. If I'm late to work, Mr. Casey will make me stay late to catch up, and—"

"And that better not happen." Arista Porter shook her finger in warning. "I'm having a little party after dinner tonight, and you'll need to do some baking as soon as you get home. Everything has to be special."

"I'll do my best, I promise." So Aunt Arista was going to start socializing. Jaime was glad. After all, her aunt had experienced much grief, and even though she could be terribly mean sometimes, Jaime felt she deserved some happiness.

Arista glared at her through tiny round spectacles. "You should be anxious to help me as much as you can. After all, if not for me, you would've been living in an orphanage all these years. That no-good father of yours certainly hasn't provided for you, so the least you can do is help out around here."

"Yes ma'am." Jaime determined she would manage somehow. As it was, she would not have time to eat breakfast herself, if she was going to make it to work on time. On days like this she envied Ella and Hannah, her co-workers. Mr. Casey let them live in a room above the laundry, and they did not have to venture out in foul weather. They could also sleep till just before time to report for work.

Arista went on. "It's a shame you had to inherit all your mother's bad traits. There's no denying she was pretty, but you, you're so dowdy no man wants to even look at you, much less marry you."

Jaime bit her lip, determined not to yield to the tears burning her eyes. After all, her aunt had been telling her for years how unattractive she was. The only dresses Jaime had were plain and made of gray muslin, even for Sunday. She had never owned a brightly colored gown, not that she'd ever been to a party or a ball anyway. And her hair had to be skinned back tightly and twisted into a bun, which made her look as old as the Rupert sisters, Ida and Inez, sour-faced spinsters who lived in the nicest rooms in the house and whined and complained about everything.

Her hand instinctively went to her breasts, uncomfortably bound with wide strips of cloth to mash them flat beneath her clothes. There were two rooms on the first floor rented only to men, and her aunt had declared she'd not have Jaime's large bosom dangling in their faces as she served them at the table.

"I even had a tutor come in and teach you to read and write, but you don't appreciate anything I've done—"

Arista fell momentarily silent at the sound of footsteps coming down the stairs, then cried, "They're coming! Hurry up, you hear me?" Snatching the coffeepot from the fire, she started out of the room, then paused to say, "At least I won't have to put up with your surly, thankless disposition much longer."

Jaime stared after her, wondering what she was talking about, then felt a sudden flare of hope. Maybe there had finally been a letter from her father, and her aunt was holding it back just to be mean.

It had been nearly a year since her father had written excitedly from California that he had found gold in the Cascade Mountains north of San Francisco. He had made other finds in the past, small discoveries that eventually petered out. But this was his first real strike, and he firmly believed the rich mother lode was located somewhere on the claim he had staked. The problem was, however, that he lacked funds to hire workers and buy the equipment for the hard-rock and deep-pit mining needed to find it. He'd had to settle for placer mining, which meant panning and sluicing on the surface of the ground only, eking out flakes and dust, enough to keep him going. The belief that a fortune waited below, if he could only get to it, had been driving him crazy.

Then he had gone on to explain that he believed he had found a way to get the money to work his strike. A man in San Francisco by the name of Stanton Lavelle was selling interests in a mine near a town called Placerville. James did not have sufficient money to buy into it, but Lavelle agreed, after looking at ore samples, to take an interest in James's strike instead of cash. Then James hoped to use the money he earned from the Placerville investment to persuade Lavelle to sell back his share in James's strike.

However, James had proudly confided to Jaime, he was no fool. He knew some men were so unscrupulous as to salt their mines to lure investors. When no gold was found, those who had staked the diggings were cheated out of their money, while the mine owner, of course, made a nice profit. Therefore, to protect himself, he had given Lavelle a map to one of his old—worthless—digging sites. If Lavelle's investment proved sound, there was nothing to worry about. If not, James would lose nothing and Jaime had the map which provided her own claim should anything happen to him.

Her aunt had reiterated her belief that James Chandler was a fool and a failure and predicted nothing would ever come of either his own strike or his investment in yet another foolish venture.

Jaime, however, hid the letter and the map in the family Bible that had belonged to her mother and prayed nightly that one day soon her dream, and her father's, would come true.

When Arista returned to the kitchen nearly ten minutes later, Jaime was surprised to notice how excited she seemed, with eyes shining and cheeks glowing. There was even a breathless lilt to her voice as she ordered, "Fry two eggs for Mr. Slawson. He doesn't want scrambled this morning."

Jaime gestured to the skillet she had just finished scrubbing. "I'll be glad to, but I've already cleaned up, and it will make me that much later getting to work."

Arista gave an airy wave. "Oh, never mind. I'll do it myself. Just make sure you come straight home this afternoon."

Jaime knew there was no time to spare but paused to ask, "Aunt Arista, are you keeping a letter from me?"

"Don't be ridiculous."

"I've just got a feeling there's been word from my father."

Arista shook her head in disgust. "I don't know what you're talking about. There's been no letter from that crazy father of yours in almost a year. It's not likely you'll ever hear from him again. He's probably drunk in some bawdy house, if he's still alive."

"But something is going on. You're acting strange. If he has sent money for me to go to California, I want it, Aunt Arista, because I want to go to him."

"Don't be ridiculous. If you only knew how I've prayed all these years he *would* send for you. If I'd had my way, you would've stayed out there with him and never come back here to cause me such grief, but no, Cyrus wouldn't leave without you. Heaven knows, I certainly didn't want you around all this time to remind me of what your mother made me lose. It's going to be a relief not to be worried with you in the future."

"Aunt Arista, please tell me what's going on." She was going to have to run all the way to work, even if it was pouring rain.

Arista giggled like a child. "Oh, all right. I was going to wait till tonight, at the party, to make a formal announcement.

"Mr. Slawson"—she paused to enjoy her moment of glory—"has asked me to marry him. We'll be moving down south. He says there's lots of construction work there, now that the war is over, and he wants to open his own lumber company."

Jaime was stunned. She had wanted her aunt to start getting out when her year of mourning ended, of

course, but to realize she was about to remarry—
well, that came as quite a shock. In the few months
or so Mr. Slawson had been boarding with them, she
had not noticed him showing any particular interest
in her aunt.

Besides, Jaime couldn't help but wonder how all
this was going to affect her personally.

She did not have long to wonder.

"I've sold the house—"

"Sold the house?" Jaime echoed. "But when Uncle
Cyrus got killed, you were terrified at the thought of
losing it. That's why you started taking in boarders
and told me to find outside work to help. Are you
sure this is what you want to do?" Jaime hoped her
aunt was not making a terrible mistake.

"I need a man to take care of me, and Mr. Slawson
will do that quite nicely. The money from the sale
will start him in business. He expects to be rich in no
time at all."

Hearing that, Jaime was sure she knew the real
reason for his proposal but did not dare say so.
Instead, she asked about the new owner.

"The Rupert sisters. I never dreamed they had any
money tucked away, but they obviously do. They
even said you could stay on and work for them. You
should be grateful, because Mr. Slawson agrees with
me I've done my duty by you, so you won't be going
with us. Now get along. But remember, I want everything to be special tonight. I've invited friends I
haven't seen in ages.

"I think some of those little butter tea cakes would
be nice," she went on to say. "The ones with the candy

roses. And maybe some chocolate cookies. Mr. Slawson loves chocolate. Do we have enough sugar?"

There was no answer. Arista looked around to find herself alone.

Jaime had quietly let herself out and begun walking in the steady, misting rain.

She had no idea what she was going to do, but she was certain of one thing—she was not going to slave for the Rupert sisters. Maybe she was unattractive and plain and doomed to be a spinster, but never, ever, would she allow herself to become as mean and cynical as those two old women.

She stomped through mud puddles, oblivious to the cold, dark water soaking the hem of her dress.

It wasn't fair, any of it. She loved her father deeply and yearned for them to be reunited. If only he would send for her, all her problems would vanish.

"You're late," Ella admonished gently when Jaime walked through the back door. Then, seeing she was drenched, she cried, "You can't work like that. You'll have to borrow something of mine. Come along, hurry."

Doggedly, Jaime followed her up the dark, narrow stairway to the tiny boxlike room Ella shared with Hannah. The furnishings were sparse: two narrow beds and a tiny table and chairs. But to Jaime, it was heaven, because once the workday ended, Ella and Hannah were free to do as they pleased.

Still lost in misery, she began to take off her clothes, forgetting about the binding cloth across her chest. When Ella saw it, she pointed. "What's that? A bandage?"

Jaime snatched up the wet garment she'd just removed to cover herself and began to babble nervously. "It's nothing. I can't afford a chemise, that's all, and —"

"That's *not* all." Ella walked over and pulled the dress away. "Your aunt made you do this, didn't she?"

Knowing it was useless to lie, Jaime attempted to explain. "She says it's not proper for me to work around her gentleman boarders without the binding, because my breasts are so large."

Ella exploded. "The old witch. You're crazy to let her make you do something so awful to your own body. Why is she so mean to you, Jaime?"

"She's not so bad," Jaime said.

"But why does she treat you like she does?"

Jaime dared confide in someone for the first time ever. "She blames my mother for the death of her sons and takes it out on me. I tell myself she just can't help it."

Ella's eyes widened. She sat down on the bed, gesturing to Jaime to sit opposite. "I don't care how mad Mr. Casey gets. I want to hear this. Go on."

So Jaime told the story, as best she could remember. Her aunt never talked about it, but Uncle Cyrus used to reminisce, once in a while. He would explain how it was back in 1849, when the East was electrified by news that gold nuggets were lying loose on the ground of the land newly wrested from Mexico. "Argonauts," as they were called, headed west by the thousands. In California, it was said, a fortune could be made in the hills and streams with hardly more equipment than a shovel and a tin pan. So thousands of men abandoned farms and jobs, and those who could not persuade their families to go along deserted them, as well.

Jaime's father wanted to make the trip, and he finally persuaded her mother to go with him and take Jaime too. Not about to see his beloved sister strike off for California without him, Cyrus badgered Arista till she agreed they and their two sons would join them.

"They made a few strikes, enough to keep us from starving," Jaime said, "but things were awfully bad those four years. Then my mother came down with a fever, and so did my cousins, and they all died. Aunt Arista was expecting another baby, and she told Uncle Cyrus if he didn't take her home she'd leave him. He talked my father into letting me go with them. I haven't seen my father since, but through the years he's written, sending what money he had and promising to come for me when he could.

"It's been a long time since the last letter, though, and my aunt says I'll probably never hear from him again," she concluded wistfully.

Ella reached to clasp Jaime's hands and attempted to cheer her. "Yes, you will. Don't pay any attention to her. But you still haven't told me why she blames your mother for her sons dying."

"Uncle Cyrus told me once how Aunt Arista was always jealous of how close he and my mother were. She said if it hadn't been for that, he'd never have wanted to go to California, and if they hadn't gone, the boys would still be alive.

"What's also sad," Jaime continued, "was how on the trip back here Aunt Arista lost the baby she was carrying and nearly died. The doctor told her she'd never be able to have another, and she blamed that on my mother too. And since she didn't have my mother to take out her resentment on all these years, she used me instead. It wasn't so bad when my uncle was alive. He only let her go so far."

"And now he's gone, and you're stuck with her."

Jaime shook her head and said dully, "Not for long," and proceeded to confide the present situation.

Furious, Ella cried, "So now she's marrying somebody else before your uncle is even cold in the ground and going off to leave you to fend for yourself."

In a gesture of bravery she did not truly feel, Jaime lifted her chin, forcing a smile as she declared optimistically, "I'll be all right. Maybe my father will send for me."

"And if he doesn't?"

Jaime struggled to keep smiling. "Like I said, I'll be all right."

Ella was silent, thoughtful for a moment, then said mysteriously, "Maybe this came at a good time, because there's something Hannah and I have been wanting to tell you but didn't know how."

For a while now Jaime had been fearing the only two friends she had would move somewhere else. They were both orphans. Hannah, seventeen, had been made a widow by the war, and Ella, sixteen, had lost her fiancé. It was only logical that they would eventually make new lives for themselves.

"Are you going away?" Jaime asked, dreading to hear the answer.

"We want to. Maybe you can go with us. Tell me, would you like to go to California to find your father instead of waiting for him to send for you?"

"Well, I guess so," Jaime replied uncertainly.

"Would you be willing to do just about anything to get there?"

"I haven't really thought about it, but I probably would."

Ella's lips curved in a mysterious smile. "Even to get married? Hannah and I have decided that's what we're going to do. Miners and other men out there are desperate to find wives willing to settle so far from home, so women are being recruited. Me and Hannah have both lived here in Missouri all our lives, and the idea of new territory, new experiences sounds so exciting we can't resist. So we've decided to sign up and join a wagon train and head out there.

"Besides," she added with a touch of sadness in her voice. "It doesn't matter who we marry now, because I'll never love anybody but Billy, and Hannah feels the same about Loland."

Jaime said doubtfully, "Well, I can understand how you both feel, but I'm not sure I could do it."

"Come on," Ella urged, "I thought you were willing to do anything to get to California."

"But marriage? To someone I don't love? A stranger?" She had heard how men out West were willing to buy a wife, due to the shortage of women

there, but she had never considered selling herself
that way for any reason.

"It would only be till you got there. Then you
could just slip away and go find your father. Do you
even know where to start looking?"

"I know where he mailed his last letter from, and I
know the name of the man he was going to do business with. He said the man was rich and prominent,
so I don't guess I'd have any trouble finding him.
But . . ." She fell silent for a moment, then shook her
head. "I just couldn't do that. I couldn't marry a man,
take his money, let him pay my way out there, and
then not show up. It wouldn't be right."

"Listen, those men have so much gold they can
afford it, but can *you* afford *not* to? Can you afford
to stay here and waste your whole life slaving for
those two old women?"

"But to deliberately swindle somebody, Ella? It's
not right."

"Oh, you can make sure he gets his money's worth
by the time you get out there. It's no more than what
he'd pay for a prostitute, probably. Believe me,
there's no reason to feel guilty about it. It probably
happens all the time."

"Wait a minute," Jaime said. "I thought the marriage took place in California, that the men out there
send for wives to meet them there. What's this about
him getting his money's worth *before* I get out there?
I'm confused."

"Listen, this is different. I heard just last night
there's a man right here in Kansas City who's come
all the way from the goldfields to find himself a wife.

His name is Austin, and he's staying at Dewar's Hotel, near the river."

She rushed to explain. "To be honest, I thought about going to see him myself. I swear, I've got to get out of here and start a new life somewhere else, before I go crazy. Too many things remind me of Billy and all the dreams we had. But Hannah and I vowed to stay together and try to marry brothers or mining partners, so we can live close to each other. I wasn't about to abandon her and go see that man at the hotel.

"But *you* can do it, Jaime." Ella suddenly exploded with her enthusiasm. "Go see him and tell him you'll marry him. What if it is sort of like being a prostitute? If it gets you to California so you can find your father, what difference does it make? You can forget it ever happened, pretend you were never married. Who's to know?"

Jaime gave a bitter laugh. "What makes you think he'd have me?"

"You're pretty, despite those drab clothes your aunt makes you wear. As for me and Hannah, our future husbands won't see us till we get there, and then they're stuck with us. Besides, we're also getting a pig in the poke, as the saying goes, 'cause we don't know what they look like either."

With an impish grin, Ella pulled a strand of Jaime's hair from her tightly wound bun and declared, "Look. It's even the color of gold. I think it's an omen. I think you were meant to go to California."

Jaime shivered. "I don't know. It's scary."

"With you in a fancy dress, that man will jump at the chance to marry you."

Jaime was starting to feel sick to her stomach. "But I don't think I could stand having a man touch me if I didn't love him."

Ella couldn't resist laughing. "You wouldn't even know how a man touches a woman if Hannah hadn't told you about her and Loland. And it didn't sound so terrible. Not to me, anyway."

"It was different for you. You were in love with Billy. You wouldn't have cared what he did to you."

Ella released her hands and placed them on her shoulders. "Listen to me. When you go to bed with him, just close your eyes and pretend it's not happening. Six months from now, you'll be in California with your father, and you won't ever have to look back. Go see Mr. Austin. Tonight."

Things were happening too fast. Jaime did not feel she could make such an important decision so quickly.

Ella sensed her thoughts. "There's not much time. There's only one more wagon train leaving Independence this spring."

Jaime didn't speak.

"Me and Hannah are going, if they'll let us sign on as brides for California. We're going to see about it tomorrow."

Jaime knew she meant it.

And she also knew there was no one she could turn to once they left.

2

Cord Austin downed the last of his whiskey. Leaning back in his chair, he yawned and stretched his muscular arms skyward. His fringed buckskin shirt strained across a broad, rock-hard chest.

Sitting opposite, swallowed within a blue haze of smoke, Pete Rowland also tossed down his drink. Beads of perspiration stood out on his furrowed brow as he gestured impatiently and snapped, "Well, get on with it, Austin."

Cord looked at his stack of poker chips, which had grown steadily through the night. Pete had lost his stake and for the past hour had been running up quite a debt. Cord knew a man didn't like to quit when he was losing, but the way things were going, Pete's luck wasn't likely to change, and it was nearly two in the morning.

Cord was holding a flush, ace high, and figured Pete was betting on three of a kind. He decided to go easy on him. "I'll stand."

Pete's face lit up in a triumphant grin, confident, at last, he had a winning hand, since Cord had not previously failed to ante up when he held the better cards. "Well, I'm gonna raise you fifty."

Cord suppressed a groan. He didn't want to take any more of his money, but Pete was too stubborn to realize it. "Listen, you're already down to me nearly a thousand, Rowland. Call this hand, and let's quit."

Pete's grin changed to an angry grimace. "Hell, no. I ain't lettin' you do that. When it's my turn, I call if I want to, and we'll quit when I say. That's the code when a man is down. You got to give him a chance to win his money back."

The crowd of onlookers shifted uncomfortably. They knew little about Cord Austin, only that he had arrived in Kansas City a few days earlier and was said to be involved somehow with the next California-bound wagon train out of Independence. Some guessed he was a hired gun; others figured him to be a scout. Nobody knew for sure what his business was, but everyone agreed there was something about him that warned them to keep out of it. However, watching the marathon poker game between him and Pete had been too good to pass up, because Pete played for high stakes and seldom lost.

Cord's eyes narrowed. Instinctively, he knew Pete was the sort whose temper would get him killed one day—but not today, if Cord could avoid it. Long ago, he had promised himself when he sent a man to glory it would be for a more important reason than an argument over a card game.

With a resigned nod of assent, he flipped a few chips to the center of the table. "Call."

He fanned out his cards, exposing his hand.

Laughter exploded as everyone realized not only that Pete had lost another hand but this time Austin had tried to go easy on him, only Pete had been too dumb to know it.

Pete locked eyes with Cord. For one frozen instant, Pete was tempted to accuse him of cheating, but he knew Cord hadn't been and decided not to risk a gunfight. Something told him the stranger's luck wasn't limited to cards. Finally, he conceded. "Well, looks like tonight's your night."

The sudden cloak of tension had silenced the laughter of the crowd, and they had begun to back away from the table. Now a few men exchanged relieved glances.

"You say I owe you a thousand?"

Cord nodded. "Any time in the next few days will be all right." He stood.

Pete held up a hand, the play of a mysterious smile on his lips. "Wait a minute. Maybe we can make a deal."

"Deals are what got you in debt," Cord reminded with a crooked grin.

Pete again bit back his rising temper. "I hear you just come from out west. I'll bet you're tired of ruttin' with squaws. How would you like to bed down with a real woman? Five hundred off my debt will give you the wildest night you ever had." He looked to the others to back him up. "Tell him, boys. Francie is the sweetest little piece of woman flesh in these parts. A real tiger. Worth every bit of five hundred, ain't she?"

One of them cracked, "Hell, ain't none of us ever been able to afford her, but if you say she's worth it, she probably is."

Pete winked. "She's worth it."

Cord shoved his chair under the table and said with finality, "I'm not interested."

He turned and walked out of the saloon and into the hotel lobby. The desk clerk was nowhere around, and he decided any messages could wait till morning. Heading for the stairs, he could feel Pete Rowland's angry glare following him.

Once in his room, he fired up the lantern, then stripped off the buckskin shirt. It was a warm night, and he opened the window wide before pouring himself one last drink from the bottle on the bedside table.

He had been too busy since arriving from California for pleasures of the flesh, but he didn't figure any woman was worth five hundred dollars.

Staring out on the shadowed, deserted street, Cord thought about the rough journey ahead. He was none too excited about herding a bunch of females all the way across the country, but he was being well paid for the trouble. Unmarried women were real scarce in California, and the man paying him kept his workmen happy by providing either wives or whores.

Wives.

Cord's soft chuckle broke the stillness of the night around him. He figured the only thing worse for a man than marriage itself was getting tied up legal to a woman he hadn't met or laid eyes on till their wedding day. The men he was delivering to, however, had different ideas. A firm-feeling woman they could touch in the night, hot cooked meals, a clean hut or cabin, and somebody to bear their children, that's all they cared about.

Love played no part in it.

Not that Cord gave a damn about love anyway. That's what had killed his father, leaving Cord an orphan, which led to his being abducted and raised by Apaches.

Bile rose in his throat at the memory.

Like so many others, Matthew Austin had taken his family and joined the mad rush to California to "see the elephant," which meant a man was heading for the goldfields. Cord was only six years old at the time, but every detail of that ill-fated journey was branded on his soul.

Because they never made it.

Halfway across Arizona, his mother had suddenly become ill and died. His father refused to continue, saying he was going to take her body back east for burial. The others in the wagon train went on without them.

Two weeks later, after following the trail in a near-constant drunken stupor, Matthew went to sleep one night and just didn't wake up. Cord, alone and terrified, could do nothing but sit beside his parents' bodies and watch the vultures circling overhead.

He was near death himself when the Apaches found him. He could remember, with revulsion, how they had stripped his parents' bodies. Then, with him kicking and screaming, fighting hopelessly with all his might, they took him along with the wagon and horses.

Thus had begun his life with the Apaches.

But despite these bad memories, Cord knew he had

come out of the experience a better man. During the war, he'd worked as a scout, due to his knowledge of wilderness survival, and there were several times he would have been killed except for what the Indians had taught him. But never, during those terrible years of his youth, did Cord ever forget he was white, and he dreamed of returning to his people.

Rescue came just before he was to endure the test to become a warrior, the year he turned twelve. He was following a group of braves out hunting, with orders to clean and carry back anything they killed, when their party was surprised by a cavalry attack. One of the officers noticed Cord was white, and he was spared from being massacred along with the others.

At the settlement where he was taken, a parson and his schoolteacher wife took him in. There he was ostracized by the other children, an object of ridicule and scorn. When he dared fight back, the parson would drag him out behind the outhouse, yank down his pants, and proceed to paddle Cord's backside till he drew blood, while he swore to beat the savage out of him.

Cord figured he lasted maybe a month there, till one day he could stand it no longer. The parson had taken a whip to him on that occasion, because he'd dared punch some kid for pushing him down in a mud puddle and calling him a stinking Indian dog. When the whip cut into his cheek, leaving a scar he still carried, he had caught the leather strip in his hand, jerking it right out of the parson's hands. He thought about raising a few welts on him, but his wife had appeared about that time to cry for mercy, so he had relented. Stealing the parson's horse, he ran away.

A loner, fending for himself in the years following, Cord had roamed the West and learned more of its secrets. When the War Between the States broke out, he sided with the Union. The prejudice and injustice suffered at the settlement school had left him with a deep respect for the freedom of all mankind, and he was willing to take a stand for it.

There had been women along the way, but Cord had kept a tight rein on his heart. If the lady of the evening hinted at anything to do with love, he was always honest, promising no more than the pleasure of the moment. More than that he would not, could not, give.

The image of his father drinking himself to death beside the body of his mother, as he cried out over and over how much he loved her, was firmly entrenched.

Love had made his father weak. Love had ultimately destroyed him.

It would not happen to Cord.

Shaking away the cobwebs of the past, Cord set aside the rest of his drink and lay down across the bed.

Maybe, he decided drowsily, if Pete's offer was still good tomorrow, he'd take him up on it. It would be nice to have a woman to love, if only for a little while.

Sometimes the nights could get real long . . . and lonely.

Almost entirely hidden from view behind a large potted plant, Jaime waited in the lobby.

It was a terrible time, she knew, to be offering herself for marriage, especially to a man she had never met, but the desk clerk had told her Mr. Austin was playing cards in the saloon and he didn't dare interrupt. Certainly, she was not about to approach him herself, not in there, so all she could do was wait for him to come out.

It had been nearly ten o'clock when she arrived. She'd had to clean up after her aunt's party, then pretend to go to bed and wait awhile before sneaking out of the house. Running all the way back to be dressed up by Ella and Hannah, she had then gone to the hotel.

She was still uncertain about the way she looked. The gown Ella had sneaked out of the laundry for her to borrow for the night was gaudy, a bright green satin with bodice cut so low her breasts were practically spilling out. But both the girls had waved away her protests, saying she had to make Mr. Austin sit up and take notice from the first instant they met.

Jaime thought of the miserable evening just past, with everyone else celebrating her aunt's announcement that she was going to marry Mr. Slawson. The Rupert sisters bragged about how they would soon be the new owners of the boardinghouse and began ordering Jaime around as though they already were, treating her like the slave they intended her to be.

But worst of all was the arrival and introduction of the Ruperts' nephew, Howard. He had taken one look at Jaime and become her shadow, which provoked teasing remarks from everyone there. Jaime had recounted it all to Ella and Hannah, and they insisted it was another reason to make a good impression on Mr. Austin—so she could escape the boardinghouse.

Finally, when they were done with her, Jaime had looked at herself in the mirror, only to to gasp, "Why, it doesn't even look like me!"

Ella cried, "See? We told you what a real beauty you are."

Well, if the desk clerk's reaction had been an indicator, Jaime decided maybe she was pretty, after all, because he had actually stammered as he spoke to her, his eyes flicking over her appreciatively.

He had promised to keep watch for Mr. Austin to come out of the saloon, so he could introduce her, but the night wore on and he failed to appear. Then the clerk politely told her he was going to his own quarters for a late supper but would return soon. "If the game has lasted this long," he advised, "it's likely it could go on till dawn. You sure you want to wait, little lady?"

She nodded her head but knew she could not stay much longer. The dress had to go back on the rack by the time the laundry opened.

Only one man had come out of the saloon and gone upstairs. She had instinctively drawn back in her seat as he passed, for there was an air about him that was almost frightening in its intensity. Yet something told her it was more an aura of power than of threat.

He was big, tall, with broad shoulders, and his open buckskin shirt revealed a muscular chest. She caught a glimpse of dark eyes and blue-black hair, and a face that was ruggedly appealing. His breeches looked to be made of doeskin, and they were tight, covering large muscular thighs.

As he ascended the steps, Jaime, with a wicked smile, could not help thinking he had nice buttocks, firm and well shaped.

He took the steps two at a time. She watched him until he was out of sight, then leaned back once more to wait.

Right after he had passed, however, two men came out of the saloon. One of them, she noted, had a very angry expression on his face as he looked in the direction of the man she had been watching. Curious, she listened as they talked.

"You think Austin was cheating, Pete?"

"Could be, but I wasn't about to say so. I got an idea he can use that gun he totes, and the way I see it, a thousand dollars ain't worth dying for. I'll pay it, but I don't mind telling you I'll be glad to see him leave town."

"How long is he here for?"

The scowling man pursed his lips thoughtfully. "I don't know. He don't say much." He gave his friend a nudge with his elbow. "Come on. Let's get out of here."

Jaime's breath had caught in her throat. The man she had watched with such fascination and found so fiercely handsome was actually the one she sought to marry.

Suddenly, she felt a mixture of emotions, for she had envisioned an older man, certainly not one so young and attractive. Why would he have to recruit a wife? It seemed to her a man like that could have his pick of women. Then she remembered how Ella said women were scarce in California, so it probably made no difference what a man looked like. Wives just weren't that easy to find out there.

Taking a deep breath of resolve, Jaime got to her feet and went to the counter. The thought of going up to a man's room and knocking on his door at such an hour filled her with dread, but the way things had developed she had no choice. It might be her only chance. And it was also best no one knew about it, like the desk clerk, who would, no doubt, think the worst of her for it.

Making sure no one was around, she quickly leaned to scan the registration book.

The name leaped out at her—*Cord Austin*—and, beside it, the room number: *Eight.*

Quickly, afraid the clerk would return any second, Jaime turned and ran up the steps.

Glancing about anxiously in the scant light provided by a small lantern hanging from a hook on the wall, she strained to see the painted numbers on the doors. Finally, she found his room at the end of the hall.

Drawing a deep breath, and pasting on what she hoped was a friendly smile, Jaime knocked softly.

Cord was standing on the other side of the door, gun in hand. The Apaches had taught him to be alert for any sound, even in deep sleep, and he was aware of the quiet footsteps approaching long before they stopped outside.

The door was jerked open, and Jaime's hand flew to her throat in terror as she found herself looking at a gun pointed right in her face.

"What the hell?" Cord swore. Then, in a flash, it came to him: Pete had obviously refused to take no for an answer. As his eyes raked over the comely young woman standing in the hall, Cord decided he was glad.

She was small, petite, but had delightful breasts, emphasized further by an incredibly tiny waist. She had a lovely face but, like most of her kind, wore too much rouge.

He found the fullness of her shiny red lips appealing and was stunned to feel a sudden tightening in his groin. Seldom did a mere pretty face arouse him.

Her hair, the color of buttercups, was piled atop her head in ringlets and held by a ridiculous cluster of satin ribbons and feathers. He found himself wanting to pull those silky tresses free, to see them fanned about her face as she lay beneath him.

He was most fascinated, however, by her eyes, a strange yet beautiful shade of turquoise. But there was something else about them he found oddly disconcerting—fear, mirrored within the enchanting depths. But why? Pete had said she was like a tigress, worth five hundred dollars for a night of unbridled passion. No doubt, he decided with a chuckle, the fear was an act. Part of her allure.

His large hand closed about her wrist, and he yanked her into the room, quickly closing and locking the door.

Plunged into darkness, Jaime waited nervously as he fumbled for a match. Only when the bedside lantern ignited did she dare speak, hardly recognizing her own voice as she endeavored to explain. "I'm sorry I'm late, Mr. Austin, but—"

He had put his gun away. His gaze moved over her again, this time brazenly as he began to circle her. He liked the hint of curves beneath her gown and could not resist confirming that her derriere was, indeed, high and round. Saucy. Impudent.

He grinned down at her, and she jumped, startled by his boldness in squeezing her buttocks. "Sir," she chided, "I don't think this is proper. I mean, we should introduce ourselves, shouldn't we? My name is—"

"You talk too much." He jerked her into his arms to silence her with hard, bruising lips.

Caught by surprise, Jaime could only stand there, trancelike, as unfamiliar yet strangely pleasurable feelings soared through her body. For one stunning instant, she actually began to yield, shamelessly enjoying the assault of his mouth.

He was shirtless, and her hands, with a will of their own, moved slowly upward to touch his shoulders shyly. The feel of his bare flesh jolted her from pleasured stupor, and she tore from his embrace. "Sir, I beg you," she gasped, lips on fire from his kiss. "I'll be a wife to you after we're married, but not before."

Cord threw his head back and laughed with delight. He always had enjoyed a prostitute with a sense of humor. He found them more adventuresome in bed than those interested only in money. "Well, let's do it right away," he said, falling into easy banter. "Do you think we can find a parson at such an ungodly hour?"

Jaime bit her lip thoughtfully. She could not tell whether he was serious but decided it was safe to assume he was. After all, that's why she was here, to marry him. "I hadn't planned on a wedding so soon, but I suppose it could be arranged. If you're sure, I mean."

"Oh, I'm sure." He grinned. He went to the bed and, folding his arms behind his head, leaned back, crossed his legs, and settled down to enjoy himself. The shy scared-virgin act was a delightful preliminary to the wild night Pete had promised. "But maybe I need a little sample of what I'm hitching up with. How about lifting those skirts? I sure as hell don't want to marry a woman with ugly legs."

Lift her skirts? Jaime swallowed hard, wondering if he could hear her knees knocking together. Hannah had said a wife was expected to do anything her husband wanted in the bedroom, and that included letting him see her undressed, of course. She had not said anything about a preview before they were married, but perhaps it was different when a man was buying a wife instead of asking her to marry him because he loved her.

A mock frown wrinkled Cord's brow. "Well, what are you waiting for? You don't have ugly legs, do you?"

Jaime shook her head and was, at once, further embarrassed. She began to stammer, "I . . . I don't know. I mean, no one has ever said." She felt her cheeks flame.

"Well, let me be the judge."

When she continued to stand there, he reminded her, "I've got to see what I'm getting, sweetheart."

She decided it was an expected ritual. Like inspecting merchandise before purchasing, he expected to see the wares. Well, she would go only so far. With a deep breath of resignation, she closed her eyes and reached to lift her skirt and petticoat to mid calf.

Cord nodded appreciatively. "Nice, so far. But take it higher. I'll just bet you've got real nice thighs." He was deliciously anticipating what she was going to look like when he had her completely naked.

"I . . . I'd rather not." She squeezed her eyes shut, unable to bear the way he was looking at her.

Cord groaned softly and wondered how long he could stand playing the game. He felt as though he was going to bust right out of his britches. "Come on. When a man is going to marry a woman, he's got a right to a few things."

Gritting her teeth, Jaime lifted her skirt higher, but only for an instant before quickly yanking it down. "That . . . that's all," she whispered.

Cord blinked in surprise. Beneath her petticoats, she wearing cotton drawers all the way down to her knees. She took this game seriously, by God.

"Well, I think it's time we got down to sampling." She was making him crazy with her playacting, even though anticipation was a sweet kind of torture. Still, a man could take just so much. He indicated her bosom. "I want to make sure they're real, not pushed out with lace hankies stuffed in your dress to make me think they're more than a mouthful. Scoop them out. Let me see."

Jaime gasped at the brazen command. "Sir, you go too far," she exploded, beginning to back toward the door, bristling with anger. "I came here to offer to be your wife, but I didn't expect to be treated with such disrespect.

"You should be ashamed of yourself," she raged on, further infuriated by the way he kept on grinning at her, obviously not caring that he had insulted her. "With your attitude, you'll never find a decent woman to wed."

She turned to go, but, with a delighted laugh, Cord bounded off the bed to grab her. He kissed her again, harder, and this time she struggled against him mightily. All part of the game, he thought, and held her face in a viselike grip as he assaulted her mouth with his tongue.

Jaime pushed against his chest but to no avail.

He shoved her back across the bed and chuckled. "Forgive my manners. Here I've been asking to see your wares, and I've neglected to show you mine."

Stunned, Jaime could only watch in silence as he rapidly stripped off his doeskin breeches to stand before her in his ankle-length underwear.

Her rapt gaze moved to powerfully molded thighs. His thumbs hooked into the band of his underwear, and he began to peel it downward. Jaime had only a glimpse of a dark mat of hair before she squeezed her eyes tightly shut and began to scream.

The sound was immediately silenced as Cord sprang to cover her mouth with his hand. Harshly, he said, "There are people around here trying to sleep, goddammit. Don't take things so far. I don't want the law crashing through the door."

And then he saw the genuine terror in her eyes, amid the glimmer of tears, and suddenly he sensed—

knew—she was not pretending. Still, he was driven to make sure. "Pete Rowland did send you here, didn't he? For five hundred dollars?"

Jaime, having problems breathing because one of his fingers was right under her nose, could only give her head a tiny shake.

He released her. "Are you telling the truth?"

Jaime sat up, turned her face to the wall, and shakily said, "Please, sir. Cover yourself."

Remembering his state of undress, he yanked up his underwear, then his trousers, and pulled on his shirt too, for good measure. "Answer me, damn it," he commanded. "It had to be Rowland who sent you here."

"I don't know anyone by that name," she said timorously. "Now may I go, please?"

She had started to get up, but he pushed her back and snapped, "No. We need to get to the bottom of this. Something is mighty odd here."

He began to pace about the room, running his fingers through his hair in agitation, then suddenly stopped to stare at her and gauge her reaction as he attempted to confirm, "You *are* a prostitute?"

"Oh, heavens no," she cried, aghast. "Whatever made you think that? It's this dress, isn't it? I told Ella and Hannah—"

"Who are they?"

"Friends of mine. Ella was the one who told me you were looking for a wife to take back to California with you."

"Not wife, sweetheart. *Wives.*"

"Ella didn't say you were a Mormon."

"I'm not. And they aren't for me, anyway. I'm taking them to California. You were obviously misinformed."

"You don't want one for yourself?" she asked, unable to keep from thinking how marriage to such a strikingly handsome man would not be so bad.

He was quick to say, "No, I don't," then shrugged and added, "Look, we both made a mistake. I thought you were somebody else—a prostitute sent in exchange for five hundred off a man's gambling debt. But since you aren't, just get on out of here and let's forget this happened."

Jaime's eyes grew round with wonder. "I didn't know prostitutes got paid that much."

"Ordinarily, they don't." He threw up his hands, not about to converse with her on the subject. "Just go, little lady."

Deciding she had already thrown pride to the wind, Jaime stubbornly persisted. "But I still want to go to California, and I'm willing to marry you to get there."

He laughed. "I'm flattered but not interested. Now it's late, and in case you didn't know it, only ladies of the night are out and about at this hour, so you'd best get on home before somebody else makes a mistake. And they might not be able to resist your charms, if you know what I mean," he added with an arrogant wink.

Jaime made no move to go. "Well, you can take me to California to be some other man's wife."

"You? You're too puny. You wouldn't make it across the Rocky Mountains, much less all the way to California. I need big women, big and healthy. Not dainty, fluffy little girls."

Jaime bristled. "I went there and back when I was still a child."

"That was different. Probably you were with your parents, and they took care of you. But I'm not willing to be your daddy on this trip."

Jaime leaped to her feet. "That's not fair! You aren't even giving me a chance. Maybe I'm not a large person, but I'm certainly not afraid of hard work. And I can make the journey. I swear I can.

"Please," she added desperately. "I really have to go to California."

Taking her arm, he steered her to the door and opened it. "I'm looking for real women," he told her irritably, pushing her into the hall, "and you, sweetheart, just don't meet my requirements. Granted, you're pretty, and men would pay top dollar to have you for a wife, but you'd be nothing but trouble for me on the way west.

"So find yourself a husband and settle down here," he said with finality. "Forget California. It's not for you."

"But—"

He closed the door in her face.

3

As promised, Ella had left the back door unlatched, so Jaime was able to slip inside the laundry. Quickly changing into her own clothes, she returned the borrowed gown to the rack. Deciding it was much to late to wake the girls and tell them about her awful experience, she hurried home.

She tried to sleep but was far too angry and upset. Wide awake, she stared into the darkness of her tiny basement room as anger continued to churn over the way Cord Austin had humiliated her.

What burned to the core was his audacity in declaring her physically unfit. Who was he to judge her strength? Her courage? Maybe she wasn't big and husky like some farmers' wives, who worked side by side with their husbands in the fields, toiling like men, but she was certainly no stranger to hard work.

Well, she brooded, maybe he would never know about it, but she would eventually make the trip to

California. She had a whole year to plan for it before the first wagons rolled out from Independence in the spring. Meanwhile, there might even be a letter from her father.

As she lay there, dwelling on the experience she knew she'd never forget, Jaime thought how there was something else about Cord Austin she would always remember—how he had held her, touched her. Thinking about it sent strange little shivers of delight up and down her spine. She told herself she was being silly. He had been expecting a woman being paid to make love to him, that's all. His behavior certainly had not been motivated because he found her desirable, for heaven's sake.

Trying to get him off her mind, Jaime sadly turned her thoughts to how much she was going to miss Hannah and Ella.

The next morning, Jaime rushed to the laundry, anxious to talk to the girls, but they had gone to see about signing up for the wagon train and did not return till midafternoon. With a grin and a nod to let her know they had been accepted, they threw themselves into their work, and there was no time for conversation.

At last, they were able to gather upstairs. Jaime didn't care that she'd be late getting home. She had been waiting all day to explain. "You were wrong. Cord Austin wasn't looking for a wife for himself. He—"

"We know, we know." Ella cut her off as she gave her what was meant to be a consoling hug. "We found that out this morning. He was there, making final decisions as to who was accepted and who wasn't, and he made it clear he wasn't in the market for a wife."

Hannah was quick to attempt to soothe by adding, "But it's nothing to worry about, Jaime. All you have to do is go to the depot where we went this morning and sign up to go with us."

"Then you're really going?" Jaime looked from one to the other.

Ella nodded. "Yes, but you can too. There's still room for more. I heard Mr. Austin telling someone he was real disappointed with the turnout so far."

With a little laugh, Hannah said, "I guess it didn't take long for him to clear things up last night, did it? I could tell he's a stern sort. Handsome, too. Some of the girls were talking about how it's a pity he's not looking for a wife himself, because they'd leap at the chance." Her words trailed off as she saw the look on Jaime's face. "What's wrong? He wasn't rude, was he? I mean, it was an honest mistake."

Jaime was not about to confide the entire encounter, afraid they would suspect she hadn't altogether minded some of it. Instead, she related only her frustration. "He says I can't go, because he thinks I'm puny."

"Puny?" Ella said.

Hannah chimed in. "What did he mean?"

Jaime gestured helplessly. "He says I'm not strong enough to make the trip, that's what he meant. Look at the two of you. You're taller, larger. It doesn't matter I'm a hard worker. He called me a 'fluffy little girl,'" she added bitterly.

Ella scowled. "He's crazy."

Hannah spoke up. "In all fairness, I can understand his reasoning. It *is* a long, hard journey. Six
months, two thousand miles, traveling fifteen to
twenty miles a day. And we've heard about all the
potential dangers along the way: Indians, outlaws,
bad weather sometimes, rough terrain, dust storms."
She shuddered to recall the tales of woe and admitted,
"I've had second thoughts myself."

"He doesn't know Jaime," Ella argued. "She works
as hard as we do, and she never complains. And when
we're done for the day, she's slaving for her aunt till
all hours of the night, then back up at dawn. Where
she's concerned, he isn't being fair."

"I agree, but he's still in charge. She'll just have to
wait till next spring for someone not quite so fussy."

Jaime asked fearfully, "Then this wagon train is
definitely the last one this year?"

"I'm afraid so." Hannah's heart went out to her
friend. How desperate she must feel.

"When will you be leaving?" Jaime dreaded the
answer.

For a moment, neither girl spoke, but Ella finally,
reluctantly, told her. "Next week."

Jaime swallowed a cry of protest. She could
already feel an emptiness in her heart.

Fighting the selfish instinct to throw her arms
about them and burst into tears and beg them not to
go, she moved swiftly toward the door. "Well, I'm
happy for you, I really am," she lied. "I guess I'd better
be going now. Aunt Arista is going to be wondering
where I am. Thanks for trying, for helping me with
the dress and everything."

Ella cried, "No, wait. Don't leave yet, Jaime. We've got to think of a way you can go with us."

Jaime turned slowly, desperately willing to listen to any ideas they had. Maybe, she dared hope, they could convince Mr. Austin to change his mind. After all, they'd said he wasn't happy with the small number of volunteer wives so far.

"What are you thinking of?" Hannah asked Ella, hoping she wasn't getting Jaime's hopes up in vain. "He said she couldn't go."

Ella's mouth spread in a mischievous grin. "Forget him. She can go with us, and he'll never even know it."

Hannah looked at her as if she'd lost her mind and bluntly asked if she had.

"No." Ella laughed, then rushed to explain. "It can work. Now listen." Excitedly, she offered a plan as to how Jaime could hide in their wagon. "I heard someone say there'll be four women to a wagon. We can squeeze her in ours and talk the others into not saying anything. She can hide during the day and slip out at night to take care of her personal needs. We'll smuggle food to her. He won't know anything, because he won't see her."

"If he finds out, he'll send her back," Hannah quickly pointed out.

"We just have to make sure he doesn't, not till we've gone so far he can't. Then he'll have to take her the rest of the way. Once she's out there, she won't have to worry about not having a husband waiting for her. She's going to find her father, remember?"

"It might not work."

"It can't hurt to try. What does she have to lose?"

Dolefully, Jaime responded to Ella's question. "Everything. The Rupert sisters would be so mad at me for running away they'd never let me back in the house. Mr. Casey probably wouldn't give me my job back either, and even if he did, I wouldn't make enough to pay for room and board anywhere. I'd lose what little security I have now."

"She's right," Hannah said. "And I don't think you should try to talk her into it. It's a big decision, and it has to be hers."

Ella agreed with that much but wanted assurance. "If she does decide to go, will you agree to help her?"

"Of course."

Jaime flashed them a small but grateful smile as she backed out the door. "I appreciate what you all are trying to do for me, I really do, but it's just too risky."

"Isn't getting to California to be with your father worth it?" Ella challenged.

Cord Austin's staunch rejection and refusal had made a firm impression. Jaime was convinced, beyond a doubt, he was indeed a man of firm conviction, and the wagon train would have to be a long, long way from Missouri for him not to turn around and take her back. "I just can't," she whispered brokenly, and hurried on her way.

The next week passed in a blur. Jaime knew she could not hold back time and threw herself into her work, wanting to be too tired to dwell on the bleak future.

Arista was obviously wanting to move fast with her wedding plans, lest Jedediah Slawson change his mind. The house was a flurry of activity as she went about making arrangements for what she hoped would be a small lovely wedding in the parlor. Ironically, the date had been set for the afternoon before the wagon train was leaving with Hannah and Ella. Jaime knew that within a period of less than a day her entire life would change.

Adding to her misery was Howard Rupert's declaration, two days before the wedding, that he intended to court her. His aunts, he explained, had made him an extremely attractive offer. If he would marry and settle down, they would will the house and the rest of their money to him.

Rupert explained he was tired of the bachelor life and felt Jaime was the perfect choice for a wife. "She can appreciate a man like me who's willing to marry her and keep her from being a spinster," he had bluntly told Arista in Jaime's presence, unmindful of Jaime's feelings.

Arista had given him her blessing. "I can start my new life now with a clear conscience, knowing my darling niece will be taken care of by a fine man like you, Rupert. That was the only shadow on my happiness, because I made a solemn vow to my dear brother-in-law I would always look after her.

"But I must warn you," she had hastened to add, after this lie, "she has this obsession for her father, and if he should send for her—if he's still alive, which I doubt—I'm afraid she'd run off to California."

Rupert's expression had instantly turned grim. "That will never happen."

"Will you allow her to keep working at the laundry?" Arista wanted to know, hardly able to suppress a gloating smile. Through Laura's daughter, she was getting her revenge.

"Oh, yes. I'll be resigning my job at the tannery, so I'll be able to keep a tight rein on things here."

Jaime knew true desperation then, because refusal to marry him would mean being evicted. But no matter. Never would she agree to be his wife. Maybe she had been willing to marry a man she didn't know in order to get to California, but that was different. With a stranger, there was always a chance she would be well treated. With Rupert, she was guaranteed a wretched existence.

Ella and Hannah had said nothing more to try and persuade her to change her mind about running away. She felt they were intentionally avoiding her. It was only natural for them to be excited over their forthcoming adventure, and they didn't want her to be hurt by it.

One morning, earlier than Jaime had expected, they drew her aside to explain that it was their last day at work. Jaime felt the world was crashing down around her. Only the night before, Rupert had told her of his decision for them to go ahead and marry right away, the day after her aunt's wedding. That way, they could make use of her aunt's flowers, as well as the leftover refreshments, sparing extra expense. It was a Sunday. They could spend their wedding night moving into her aunt's vacated quarters, and Jaime would not have to miss a day at the laundry.

Faced with the reality that she had to move out of the house as fast as possible, Jaime had approached Mr. Casey as soon as she got to work that morning, begging him to let her have Ella and Hannah's room. Sorry, he said, but he had already hired two of his wife's relatives to replace the girls, and they would be moving in.

So it was that Jaime could no longer keep her emotions under control and burst into tears. "I'm sorry, so sorry," she whispered, shaking her head from side to side as they put their arms about her. "It's just that I'm going to miss you so much, and you're leaving sooner than I'd thought."

Ella explained how they would not be departing until Sunday morning but had been told they needed to move into their wagon by Friday to settle in, as well as hear all the orders and instructions to be given.

"Listen, there's a big party Saturday night," Ella told her excitedly. "Why don't you come? Everybody is gathering to say good-bye to all their friends and relatives, and Hannah and I would like for you to be there."

Hannah chimed in to urge, "Oh, please say you'll come, Jaime. We probably won't ever see each other again." She was close to tears herself.

Jaime promised she would be there. Where she would go after that, she had no idea, because she had to escape from Rupert. But she did not confide her misery to Ella and Hannah, not wanting to burden them with her problems.

*   *   *

Saturday night, when all was quiet in the house and Rupert had left, thinking tomorrow was his wedding day, Jaime packed a change of clothing in a small satchel, along with her Bible, and quietly left the house.

Her intention was to seek a church later that night and ask for shelter till she could find work and somewhere to live. She made up her mind not to worry, because she was determined to find a way to survive despite everything.

She had unbound her breasts and felt a strange sense of freedom as she walked along in the night. Maybe her future was uncertain. At least from now on she would be making her own decisions, and there would be no one nagging at her. That alone was worth any struggle that lay ahead.

A kindly man slowed his wagon and asked her destination. She told him, and he held out a hand.

As they drew closer to the departure point, they could hear the music of the banjos and guitars. When they arrived, she thanked the stranger and hurried toward the festivities but soon slowed in charmed fascination over the scene before her.

Prairie schooners, she'd heard them called, these wagons with white canvas covers supported by a frame of hickory bows, now drawn into a circle. Within, gathered around their campfires, were too many people to count. Laughter, singing, and music rang out in the cool spring night. Herded into a crude corral, oxen waited to be hitched up at daybreak. She could hear cattle lowing, also, and now and then the bray of a mule or a horse's restless whinny.

All about was an air of excitement, yet when she drew closer she could hear some women crying as loved ones about to be separated gathered to say good-bye.

Jaime kept to the shadows just beyond the firelight. She moved along slowly, searching anxiously for Ella and Hannah. She wanted to get the farewell over with and begin to put the sadness of parting behind. She knew she also needed to find shelter as soon as possible.

Cord leaned against the side of a supply wagon, quietly observing the festivities. He wanted no part of it. Let them have a good time, even if it meant they'd feel like hell at the crack of dawn, when he planned to roll them out. It would be their last party for a while. Sure, for the first weeks or so, every evening when they drew the wagons into a circle to bed down for the night, there would be some revelry. But that wouldn't last long. Soon they would be so tired at the end of the day all they'd want was a bite to eat and a place to lie down. So he would not interrupt them. They could stay up till sunrise for all he cared.

The girl caught his eye. She was obviously looking for somebody. Then, as she passed by one of the campfires, he got a glimpse of her face. She looked familiar, but he couldn't place her. Certainly, she wasn't one of the future brides. He hadn't signed up anybody that small. And she wasn't one of the prostitutes he'd been asked to take out to work in the big saloon owned by the man financing his trip. Too plain and dowdy.

He decided she was searching for a relative, but a closer look made him blink in disbelief.

He could see her eyes in the fire's glow, and there was no mistaking that strange color, like the greenish-blue stone the Indians polished to a sheen and used in their jewelry. No other woman he had ever seen had hair the exact color of a coveted gold nugget, either.

No doubt about it, that pristine little filly was none other than one he had mistaken for the infamous Francie.

He knew her name now, thanks to the two girls named Ella and Hannah. They had begged him to take her along, and finally he'd had to be a little harsh to get them off his back. No matter that Jaime Chandler was a beauty beneath that homely façade. He had endeavored to sign up only the heartiest of women, because he would be responsible for all of them and did not want any dainty ones who would need extra tending to. Besides, the men out in California wanted big, husky wives.

Some parts of that night made him laugh to remember, Cord mused, as he watched Jaime. And the fact was, he had never been aroused so easily. What he had thought was feigned innocence had delighted him at the time, but, thinking back, he was touched to recall how he'd felt her yielding, despite herself. The other women in his life had been experienced. And far too many had been actresses, pretending desire in order to please a man. Those he had enjoyed pleasantly torturing till they begged for it. But there was something about Jaime Chandler that made him think, with the right man, she might turn out to be the tigress Pete had promised in Francie.

Tossing aside the cheroot he had been smoking, he silently moved up behind her. "Looking for your friends, Sunshine?"

Jaime spun about to gasp in recognition, "You!" and found herself mesmerized by dark, mocking eyes.

"Haven't you learned your lesson about being out at night by yourself?"

Jaime managed to keep her voice even as she fired back. "Not every man I meet mistakes me for a prostitute, Mr. Austin."

"Not the way you're dressed tonight, for sure."

She said primly, "I don't think you should concern yourself with either my appearance or my nocturnal activities." She turned away but paused as he spoke.

"I saw Ella and Hannah on the other side a little while ago. They'll be glad to see you. I don't think anybody else came to tell them good-bye."

She whipped about. "How did you know I was looking for them?"

"They nearly wore my ears off begging me to take you along."

"I'm sorry. I didn't ask them to speak on my behalf."

Disconcerted to realize he actually found himself wishing she was going too, Cord's next words came out sounding harsher than he'd intended. "Instinct can mean the difference between life and death, and my instinct tells me you aren't cut out for a trip like this. Good night, Miss Chandler."

He started away, but fury flashed; Jaime reached out and caught his arm. He turned to glare with equally fiery eyes.

Undaunted, she stood on tiptoe, pointing a finger under his nose. "Let me tell you something. You don't know anything about me. I've had to work hard all my life, and I'm probably better able to cope with a trip like this than half the women you're taking. I'll make it, too. But not with you, thank God. I'll leave next spring, when I'm sure I can find someone to take me who isn't so pigheaded.

"And I'm glad you weren't looking for a wife." She went on, pausing only long enough to take a ragged breath. "I'd rather die than have you for a husband."

He fired back, "Well, pity the man who takes on a stubborn filly like you."

"Then we feel the same about each other, and there's no need to continue this discussion. Good night, and good-bye."

His hands clamped down on her shoulders, preventing her retreat. Jaime was too mad to be intimidated. "If you don't let me go this instant, I'll scream."

He released her, started to turn away, then yielded to impulse. Jerking her into his arms, his mouth claimed hers in a bruising kiss. Then, just as abruptly, he released her and gave her a gentle shove away from him. "Now get out of here."

He disappeared into the shadows.

Touching her fingertips to her mouth, Jaime felt rage washing over her for his audacity but could not deny being shaken by the surprise of his kiss.

Just then, Ella and Hannah saw her and descended in swooping hugs.

"You came!" Ella's delighted cry broke the spell. "Thank goodness. We were afraid you wouldn't."

Hannah grabbed her hand. "Come on. We want to show you our wagon."

Jaime took the glass of wine Ella handed her, anxious to do anything to get her mind off Cord Austin.

They introduced her to some of the others and gave her more wine, and soon, dizzy and mellow, Jaime joined in the merriment.

The celebration grew wilder and happier. Jaime did not know exactly when her head began to spin, and she lost all sense of time. There was dancing, and the girls spun one another around, giggling shrilly.

After a time, Jaime began to feel sick. Finding her satchel where she had left it, she carried it with her to Ella and Hannah's wagon. She crawled in and lay down, immediately falling into a deep sleep, and awakened only to realize it was nearly morning and preparations were under way for the wagons to roll out.

"Why not stay with us?" Ella said when she saw Jaime was awake. "Where else do you really have to go?"

Jaime's head was hurting terribly, and her mouth felt as though it were filled with cotton.

Hannah also urged her to stay. "You're probably

in a lot of trouble, anyway, for being out all night. You might as well come with us."

Jaime felt too awful to argue. With a nod and a faint smile, she closed her eyes and drifted away once more, telling herself Cord Austin's brazen kiss had nothing to do with changing her mind.

4

Named for the sailing ships they resembled with their high white covers of heavy cotton twill, over forty prairie schooners lined up in single file just before dawn. Gone was the festive air of the night before and, in its place, sober contemplation of the momentous pilgrimage ahead.

Overcome with excitement, Jaime had slept little after all. There were two other women, besides Ella and Hannah, in the wagon: Ruth Winslow and Martha Lowery. Like Hannah, they had been made widows by the war. Still grieving, they viewed the journey to meet a new husband as necessary for their survival, not as an exciting quest. Fortunately, neither expressed any reluctance to help Jaime stow away, apparently viewing it as a welcome diversion to what was sure to be a long and grueling experience.

Ruth had explained a bit about the construction of the wagon. Her husband, before his death, she'd said, blinking back tears, had worked as a wagon builder. She knew a few things, like how the schooners had descended from the Conestoga model, which had originated in Pennsylvania. Intended to haul heavy freight over rough and muddy roads, the Conestoga was curved at each end to prevent the contents from shifting about, while the prairie schooner had a flat body and lower sides. The hoops supporting the canvas were about the same, she'd said, around eleven feet high.

A schooner had to be light enough to keep from putting undue strain on the animals pulling it, yet strong enough not to break down under heavy loads. Therefore, iron was used only to reinforce parts that would take the greatest pounding, with the rest constructed of hardwoods such as oak, hickory, and maple.

There was hardly any place to sit. Most space had been taken up by cargo, such as cooking utensils, clothing, sewing necessities; in addition to staples like flour and corn meal, salt and sugar, there was an ample supply of hardtack, dried beans, fruit, and beef. The women had protested but Cord filled one corner of their wagon with tools anyway—shovels, spades, ox shoes, and extra axles. As a result, Jaime was squeezed in tightly, with hardly enough space to lie down, for she couldn't expect the others to put themselves out for her.

Warily, she eyed the cover, about five feet over her head. It had been waterproofed with linseed oil and was meant to shield from rain and protect from sun and dust. Yet when they encountered midsummer heat, it would have to be rolled back and bunched to provide air circulation. How would she go undetected then? As they sat up talking throughout the night, she had finally voiced her fears.

Ella had dismissed her concern. "We're all going to be wearing slat bonnets. They're called that because they've got wooden splints on the sides. They almost hide your whole face. I've got an extra one you can use. You'd better keep your hair pinned up, though, because nobody else has hair the color of yours."

Jaime remembered pleasantly how Cord had called her Sunshine. No doubt he had been thinking of her hair.

"Besides," Ella had gone on, "nobody stays in the wagon all the time anyway. Mr. Austin told us how everybody should walk on the footpaths as much as possible, because there aren't any springs in these things, and it's worse riding than walking when you hit a rocky stretch. So you can probably move around a little more, because everybody will be spreading out, and you won't be noticed."

"How many wagons is he taking?"

"Ten. We heard they cost around a hundred dollars each. Some have mules pulling them, which were fifty, and some, like ours, have oxen. They cost the most—ninety. Ten wagons of women," she calculated brightly, "and thirty-one others with families."

At the first faint light of dawn, Cord had come to hitch up the oxen.

Ella had seen him and nudged Jaime. Together, they crouched to peek out from behind the cover, which had been closed by drawstrings for privacy.

"He is a handsome devil, isn't he?" Ella whispered against Jaime's ear. "Look. He isn't wearing a shirt. See how big his chest is? He's strong, I can tell. I'll bet you've never seen a man half naked before, have you?"

Jaime was glad it was so dark inside the wagon Ella couldn't see her face. She could feel her cheeks flaming to think how she'd seen much more, like how he looked in his union suit.

"Are you cold? You're shivering."

Not shivering, Jaime could have corrected, trembling. And she hated herself for it, but no matter how she despised Cord Austin for his smugness, there was no denying he set her pulse to racing. Surely, during the arduous times ahead, she told herself, that kind of silly nonsense would stop.

There had been one terrifying moment when Jaime thought her quest had ended before it even began. Shortly after a bell clanged to signal it was time for everyone to wake up and make final preparations to leave, Cord had again come to the wagon. Carrying a barrel, she heard him explain to Ella how it was filled with cornmeal and packed with eggs. "When the eggs are gone, you can use the meal to make bread. I'll be back with another in a minute. That one has slabs of smoked bacon packed in bran. The bran protects the bacon from the heat. It keeps longer."

Balancing the heavy barrel on one broad shoulder, he had been about to hoist it inside and crawl in behind to position it. Jaime, drawn up in a corner, had no time to scramble beneath anything and would have been discovered when he poked his head inside.

Hannah, however, was quick to lunge for the end of the wagon to stop him. "You can't come in here now. We aren't all dressed. And really, Mr. Austin," she continued, feigning indignation, "you're going to have to remember there are ladies in here, and you can't just barge in any time you like."

He set the barrel on the ground. "Don't worry. I'll be too busy."

When he had gone, Ella snickered. "He'll be busy, all right, busy with the prostitutes. I'll bet that's where he beds down every night."

Jaime struggled to keep her voice even as she asked, "What are you talking about? What prostitutes?"

Ella obliged to tell her. "Both wives and prostitutes are scarce in California. Didn't you know that? There's only four whores, though, and they're in the wagon right behind us. You haven't seen them, because they didn't join the party last night."

Ruth commented airily, "They knew they wouldn't be welcome around decent folk."

Hannah frowned. She didn't like such remarks about anybody. "It's going to be a long trip, and we're all in this together. It's no time for snobbery."

"Snobbery has nothing to do with it," Ruth fired back. "I don't mingle with whores."

Hannah said nothing more and exchanged disapproving glances with Jaime and Ella. They knew they could not risk making an enemy, lest Jaime be exposed out of spite.

The call was given for everyone to assemble one last time, and Jaime tucked her hair beneath a bonnet and squeezed in between Hannah and Ella. Along with everyone else, she was surprised by Cord's announcement that he was the new wagon master. At once, several of the men wanted to know why Captain Wingate was being replaced, as they had met him and liked him.

Cord was not the sort to mince words, as everyone was soon to learn. Neither did he believe in softening the truth. The way west was harsh. It did no good, he felt, to give hope it could be any other way, so he came right out and told them. "Captain Wingate decided it was too late to be leaving. He felt too many other trains had already left, trampling grass and fouling water holes."

Someone shouted irately, "Well, is that true?"

"It's a possibility," Cord admitted. "If we'd left earlier, though, there's a chance there wouldn't have been enough grass to graze the livestock. They'd get sick, slow their pace, which leads to more problems later. There is no one perfect time to leave. We take what comes. That's how it is.

"And as you've already been told," he continued, meeting hostile glares in challenge, "if you don't think you can take it, stay here. It's better to pull out now than later. After we've gone so far, it's too late to turn back, because it would be dangerous to be alone out there. The Army is even talking about banning travel by single wagons because of Indian danger. There's safety in numbers, despite renegades and ruffians."

Jaime smiled and hugged herself. That was the time she was waiting for, when they were too far along to do anything but keep on going—with her right along with them. Surely Cord would not abandon her along the way in a strange settlement where she knew no one.

Fifteen wagons, the owners either sharing Captain Wingate's fears or not absolutely certain they wanted to go at all, did pull out. The others rolled forward, taking a previously assigned position in line. Jaime crouched behind Hannah, who sat on the wagon seat, anxiously holding the reins of the four oxen, yoked two by two. "Are you sure you can handle them? They're awfully big."

Hannah tightened her grip and said confidently, "I've got to. All but two of Captain Wingate's sentinels resigned with him, and all the teamsters. The sentinels will be kept busy riding the line. But I think I can do it. I've worked with these monsters before."

"Look back there." Ruth pointed to the rear, where two men were loudly arguing outside the prostitutes' wagon. "Looks like the remaining sentinels are fighting for *their* reins."

They watched with interest as Cord appeared, just as the blows started. Slinging each man in turn to the ground, he towered above them, fists clenched. "No more. You get into a fight on the trail, and you're finished, then and there. I won't tolerate bickering and fighting, understand?"

Mumbling, the men struggled to their feet.

"You. Fletcher." Cord pointed to one of them. "You take the reins. Henderson, you go ride herd on the cattle."

He was about to turn away when a pinch-faced

woman stepped from the onlookers that had gathered. Firmly planting herself before him, she lashed out. "There wouldn't be any trouble if you'd get rid of those Jezebels before we even start. As long as they're with us, the devil is going to be working on our menfolk, filling them with lust. It's not good for decent folk to be around such women."

Cord looked into the furious face of Mrs. Wilma Turnage and again wondered miserably what he had got himself into. He had agreed to take wives and prostitutes to California, not coddle and cater to a hundred other people on the way. No time like the present, however, to set a few of them straight. "I'm sure, Mrs. Turnage," he told her with forced politeness, "that the Lord depends on good women like you to keep your menfolk from temptation.

"Now let's roll," he said to no one in particular, dismissing her as he brushed by.

Jaime and the others in her wagon giggled as one of the prostitutes leaned out to needle Mrs. Turnage. "Don't worry, lady. We've seen your husband. Satan himself couldn't make me take a tumble with *him*."

With a red face, Wilma Turnage angrily scurried back to her own wagon.

Excitement and tension was in the air as everyone awaited the signal for departure. Cord rode down one side of the single line and up the other, making sure all were in position. Most people were planning to walk beside their wagons, especially as they left Independence. With relatives and friends lining the road out, some carrying flags and waving banners, it would be quite a parade to the edge of town.

Jaime could hear her own heart pounding as she sat inside the wagon. The others had joined the caravan walking, but she did not particularly long to be with them. So many emotions were churning within her that she relished the time alone to try and sort them out.

What if she didn't make it and died en route as some people did? If anything happened, no one would ever know what became of her. But did it really matter? After all, her father could already be dead, and she could arrive in California to find herself truly alone, destitute, with nowhere to go. She had the map but it might be worthless. Ultimately, she might become desperate enough to marry any man willing to give her a home.

But I won't let that happen, she vowed. She would find a way to take care of herself. Meanwhile, she was going to taste life and experience all it had to offer. Too long, she had been sheltered and restrained, but no more. This was truly the start of a great adventure.

Free. Dear Lord, she had never felt so free.

A gun fired, exploding the stillness. With whoops and hollers, outriders galloped far ahead, unleashing some of their pent-up impatience. Reins popped, and oxen and mules began to plod forward.

The cries rang out.

"God bless!"

"Farewell!"

"May the Lord have mercy!"

"Good-bye!"

"Godspeed!"

The sun made its final leap from the horizon.
There was not a cloud in the bright blue sky. A cool
breeze assaulted, rippling the canvas tops.

It was a motley scene. Some wagons had cows tied
behind. A few had pigs. There were crates of chickens
fastened on the sides. Children skipped along happily,
hand in hand, the womenfolk following, some carrying babies and the ones too little to walk. There were
banjo and guitar players. Someone even had a flute.

"Oh, I wish you could be up here with me, Jaime,"
Hannah called. "It's so exciting. But I can tell lots of
people are scared. I just saw another wagon pull out
and turn back. And some folks are crying. But for the
most part, I think everybody is happy. I know I am.
How about you? Any second thoughts?"

"None at all." Jaime drew back as she spotted Cord
up ahead. The horse he was riding was magnificent,
sleek and black. Suddenly, the animal reared up on its
hind legs, forelegs pawing the air as though it, too,
wanted to share in exultation over the trip's beginning.

Hannah said, "Look at him. He's quite a rider,
isn't he? But then, I've got a feeling he's also quite a
man. I think we're in good hands."

Jaime pulled even farther back in the wagon.

Cord took off his hat to give a final wave to the
cheering onlookers. It was time for the wagons to cut
toward the trail that would lead northwest to Nebraska
and the Platte River.

He held back, counting the schooners as they
passed. Twenty-five remained, including his ten. All

the men had weapons and knew how to use them. They were large enough in number to be safe. Still, if it hadn't been for the money waiting when he got the women to San Francisco, never would he have agreed to be wagon master. But it was either that or wait till next spring. There was no way he would have tried to take them alone. Even if he'd hired some mule skinners, it would be asking for trouble.

The wagons passed carrying the future brides, and the one called Hannah threw up her hand at him. She was big-boned, appeared healthy, and would make some prospector or farmer a good strong wife. But there was always the possibility she and some of the others might fall out at some village or post along the way. He'd been told that always happened with a few.

Suddenly the image of the one with the golden hair came to mind. He laughed out loud to think again of that crazy night in his hotel room. And, once again, he could not resist thinking how nice it might have been if she were along.

Maybe too nice, something warned from within.

He spurred his horse to gallop forward, wanting to position himself to observe the crossing of a small creek just ahead.

There was no time to dwell on what might have been.

"He's laughing."

"Who?"

"Captain Austin. He waved at me and sort of chuckled. Wonder what that was all about. I can count on one hand the number of times I've seen him smile. He's always so serious." Hannah was quiet for a moment, then asked, "What *really* happened that night you went to see him? You never told us any of the details."

"He just said I'd made a mistake, that's all." Jaime hedged, not about to tell her the truth. "And then when I asked could I come along, he said I was too small, like I told you before."

Hannah wriggled on the hard wood seat, thinking how her discomfort had not even begun. "Well, it doesn't matter." She dismissed her interrogation of Jaime. "You're here, and by the time he finds out about it, he'll have to accept it. We're on our way now."

Jaime settled back, feeling as though every bone in her body were rattling as the oxen pulled the wagon down the first bumpy path.

Her new life had begun, she told herself, in blended emotions of anticipation and fear, and nothing would ever be the same again.

5

On schedule, they reached the Big Blue River. Cord was relieved to find the water down, enabling the wagons to ford rather than be ferried. The trail then carried them into Nebraska to meet the Platte River, where they turned west to follow its south bank.

Farther away, the land began to creep upward in cliffs of sandstone, which became higher and broke apart as they moved deeper west.

They marveled at the terrain, so different from the forested regions of the East, but were even more awed by the wildlife they saw from time to time— antelopes and coyotes, grizzlies and black bears, prairie dogs, rabbits, and buffaloes.

The day they saw buffalo for the first time, Cord spread the word for the women to join the men at the nightly meeting after supper. When the usual problems and complaints had been dealt with, he drew disgusted cries with his announcement that the ladies should carry baskets and pick up buffalo dung as they walked alongside the wagons during the day.

"What on earth for?" Wilma Turnage screeched above the immediate wave of disgust. "Why would we want something so nasty?"

"You've seen the prairie," Cord said, glancing about to note almost everyone shared her revulsion. "Wood is scarce. It's going to get worse. Dry dung—chips, they're called—makes good fires. We'll reach a point where chips are all you have to cook with. You'll use them or you go hungry."

"I won't do it," Wilma cried. A murmur of support rippled through the other women, with a few men also chiming in. The thought of cooking their food over animal excrement was repulsive.

Ignoring her, Cord went on to explain how buffalo chips were also used in smudge spots to keep off mosquitoes and gnats. "This pleasant spring weather we've been blessed with since leaving Missouri won't last. It's going to get hot, and we're going to have rain. You'll be eaten alive by bugs at night unless you have the smudge pots going. You ladies suit yourself. If you're too squeamish to take my advice, you'll suffer the consequences.

"You'd be wise to stock up now." He raised his voice above the displeased mutterings. "We'll hit some trails, when we get farther southwest, where both trees *and* chips are in short supply. The only fuel then will be mesquite roots, and looking for them would take time we might not have. You all know we've got to keep on schedule if we're to make the Sierras before the first snows."

Cord was standing on the open tailgate of the supply wagon. Wilma maneuvered her way forward to stare up at him. "You should have told us all this ahead of time, Captain Austin. Seems to me you've got a little surprise for us most every day. Like yesterday, the Lord's day. Captain Wingate told us we wouldn't have to travel on the Sabbath. It'd be our layover day. We agreed if we had time for a devotional service, we'd spend part of the day working— laundry for us women, and catch-up chores for the men. But you!" She scowled. "You made us do fifteen miles just like it was any other day of the week."

His face void of expression, Cord advised, "You can do a lot of praying while you're covering those fifteen miles, Mrs. Turnage.

"All of you"—he swept the crowd with a commanding gaze—"had better get this straight, once and for all: I don't intend for anybody or anything to hold us back. It's my job to get you to California, and I intend to do it. We'll take layover days only after a rain, to clean and air the wagons and to dry bedding and clothing. Otherwise, we keep rolling."

He broached the other reason he had requested the ladies' presence. "I've noticed some of you ignored the packing list you were given back when you first signed on, and you're overloaded. In another week, we're going to have to cross the south and north forks of the river. After that, we're out of flat country. We've got a sharp uphill climb, then twenty miles or more across a tableland before the trail drops into the valley of the North Platte."

He described the steep drop, how special care was needed to take the wagons down. Wagon wheels would have to be locked by chaining them to the wagon boxes, then slowly skidded by ropes down to the bottom of the forty-five-degree grade. "If a wagon is too heavy and breaks the rope, it hits the bottom in splinters. To keep that from happening, the wagons have to be as light as possible. This is a good time for you to lighten your loads and get rid of some things you were told not to bring anyway."

Wilma was fast to challenge him. "Like what?"

"Your sheet-iron stove, Mrs. Turnage." Then, having to raise his voice to be heard above her shouted protests, he went on to tell Amy Dunbar to abandon her claw-foot table; the Ward family, as well as the Proctors, needed to unload anvils. Reading from the list he'd made, he called out other names, other possessions: crates of china, books, other heavy pieces of furniture.

Fury shot through the crowd like a bullet. Cord was adamant. Either they discarded heavy pieces or they risked losing their wagons. Eventually, a few men saw the wisdom of what he was saying and agreed to cooperate. The women, however, remained reluctant to give up their precious possessions.

In the midst of it all, Wilma shouted, "What about the whores, captain? What do they have to give up? We didn't even know they were coming along till the last minute, and that wasn't right. I'd never have agreed to me and mine being in the company of strumpets."

Several of the women cried out to agree.

"Have any of them bothered you, Mrs. Turnage? Or your family?" he asked evenly, though he could feel himself tensing as she continued to try his patience.

With a sneer, she fired back. "They know better. They think they're too good to walk anyhow, so all they do is sit in their wagon and primp all day. But if we got to get rid of some of our belongings, they've got to give up theirs too."

"They only have their clothes. They aren't bringing furniture," he told her.

Amy Dunbar snickered. "Why should they? All they need is a hotel room."

The crowd broke into gales of mocking laughter. Cord could see the prostitutes standing at the rear and noticed they were exchanging glances of annoyance. Crammed into one wagon, they were uncomfortable enough without being singled out for ridicule and scorn. He watched as they all drifted back into the shadows except for the spunkiest of their number, Imogene Newby.

Cord groaned inwardly as Imogene started pushing her way forward. Hoping to avoid a scene, he announced the meeting was over.

But it was too late.

Imogene stepped in front of Wilma Turnage and jabbed at Wilma's bosom with an angry finger. "For your information, we'd rather be outside walking. It'd be a damn sight better than bumping our butts every time the wheels hit a rock. But we stay inside to keep out of trouble, 'cause we're sick of the hateful remarks you make every time you think we can hear you. You leave us alone, and we'll leave you alone."

Wilma had no intentions of backing down. "You've no right to be among decent folk. Even the

Good Book preaches to avoid the temptations of evil, and that's what you are, evil. And you're tempting our menfolk to commit sins of the flesh."

Cord stepped between them. "That's enough, both of you."

Imogene wasn't through. With a look of contempt in Harry Turnage's direction, then at Wilma, she said, "You ain't got nothing to worry about, lady. None of us are that hard up for money."

It was all Cord could do to keep from breaking into laughter with everyone else. He steered Imogene away, leading her out of hearing range of the others. "You know it's best to just ignore her kind."

"I can take only so much." She wrested from his grasp. "The others feel the same. We shouldn't have come till there were more of us and fewer of them."

"Which would be next year," he pointed out.

Warmed by his nearness, Imogene's anger was fading fast. Since the first time she'd laid eyes on him, she had wanted him in her bed. She reached to brush her fingertips down his cheek, felt the roughness of his morning shave growing out. "Let's don't talk about unpleasant things. It's a beautiful night. I've got a jug of whiskey back in the wagon. We could go for a walk down by the river. Get to know each other better." She stepped forward, pressing her breasts against him. "Maybe I'll even give you a free one."

He moved away. "You know my rules. We talked about that when I signed you girls on. I don't mix pleasure with business."

Her laugh was husky. "But this *is* my business."

"Not till you get to California. Another rule is that you don't do it with anybody till we get there, remember? But I think I will have that drink. I need to talk to all you girls to get you calmed down so you won't let Wilma and the others get under your skin."

"They already have," Imogene whispered, not giving up. "So how about you getting *inside* it?"

"Forget it, Imogene." He took hold of her again, this time leading her in the direction of her wagon.

Jaime listened with interest as Hannah and Ella recounted the events of the meeting. She envied their freedom to move about, because the past few weeks had taken their toll. She wasn't able to walk as much as she wanted, because the others did not want to give up their turn. In fact, Ella was the only one who would allow her to walk in her place. Everyone was becoming grumpy and irritable as the trip wore on, and she had grown weary of hiding by day, stiff and sore from the wagon's jouncing.

She lived for the night, when, after the others made sure it was safe, she could slip outside to stretch her legs and, every once in a while, take a bath in the river if they were camped close enough. But always she had to hurry, limiting her time outdoors, for the risk of discovery was too great. She had to be careful lest Cord see her hair; she had also swapped her drab dress for something bright of Ella's, even though it hung large and loose.

Hearing of the argument between Wilma Turnage and the prostitute known only as Imogene was fascinating. Jaime also secretly enjoyed hearing how Cord had stood up to everyone. Watching him from afar whenever possible, she had come to respect him, despite her resentment for the way he'd so easily denounced her. His job, she knew, was not easy. It was said he was up before sunrise, and if there was work to be done, he did not make his bed beneath the supply wagon till the wee hours.

"How much longer?" Ella asked Hannah as they waited together for the right time for Jaime to sneak out.

Hannah said she had no idea. "I don't know where Austin is. I lost sight of him when the meeting ended. I think he took Imogene off to try and calm her down before she started pulling out Wilma's hair."

"I wasn't talking about that. I meant how long do you think it will be before Jaime can come out of hiding for good?"

"Not till after Fort Laramie. He might make her stay there. Frankly," she added with a sigh, "there are times when I wish he'd throw me out."

Jaime, quiet till now, gasped. "You don't mean that."

Hannah assured her she did. "I know the trip isn't as rough as it used to be, back in the first days of the gold rush, but it's still brutal. And I swear, if I was to meet a man standing alongside the trail who wanted to marry me and settle down then and there, I think I'd do it to keep from having to go all the way."

"Me too," Ella chimed in.

She could see their faces in the moonlight streaming through the end of the wagon and realized they

were serious. If she had shared their motives for having left Kansas, Jaime knew she might feel the same
way. Still, she hoped they did not change their minds
and drop out.

They moved back as Ruth climbed up. She had
taken a bath in the river despite its being muddied.
"Still waiting for Captain Austin to finish up with
Imogene?" she asked, settling down in the spot
where she made her bed.

Hannah said they hadn't returned from their walk.
"We can't chance Jaime going outside till we're sure
where he is."

Ruth said airily, "He's right behind you, silly. I saw
him follow her into her wagon as I was leaving to get
my bath. You all must not have been watching."

Ella was stunned. "Isn't that rather brazen? I mean,
I hate to sound like Wilma, but it doesn't look nice. The
wagon master should have some sense of decorum."

"Oh, I agree." Hannah nodded briskly. "After all,
how can he watch out for all of us if he's over there
carrying on with a wagon full of prostitutes? You
might as well get on out and take your walk, Jaime.
He'll be busy all night, for sure."

Jaime hastily crawled out of the wagon, to disappear into the night. As she paced about, giving her
stiff legs much-needed exercise, she told herself the
anger boiling within her came only from indignation
over Cord's shirking his duties to yield to the temptation Wilma Turnage preached about, not because she
personally cared what he did.

Finally going back, Jaime squeezed into her space
in the wagon. All was quiet. Evidently Cord had fallen

asleep. Maliciously, she hoped he did not wake till the arise shot was fired at four o'clock. Maybe then others would see him emerge and know what he'd been up to. Maybe they would be so mad they would ask him to resign when they got to Fort Laramie. With a new wagon master, she could come out of hiding, and Cord Austin could just go to hell for all she cared.

She drifted away to restless dreams of revenge, mingled with helpless desire for the man she was trying so hard to despise.

Promptly at four, the sentinel on duty fired his rifle. At once, people began to pour out of wagons and tents. Slow-kindling smoke began to rise. Breakfast was prepared and eaten, tents struck, wagons loaded, and teams yoked.

They had three hours to fall in their places in line, for the bugle to roll sounded exactly at seven. Those not ready were left behind to catch up, and everyone scrambled to keep that from happening, for it was not safe for a single wagon to straggle.

In the first moments of activity, Jaime stared out at the wagon behind, watching as Imogene and the others emerged to head for the bushes for their morning privacy. There was no sign of Cord, but she had not expected to see him, anyway. He was far too smart to get caught.

Imogene spotted her and gaily called "Good morning." Jaime nodded, then ducked back inside. The prostitutes had discovered her presence some weeks earlier but had been sworn to secrecy. Jaime found Imogene to be quite friendly and actually liked her, but that morning, as she watched her walk toward the bushes, she chided herself for actually feeling a twinge of jealousy. Cord Austin's kiss, unfortunately, was still a vivid and pleasant memory, and looking at the woman who had obviously known it last was unbearable.

"I'll get over it," she muttered under her breath.

Ella heard and patted her shoulder. "Sure you will. Before you know, we'll be far enough along for you to thumb your nose at Captain Austin, and he won't be able to do a thing about it. Won't that be wonderful?"

She skipped along toward the bushes with the others, not waiting for an answer.

Jaime had nothing to say. With a sigh of resignation, she settled down, resolved to make it through another day.

On schedule, they reached the steep drop Cord had warned about. There, with many of the women weeping and wailing over being forced to leave family heirlooms behind, the wagons were lowered to the bottom one by one.

Jaime, wearing a slat bonnet, blended in with the other women. Cord was far too busy to take note of an extra person.

All around, they could see evidence of other wagon trains having gone before them, for the area was littered with discarded items: weather-beaten furniture, rusting iron stoves and cooking utensils, and even luxury possessions, like ornate clocks, fine china and silverware, musical instruments, and books. In the valley below, however, lay the skeletons of wagons that had broken the ropes and tumbled downward to crash and splinter—a sobering sight that somewhat helped to ease remorse over abandoning cherished belongings.

A cool woodsy glen awaited, where Cord allowed a layover day for everyone to gather up the belongings that had been lowered by separate ropes and repack their wagons.

For the next fifty miles, the trail was an uphill grade, slight but constant. It was late June, and the nights were growing steadily colder with the rising altitude. On the distant horizon, they could see the snow-patched Laramie Mountains, which formed nature's stepping stones up into the rugged Rockies.

The scenery was spectacular, with strange formations of earth and rock. Jaime wondered wistfully if her family had taken the same trail when she was only two. She had no memories of the journey out and only vague recollections of the return.

On they traveled, weeks passing in misery. July came and, with it, tempers to match the soaring temperatures. They had covered over six hundred miles since leaving Independence. Everyone was tired; both strength and patience were growing thin. Animals were exhausted, as well as a third of the supplies. There were fights among the men, arguments among the women.

Sometimes, when things got out of hand, Cord stepped in to break up an altercation. As a result, anger was transferred to him, and as the wagon train approached the frontier outpost of Fort Laramie, he found himself the brunt of much animosity and resentment.

Increasing the tension, some of the men began to share the horrible tales they'd heard of how the trail got worse beyond Fort Laramie. The night Cord overheard Harry Turnage talking about the Donner party, he exploded.

It was a real horror story. Blocked by snow in the Sierra Nevadas, the pioneers had been forced to resort to cannibalism to survive.

"Why waste your time talking about something that happened twenty years ago? It was sad, but they made the wrong decision when they tried to take a shortcut that hadn't been proven. They paid the price for their mistake. Things are different now. It won't happen to us, because we're going to keep on schedule, follow the trail, and not let the snows catch us. Why stir everybody up?"

Harry spit a wad of tobacco juice dangerously close to Cord's boots. "It damn well better not happen to us, captain, 'cause if you get us snowbound and we run out of food, I promise you'll be the first one we put in a stew pot."

Those around him laughed, but Cord felt the undercurrent and also noted the hatred glowing in Harry Turnage's eyes. Fighting the impulse to smash his fist into the scowling face, Cord told him, "Any more talk like that, and you'll find yourself left at Fort Laramie, Turnage. I don't need rabble-rousers stirring folks up."

Harry snickered. "Well, you might be interested to know me and the missus have been talking about dropping out there anyway. Lots of others, too. We figure we might just hole in for the winter and wait till next spring to make it the rest of the way. My missus don't like traveling with whores."

Cord stalked away. Damn it, all he'd set out to do, been hired to do, was get the women to California. It had never been his intention to wind up mollycoddling a bunch of whining settlers. In a way, he didn't care if they did pull out, but he knew it was best to have as many wagons traveling together as possible.

It was late. As much as he needed a drink, he didn't want to join Imogene and the whores as he had got in the habit of doing. They might suspect his bad mood had something to do with more complaints about their presence. But he didn't want to go to bed quite yet, either. It was the perfect time for a swim. Everyone else was afraid of snakes and stayed out of the river after dark, but right then Cord was so blasted mad, he felt sorry for man or beast that crossed his path.

He headed for the river.

Jaime saw him and held her breath. Only moments before, she had finished her bath at water's edge, retreating to the cover of rocks to dry herself and dress. As soon as he passed, she crouched down and darted through the scrub brush toward the ring of wagons.

She did not see Wilma Turnage squatting in the bushes till it was too late to keep from crashing right into her.

6

"*Why don't you watch* where you're going, you little upstart?" Wilma whispered harshly, righting herself and yanking down her gown.

Jaime murmured a hasty apology as she tried to scramble away, but Wilma grabbed her ankle and held tight. "Who are you, anyway?" Suspiciously, she scanned her face in the moonlight. "You're one of the whores, aren't you?"

"Oh, no, ma'am," Jaime was quick to say, afraid Mrs. Turnage was going to start screaming and bring everyone running, including Cord. "I'm with the women going to get married."

Wilma shook her head. "No, you aren't. I've seen all them. Know them by their names. Who are you? And why haven't I seen you before?"

Jaime knew she had no choice and admitted she was a stowaway.

Wilma chuckled as she listened, pleased to hear of

a conspiracy aimed at the smart-alecky wagon master. "Well, now." She beamed at Jaime. "I think you're real smart to get away with it all this time. You sure don't have to worry about me saying anything."

Jaime needed reassurance. "You promise?"

"Of course. I got no use for that man and how he brought them whores along, and I'll be looking forward to the day he finds out you tricked him. When do you plan to come out of hiding?"

"I'd like to make it all the way past Salt Lake; then there wouldn't be any big town to leave me in before Sacramento. I believe he'd let me continue on."

"You really think you can hide out till then?"

"I've come too far to fail now," Jaime said confidently.

"Well, quite frankly, not much gets by me, but you did, so I reckon you'll succeed."

Jaime turned to go, anxious to end the conversation.

Wilma called, "You let me know if you need any help, hear?"

Jaime kept on going, praying she would never have to accept her offer.

She knew something was going on between Ella and Hannah long before they reached Fort Laramie. While everyone else talked excitedly, constantly asking Cord how much farther till they got there, Ella and Hannah hardly spoke to each other and had little to say to anyone else. She prayed they were not arguing about turning back, for Hannah's discontent had steadily been worsening.

It was their last night on the trail before their

planned arrival at the settlement the next afternoon. As the sun sank low in the west, Cord sent Fletcher ahead to make ready to guide the wagon into a circle. The ritual had been performed so many times the measurement was perfect, and the hindmost wagon precisely closed the gateway. In less than ten minutes from the time the lead wagon halted, the barricade for the night was formed.

Everyone scrambled for the chores they knew by heart. The women busied themselves preparing fires of buffalo chips to cook the evening meal, while older children helped their fathers pitch tents, unyoke the oxen, unharness the mules, and feed all the animals.

Not too many days after leaving Independence, all the women Cord had signed on had decided to pool their resources and prepare their meals together, including the prostitutes. Usually, they took turns cooking, but this time Hannah found herself alone with the chore as the others took off to the riverbank to do their laundry. They knew there would be soldiers at the fort, perhaps a party and dancing, and they were all anxious to have a clean dress to wear for the festivities.

"I never want to see another potato as long as I live," Hannah grumbled as she dropped them, one by one, into a kettle of water to boil.

She was talking to Jaime, who crouched inside the wagon, counting the minutes till it was dark enough to slip outside and join the others. She ached all over from the cramped, bumpy ride. Everyone had wanted to keep going, anxious to cover the remaining distance to Fort Laramie, so they had not stopped as long, during the nooning time, for lunch and to water and rest the animals.

Hannah continued her griping. "It wasn't my idea to join up with those whores," she said.

Jaime knew then that Hannah was really at the breaking point. Normally, she was more tolerant.

"They're just anxious to get their laundry done too," Jaime said, in an attempt to pacify.

"That's not what I'm talking about. If it weren't for them, some of the husbands would give us some meat when they kill a buffalo or a deer. All we have is potatoes and onions and what's left of the meal to make johnnycakes. I can't remember the last time I had a bit of meat, but the men aren't going to come near us, thanks to the whores. Their wives would have a fit."

Jaime tried to lighten her mood by teasing. "Would you even know how to cook buffalo, Hannah?"

"Of course I would. I see the other women. They cook it just like regular beefsteak, only a little bit longer. It smells wonderful." She swiped at her hair with the back of her hand, pushing it back from her forehead, then reached for the bag of onions, winced as she began to peel them, and wailed, "Look at my hands. It makes no difference if I wear those hot and heavy buckskin gloves. I still get blisters. Somebody else needs to take a turn with those reins—"

Jaime's eyes bulged and every nerve went taut as she shrank back into the shadows. Hannah had not seen Cord approaching, but she had, thank God, in time to keep him from spotting her. But a chill of horror swept as she thought of the consequences if Hannah wasn't soon aware of his presence, for she might speak her name, and he was staring at her like she'd gone daft anyway, thinking she was talking to herself.

". . . not right I have to do all the work around here, anyway. If you—" Hannah turned to glare at Jaime, and tell her once again it was time she let her presence be known, and saw Cord standing there, a strange look on his grime-streaked face. "I . . . I didn't know anyone was around," she stammered.

"Obviously." He flashed a crooked smile and held out a bowl containing a hunk of dark red meat. "Here. One of the sentinels killed a buffalo earlier in the day and just caught up with us. You and the other ladies should enjoy some meat."

Hannah broke into a grateful grin and without thinking blurted out, "I was just saying how we never have any meat—" then caught herself and countered self-consciously, "There I go. Talking to myself again. I guess I'm more tired than I thought."

"We all are." He reached out, gently took her wrist, turning her palm up, and frowned to see the oozing blisters. "I'm going to try and hire some extra teamsters at the fort to help out, and I'll also work it out so I can take a few hours every day. Meanwhile, it's time the other women on your wagon started taking turns at the reins, whether they like it or not."

She drew her hand back. "I'll be fine. Don't worry about me."

After he left, Hannah angrily turned to the wagon, knowing Jaime could hear her. "See what trouble you cause? If he can't hire extra men, I'll have to keep at it myself. The others won't do it; they've said so. And it'd be taking too big a chance for him to do it with you hiding inside. He'd probably roll back the cover like he's been after me to do anyway. I'd sure get a better breeze coming up behind me, but no, we have to keep it up 'cause of you."

She railed on and Jaime kept silent, washed with guilt to be the cause of such discomfort. Still, she had come this far and felt compelled to hide out a little longer. It would be horrible to have to turn back now, and Cord might just be angry enough to see that she did.

Toward sundown the next day, slightly above the gentle rolling prairie, whoops and cries went up from the weary pioneers as the turreted and picketed ramparts of Fort Laramie came into view.

An adobe wall, fifteen feet high, surrounded the fort. Long before the wagons began to roll into a circle on the green meadows just east of the wall, those walking broke into an excited run and fell into the welcoming arms of strangers amid shouts and laughter of greeting. Cord had announced at the previous night's meeting that he would allow two layover days, instead of one, and everyone was in a festive mood.

Jaime could only stare wistfully from inside the wagon as activities got under way inside the fort. During the day, wearing the big slat bonnet, she didn't worry about being noticed so much anymore, but she still dared not mingle socially. Through the open gates, she could see the dancing as the soldiers were given liberty to socialize with the unmarried women. The lively music of banjos, guitars, and har-

monicas filled the air, along with the tantalizing odor
of pigs being roasted over open pits.

She had hoped Ella and Hannah would bring her a
plate of food, but as soon as they found out there were
bath facilities—barrels of water with pull ropes positioned over a neck-high wooden pen—they grabbed up
the gingham dresses they had washed in the river the
night before and took off. Joining the merriment, they
forgot all about their hungry stowaway.

But Wilma Turnage remembered. As soon as it
was dark, she carried Jaime a tin plate, heaped with
meat, boiled cabbage, crispy fried bread, and a delicious mug of cold cider.

Jaime ate ravenously as Wilma enthusiastically
described the inside of the fort. "The men have the
means to mend both wagons and harness, shoe
horses and oxen, and there's also a trading post.
Flour is going for fifteen dollars a hundredweight,
and a dollar will get two cups of sugar or two cups of
coffee beans."

"Oh, I wish I could go inside. I'd give anything to
be able to dance—not that I even know how," she
added.

"Well, your friends certainly know how. Hannah
latched up with one of the army scouts and hasn't let
him out of her sight. Ella is just as bad. It's a sight.
And I can tell you, the captain doesn't like it. I saw
him standing off to one side watching, face like a
thundercloud, because all them promised brides are
having themselves a time. I'll bet he's wondering if
he's going to be able to get any of them out of here."

Jaime shivered, but not from the chilly night of

late July. Cord didn't know it, but he wasn't the only one concerned.

Feeling terribly worried, she wrapped a blanket around herself and finally drifted off to sleep. Sometime later, she was abruptly awakened by angry voices outside and hurried to peek out. Cord, she soon realized, was telling three irate soldiers they could not enter the prostitutes' wagon. And once again, despite everything, her heart went out to him for the burden of the responsibilities he had inherited.

"I've got an agreement with the commander that the ladies won't conduct any business on the post," Cord informed the men.

"This ain't the post," one of the soldiers grumbled. "We're outside."

Cord told him it didn't matter. "He agreed they could visit inside. That's all. If I let you boys come here for pleasuring, the ladies living on the post are going to raise hell, and I've heard enough already from the ones on the train."

"Well, you shouldn't have let 'em come in, captain, and get us all stirred up," another furiously protested. "You seen the way they was dancin' and flirtin' and carryin' on. If you wasn't gonna let 'em take care of us, you shouldn't have let 'em inside in the first place."

The others grunted in agreement.

The first man who had spoken complained again. "Some of us ain't had a woman in months."

At that precise moment, Imogene stuck her head out and laughed shrilly. "Oh, come on, Captain Austin. We need a little fun. Besides, we could use some money to spend at the trading post tomorrow."

Cord swore. She was deliberately teasing them, allowing her breasts to spill from her robe as she held it together just enough to cover her nipples. "Get back inside," he ordered harshly, reaching to yank the canvas closed.

"Hey, you leave her alone."

Cord was caught off guard by the man's sudden shove.

Stumbling backward, Cord rebounded to clip the man's jaw with his fist before whipping out his gun, all done so quickly that those watching would later swear they never saw him move.

"All of you. Out of here," he commanded through tightly clenched teeth. "And don't come back around this wagon."

Wilma Turnage, having heard the commotion, came rushing up. Seeing Cord with his gun pointed at the soldiers, she shrieked hysterically. "I knew it. I knew sooner or later there'd be trouble over those strumpets. You had no business bringing them along with decent folk."

Cord kept his eye on the enraged soldiers as he quietly directed Wilma to get back to her wagon and mind her own business.

Undaunted, she fired back, "This *is* my business. It's everybody's business. For over two months and six hundred and forty miles, we been looking forward to getting here so we could relax a little and celebrate going a third of the way, but it's being ruined by them whores. I say you leave them here."

Others were gathering, women in robes or shawls

wrapped about their gowns, the men bare-chested and wearing long johns. A few were emerging from their wagons carrying weapons.

Cord saw that sentries at the fort had noticed the goings-on and alerted others. Soldiers were starting to run across the grassy slope to investigate.

Jaime groped in the darkness for Hannah and Ella, softly calling to them. Only Ruth and Martha were there, and it was Ruth, beside her, who whispered that Hannah and Ella were still inside. "They met two men and seemed to really like them."

Just then, Jaime saw her friends coming from the fort. With a stab of apprehension, she noted that Hannah was clinging to the arm of a man clad in buckskin, while Ella held hands with one wearing the uniform of an officer.

Outside the wagon, Fletcher and Henderson showed up to stand beside Cord. The drunken soldiers had been gathering their nerve to jump him, but they began to back away.

Holstering his gun, Cord said, "All right, everybody back to your wagons and tents. It's over."

"Not as long as those whores are around," Wilma cried, striking the air with her fist. It made her even madder the way Imogene continued to poke her head out the wagon, watching with a smirk on her ruby lips. "We're going to keep on having trouble. It's time you did something about them, got them away from decent Christian folk."

Wearily, Cord attempted to reason with the woman. "Mrs. Turnage, this isn't the first time prostitutes have been transported to California. It won't be the last. And you're wasting your time and mine griping about it."

Muttering to those around her, she joined them in leaving.

The officer who had been walking with Ella left her to ask what was going on. Cord told him, saying he thought it would be best if the wagon train was declared off limits to army personnel.

The officer assured Cord it would be done. It was the policy of the Army to maintain good relations with the passing wagon trains. Since Fort Laramie had become an official government post in 1849, between nine and ten thousand wagons had come through each year. From time to time, there were incidents and altercations, but for the most part peace prevailed.

Jaime was disappointed when the officer led Ella back to the fort, with Hannah and her scout right behind. She was lonely and wanted to hear all the details of the party.

But something else happened to keep Jaime and the others peeking out of the wagon.

Once everyone was gone, Cord, careful to keep his voice low despite his fury, whirled on Imogene. "You almost started a riot. I told you before we left Independence you wouldn't carry on any business till we reach California. I should have known better than to let you go inside, but I thought you could behave yourselves. No more, understand? You and the others are not to leave this compound."

Imogene gave her long hair a haughty toss and downed the rest of the whiskey she was drinking before informing him airily, "There won't be a next time, captain. I've talked to the other girls, and we're fed up with being treated like lepers. We're not going any farther."

Any other time, Cord might have argued, but right then, he just didn't give a damn. A seemingly simple assignment had turned into nothing but aggravation, and he wished he could just saddle his horse and ride out and let them all go to hell. "Fine, if that's what you want, but I hope you realize you women won't stand a chance out there alone."

She gave a careless shrug. "So we'll stay here till we decide what to do."

"And I don't suppose you care about the money that's been spent to get you this far."

"Honey," she drawled, smiling, "you know I'll be glad to let you take it out in trade."

Cord knew then what the oxen must feel like at day's end when the yoke was lifted from their shoulders. He didn't care about the whores or the money. All he knew was relief to have one less problem to deal with.

Without another word, he stalked away.

And Jaime, still spying, felt a great wave of compassion as she watched him go.

The news that the prostitutes were staying at the fort spread like wildfire. The post commander was just about to declare it would not be allowed when several families announced they were turning back. The prostitutes decided to join them.

When the commander learned that Cord had never led a wagon train before, he told him he should not feel bad to be losing some of his people. "Every time a caravan comes through, it happens.

They're worn out and weary and homesick. Don't blame yourself."

Cord was quick to answer. "Believe me, I don't. To be honest, it would suit me fine at this point if they all wanted to turn around. But they can damn well find somebody else to lead them. This is my first and last wagon train."

Jaime was deeply disappointed to hear that Imogene and her friends would not be continuing. Despite everything, she had liked walking with them from time to time. They had known her secret and kept it well.

Ella and Hannah had not been around much during the layover, but they came to the wagon the night before they were scheduled to depart and she was able to bring up the subject of the prostitutes and how she would miss them.

Ella and Hannah exchanged uncomfortable glances. They were dressing to join their new men friends for dinner at the fort. Jaime wondered why they were acting so strangely but, before she had a chance to ask, Ella made a shattering announcement. "We aren't going on to California either. We're staying here, at Fort Laramie. Tom has asked me to marry him, and Charlie proposed to Hannah."

Hannah added, "Most of the other brides are staying too. If they haven't already found somebody to marry, they will. There're lots of men looking for wives right here. Why should we keep on with this miserable trip?"

Jaime went pale and could only stare at her two friends in stunned disbelief.

"You see," Ella rushed on, putting an arm about Jaime in an attempt to console her, "Hannah is just plain worn out. And since the whole idea was for us to make a new life somewhere else, it doesn't have to be all the way out in California."

"But here?" Jaime gestured, eyes wide. "An army post in the middle of nowhere? And you only met these men two days ago—"

"At least we *met* them," Hannah defended. "We were on our way to marry complete strangers, remember? At least I've had a chance to get to know Charlie and see what a fine man he is. And it's the same with Ella.

"It's our lives," she said, lifting her chin, "and we can do what we want."

Ella spoke up to remind her. "Once you get to California and find your father, you'll have a new life too. You won't need us then, and you really don't need us now. You've got Ruth and Martha. Even Wilma is your friend, and though she and her husband grumble a lot about Captain Austin, they've decided to keep going since Imogene and her girls are turning back.

"You'll be fine," Ella went on, giving her another hug. "You've got believe that."

But Jaime did not know what to believe anymore, for emptiness had already begun to gnaw at her.

And all of a sudden California seemed farther away than ever.

7

As they continued onward, with Ruth and Martha finally taking turns driving the oxen, Jaime saw the road beyond Fort Laramie was littered with still more discarded household goods from those who had passed before. Soon they learned the reason, for they had begun the ascent of the Rockies in earnest, and it was better to lighten their loads as much as possible than to curse and beat the exhausted animals onward.

Barren land surrounded them. From a distance the mountainsides appeared green and lush, but as they drew closer, reality became dry sand and rocks, accented by stunted sage clumps and greasewood. A fifty-mile trek along the North Platte took them to the Sweetwater River; from there, the trail led deeper into the Rockies, and the scenery became more spectacular.

With so many having turned back, and only two women supposed to be in her wagon, Jaime had to be very careful lest she be noticed by Cord and his sentinels, Fletcher and Henderson. Gradually, the others learned of her presence, and they all conspired to keep her secret. As a result, she started feeling as though she were part of a huge family. It was wonderful. Despite the grueling trip, she was happier and felt better than ever before.

She had taken to spying on Cord whenever possible, a diversion she enjoyed. Hiding in the shadows, she would watch for him to drift away from the circle of wagons to take his nightly walk. She would follow, keeping a safe distance. Eventually, he would stop—to meditate, she supposed. If they were near water, a river or a stream, he would sit down, light up a cheroot, and stare quietly into the night.

Sometimes he would stay for hours, and so would she, playing a game with herself as she tried to guess what he was thinking. If it had been a particularly grueling day, she could tell by his restless fidgeting, the occasional sighs of disgruntlement. But after a good day, which meant one without incident, such as a broken wheel, collapsed animal, or sickness, he would sit quietly, obviously at peace with himself and the world around him.

She had come to realize there was a side to him others never saw. By day, he was unflappable, coldly reserved, forceful, and unyielding. But observing him as she did, she felt he was deeply concerned about his responsibilities. Maybe some felt he ruled with an iron fist, but she suspected that beneath the harsh façade he was a very sensitive man.

Some nights, despite the chill, he would strip off his shirt. When there was moonlight, she was awed by the sight of his muscular chest, powerful shoulders, and sinewy arms. Sometimes, he would take off everything and go for a swim or take a bath. And, again, if there was ample radiance, she would marvel shamelessly at his tight, sculptured buttocks, the backs of his rock-hard thighs.

The spying caused her no particular feelings of guilt, for no one knew. Her dreams were all that bothered her, stirring and haunted by wonder over what it was really like to be loved by a man. Images. Fantasies. She would awaken bathed in perspiration, feeling as though she were glowing inside and out. On those mornings after a passion-ridden night of imaginings, she felt a strange affinity for Cord she could not understand that evoked delighted shivers if she happened to see him. And, as always, she chided herself for such weakness.

Finally, they reached the eastern boundary of the Oregon Territory, but many did not rejoice over the milestone. Some wished they had turned back at Laramie, while others no longer looked to California as a land where hopes and dreams would be fulfilled.

Due to the increasing discontent, fueled by exhaustion, Cord found his job even more difficult. Like dry grass waiting to be struck and ignited by lightning, the atmosphere of the wagon train became volatile. Arguments increased, along with fist fights. Some of the women even engaged in hair pulling over trivial incidents. Accordingly, he had come to dread the nightly meetings, for they always turned into trying to resolve some dispute between families. Fighting seemed a welcome diversion to the misery of their existence.

The night Harry Turnage asked how long a layover they would have at Salt Lake, Cord knew what the reaction would be when he replied, "Two days."

"Two?" Harry echoed above the angry rumbling around him. "But it's our last big stop before crossing the Sierras."

Another voice else joined in, also irate. "He's right. We deserve to stay longer than two days, for God's sake. We got to cross the Sierras, and we deserve a rest."

With a sigh, Cord asked wearily, "How many times do I have to say it: we've got to cross before the snows come? We could be blocked in the passes till the spring thaw. Even the relay riders suspend mail runs when the worst weather comes, and they've got those newfangled snowshoes for their horses. We've got to keep moving. Every day counts."

Wilma Turnage yelled, "I say we take a vote. Let the people decide how long we stay."

Cord felt his ire rising but managed to respond calmly. "As long as I'm wagon master, I'll make the decisions."

"Well, if enough of us decide we're laying over, you can't do nothing about it."

"I can leave you behind, you and anyone else who doesn't roll when I give the signal."

"Well, maybe we don't care," she fired back, shaking her head at her husband's whispered urgings for her to be quiet and resisting as he sought to pull her away from the gathering.

"Do what you want," Cord declared in disgusted conclusion. "Two days after we make Salt Lake, I'm pulling out."

With two days left before they were scheduled to reach the Mormon settlement, Jaime again followed Cord after dark. Maybe it was wrong, she reasoned, but it was something to do to while away the boring hours. This time, however, there was no moon and she could barely see him, so she did not tarry. Besides, she was overcome by excitement, having long ago decided that once they left Salt Lake she would come out of hiding.

Cord heard the sound of someone creeping away through the bushes, just as he had heard the approach. He had known, each and every time, when he was being watched, and he knew it was a woman from her fragile movements. In the beginning, he was tempted to trap her and discover her identity, but then it became a novelty. Let her look, whoever she was. When he got tired of being spied on, he would make his move. Till then, she could have her fun, and, besides, he had enough on his mind without concerning himself over some old busybody, probably Wilma Turnage, who, no doubt, was hoping to catch him doing something she could bitch about. Like secretly meeting somebody's wife, or maybe getting drunk.

Well, to hell with her, he thought, disgusted. To hell with all of them.

He stayed a while longer, then headed back to the supply wagon to bed down. Seeing Fletcher and Henderson waiting, he slowed his pace in apprehension. Jasper, their supply driver and cook, was nowhere in sight, but he'd left a good fire going, and in its glow Cord could see by the men's faces that something was up.

A pot of coffee was set near the fire to keep warm. Cord walked over, got a mug, and poured himself a cup.

Fletcher and Henderson murmured nervous greetings.

Cord sat down and said tonelessly, "All right. Something is wrong. Let's hear it."

Henderson gave Fletcher a jab with his elbow, indicating he was to do the talking. Fletcher cleared his throat and began uneasily. "There's talk, captain, about how a lot of wagons are gonna pull out at Salt Lake."

Cord shrugged, sipped the coffee. "I'm going to California, with or without them. What's your problem?" he asked with narrowed eyes.

When Fletcher did not immediately respond, Henderson gave him another jab. "Well, we figure you won't be needing us no longer, since probably everybody is gonna drop out."

"Everybody?" Cord had not anticipated that, but neither did he care. Still, he reminded, "You two signed up to go all the way. I've still got Ruth and Martha to get out there. I'd like to have you along."

Fletcher swallowed hard and glanced away, not wanting to be the one to tell him. Henderson, ready to get it over with, lost his patience and blurted out,

"They ain't going either. I'm marrying Ruth and Fletcher's marrying Martha, and we're gonna find us a place to homestead."

For long tense moments, no one spoke. Cord stared into the fire, teeth ground tightly together, every nerve in his body tensing as he resisted the impulse to leap to his feet and crack their heads together. But as he sat there, he slowly got hold of himself and thought once more how he really didn't give a damn. He had tried. Done his best. The man who hired him wouldn't like the money he had lost, but he was rich and could stand it. No need to be upset. If they all dropped out, fine. He would keep on going.

"You know," he felt the need to say finally, "those women agreed to get married in California. Not along the way."

"Sorry," Wallace and Fletcher murmured in unison.

Cord stood and flung his empty cup into the darkness. Then he walked away, still tempted to knock the hell out of both of them.

Jaime watched as Ruth and Martha gathered their things, preparing to move out. They were on the outskirts of Salt Lake and would arrive the next day, but Henderson and Fletcher wanted to pull out then and there.

"I still can't believe it," she said, shaking her head in wonder, having heard the story of their romances. "I had no idea all of you were . . ." She trailed off, not sure what to say. Though she was terribly upset by the news, it was still none of her business.

"It was a gradual thing," Ruth said. "But you don't have to worry. We never let them know about you."

Martha agreed. "No. We kept your secret, honest." She then went on to point out, "But you know you can't stay here by yourself, and if you go to Captain Austin now, he's not going to let you go with him. He's not going to care what happens to you."

Sounding braver than she felt, Jaime lifted her chin. "I'll find a way to get there somehow."

Martha exchanged a worried look with Ruth before asking, "Well, what are you going to do now? Everybody is quitting the wagon train."

"That's right." Ruth joined in. "There's nobody left for you to ride with."

Jaime lowered her face to her hands. After all she had been through, all the weeks and months of hiding, it had come to this. What could she do?

Just then Wilma Turnage poked her head through the opening in the laced canvas at the end of the wagon. By lantern light, she saw their faces and knew they had to be discussing Jaime's fate.

Ruth confirmed it by telling her, "She won't say what she wants to do."

In her no-nonsense way, Wilma snapped, "She has no choice. She's going with me and mine." To Jaime, she said, "Come along, child. Harry isn't sure where we're going, but you can go with us. We'll make sure you're looked after."

Jaime wiped her eyes with the back of her hand. God, she was fed up with having no choices in her life. Once, on the trail sometime back, she had seen a team of horses spooked during a thunderstorm. They had run wildly across the plain with no aim or direction, galloping furiously to try and escape an unknown fear. By so doing, they had destroyed themselves. The driver had jumped in time, realizing there was no hope of bringing them under control before they ran off the edge of a precipice to certain death below.

That was not going to happen to her, Jaime vowed. She was not going to run merely because something had happened she could not control. Somehow, some way, she would find an answer to her dilemma. Till then, she would have to endure as best she could.

Finally lifting her head, she thanked Wilma quietly, then gathered what few belongings she had and followed her to her wagon.

It was late when people finally bedded down. Jaime could not sleep, far too worried over her plight. Creeping out into the darkness, she made her way to the tiny stream where earlier the women had gathered to bathe themselves and their children in happy preparation for arriving in Salt Lake.

Hearing voices, she ducked behind a large rock. She was about to turn back when she recognized Cord. She could tell he was fired up.

"They signed on for the long haul. What I ought to do is put a bullet in them for desertion. That's what we did in the war, by damn."

"This ain't war, captain. And if you'd been on as many wagon trains as I have, you'd understand it happens all the time. Folks drop out. Change their minds. And they don't care who gets hurt when they do. And you can't blame the promised brides, neither. A husband is a husband, the way they see it, no matter where they find him."

"Well, Jasper, at least you're here," Cord said.

Jaime's heart slammed into her chest as the idea struck. The supply wagon. Of course! All she had to do was slip inside it and hide among the crates and barrels, and as soon as they were a little way down the road, she'd let her presence be known. They would have to take her on to California with them.

By God, she told herself amid the thrilling rush, she was going to make it, after all.

She heard Jasper say he had to go check on the animals; then came the sound of his footsteps fading in another direction. She tarried but a moment longer, wanting to make sure Cord was not coming her way. Then she turned and started quietly back, anxious to slip her satchel out of the Turnage wagon and settle into Jasper's. In the morning, Wilma would wonder what happened to her but not for long. Like everyone else, Wilma was excited and anxious to get to Salt Lake and would quickly forget all about her.

Cord was sprawled on the ground but suddenly he sprang to his feet to cry out, "All right, dammit, who are you? I think it's time you showed your face."

Terrified, Jaime broke into a run.

Cord started to follow, then swore and dropped back to the ground.

After tonight, she wouldn't be bothering him again. Nobody would. Because Jasper didn't have him fooled, not a bit. He knew the traitorous son of a bitch was deserting to go with the others. He just didn't have the guts to tell him so.

Cord closed his eyes and let sleep take over. He was going to spend the night right where he was, and when morning came he was leaving. He would take the supply wagon and continue on by himself.

He didn't need anybody, by damn.

He would make it on his own—like always.

8

Jaime burrowed beneath sacks of flour and sugar and then spread a canopy, completely covering herself. Two days at the most, she figured, and she would be able to come out of hiding for good. She had a canteen of water and some buffalo jerky. She could survive. The greatest risk of discovery would come at night. She would have to slip out then to relieve herself. But surely Cord and Jasper would have things to take care of, like tending the animals and such, that would take them away from the wagon.

She harbored no hard feelings for the others and wished them well. They owed her nothing and had already helped in many ways.

The night air was cool, but lying between the burlap bags, Jaime was warm and cozy. Soon, despite the sound of laughter and merriment coming from the distant encampment, she felt herself drifting away.

*   *   *

It was still dark. To the east, there was not yet a hint of dawn. Cord hitched the mules to the wagon and tied his horse behind. He wanted to be on his way before the others began stirring about, knowing there would be those, like Wilma Turnage, who would gloat over his being completely abandoned. Not that he truly gave a damn. He just didn't see giving her the satisfaction of thinking he did.

Some wagon trains succeeded. Some didn't. He was just glad it was over.

He popped the reins and set the mules lumbering forward, skirting around Salt Lake. He could have made faster time on horseback but took the wagon so he would have supplies if bad weather made it necessary to hole up a spell.

Dawn came, the sky overcast. Cord welcomed the chilling wind. He was heading for the Great Basin, a killer of men. Isolated and rimmed, it formed a cauldron of white salt sands, baked clay wastes, and the circling mountains reflected the heat of the sun like a mirror. Bleak and desolate, the Humboldt River did not flow, it oozed, disappearing eventually into a thick sponge of alkali dust. But till then, he looked forward to a fairly smooth trail amid the cool green foothills composing the basin's outer walls.

He was not too concerned about Indians, even though he traveled alone. He had his weapons beside him: two Spencer repeating rifles, as well as double-holstered guns. He could also speak the language of the two tribes he might possibly encounter—Paiute and Shoshone. Being able to tell them he intended peace, and offering them a few beads and trinkets, should get him through without incident.

Frankly, he could understand the Indians' anger over the white man's intrusion. After all, the first gold seekers had left devastation on the plains in their wake—dead buffalo by the thousands, death from the cholera they brought, as well as trampled and dying grass caused by the wagons and animals.

Late in the day, rain began to fall. He set his sights on a craggy formation in the distance, figuring he would camp there for the night and have shelter beneath the outcropping rocks.

Inside the wagon, Jaime had been dozing off and on all day. Her stomach gave a rumble, and she ate a piece of buffalo jerky, which made her thirsty. Finding her canteen, she took a long sip of water.

Stiff and sore, she longed to stretch her aching limbs. Slowly, cautiously, she pushed away the sacks and peered about. The canvas had been laced and drawn together tightly at both ends, but rain was still blowing in. Crawling forward, careful not to knock over crates or barrels, she looked first out the rear but saw nothing but empty wasteland.

Moving to the front, she saw Jasper hunched forward, hat pulled down over his head. He was drenched, and she felt sorry for him. At least she was reasonably dry, although if she didn't return to shelter beneath the canopy and sacks, she would also be soaked by the rain.

She was about to turn away when Cord saw a big rock in the road just ahead. With a curse, he snatched at the reins and yelled out at the mules, "Whoa, easy!"

In that heart-stopping instant, Jaime's hands flew to her mouth in a futile attempt to stifle her gasp of horror. It was Cord at the reins, not Jasper!

Cord heard the sound. With one hand, he jerked the mules to a complete halt, at the same time drawing his pistol and whipping about to demand sharply, "Who's there?"

Jaime dove beneath the sacks, frantically, wildly, daring to hope he might think a wild animal had got inside but ran away when he yelled. It was too soon for him to find her. They had not been gone from Salt Lake even a whole day. He could turn around and take her back without losing hardly any time at all. And where was Jasper? Dear Lord, surely someone else was about.

She sank down and held her breath.

Cord dropped to the ground. Only an Indian could have been quiet enough to sneak inside without his hearing. In the language of the Shoshone, he commanded, "Come out. I mean you no harm. I will let you go in peace."

Jaime had been crouched with eyes tightly closed, dreading the moment she would have to stare up into his livid face. But when she heard the strange-sounding, guttural words, her eyes flashed open.

Cord repeated himself, then changed to the Paiute tongue. Both tribes could be found in the area, though he'd not seen any. Buffalo hunting was better farther south this time of year. Few braves ventured this far till spring.

Jaime was even more terrorized by the bizarre sounds.

Expecting a knife-wielding savage to leap out, Cord cautiously approached the rear of the wagon. "All right," he whispered. "You had your chance."

His right hand held a pointed rifle. With his left, he drew a knife from his boot. With one quick slash, he severed the gathering cord of the canvas, and it fell open, exposing the interior. He knew whoever was in there had to be hiding beneath the sacks, so with another slice, he ripped open the top bag.

Flour spilled down to cover Jaime in a cloud of white dust, and she couldn't help herself; as the thick powder covered her face, she began to gasp and cough.

"What the hell?" Cord froze for only an instant before jerking away the ripped bag, which filled the inside of the wagon with flying powder. "Who in thunderation are you?" he bellowed, grabbing her arm roughly and jerking her out.

Jaime struggled in his grasp. Hacking, wheezing, she felt as if she were choking to death. He was hurting her, the way his fingers were pressing so brutally into her flesh as he pulled her from the wagon. "Let . . . let me go," she sputtered amid a snowy spray of flour. "You almost killed me with that knife, you idiot."

"If I'd wanted you dead, you would be." Holding her with one hand, he swiped roughly at the mask of flour. "You aren't Indian, that's for sure. Not with this pale face."

"Very funny." She twisted in his grasp, but he held tight. "Let me go, I say."

"You say," he snorted. "*I'll* say when I'm done with you. Now start talking. I want to know who you are and what you're doing stowing away on my wagon. If you wanted to go along, why didn't you say so?" He studied her as best he could, with the flour caked on her face. Only her wide, angry eyes were visible, ringed with white. "I don't recall seeing you before, but that hair . . ." He lifted a strand of gold.

Jaime continued to squirm. It had stopped raining, but the flour was clinging to her damp clothes and was extremely uncomfortable.

He released her to stand back and stare in wonder. There was no mistaking the turquoise eyes. He'd thought of them again when he'd traded a necklace made of the blue-green stone to the Cheyenne. And that hair, the color of gold.

"You!"

"Yes, me." Jaime indignantly began wiping her face with the hem of her calico dress. It was one of her favorites, given to her by Wilma Turnage, whose daughter had outgrown it. Now it was going to be difficult to wash. "Why didn't you just yank the sacks away if you knew I was under there? Why did you have to act like some kind of crazy savage?"

Grabbing her elbow, he steered her to the side of the trail and all but threw her down on a flat rock. Towering over her, he pointed a buckskin-gloved finger at her, and, with nostrils flaring, every nerve in his jaw jumping, he ordered, "Talk, damn it. How did you get here?"

She enjoyed the gloating triumph of being able to tell him that, thanks to a slat-side bonnet to hide her hair and too many friends to count, it had been quite easy. Uncomfortable at times, because she couldn't have all the freedom she wanted to move around, but it hadn't actually been too bad. She watched smugly as he ran agitated fingers through his hair.

"Why now?"

"Why now what?" She blinked.

"Why did you come with me now? Why didn't you stay with the others?"

Hastily, she explained how she was going to find her father, adding, "And since I'd made it this far, I had to try and go the rest of the way. Besides, I thought Jasper was going with you. I heard—" She fell silent, embarrassed to admit she had spied on him.

He smiled for the first time. "So it was you all those nights."

"You knew?" she cried in wonder. "But you never gave any indication."

"What? And spoil your fun? I wanted to see how long you'd keep it up. Usually, it's the other way around, men looking at women, but I don't guess I should be surprised at anything you do."

"It was just a game, something to pass the time and—oh!" She turned away, unable to bear the way he was staring down at her.

He was not about to show mercy, enjoying his torment for her having made a fool of him all this time. "You have to admit you keep turning up in the most unlikely places. First you come to my hotel room, wanting to marry me. Then you follow me across the wilderness to spy on me. You're a strange one, all right, but that still doesn't tell me why you crawled in the supply wagon. Surely you don't think I'm taking you the rest of the way?"

"You have to," she cried, anguish shimmering in her wide, frightened eyes. "Don't you see? I've nowhere else to go. You're my only hope.

"And surely you can see now you were wrong about me," she hastened to add. "I'm not puny, like you thought. I haven't been sick a day. Not the whole trip. And even though you didn't know it, I did my share of the work, as much as I could without risking you or your men seeing me. Please. You've just got to take me with you."

A tear rolled down her cheek. She swiped at it viciously, determined not to cry, lest he think her weak despite her accomplishments.

"This is crazy." He shook his head, looked at her thoughtfully, then shook his head again as he laughed at the ludicrousness of the situation. "Absolutely crazy. I can't take you with me. On down the trail, I'll abandon the wagon to move faster. You'd have to ride a mule and—"

"I could do that," she interrupted him to say.

He scratched his whiskered chin. "Yes, I'll just bet you could."

"Then why won't you agree?" She felt like grabbing the front of his fringed shirt and giving him a frustrated shake but thought better of it. "I tell you, I've proved I'm strong enough."

When he did not say anything, but merely stared at her as though he might actually be considering it, she pushed on.

"I can help you. I even know how to cook. I won't

be a bother at all. Believe me, if I have to ride a mule, I will. And you'll never hear me complain, I promise."

"I've a mind to put you on one right now, and I won't hear you if you do gripe, because you'll be on your way back to catch up with the others."

"You can't send me back," she argued. "Are you so stubborn you won't admit I'm strong enough to make it?"

"That doesn't mean I want to be saddled with you."

As he spoke, he was wondering what in hell to do with her. She had indeed proved she could make it, but he was fed up with having anybody to look after but himself.

Jaime felt her temper abating. From afar, so many nights she had secretly shared his frustrations and weariness. With heartfelt compassion, she said, "What they did was wrong. They shouldn't have deserted you."

He stopped pacing to regard her in silence. She was not the demure young woman he remembered. Life on the trail had not only matured her but improved her appearance as well. She was robust, skin tanned to a soft bronze, her cheeks pink and glowing. With a warm rush, Cord realized he found her even more appealing than before.

Jaime didn't like the way he was staring at her and prodded, "Are you going to let me go?" She took a step back towards the wagon. "It's starting to rain again. You won't make me go back in the rain, will you?"

"Get in," he ordered brusquely. "And hang on. I'm going to get us to the crag up ahead. Then I'll decide."

She moved all the way forward to crouch behind him as he took the reins again. "I won't be any trouble. Actually, I'll be a big help, because I've learned a lot."

"Have you now? Seems to me the only thing you've proved is that you can stay hidden. And why don't you show me how well you do that by making yourself scarce for a while? I've got to watch where I'm going in this rain, and I don't need you at my ear nagging."

Jaime made a face he did not see and withdrew.

Cord did not like thinking how she had managed to make a fool of him or how most of the others had probably laughed at him behind his back. Well, by God, he would see how hard she laughed when he sent her on her way to try and catch up with the friends who had aided in her little scheme. She wouldn't think she was so smart or brave if the Indians caught sight of that long gold hair.

Instinctively, he shuddered to think of her in the hands of savages. He knew what they could do to white women, and he couldn't risk her suffering such a fate. That meant he would have to turn around and give her safe escort. His approach to the Sierras would be delayed, and he would also have to face the grinning, gloating faces of those who had deserted him.

But what if he allowed her to go with him? Evidently it meant a hell of a lot to her to get to California. Maybe, he grudgingly reflected, she deserved to make it the rest of the way. He wasn't about to tell her so, but he was plenty impressed with how she'd fared so far. Still, he was entitled to the sweetness of revenge and intended to erase that smug look on her face.

"If I let you come along," he said thoughtfully, "there's something we have to get straight."

At once, Jaime was on her knees, practically breathing down his neck. "Anything."

"Well," he drawled, enjoying the moment, "I have to know—which do you intend to be?"

"What. . . ." She stammered, confused. "What do you mean?"

"My wife or my whore?"

He swallowed to keep from bursting into laughter as he heard her sharp gasp, felt her instant recoil.

He made his voice gruff. "Don't be so naive, Jaime. Once upon a time, you offered to be my wife, remember? And I thought you were a whore. So if I trouble myself to take you the rest of the way, I think I should be pleasured one way or the other."

Jaime felt her confidence slipping away. "You want me to"—she swallowed hard, barely able to confirm his ultimatum—"sleep with you?"

"Of course," he said brightly. "Your free ride is over, Sunshine. From here on out, it's pay as you go, or I'll leave you stranded on the side of the road."

"You . . . you would do that?" she asked shakily, fearfully.

"Of course," he lied. "I wouldn't hesitate to stick you on a mule, give him a slap on his rump, and send you home."

She could have told him she had no home, but she kept silent, not wanting his pity—if he was even capable of the emotion, she thought bitterly.

"Come now," he prodded, lips twitching. "You were

willing to marry me to get there. What's happened to change your mind?"

"There . . . there's no preacher," she floundered, trying to think of a way out of her predicament.

"We can live as man and wife and get married the day we get to California. But I'm giving you a choice. You can be a prostitute, pleasure me whenever I want, and when we get there, I'll pay you for your services.

"One choice gives you respectability and security," he pointed out. "The other gives you money, and you'll be rid of me when we arrive. It's up to you."

Jaime glared angrily, sullenly, at his back, the soaked buckskin shirt stretched across taut muscles. "I'm not surprised you would attempt to take advantage of me. You're just as ruthless as the Indians I've heard about. You . . . you're probably no more than a savage yourself."

Cord winced at the barb. Popping the reins, he set the mules to trotting faster. "I think we'd better finish this conversation when we get to shelter."

"There's nothing more to discuss." She settled back, washed with anger. She would beg no more, by God. "I'll find my own way out there, all the way on a mule, if need be. The company of a jackass would be preferable to yours, anyway."

Cord paid no attention to her, concentrating on maneuvering the wagon. Through a blinding sheet of rain and mist, he urged the team onward. Reaching the first protective outcropping of rock, he leaped down and grabbed the mules by their harness to tug them on. They resisted, leery of the overhang and the dark cavern beyond, but he jerked and pulled till they and the wagon were under shelter.

"We'll dry out and camp here for the night," he told Jaime. "The storm is already breaking up."

She had got down by herself and stood watching him warily, hands on her hips.

Cord glanced around in the dim light. "I think I can find enough dry wood to build a fire. It's going to be a cold night." He unhitched the mules, knowing they would head out into the rain to start grazing on the bunch grass beyond, then tethered the horse.

Noting the wagon rested on a slight decline, Jaime picked up a large rock and braked one of the front wheels.

Cord saw her and snapped, "You should have let me do that."

"I've done it before," she enjoyed informing him. "Only you didn't see me then."

"Be glad I didn't. You'd be back in Missouri by now."

"Why?" she flared, ready to face the inevitable confrontation and get it over with. "Once I proved I was as strong as any of the other women, why would you have turned me back? I'd really like to know just exactly what it is about me that rankles you so."

"All right, I'll tell you—it was your deception, damn it. Your friends told me you were desperate to get out there and meet your father, and when you came to me that night, you were planning to dupe me and you know it."

"That's one way of looking at it, I suppose, but I would have married you. I wasn't lying about that."

"Oh, you would have married me, all right, and then walked out on me once we got to California.

That's what made me mad, little lady, and that's why I made up my mind you weren't going."

"If Captain Wingate hadn't backed out at the last minute, he might have decided different."

"That wouldn't have mattered, because he wasn't the one paying passage for the women I signed on. It wouldn't have been up to him."

The air between them crackled with animosity.

"Well," Jaime said finally, lifting her chin, "you can't make me go all the way back to Missouri."

"But I can refuse to take you the rest of the way to California."

"No, you can't, because I'm not asking. I've changed my mind about wanting to go with you. I'd rather face Indians, bears, whatever is out there, than be forced to endure your insufferable company for even one day, Cord Austin.

"And if you won't be gentleman enough to at least give me one of your mules"—she stared up at him through a veil of angry tears—"I'll walk, by damn."

She turned away, but he grabbed her arm and yanked her back. "No, you won't, and stop that cursing. Is that something else you learned on the trail?"

"What I do or say is none of your business." She twisted futilely in his grasp. "Now let me go. You've no right to stop me."

He was fighting to keep from smiling. "Are you really sure you'd rather be raped and scalped by Indians?"

"Your ultimatum as to my either marrying you or being your whore is the same as rape, because I'd never give myself to you willingly. As I said, you're nothing but a savage like the rest of them." She clenched her fists, fighting the impulse to punch him right in the face, because she could see laughter dancing in his brown eyes and knew he was enjoying her humiliation. "I'd rather die," she said with cold finality.

Cord's humor disappeared in a flash. "Hear me, Jaime. I don't rape women. As for what I said back there, I was joking, paying you back. Not that it makes a damn now." He released her so abruptly she stumbled backward a few steps, fighting to keep her balance on the rocks.

"If you want to go back to Salt Lake, I'll take you in the morning.

"Frankly," he added, "I pity the man or beast that dares cross your path, but I'd be remiss in my duties as a gentleman not to offer safe escort."

Jaime watched, boiling with fury, as he turned away, dismissing her to begin searching for dry twigs. Finally, at once realizing how childish it sounded, she retorted, "Well, I'd be desperate to want a man like you."

"Fine. We understand each other." He glanced at her and frowned. "Do you have any other clothes?"

"I have one other dress, but it's still damp from washing."

"You need something dry. One of the prostitutes' bags was stored in the supply wagon and she forgot to take it out. See what you can find."

Jaime declined, petulantly saying she doubted she would find anything decent.

"Then stay wet and get sick, if you're so almighty proud."

Jaime knew she was being ridiculous. Her clothes

were damp, and she was starting to shiver in the chilly cavelike shelter.

Climbing back up into the wagon, she looked about in the faint light and finally found a bag amid the sacks and barrels. Opening it, she took out what looked like a pair of ruffled trousers and stared curiously.

"Bloomers."

She jumped, startled, unaware that Cord had slipped up behind her soundlessly and astonished he had been able to do so. "You move like a cat," she grumbled.

"Bloomers," he repeated. "Didn't you see some of the women wearing them under their skirts on the trail? They learned real quick that hoops are cumbersome but, without them, dresses drag on the ground and get dirty, pick up sandburs. How did you manage?"

"I pinned rocks in my hem and got black and blue shins like everyone else," she admitted irritably.

"Well, you'll be more comfortable in these." He picked up the rifle he had come to retrieve from where he had stashed it out of the rain. "I'm going out to see if I can shoot our supper. The fire is going good, and I left some wood stacked nearby. Don't let it go out."

When he was gone, Jaime changed into the bloomers and shirt. Though a bit large, she was amazed at the comfort the clothes provided. Unpinning her hair, she combed it to hang straight down her back to dry, then went to see about the fire.

Time passed, and she alternated between piling on wood and wandering about inspecting her surroundings. The rain had stopped, and the late-afternoon sun was shining. Venturing outside, she walked up the crest of the ridge, drinking in the sweet evening air in the quiet aftermath of the storm.

She could look out over a long shallow valley ahead. It skirted a narrow creek, and here and there the grass was pocked with clumps of cactus, glistening in the rain-washed radiance.

Her stomach rumbled with hunger. The buffalo jerky was all she'd eaten since the day before and very little of that. Spotting a patch of pigweed, she gathered an armload and returned to the campsite. Taking a kettle from the wagon and hurrying to fill it in the creek nearby, she soon had the greens boiling over the fire. While they cooked, she found meal and stirred up a batch of drap dumplings.

From somewhere in the distance, as shadows fell, a shot rang out. She hoped it meant there would be meat to go with the greens.

When Cord returned, he paused outside the shelter to stare at Jaime, her long golden hair shimmering by firelight. He could not help thinking maybe it was a shame they weren't continuing on together. Having someone so lovely along would have been nice, even though he would make better time by himself.

Looking at her, he could not deny wanting her, just as he had the first night they had met.

Suddenly he felt the need for a drink.

He made his way on down to the camp and dropped a rabbit next to the fire. "I'll clean it in a minute," he said, turning to the wagon where Jasper kept bottles of whiskey stashed inside barrels of meal.

Inside, he took several swallows, grimacing against the burning taste. Jasper had drunk the hardest stuff he could get his hands on, and Cord felt as if his stomach was on fire, but only for a little while. Soon, he could feel the tension easing. Leaning back against the crates, he closed his eyes and tried not to think of the rough trail ahead. Instead, he conjured up visions of reaching California and the comforts of a hot bath, his own bed, and a warm and willing woman in his arms.

He did not realize he had drifted away, yielding to exhaustion. Only when Jaime spoke right outside the wagon did he sit straight up, hand instinctively going to his gun. Drink and weariness were what got men killed. "What is it?" he said crankily.

Equally curt, she replied, "The food is ready."

He scrambled out of the wagon, still holding on to the bottle of whiskey, absently grateful he hadn't dropped and spilled it while he slept. Taking a few steps toward the fire, he froze and blinked incredulously. "What have you done?" His eyes bulged at the sight of the rabbit. Skinned and cleaned, it was skewered on a spit and done to a turn.

"What does it look like? We've got rabbit and pigweed greens and dumplings. If you don't like my cooking, too bad."

He was visibly impressed. "I don't believe it." He watched as she took the rabbit off the spit, pulled off the meat, and handed him a plate. Then he ate ravenously, talking around mouthfuls to heap praises upon her.

Jaime was nonchalant, though secretly enjoying the compliments. "I told you. I wasn't hiding in the wagon all that time. I watched the other women and learned how to cook outdoors. I'm still not real good with the bake kettle over an open fire, but I don't scorch much anymore."

"Everything is delicious." He turned up the bottle to wash down a dumpling, then saw her looking at him. "You want a drink? Or I can get you some water from the creek if you'd prefer."

Jaime pursed her lips thoughtfully; then, feeling a stab of daring, she reached for the bottle. "Maybe that's what I need. I've never tasted hard liquor before." She turned it up to her mouth, took a large swallow, then choked and spit it out in a spray that caused the flames to sizzle in protest.

Laughing, Cord patted her back. "Better sip it, Sunshine. It goes down easier that way."

She dared to try again, but by the time the liquor hit her stomach in a hot wave, she handed the bottle back. "I don't think I like it."

Cord went to the wagon, rummaged in another barrel, this one partially filled with flour, and returned with a half bottle of wine. "I thought I saw Jasper with this one night. Here. You'll find this more to your liking."

She did, admitting she had shared wine with Ruth and Martha the night of the farewell party and on a few other occasions till their supply ran out.

Between the two of them, they devoured all of the food. Cord built up the fire once more before bringing out blankets, which they wrapped about themselves to help ward off the night chill. Then, mellow and relaxed, he yielded to curiosity and asked bluntly, "What are you running from?"

"Nothing. I guess you could say I'm actually running to something—my future and whatever it holds."

"You have no family back in Missouri?"

"My family consists of an aunt I would never be able to locate, even if I wanted to, which I don't. And I have no home. She sold it before she left to move south."

Cord gently pointed out, "Surely you've got friends back there."

"No. That's why I have nothing to lose and everything to gain if I can find my father."

He did not speak, staring at her in deep contemplation, which she found unnerving.

"Is something wrong? You look angry. I know it's a great inconvenience for you to take me back, and I'm sorry. I really am. But it's not my fault everyone else stayed behind, you know."

He leaned forward, his stare even sharper. He had not been thinking that but, instead, how much he was enjoying her company. "Whose fault is it then? I think we both agree you were never asked to come along in the first place."

"True," she conceded primly, "but I didn't know I would wind up alone with you, either. Last night, when I heard you and Jasper talking, I thought he was going too. If I'd known different, I'd have stayed with the others, believe me. So you can't blame this part of the trip on me. It was a mistake."

Amused, he asked, "What made you think Jasper and I both wouldn't take advantage of you?"

"I never met him, but from a distance, he seemed nice. I think he would have been a gentleman. And I also think he would have protected me from you," she added.

Cord's smile faded. Damn it, no matter what he said or did, she was bound and determined to consider him untrustworthy. But so what? After tomorrow, he would never see her again. Therefore, talking to her was a waste of time.

Jaime watched him uneasily and thought how the night loomed ahead, long and frightening. "I'm really very tired," she told him quietly as she got to her feet. "I'll clean up everything in the morning." She turned away.

"You can sleep by the fire."

"No, I prefer the wagon." She noted that he looked settled where he was, and she had no intention of bedding down anywhere near him.

She had taken only a few steps when an eerie howl split the silence of the night. With a scream, she stumbled back toward the campfire.

"A wolf," Cord murmured. "Sleep here by the fire, like I said. He might decide to leap in the back of the wagon looking for food . . .

". . . and find it," he added grinning.

"I'll take my chances." With a deep breath of resignation, she headed into the shadows.

Cord stared after her, fury smoldering. Did she really think he would attack her while she slept?

With the spring of a cougar, he was on his feet to stalk to the back of the wagon and jerk open the canvas.

Startled, Jaime drew the blanket up to her chin and whispered in panic, "Don't you dare touch me," and then lied, "I've got a knife. I'll use it, I swear."

"Don't miss your mark if you do. You won't get a second chance." He swung up into the wagon and swooped her into his arms. Holding her against his chest, he dropped to the ground and returned to the campsite.

He fought the impulse to drop her right on her arrogant bottom. "You're sleeping here, where it's warm and safe. And you have nothing to fear. Believe me, I'd as soon tangle with that she-wolf out there screaming for a mate. Probably be a damn sight more enjoyable too," he added, dropping back to his own bedroll nearby. "Now settle down. It's enough you're making me lose time. Don't make me lose sleep too."

Jaime bit back an angry retort. Secretly she was glad he had gone and got her, for she had not relished thoughts of sleeping out in the wagon alone.

Several moments passed in silence, but she could tell by his harsh breathing he was still awake. Finally, she ventured to tell him, "You know, if you weren't so stubborn, you wouldn't have to lose time taking me back."

He drew an exasperated breath and let it out slowly. "All right. What are you talking about now?"

"Well," she began, framing her words carefully, "since I do need to get to California, I'd like to make you an offer."

He tensed, wondering what she was up to. "Get to the point."

Recalling how she had long ago fiercely made the decision she would use any means necessary to achieve her goal, she explained. "If you will honor my virtue . . ." She paused and winced, thinking how priggish that sounded, but felt it was necessary. She continued. "We can make a pact. You take me the rest of the way to California, and when I find my father I know he'll reward you. Meanwhile, I'll help on the trail."

Cord smiled in the darkness. He knew, despite her attempt at nonchalance, that she was desperate. He decided to make her squirm. "I'm sick of whining, complaining women."

"If you had been around me, you'd know I never once complained about anything."

"Well, frankly, I wasn't planning on taking the wagon all the way. I figured farther on I'd ride my horse and have just a pack mule."

"I told you I'd be willing to ride one."

Cord turned his back on her, and she had to strain to hear his next words. "I'll sleep on it and let you know in the morning. I still think you'd be a nuisance. And who knows?" he could not resist a final barb. "You might attack me in the night."

Jaime did not respond. She was far too happy. Something told her he was only teasing and had already made up his mind she could go. For the first time in a long time, she slept peacefully.

9

Jaime gradually relaxed when it appeared that Cord intended to honor their agreement.

Pushing hard by day, they fell asleep, exhausted, as soon as the evening work was done. Jaime slept in the wagon while Cord camped out in the open. However, in bad weather, if there was no other shelter, he bedded down beneath the wagon.

Jaime quickly learned how to handle the mules, but even with thick buckskin gloves, the blisters came on her hands. When Cord saw her applying lard, he scolded her. "Why didn't you say something? That's not going to do any good." He rummaged around in the wagon and brought out a bottle of foul-smelling liquid.

As he smeared it on her palms, Jaime admitted it was soothing and, with wrinkled nose, asked what it was.

"Skunk oil, mixed with beeswax and tobacco. It's

an old Indian remedy. They use it for sores on their legs from riding too long."

The mention of Indians reminded her of the strange language he had spoken the day he found her hiding in the wagon. She asked what it was.

"Paiute. Shoshone. The tribes around here. I thought one of them might have sneaked in."

She was impressed. "You speak both languages?"

"Enough to make myself understood." He had been wrapping her hands with lint and tied a final knot before adding with a lazy smile, *"Come out or die* is pretty much the same in any tongue."

Jaime persisted. "But how come you know their language? So much about their ways, like this potion?"

"I grew up in the West." That was all he was willing to divulge about his past. Long ago, he had locked the misery deep inside.

"It's still unusual to know so many different—" She fell silent as he walked away without another word.

The days were long and, at times, boring. Surrounded by white salt sand, at times she felt as though she were drinking dust instead of water. To while away the hours, she found herself watching Cord when he wasn't looking and wondering all sorts of things about him. Had he ever been married? Did he have a family? Why was he so reluctant to talk about himself, his past? Was he hiding a deep dark secret?

So many questions—and so much idle time to ponder the answers.

On occasion, when the day had not been too grueling, Jaime would tarry about the fire a little longer before retiring. They talked more, and she started thinking they were on the threshold of becoming friends.

One night, when they were enjoying the last of Jasper's wine, he surprised her by asking about her father. Something told her it was best to keep the information about the map and her father's fears of a dubious investment to herself for the time being. All she was willing to tell him was that her father was a prospector, explaining, "He's been out there since the early days of the rush. I was sent back east to live with my aunt and uncle when my mother died."

He knew her uncle died in the war and her aunt remarried and moved away, but he was unconcerned with that part of her past. What he wanted to know was, "Exactly where is your father living now?"

"I'm not sure." Actually she knew his mine was located near a place called Drytown, but she was reluctant to share even that much.

Cord frowned. She did not seem stupid enough to come so far without knowing where to look, and he said as much.

Stiffening a little, she defended herself. "He was doing business with a man in San Francisco. I plan to see him and ask him if he knows where he is."

"And if he doesn't?"

"I'm no worse off than I was back east, I suppose. I had no one there either. I'll survive."

"It's a rough place, San Francisco," he warned. "Lots of money there, but violence to go with it. It's no place for a woman alone."

Jaime's laugh was short, bitter. "I'm beginning to think you consider a woman useless anyway, unless she's clinging to a man."

Cord raked her with insolent eyes. "Isn't that what you're doing now to get out there?"

"This . . . this is different," she stammered, swallowing against indignity. "Once we arrive, I can take care of myself."

"Good." He tossed down the rest of his wine and stood. "Because I've got other things to do besides look after you, Sunshine."

Cord walked away from the camp, wanting to be alone. Lying down on the ground, he gazed pensively at the curtain of stars spread above him.

He was drifter, a loner. Home was wherever he happened to be. He had no intention of getting tied down to any person, place, or thing.

Once in a while, when he happened to take a tumble with a woman who particularly pleased him, he would hang around a bit. That's what had happened in San Francisco, which eventually led to his agreeing to go east to recruit wives and whores, because he needed to get away and let things cool off. The wild little filly he had been sleeping with had got a little too possessive and demanding, so he had felt the need to take temporary respite before things really got out of hand. Not that he was falling in love. No chance of that. But it was dangerous, being as she was the mistress of the man he had been working for.

But now he was looking forward to returning to her, because being around Jaime was starting to get to him.

The days weren't so bad. He was always aware of Jaime's presence, of course, but it was the nights that anguished. Burning with hunger, it was torture to know she was so close, yet he was unable to touch her.

He wanted her fiercely. And though he was sure she was a virgin, instinct told him she was ripe and ready. The fires of blazing passion were just waiting to ignite.

And he wanted to be the man to strike the match, by God.

That was the way it should be, he brooded. They should be enjoying each other for the duration of the trip. And why not? Out here, with every day a struggle for survival, they needed to grab every pleasure they could, every golden minute of happiness to make up for all the misery and hardship. Tomorrow didn't matter. It was only the here and now that counted.

Only Jaime didn't see it that way.

She was too damn proud. In a way, so was he, knowing he'd rather be dipped in hot tar than give her the satisfaction of being able to say she was right to call him a savage.

Though she would never know it, she had cut him to the quick.

Savage.

Always, the word provoked deep, burning rage.

And he had no intentions of making it so.

He prided himself on being a man of great self-control. He would not yield to his desire and instead would look to California and the willing female who waited.

In addition to his smoldering desire, his admiration for Jaime grew with each passing day. No matter how rough things got, she never complained. If there was work to be done she could help with, she was right beside him. He marveled at her spunk and spirit.

Because of his respect he became less reserved, and a gentle camaraderie began. He pushed aside chagrin over her ability to conceal her presence all those weeks. Wanting to hear of her experiences, he laughed as she recounted humorous episodes, like the night she had crashed into Wilma Turnage at the most private of times.

"You would have made my life so much simpler if you hadn't been so stubborn," Jaime told him.

Jovially, he countered, "Maybe you're the reason everyone abandoned ship. You got them to mutiny for revenge."

She laughed, a sound like silver bells in the wind, and he found himself thinking she was even more lovely now that the sparring between them was a thing of the past. No longer did she glower or frown or brood. They were both lighthearted, making the best of a trying situation, and the days spent with her were a delight.

But the nights were still hell.

Jaime went on to say, "Of course I did. I didn't want them around to help with the work. I wanted to do it all, and—oh!" She cried out as the rear wheel suddenly broke, bringing that side of the wagon sharply down.

Riding his horse alongside, Cord was quick to react and reached to pluck her from the bench and lift her up and out of harm's way.

A few seconds passed before Jaime calmed to realize she was being held tight against his chest.

"Damn," he swore, holding her with one arm while he reined the horse in a sidestep to the end of the wagon to inspect the damage. "Looks like the whole axle assembly is busted, and the bolster is cracked. The hound is ruined too."

Jaime, trying not to be unnerved by his nearness, managed to keep her voice even as she asked, "Do you have the parts to repair it?"

"Afraid not. Jasper took care of things like that. He was supposed to see to it in Salt Lake, and I was so mad at everything going on I didn't check to see if anything was needed when he deserted. Maybe it's just as well. We were going to have to abandon it in a few more weeks, anyway. We'll make better time with the mules."

"And if it snows, what do we do for shelter?" she asked, though her actual concern was over her future lack of privacy. With no wagon, she'd have to sleep outside, with no place to dress or undress except behind bushes.

"I don't intend for us to get caught in the snow. We've got to keep moving. . . ." He had turned to look at her, and his voice melted away.

Her face was streaked with sweat and grime, and her golden hair had come loose to billow about her

shoulders and down her back. He could see the tantalizing protrusion of her nipples through the thin
fabric of the perspiration-soaked blouse. With a
ragged gasp, he knew, beyond all doubt, he had never
wanted a woman more. Her mouth was mere inches
from his. He could feel her rapid breathing upon his
flesh and felt desire sweeping like hot, desert winds.

As he had grabbed her from the wagon, Jaime had
thrown her arms about his neck to cling tightly. She
had not relinquished her hold. Now, pressed against
him, she could feel his sudden hardness against her
hip.

Time stood still as their gazes locked and held in
mesmerized wonder.

Dizzily she wondered whether he was going to kiss
her, whether she wanted him to, all the while knowing she did, very much.

Cord felt a yearning within like nothing ever
before. Desperately he wanted to crush his mouth
against hers, to devour and probe with his tongue and
drink of the passion he knew awaited.

Savage.

The word was like liquid thunder in his blood,
coursing through his body.

Savage.

He could take her here and now, and if she resisted
he had ways of making her beg and scream for more.
He would ultimately feel her nails digging into the
hard flesh of his back, would see her head thrown
back and pressed into the sand and rocks as her spine
trembled in ecstasy, legs wrapped tightly about his
buttocks to spur him onward.

He knew he could make her revel in the glory of her own body and the joys it could bring with the explosion of climax—again and again. For he had long ago discovered it only increased and intensified his own pleasure when his lover reached ultimate ecstasy.

But he held back, for he knew when it was over, when she lay spent and sated in his arms, he would hear that hated word once more.

Savage.

She would condemn and damn him to assuage the betrayal of her own body, and that reality gave him the strength to resist.

Jaime, however, was not concerned with pride for the moment. It was as though this moment had been there all along, smoldering, just beneath the surface, waiting to erupt at the right time.

And that time was here and now.

As she had so many times in her dreams and fantasies, she kissed him. Hands moving to clutch his shoulders, she clung to him, lips parting to receive the sweet assault of his tongue.

For endless moments he held her, then drew away with a ragged sigh and a lazy grin. "Sunshine, if you want me to stick to our bargain, you've got a hell of a way of showing it."

Jolted by his candor, she all but fell from the horse as she struggled to get down. He helped her as much as she would allow but still she stumbled, almost fell.

Turning away from him, washed with embarrassment, she smoothed her skirt, straightened her blouse, and said nervously, "I . . . I don't know what came over me. It's hot. I . . . I think I need some water, some shade. People do crazy things in this awful heat."

He had dismounted. Jaime did not realize he was so near till his hands clamped on her shoulders. He drew her back against him gently. With his breath warm on her ear, he whispered, "You're right. They do crazy things. Wonderful things. I'd like to show you. But only when you're ready."

She knew it was his way of telling her that he would not make love to her until she was so bold as to make the first move, which, she realized with chagrin, she had just done. Only it did not have to go any further. She could pretend it had not happened.

It was the way it had to be, she told herself as she hurried toward the river and the scant shade of the taller greasewood.

Eyes misting with tears of humiliation, she took off her shoes and waded into the river. Kneeling, she took a long, cool drink, then withdrew to the sparse shade to try and get over the upset.

After a time, she returned to the wagon and found Cord busy unloading and sorting what could be taken, what had to be left behind.

Without so much as a glance in her direction, he spoke as though nothing at all had transpired between them. "I'm leaving everything but the barest essentials. The lighter the pack, the swifter the mule can move.

"We'll swap mules every day," he went on, intent on what he was doing. "No need in one bearing the burden all the time."

She saw he had put her satchel to one side and quickly went to retrieve it.

A few moments of awkward silence passed, then he asked, "Are you feeling better?"

"Fine," she murmured. "It was the heat."

"It always is."

The grin he flashed was maddening, and she clenched her fists and fought against her temper bubbling. "It shouldn't have happened. I'm sorry it did. It won't happen again, and I'll thank you not to mention it." She turned away, not knowing where she was going but determined to escape till her pulse stopped racing.

"Hey, Sunshine," he called, a lilt to his voice, obviously unmoved by her scathing decree.

She paused but did not turn around.

"I've been told when folks reach their destination they put the trip behind them."

Timorously, she asked, "What's that supposed to mean?"

"It's still a long way to California. A lot of things can happen. If you get a little crazy in order to make things bearable, later you can just forget it happened." He knew he was goading her but didn't care. Hell, let her suffer a little too.

"I already have," she lied, glad he was not standing closer lest he hear the guilty pounding of her heart.

10

The first night they camped after abandoning the wagon, Jaime took her blanket far from the ring of fire.

Cord watched in brooding silence, then asked what she thought she was doing.

"I intend to have my privacy," she informed him. "And besides, it isn't proper for us to sleep so close together anyway."

"Do you walk in your sleep?" he asked with mock innocence.

"And what is that supposed to mean?"

"Unless you do, you won't wind up in my bedroll, sweetheart."

Her temper flared. "I didn't mean that's what would happen. I meant—"

"It doesn't matter." He cut her off. "All I know is you aren't sleeping out there in the dark. In case you haven't noticed, those are wolves howling. And they're hungry. But they don't usually come around light or fire, so they'll probably stay away. Now get over here and lie down before I drag you."

They regarded each other in frosty challenge, but only for an instant. When a chilling howl shattered the heavy silence, Jaime needed no further prodding. Spreading her blanket only a few feet away from him, she took comfort in seeing that he kept his rifle within easy reach.

Soon, his even breathing told her he was asleep, while she was annoyed to be wide awake. How could she rest with him so close? Despite cursing herself over and over for her weakness, all she could think of was his kiss, how good it had felt, and how wonderful it would be to lie in his arms all night and have him make love to her in the way Hannah had described her husband doing. Jaime knew she wanted him and was infuriated at her own weakness.

How much longer, wondered raggedly, till they arrived in California to end this madness?

Cord only pretended to sleep. He could hear her tossing and turning, her occasional frustrated sighs. She wanted him. There was no doubt in his mind. But if she could stand the agony, so could he, by damn.

The stalemate continued, taking its toll in short tempers and intolerance.

Cord was well aware of the root of his bad mood and found himself wishing he had never allowed her to come along. As stubborn as she was, she'd rather die than give in to her own desires. And here he was, in the wilderness with no other woman around to free him of his misery. But hell, he doubted that would help anyway, because it wasn't just sex he wanted. It was *her*.

All day, he pushed them with a vengeance, trying to cover as much ground as possible. At night, no matter how blasted tired he was, her closeness made his gut ache.

It was probably a good thing he had no liquor left, or he would have drunk himself into a stupor. That wouldn't solve anything, but at least he'd be able to fall asleep instead of tossing and turning all night.

To hell with her beauty and the way she could lift him to the sky with just a smile. He was a damn fool to let her affect him the way she was doing.

"You don't have to snap!" Jaime wailed one evening when she'd had enough of his ill temper.

She had been trying to skewer a prairie bird he had shot for roasting over the fire, but it was small. She was having trouble pushing in the stick, and he was harping about how she had to hurry up, while the flames were burning just right.

"I'll never get this done if you don't stop nagging at me, Cord. What's wrong with you?" She turned to give him a condemning glare. "Nothing I do pleases you. All you do is fuss at me and criticize. You haven't spoken a pleasant word to me in days."

"There's nothing wrong with me except being fool enough to think you could do your part." He snatched the bird and stick away from her and speared it himself, then handed it back. "You're worthless."

That was the last straw. Declining to take the skewer, she leaped to her feet to shout, "Then do everything yourself, dammit. If you don't think I'm doing my part, I'll just quit trying."

"No, you won't," he warned, nostrils flaring as he met her fiery glare with one of his own. "You'll do exactly what I tell you to do, and you'll do it right."

The resentment she had been holding back the past days spewed forth. "I'm not your slave, and you get something straight, mister. I'm as sick of you as you are of me, and this trip can't be over soon enough to suit me. I never want to see your arrogant face again."

"Fine." He propped the bird over the fire. "We understand each other. And somebody ought to kick my butt all the way back to Independence for bringing you along."

With a mocking toss of her hair, Jaime returned, "Why do I have to keep reminding you you didn't bring me? I outsmarted you all the way beyond Salt Lake, and you can't stand it."

"I wasn't talking about that." Damn, she was making him mad, and maybe that was good. Maybe learning to despise her, hate her, would dissipate the gnawing desire, but even now, with them squared off and ready for a battle royal, he wanted her fiercely. Anger made her cheeks flush and caused her eyes to sparkle with flecks of gold and red amid the greenish-blue depths. Her chest was pushed forward, making her lush breasts even more enticing, and the petulant pout of her lips made him want to devour them. "I meant I shouldn't have let you talk me into letting you stay once I found out you were along. It was a mistake."

"Why? I've helped you. I've cooked—"

"Who cares? I've never had a woman along to cook for me before, and I got by just fine."

"Well, get by the rest of the way without me doing it. Take care of your food, and I'll take care of mine. And from here on out, leave me alone. Don't even ride your horse near me. I'll follow far enough behind you won't even know I'm around."

"You get on my nerves with your jabbering anyway."

"I don't jabber, and you know it. I hardly talk to you at all. I'm too busy trying to stay on the back of a mule while you ride your big fine stallion."

"If I thought you could stay on him, I'd let you ride and I'd walk."

"Don't do me any favors, Mr. Austin."

"I won't." Angrily, he threw the skewered bird into the fire in a shower of flying sparks.

Jaime watched him disappear into the shadows. She hadn't wanted a cooked prairie bird, anyway. The last one had been tough with practically no taste. Besides, the argument had ruined her appetite.

Laying down on her blanket, she blinked back frustrated tears. In the beginning, he had been pleasant company, enjoyable and humorous. They'd had good times on the trail and shared warm conversations at night. So what had happened to make him so cranky and mean?

Probably, a little voice inside needled, the same thing that had made her so crotchety of late. Being alone together was a strain on both of them.

She tried to dwell on other things to get her mind off the misery.

The haze of a purple sky descended. They had camped where others had been before them. Cord had pointed out the remains of other cooking pits, and Jaime had been saddened to see a cluster of stone-covered graves.

"That meant cholera hit hard as they were passing by," he had explained. "They probably stayed longer than usual due to so many being sick. Looks like they even made a hut of some kind."

Jaime wished it were still standing, but there was nothing left but a small pile of rotting boards. However, beside a small stream, it appeared someone had once tried to plant a flower garden. Cord had told her how pioneers brought along all kinds of flower seeds and cuttings, wanting to have something from their old home to take to their new.

She had wanted to tarry, to look around for even more evidence of those gone before, but he had kept after her to prepare for the night. They had to get an early start, he'd said, at first light. There was no time to dawdle.

Wriggling around, trying to find comfort when there was none, she thought how he would be even crankier in the morning after stalking about all night pouting. Maybe he would fall in a hole and break his leg, and—

She shook her head to dispel such a horrible thought, especially when it frightened her to think of him injured or in danger.

And smoldering just beneath the surface was her own awareness of how, like it or not, she had come to care for him deeply.

A cool wind was blowing, and she snuggled beneath the blanket. Above, opaline clouds hurried across the sky, bowing to the radiant glory of the full moon. The world about was bathed in silver, an air of magic shimmering across the landscape.

Now a familiar intrusion into the silence, the wail of a prairie wolf made her feel terribly lonely. She resolved, then and there, to make Cord see they needed to talk about their sniping at each other. Surely, if they both tried, they could be civil to each other for the duration. They would just have to mutually agree to avoid sarcasm and sniping, and—

Suddenly he was there, having approached, as always, in silence. He sat down, cross-legged, near the fire, staring down at his right wrist, which he held with his other hand.

Then she saw it.

Blood!

Scrambling forward, she crouched beside him. "What happened? What did this?"

"Snake," he said tonelessly, then quietly added, "I'm right-handed. It'd be best for you to do it."

Jaime shuddered, knowing what he wanted.

"Cut it. Take my knife out of my left boot and stick it in the fire. Then cut."

She reached for the knife, washed with dread as she offered a silent prayer.

In that instant, nothing else mattered.

She was not concerned over her fate if he died, only how much she had grown to care for him. And, yes, loved him.

Swallowing against the rising hysteria, she resolved

to do whatever was necessary to try and save his life. "I know about snakebites," she said, in a voice so controlled she could not recognize it as her own. "Wilma Turnage told me how it has to be cut and then the poison sucked out. Don't worry. I can do it.

"And I know to pack it with chewed tobacco," she went on nervously, taking out his knife to hold in the flames as he had instructed. "Only I'm afraid we don't have any. Maybe you know some Indian potions. Just tell me what I need, and I'll make a torch and go look. Maybe whoever planted that little flower garden also planted some herbs we can use."

She was talking, rambling, to try and steady herself, but finally it was time. She approached him with the knife, the tip poised and ready to slice into his flesh.

His left hand shot out to close about her wrist, and she froze, eyes wide with frightened confusion. Then, in the rich glow of the fire, she was further puzzled to see the play of a smile on his lips as he looked up at her in wonder.

"You were going to do it, weren't you? I wanted to see how far you'd go before you started screaming, but you were actually going to cut my wrist open and suck out the wound, weren't you?"

Baffled, she nodded. "Yes. That's what Wilma said—"

In a lightning-quick movement, he took the knife from her and tossed it aside. In the same instant, he grabbed her and pulled her against him, taking them both to the ground. Rolling over, pinning her beneath him, he looked down at her and grinned. "Sunshine, you never cease to amaze me. I was all set to laugh in your face and prove myself right when I said you were worthless."

Jaime was still confused—and also starting to get mad. "But you said you were bitten by a snake."

"But I didn't say what kind. It was a whipsnake. They aren't poisonous. I was lying down, trying to go to sleep, and I guess I put my arm right on top of him. He did what comes naturally, and, being a whipsnake, quick as hell he was gone the second he bit."

"Are you sure that's what it was?"

"I've got teeth marks, not fang marks. If you'd ever seen a rattlesnake or copperhead bite, you'd know the difference."

Testily, she murmured, "So it was just your idea of a joke, to scare me to death, hoping I'd start screaming and run."

He did not answer right away. Instead, he continued to hold her, gazing down into her face, so lovely bathed in moonlight, enjoying the moment, reveling in the feel of her heaving bosom against his chest. "Now I'm not so sure. I'm starting to think maybe this was what I was hoping for all along, to somehow wind up with you beneath me."

Jaime felt his hardness pressing into her just as she was forced to acknowledge the sweeping rush of her own arousal. Cursing herself for not trying to push him off, instead she dared to tease. "I thought you said you didn't seduce women."

He released her and rolled to lie on his side. "I don't. I was hoping you'd seduce me."

Jaime urged the smoldering anger forth, to sweep

her up and away with indignant rejection, but her body, her heart, betrayed her.

Slowly, easily, as though in a trance, she moved into his arms.

He kissed first her temple, in tenderness, then moved his lips to each cheek in turn. "I think we both knew this was coming," he said softly, brushing his mouth across hers. "And you don't have to be afraid. I know it's your first time. I'll be gentle."

He probed her mouth with his tongue, delighting in the taste of her, the feel of her. He had waited a long time for this moment and intended to savor each and every sensation.

Responding, welcoming, she drew him deeper inside, fingers dancing into his long hair that touched his shoulders, gingerly pulling him closer.

Her soft whimper came from deep within as she gloried in the kiss. Cord lingered a moment longer, devouring her with his lips before allowing his hands to move with a will of their own. In near slow motion, he touched her chin, then her throat, finally maneuvering to use both hands to cup each breast simultaneously.

"I want to feel you," he said raggedly, pausing anxiously in disciplined assault to open her blouse. With one quick jerk, her chemise was open, spilling forth her breasts. "I want to touch you, feel you, all over. . . ."

He dropped his head to take as much of her in his mouth as he could, sucking hungrily, voraciously, before withdrawing to pucker against her nipple as he flicked wildly with his tongue.

Jaime entwined her hands in his hair even tighter,

arching her back and urging him to continue feeding his hunger, for the sensation was a hot burning knot in her belly that she wanted to last forever.

As he suckled, his fingertips tormented her free breast, kneading, rubbing his thumb over and around in a circular motion that made her gasp out loud. He began to switch from one to the other, assailing first with his tongue, then taking all of her, only to withdraw and flick to and fro upon her nipple once more in a torturous rhythm.

Finally, when her ecstatic whimpers had become a long continuous moan, he drew back to look down at the tightly beaded nipples as he continued to work the firm, smooth flesh. "God, you're beautiful," he murmered. "I knew, the first night we met, your body would drive me insane."

Hotly, he took her in his mouth again, and she cried out in sweet joy, twisting against him, reveling not only in the luscious attack upon her breasts but also trembling to feel the hard pressure of his manhood as it demanded to be unleashed.

He jerked at her bloomers, yanking them downward, as she wriggled to help. In the night glow, he feasted on the slender curve of her hips, the honey-colored thatch of pubic hair, as he swiftly tore off his own clothes.

She lay back and he caught her mouth with his, scorching, searing, till she was shaking and limp and clinging to him in helpless surrender. He could feel her fever and rejoiced to confirm it had been there all along. This night, while she succumbed to her desire, he would take charge, knowing she was afraid. But later, during the lonely nights ahead, he would teach her everything she needed to know to please a man.

"Easy . . ." he coaxed, when, instinctively, she closed her thighs at his first touch there. "I won't hurt you. Open your legs to me, Jaime. I'll be easy, I swear."

Only partially did she relax. She felt one tiny jab, one sharp pain, and then only a warm spreading that told her, somehow, the last barrier to her innocence was well on the way to oblivion.

Cord thought he was going to explode. Using every ounce of self-control he could muster, he held back. God forbid he should hurt her. She had to be ready, ripe for his penetration. Some women, he knew, from listening to their besotted husbands in smoke-filled saloons, merely tolerated sex. They spread their legs long enough to be rutted, then snapped them shut and turned their backs and prayed a lot of time would pass before they were again required to succumb to marital duty. Cord did not want it to be like that for Jaime. He hoped she would learn to crave it as much as he did; only then would they both know true fulfillment and pleasure. Frankly, he didn't care if they did it all day, every day, and took the next year to get to California, because he sensed, somehow, she had been waiting for the right man to come along and awaken all her carnal senses.

He was damn glad to be that man.

She was moving her hips, undulating as he brushed his thumb across that nuclei of sensation, the crest of her womanhood. She was enraptured, drowning in a sea of ecstasy unparalleled. Opening her mouth, she clung to him as he claimed her once more in a bruising kiss.

If life ended here and now, Jaime knew she would

have no regrets. And she told herself he had to care about her, if only a little.

Cord could resist no longer, had delayed as long as possible. The heat had built beyond control.

Raising up, he clutched her waist and stared down at her face, a mirror of yearning and wonder. Her hair and flesh was damp, wet with perspiration, despite the night chill. They were both naked, the cold wind delicious against burning skin.

As he lowered his mouth to hers, she felt his first hard jab and instinctively, sensuously, lifted her legs to wrap around his thighs and hips. Digging in her heels, she received him.

Cord sensed he was hurting her and started to withdraw, but, feeling his reluctance, she clawed at his back to hold him tighter. Helplessly, all resistance melting beneath her eager invitation, he drove into her. Again and again, he rocked to and fro, and she met his every thrust by lifting her hips.

Jaime could feel the crescendo building, awed by the intensity of raging delight, as though molten lava coursed through her veins, up and down her spine, twisting, twining, jerking her about like a puppet on a string. She had no will of her own any longer, was powerless to withdraw from the hypnotic power that held her in its velvet grasp.

Cord felt her shuddering within and lifted his mouth from hers to allow her to unleash exultation's cry.

Only then did he push ever deeper into her, no longer able to be gentle, for he was lost in his own glory.

But Jaime felt no pain, only the supreme fruition of her body, her spirit . . . her heart.

11

Cord thought how beautiful she was. Long sweeping lashes brushed soft, heated skin. Her swollen lips were still wet from his kisses. His gaze dropped lower, to the perfect breasts, bare now that the blanket he'd wrapped about her had dropped away as she slept through the night.

Dawn had broken, bathing the earth in blue and pink ribbons of a new day. He knew they needed to be getting started but was reluctant to end the moment. As he pulled her against him, she moaned softly, drowsily, and he delighted to see the peaceful smile that touched her lips.

They had made love the night before too many times to remember, but Cord's real pleasure came from knowing she had given herself freely, without reservation. It made it all special, and he was awed to realize it was the first time in his life he had ever experienced such a tender bonding. They had not come together as the result of a night of revelry and drinking in a saloon, nor had it been a cut-and-dried business deal. It had happened naturally, without forethought, and he was shaken to know it was the best he had ever had.

Pushing the blanket farther down, he exposed the long line of her hips and shapely thighs. Kissing the firm skin of her belly, his lips whispered against her flesh, and he felt her quivering.

She was awake, watching him with an almost glazed expression of heat.

His tongue was doing crazy, wonderful things to her stomach, and she was thrusting her pelvis against his assault. "Touch me," he urged. "Touch me and feel how much I want you."

Jaime did not hesitate, for she was well aware of his hardness against her flesh and yearned to touch, to savor, the energy and hunger she had birthed. Closing about his shaft with nimble, eager fingers, it seemed only natural to begin to stroke him, up and down, squeezing ever so tenderly.

Exploring, her hand wandered, delighting in the sensuous power exuding from the hot flesh. She trailed on to feel and revel in the molded perfection of his muscular thighs. Finally manipulating to cup and squeeze his buttocks, she strained ever closer, wanting all of him deep inside her.

He felt her need, knew she was ready, and moved to oblige. Easily he mounted, lifting her legs up and wide. She snuggled against him, sighing deep in her throat as he entered with a single swift thrust.

Making his arms straight on each side of her, he held himself rigid so he could see her face.

She met his hungry gaze of wonder as she clutched his shoulders, her hips matching his mighty rhythm. He held back his own zenith, waiting to feel her quickening before driving himself to furious release.

Together, they climaxed, then clung together in wonder for long moments. At last, he kissed her long and deep, then rolled to the side to proclaim, "You're one hell of a woman, Sunshine."

"Well, you should get a little of the credit, sir," she told him lightly. She managed a smile, despite disappointment to recall how Hannah had talked of closeness and sweetness with her husband, not humor and mirth after lovemaking. Jaime told herself she was foolish to expect Cord to treat her as he would a wife. After all, they were just two people, alone in the wilderness, coupling out of loneliness and desperation.

Yet, she knew she was falling deeper in love with him. If she didn't want to wind up with her heart smashed to bits and pieces, she had to start regarding him as just a man to give her pleasure and hold her close on a long and dreary night.

The day passed pleasantly. They joked and laughed and talked about trivial things. Then, climbing up a steep slope to a flat, grassy meadow, they sobered at the sight of bleached white bones—the skulls of cows and the curved rakes of rib sides.

"Looks like somebody lost a whole herd," Cord said, squinting in the late-afternoon sun.

Jaime gaped at the sight of what looked like the scattered remains of a human being next to a gaping hole.

Cord confirmed grimly. "The body was probably buried but without enough rocks on top of the grave. If wolves can smell anything, they dig."

She did not need persuasion to leave the grisly scene.

The road stretched before them in a thin crescent strip, winding through grass and sand. Pointing to the distance, where the plain broke up into a slab of mountains, he announced, "The Sierra Nevadas. We're almost there."

Jaime marveled at the spectacle. In a play of dramatic light that sent rose and gold shadows dancing across the landscape, the majestic peaks stretched skyward. Though ominous and foreboding, she nonetheless felt excitement racing up and down her spine as she stared at the rugged mountain range and thought how her quest would finally end somewhere beyond.

By the time the sun began to sink behind them, casting splaying purple and gray shadows in its wake, Jaime was already yawning. When Cord looked at her quizzically, she felt herself blushing to admit, "We didn't get much sleep last night."

"Probably won't get much tonight either." He winked, then went on to say there was a campsite not far ahead. "I've been pushing to get there to stop for the night. I think, once upon a time, it might have been somebody's idea of a homestead, because there's a small shack there. When I came through, I took time to patch the roof, so it might still be in good shape. There's also a little pool, made from the offshoot of the river. It'll be a good place to get a bath."

It was nearly dark when they came out of the head-high grass, and he was happy to inform her, "We've seen the last of our travel on the plains. From here on, we'll be climbing."

Jaime had been walking, and she dropped the mule's rope as they reached the clearing, delighted to see a crystal-clear pond. "I can't wait," she cried, beginning to peel out of her clothes.

"It's going to be plenty cold," he warned. "You'd better get a fire going before you plunge in so you can warm in front of it when you get out. I'm going to try and find something to eat before it gets any darker."

He walked away, disappearing over a little rise. Jaime busied herself gathering twigs and sticks and soon had a nice fire going. Stripping, she grabbed a bar of lye soap and a change of clothes from the supply pack, then ran into the frigid water, squealing out loud as the chill washed over her bare flesh.

Quickly, knowing she couldn't stand it for long, she dipped her head to wet her hair, then scrubbed herself all over.

Night was rapidly descending, but a full moon was already bathing the world in liquid silver.

Finally, teeth chattering and shivering from head to toe, she waded to the bank, straining to see where she had left her clothes. They'd had to abandon their supply of linens and so used their soiled garments to dry off. She would put on clean clothing, then wash what she could and hope they would dry by morning in the brisk night wind.

Jaime froze. She could make out the figure of someone in the shadows, watching. "Cord?" she called softly, hopefully, every nerve tense. "Is that you?" There was an annoyed edge to her voice, sure he was trying to scare her.

She saw movement and frantically called out again. "This isn't funny, Cord."

Fumbling for her bloomers, she was shaking as she struggled to put them on. Then, just as she reached for her blouse, cold terror seized her.

Out of the shadows, they came at her. She opened her mouth to scream, but a hand clamped over her mouth to stifle the sound.

Struggling wildly, she felt terror rock through her insides as she saw there were two of them.

Indians!

Long dark hair streamed down their backs, and feathers drooped from some kind of skin wrapped about their heads. They spoke a language she could not understand, low and guttural, as they wrestled her to the ground and stuffed a gag in her mouth.

In wonder, one lifted a strand of her wet, golden hair and spoke to his accomplice in their native tongue. A chill shot through her as she remembered Cord saying Indians were especially fond of yellow-haired women. Against the gag, she cried in horror as one produced a knife and swiftly cut off a lock to hold high in triumph.

A necklace made of bones and beads hung from his neck, brushing his hairless chest. Above her, the other one stood with his moccasined feet mashing down on her wrists. He wore leggings, open in front and fastened to his belt by thongs, and, like his friend, a breechcloth between. He spoke, pointing to her breasts, still wet and glistening in the firelight. She hadn't had time to put on her blouse and lay vulnerable, exposed.

Dear God, she wondered frantically, what was to be her fate? Did she dare hope they would only cut off more of her hair and be gone? Cord had told her they were on the fringes of Shoshone territory but said the tribe always headed south in the autumn, and he'd anticipated no trouble.

They continued to grunt and mumble between themselves, as though undecided as to what to do with her.

With a sudden new wave of terror, Jaime felt one start to tear at her bloomers.

She knew it was now or never.

Instinct for survival took over.

She dropped her chin to her chest, then swiftly brought her head back up to smash into his crotch. With a shriek he slumped forward, slamming into his partner and catching him by surprise. They both fell from her in a tangled heap and cries of outrage.

Twisting with all her might to the side and scrambling to her knees, Jaime sprang upward as she spat out the gag, then immediately bolted forward. At the same instant, she screamed, long and loud and piercing in the stillness of the night.

The Indians came alive amid shouts of fury and were right behind her.

She plunged into the night, running blindly.

She felt him before she saw him, one strong arm sweeping about to lower her gently to the ground behind him.

He stood bathed in moonlight, legs wide apart, his face a mask of stony resolve. Dark eyes flinty, mouth set in a tight line, he fired one shot into the air as the Indians charged.

In their language, Cord told them angrily that Jaime was his woman.

Jaime was on her knees, clutching Cord's right leg as she watched and listened. "Why . . . why don't you just shoot them and be done with it?" she surprised herself by asking bluntly.

"They're not really vicious," he told her calmly. "They're Pah Utes, young bucks probably out on their first hunting trip for wild sheep. This is the time of year the rams lead the herd down from the higher elevations, because they sense the snows are coming. Seeing you, they went crazy. I think they'll back off, but one of them worries me. He looks real angry."

"That must be the one with the sore crotch."

"What are you talking about?"

"He was bent over my face, and I butted him with my head. That's how I was able to get away from them."

Cord winced at the thought. "Christ, Jaime. If you'd shot him, he wouldn't be half as mad."

"I didn't have a gun. They had me pinned down. I was desperate."

"Obviously. If you hadn't managed to get away, he'd probably have cut your throat." He spoke to them again in Pah Ute.

When they exchanged nervous glances and began to take a few steps in retreat, Jaime tugged at Cord's trousers and demanded, "What are you telling them?"

"I told Sore Crotch he has no right to be mad, because you were only defending yourself."

"But why do they look scared?"

"I also told them you were tetched. Indians think crazy people are bad medicine, so they want no part of you." He motioned them to go, and they took off running.

Jaime watched them disappear into the darkness, then said, "If I weren't so relieved, I'd take offense at being called crazy. Do you think they'll be back?"

He pulled her to her feet. "No. They figure if I know their language, I also know a little of their ways, and I'll be ready if they do. Besides," he added with a chuckle, "don't forget they think you're crazy."

They started back toward the fire.

"I'm glad you got back in time,"

"You were doing all right. After all, you used your head."

She ignored his pun. "I had no choice. They caught me off guard. I'm not an old hand at the ways of savages like you."

She did not see him wince at her unintentional barb, and he swiftly changed the subject. "Sorry I didn't find any meat. It'll be beans and jerky again."

"I don't care. I'm just grateful it's over." And she gave him a warm hug, which he returned obligingly.

Later, the wind picked up, and though the air was not as cold as previous nights, Jaime looked longingly at the little hut. Cord knew what she was thinking and said sleeping inside was not a good idea. "In case they did come back, we'd be trapped."

He found a place not too far away, on a slight rise

where he could observe the silvered night. He could see anyone approaching and felt safe.

Jaime eagerly took her place next to him on the bedroll. With her head on his shoulder, cradled in his arms, they lay quietly for long moments staring into the velvet heavens, the stars glittering like diamonds scattered to infinity.

His hand dropped to caress the softness of her hip as he turned his head to claim her mouth once more. This was not the fierce urgency of other kisses, rather a melding of tenderness, mingling with desire.

Easily, as natural as breathing, Jaime answered with her body. Rolling to her side, she began to explore him, touching the hard curves of his thighs, the sinewy muscles of his arms, his smooth back.

Even as he lowered his lips to nibble softly and whisper how much he wanted her, a part of him was ever alert should the Indians return. With his hands cupping her bottom and drawing her closer, she squirmed deliciously to feel the hard, rigid length of him against her belly.

He inhaled her fragrant softness, the damp sweetness of her hair. With his tongue, he trailed a path of fire to her ear, to drive her to fever pitch with his hot, wet assault.

Jaime could wait no longer; she trembled from wanting him. No longer shy, no longer able to hold back from yielding to her own incessant urge, she boldly mounted him.

Smiling with delight, he grasped her by her tiny waist and settled her down upon him. She gasped softly but reveled in the ecstatic wonder of how he filled her.

He reached for her breasts, and she leaned forward to render her all. He drew her to his hungry lips to suckle, and she arched her back and pressed her fingertips against his chest to stroke, urging him onward.

"Never," she whispered throatily, her face raised to the night and bathed in moonglow, "never have I known anything so wonderful."

He caught the tip of her nipple between his teeth and bit just hard enough to make her bottom wriggle delightfully upon his shaft. "It gets better and better," he promised, flicking his tongue to and fro, sending rivulets of torturous delight into her loins. "It hasn't even started."

Afterward, when she had joined a shooting star to soar across the heavens in glorious explosion, and he had emptied himself inside her in his own soul-searing climax, Jaime lay quietly in his arms and pondered his words.

It hasn't even started. . . .

Locked in her throat were many words of endearment she yearned to speak in that quiet moment of awe and splendor but dared not.

She had tried not to fall in love but to no avail. Now all she could do was savor the time they had together and keep him from knowing how she felt, lest he regard her with pity for her foolishness.

Wanting to break the rapturous spell that had enveloped her before she did yield to impulse and confess what she was feeling, Jaime rolled over on her stomach to prop her chin on her hands and stare out at the glowing landscape below.

Something caught her eye.

Mere inches away, a strange flower was growing, and she was at once awed by its graceful beauty. It had three upright petals and two drooping, with a delicate ragged throat. In the moonlight, it seemed to glow with a silver hue, although she could see it was a bluish purple color with fingers of white at the base of the petals. "I don't think I've ever seen anything so pretty," she whispered reverently.

"Neither have I." Cord smiled. He was not talking about the flower.

"I think it's called an iris." She touched her fingertip to a satiny petal. "I saw some sketches of different flowers in a book once, and I remember seeing one like this."

He turned to join her in scrutiny. "Actually, it's an orchid. Someone has to have planted it here. Remember me showing you flowers all along the trail that pioneers passing through had set out? This one is what they call cultivated, or hybrid. I don't know why anyone would leave it here and expect it to grow. The last one I saw was in a greenhouse in California."

"But it *is* growing, and it's beautiful."

He reached out and plucked the blossom, then turned on his back to drink in the sight of her as he tucked it above her ear.

As he traced his thumb across her lower lip, she smiled ever so shyly as he murmured, "Orchids in moonlight . . . and you."

He pulled her face toward his. "What man could ask for more?" And he claimed her mouth in a searing kiss.

12

By day, *they concentrated* on the journey at hand, covering as much ground as possible between dawn and dusk.

By night, they slept in each other's arms, spent with passion.

Yet while Cord treated her with tenderness and affection in so many ways, Jaime was disappointed that he never murmured a word of personal endearment. So she bit back her own utterances and avowals of affection, even though she could feel her love for him growing deeper.

Sometimes, compounded by the weariness of the grueling trek, her frustration would become unbearable. She would lag behind, eyes boring into his back as though trying to see inside to his very heart and discover what made him hold that part of him distant.

She had pressed the orchid between the pages of her Bible, and one afternoon, trying to take her mind off how much she adored him, Jaime asked about it, reminding him, "You said you saw one in a greenhouse."

"In California," he confirmed. "The man who built it cultivates orchids, but he also grows a variety of other flowers for his bees."

"Bees? For honey?"

"That's right. The climate is great for bees and flowers. Wild roses, violets, mint, clover. Everything bees like. Certain kinds grow year round, but with the number of homesteaders coming to clear fields and graze sheep that eat everything by the root, flowers are dwindling. That's why cultivation started, to plant alfalfa, honeysuckle, even groves of oranges.

"But orchids don't give off a fragrance," he went on. "The bees don't want them, so they're grown just for their beauty. Probably the one we found was planted there as a lark by a botanist passing by."

"Well, it doesn't matter who left it. I'll always treasure it."

When he did not respond, Jaime bit back disappointment to again be reminded how he avoided any nuance of romance or intimacy—except in bed.

As they wound their way higher into the Sierras, the air became colder. Warily, Cord watched the skies in fear of snow clouds gathering, while Jaime wrapped a blanket about herself to try and keep warm as she rode.

The day the Indians appeared, Jaime nearly fell off the mule in fright, but Cord snapped, "Don't move. Don't scream. Don't make a sound."

He held his rifle across his lap in readiness should the Indians make an aggressive move. There were five of them, and they did not seem hostile, for it was Jaime they were looking at, and Cord saw the fear etched on their faces. As if by instinct, their ponies began to back away.

He spoke to them in their language, and they all tried to respond at once, pointing at Jaime as they did so. He laughed. "News travels fast out here. All the Pah Utes for miles around have heard about the crazy woman with gold hair. Of course, the story has grown a little with each smoke signal, and now you're considered not only tetched but heap bad medicine, as well."

Jaime did not like the way they were gawking at her but knew it was better than being scalped and said so.

"Actually, scalping would solve the problem." He was able to tease her, despite the tension. "Your hair gives you away."

The Indians were turning to leave. Jaime saw the dead sheep slung over the rumps of their ponies and knew these were hunters, like the two they had encountered previously.

She was startled when Cord called out to stop them, pointing at her while he communicated in the strange gibberish.

"What are you doing?" she cried. "Why did you stop them? Let them go. I don't like this. . . ."

"You will," he said confidently. "I just made a trade."

Astonished, she watched as one of the Indians

removed the big thick buffalo-skin coat he was wearing. Keeping his eye on her lest she cast a spell, he handed it over to Cord before rushing to join his fellow braves, who were already hurrying away.

Cord helped her put it on. It was bulky and heavy and smelled to high heaven, but the warmth was welcome.

As the Indians disappeared around a bend in the trail, she wanted to know what he had given them in return. "I didn't see you offer anything."

"Yes, I did." He flashed a grin. "I told them you promised not to work bad medicine on them if they'd give you a coat."

She tried not to laugh. "That's swindling, and you know it."

"Not really. They think they got the best part of the deal.

"And maybe they did," he added, wrinkling his nose as he caught a whiff of the smelly coat. "But you probably won't need to wear it after the next few days. Not for a while, anyway. It's time for what's called Indian summer." He went on to explain how, even though they were almost into late autumn, the weather could turn surprisingly mild and warm for the next few weeks. "It's like nature is giving one last chance to get ready for the bitter cold of winter."

A few days later, his prediction came true, and Jaime reveled in the sweet warmth of sunshine streaming down on her face. He made her pull out the slat bonnet she had used to hide from him in the beginning, remarking that her face would blister.

"It just feels so wonderful," she argued, twisting her hair up to cool her neck and back. "We went through some really cold weather for a few days. We saw ice, remember?"

"And we'll see more, just beyond that next pass."

She squinted in the midday sun to see what looked like a tall thin crevice running between two mountains and wanted to know what awaited.

"The roughest part of the trail. Almost straight up. And it's bitter cold, because little sunlight shines through the trees. The firs and pines are real thick there, because we're below the timberline."

As much as he hated to take the time, Cord said they would lay over the day before entering the pass. Since the river cut through a narrow gorge, they would be away from it for a spell as they climbed upward. He wanted to catch some river trout and dry the skinned fish in the sun for jerky, as well as give the horse and mules time to rest up. He added she looked like she could use some rest, as well.

When they made camp, he drifted away to fish and hunt, and Jaime soon grew bored. She decided to look for any vegetation that could be used for food. They still had a few sacks of beans, but any variety in their diet was welcome.

She moved through the forest, savoring the pungent sweetness of the fragrant pines. Yielding to autumn, the night frosts had begun to sting, bronzing the grasses and ripening the leaves of the creeping heathworts along the banks of the stream to crimson and reddish purple. Where once wildflowers were abundant, only a few daisies and goldenrods remained.

Warmed by the sun, butterflies had come out to hover and dance above her, and the air was alive with the sound of hummingbirds frantically searching for a last drop of nectar.

Jaime began to gather pine nuts. Only a half inch long, the white kernels turned brown when roasted and would make a delicious treat for them as they doggedly followed the trail.

Intent on what she was doing, she ventured deeper and deeper into the dense woods without realizing it, forgetting Cord's warning to stay close to camp. It was only when she had to strain to see in the darkness that she realized she had wandered so far.

Turning, she lost her bearings and felt a stab of panic to think she might be lost. Then she spotted her marker, as Cord had told her always to do. Fixing on the tiny sapling jutting out from the overhang near the campsite, she made her way back through the brush and foliage, heading for the clear path.

She did not see the rabbit hole. All of a sudden, her foot dropped belowground to her ankle. Flailing, she managed to keep from pitching forward onto her face and instead fell to one knee, while her other leg remained stiff, her foot stuck.

She heard the loud, angry buzzing sound at the same instant she felt a sharp white-hot stab into her flesh.

"Damn bees," she cursed, gritting her teeth against the stinging pain. How could a bee hurt so badly, she wondered dizzily.

Clutching her leg, she yanked mightily, finally jerking free. Staring into the hole, she saw only darkness, but the buzzing continued. Then, with a creeping chill, she realized the sound was more of a hissing, and she could also hear slithering, as though something was wrestling about, trying to climb out.

With fear-widened eyes, she looked at her ankle and saw a yellow venom oozing from two tiny puncture wounds.

"Dear God, no," she breathed in horror. Just then a snake slithered upward from its den to disappear into the brush.

Hobbling backward away from the hole, panic squeezing to choke and strangle, Jaime prayed for strength to make it back to the campsite. If she passed out here, Cord might not find her till it was too late. It might already be too late, she realized, dread washing over her.

The pain was excruciating. Daggers of agony were shooting up and down her leg. She ran a little farther before slowing as she remembered one of Wilma Turnage's warnings—anyone bitten by a poisonous snake should try to remain calm, lest the poison spread quicker.

Several times, she paused to call out to Cord, as loudly as she could, but the sound merely bounced back at her within nature's shielding shroud.

She was getting dizzy, and it was becoming more difficult to move due to the numbness spreading from the wound. She fell, scraped her head on something, and saw it was a long curved stick. Hoisting herself back up, she pressed her weight against it and continued limping onward.

She did not know when she reached the site, for her mind had taken her away from the horror of the moment. The ground smashed into her face, and she was taken to merciful oblivion.

Cord lay on his stomach, stretched across the rocks. Below him, in the crystal-clear water, a large, lazy trout swam in the shallows. He waited for what he felt was the right moment, then plunged his hand downward—and missed. With a triumphant flip of its tail, the fish darted away.

Cord didn't really care. Already he had landed a dozen, which would slice up into a generous supply of jerky. Now he was just passing time, wanting to be alone to try and sort out his thoughts.

Something was happening deep inside him, something he did not want and fought against, using the painful lessons of the past as ammunition. It didn't help any to feel that Jaime was starting to care deeply for him, as well. But—he gave a bitter laugh—he knew all too well how that would change if she knew the truth about his background. Besides, he had made a vow to neither give nor receive love, and that's the way it had to be. Maybe some men could, but not him. It just wasn't in his blood, due to his father's weakness.

Where he had chosen to fish, the stream was narrow and jutted off from the river. With the spiky mountains as a frame, gazing up was like looking from out of a deep tunnel. Ringed by mighty firs and pines and a few oaks lower down was the bluish gray sky,

Dolly Sister

Back Home -
again Indiana

Daughter of Rosie
ogrody

New FOX
387 - 2669

the Gossamer
Cord

continued

we'll   meet ~~again~~
                again

by   ~~Philip~~
      Philippa
       carr

on Victoria Holt.

943

3557
35_00

292.00

and Cord knew he should be heading back to camp.

Yet he tarried. Thinking of how Jaime would react if she knew of his Indian background, he allowed painful memories to surface.

The summer he was seventeen seemed a lifetime ago. He was hanging around a military post in Texas by then, earning his keep as a scout. He was a good one too, thanks to all the Apaches had taught him. But back then, he was too naive to fully understand what a stigma it was to have lived with them.

He learned quickly, however, and painfully, thanks to the daughter of the post commander.

Her name was Nora Lansing, and the day she and her mother arrived at the post, Cord had taken one look and stupidly forgot his vow never to love. He was smitten, hard and hopelessly.

With so beautiful and vivacious a young woman on the post, every unmarried officer, and even some of the single enlisted men, beat a path to her door. Cord watched from afar, figuring he didn't stand a chance, but when she began to smile and flirt with him he decided to pay her a call too.

He had put on clean buckskins, washed and brushed his shoulder-length hair. He even splashed on some rose water after scraping his face with the shaving stone. He'd picked a bouquet of daisies for her from outside the gate. She had been delighted and boldly kissed his cheek in gratitude.

Then his bubble of happiness burst with a loud bang.

Major Lansing loomed up behind her in the door-way of their quarters, took one look at Cord, and angrily bellowed, "What's that half-breed doing at my door?"

Nora had dropped the flowers as if they were covered in spiders. Pressing back against her father she had glared at Cord in revulsion.

The major was pulling her back, and Cord had tried to explain. "No, Miss Nora. That's not true. I don't have a drop of Indian blood. . . ."

Major Lansing's lips had curved in a contemptuous sneer. "It doesn't matter. You were raised by the murdering Apaches. That makes you one of them, no better than a savage."

Cord had defended himself. "Sir, that's just not so. Please. I mean your daughter no harm—"

"Shut up," Major Lansing had yelled, temper boiling over. "How dare you argue with me? I agreed you could work as a scout, because you know the area, but you're still an Indian, as far as I'm concerned, and I won't have you coming near my daughter. Now get out of here. And get off the post. I won't stand for any half-breeds that don't know their place."

Cord knew if he lived to be a thousand years old, he would never forget the look on Nora Lansing's face as the door slammed on him.

If Nora had not joined her father in rejecting him, if she had said just one word in his behalf, he knew it would not have hurt so bad.

He had left the post that night and moved on.

Renewing his vow not to feel anything beyond passion for any woman, he made sure he sought out only the soiled doves, the ladies of pleasure, the ones he could pay for their services.

That was how he regarded Jaime. Her payment was his getting her safely to California. After that, he would put her out of his mind forever.

There could be no other way.

He headed back to the camp, confident he again had a hold on his emotions.

As he approached the camp, he frowned to see there was no campfire burning. Jaime knew to get one going before dusk, and he had never known her not to do what was expected of her.

With a stab of apprehension, he quickened his step, calling out to her, alarm thick in his voice.

Then, in the twilight, he saw her.

With a furious oath, he dropped the fish he was carrying and broke into a run the rest of the way. He knew something was badly wrong by the way she lay in a crumpled heap.

Kneeling beside her, he saw no blood on her head, except for where she'd scraped her face when she hit the ground. He began to look for another wound and drew a sharp breath when he spotted the swelling above her left ankle.

Closer examination revealed venom oozing from the puncture wounds, and he knew, with bone-chilling horror, she'd been struck by a rattler.

"Just hang on, Sunshine," he murmured, yanking off his shirt. Ripping along the bottom, he wrapped the strip of material below her knee.

Drawing his knife, he sliced an X across each hole and began rhythmically to suck and spit both blood and venom. When he felt he could draw no more, he ran to his saddlebag where he had always kept remedies for snakebites and other emergencies.

Taking out a pouch of thick, black, foul-smelling salve, he rubbed it into the wound. He had learned from an Apache medicine man how to make a potion that would draw out the rest of the poison, as well as take down the swelling that might otherwise cause gangrene to set in. And Lord, he could not let himself even think of the possibility of having to amputate her leg.

He knew the chills would start soon, so he set about gathering wood to build a roaring fire. Settling within the ring of warmth, he covered her with blankets as well as the thick buffalo coat.

There, beneath the canopy of trees, darkness came quickly. He had no thoughts of eating, forgetting about his own needs as he continued to hold her tightly in his arms.

She began to tremble, teeth chattering, body convulsing with chills to the marrow of her bones. From time to time, she would cry out loud, arms thrashing about wildly, but he held her down.

Fever came, and she began to mumble crazily. He left her only long enough to bring cups of cold river water to drip upon her parched lips. Sometimes she would rally to drink, only to lapse back into delirium, head lolling.

Once in a while she would call his name, which evoked conflicting emotions. Part of him was moved, while remembered resolve warned not to care.

The night wore on, and finally her fever broke, and she was soaked in perspiration. He took away the buffalo coat, tucking only a blanket about her. It was still too soon to be confident she would make it. If she lasted till morning, with no more chills, and regained consciousness, he knew he could start to breathe easy.

Not about to fall asleep himself, he paced restlessly for a time. Then, noticing her satchel, he hesitated only a moment before looking inside. If she did die, God forbid, he would feel an obligation to find her father and let him know. He was curious to see whether she had brought any of her father's letters with her, though he had no intention of reading them unless it became necessary in order to figure out where to start looking.

At first, he thought there was only intimate items, underwear and such, her spare clean dress neatly rolled, a few hair ribbons.

When he saw the Bible, he took it out and began to leaf through. Inside the cover there were names scrawled. No doubt, her family. Her own name was penned: *Laura Jaimelle Chandler, December 10, 1848.* They'd never discussed age, but he had guessed she was about five years younger than he was; now he knew he was right.

He saw the envelopes and was satisfied to know there were letters.

As he was about to put the Bible away, it fell open to the pressed orchid.

Cord felt a tightening in his chest.

Somehow, he knew she had saved that flower because it had special meaning, which confirmed his suspicions that she did not look on their relationship merely as two people clinging together for strength and affection during a difficult time.

It meant much more to her than that.

But he could not, would not, allow it to mean the same to him.

He put the satchel back where he had found it and went to kneel beside her.

She would live.

He would get her to California.

But after that, it was over.

And now he felt like a damn fool for having ever let it begin.

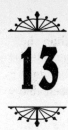

13

It was on the morning of the second day after the incident that Jaime said she felt strong enough to travel, but Cord was not as optimistic and said they would wait a few more days.

"I'm sorry," she said between sips of the coffee he'd made. "The last thing I wanted was to hold us back."

Cord did not look up from where he sat working on a broken harness strap. "Can't be helped now."

"I feel fine, really," she lied. "If you want to get started tomorrow, I'm sure I'll be up to it."

He shook his head. "No. That'd be asking for trouble. That foot needs to heal a few more days before you start riding and jouncing it around. And you sure as hell can't walk on it for a while. Besides, we've got a good campsite here. Lots of game come to get water, so we've got food without going into our supplies. We'll be fine for a few more days."

"But I can travel now," she said, braver than she felt. She looked down at her ankle, the flesh still bruised and swollen. He had removed the bandage that morning, and it was the first time she'd been able to see the wound. "It's ugly, isn't it?"

"It will heal. You were lucky. It could've been worse." She had told him how it happened, and he knew she'd stepped into a den of rattlesnakes. It was not uncommon for the deadly pit vipers to take over another animal's burrow for the winter.

She laughed softly, nervously. "Next time, I'll know the difference between bees buzzing and a snake rattling."

He did not respond to her humor, but said gruffly, "Next time, you'll remember not to stray off in the woods. You don't know enough about the wilderness to be alert to all the dangers. Do as you're told from now on, and don't be so bullheaded."

Jaime was bewildered by his scolding. His voice had an edge to it, as though he were trying to hold his temper.

"I said I was sorry," she repeated coolly.

A few moments passed in tense silence. Cord continued to focus his attention on the task at hand, while Jaime, her feelings hurt, wondered what to do to smooth things over.

"Are you mad at me for holding us up?" she asked finally. "I've told you over and over I'm sorry, and you know I didn't do it on purpose."

"Nobody said you did."

"Well, you act as if it's all my fault."

"No, it's not your fault. It's mine, for bringing you

along. If I'd taken you back to Salt Lake, you wouldn't have damn near got yourself raped, scalped, and killed, and you wouldn't have almost died from a snakebite.

"I'm the one to blame," he concluded flatly. "Not you."

Indignant, Jaime retorted, "Well, who's to say it wouldn't have happened anyway? Probably I would have got me a horse and set out on my own, because I don't think you realize even yet just how determined I am to get there."

He looked at her then, his face purposely void of emotion. "Well, the fact is, that's your business, and if I'd been smart, I'd have seen it stayed that way instead of letting you talk me into changing my mind."

"It hasn't been all bad," she reminded him tightly.

Cord held back a frustrated sigh. He did not want to hurt her, but his mind was made up to steer clear of intimate talk. "I guess we had our moments," he said, as though it didn't matter very much.

Jaime pressed on. "What would you have done if I had died?"

"Buried you and kept on going."

"Is that all?"

His eyes were dark and inscrutable. "What would you expect me to do?"

Attempting to lighten the mood, she said, "Oh, you could say a few prayers—"

"I'm not a praying man."

She stamped her uninjured foot and scolded lightly, "But you could do it for me, couldn't you? I mean, I am a little special, aren't I? And you *would* miss me."

She went on, seeing how he held back a smile. "After all, it's still a ways to California and all those women you've got waiting for you out there. Who's going to keep you warm at night?"

He saw how she pretended to frown, her finely drawn brows wrinkling over the bridge of her saucily tilted nose. They'd had their moments, all right, and not altogether in bed. They had laughed together, played together, and had some good times. She had made what would otherwise have been a lonely time an enjoyable experience. And now he found himself wishing he could join in her little game, grab her and wrestle her to the ground, tickle her into a fit of giggles till she screamed for mercy. Eventually, passion would ignite, as always, and they'd wind up naked in each other's arms.

He could not resist teasing. "Who says I need anybody? I could use your buffalo coat. You don't think I'd bury it with you, do you?"

"You're disgusting." She wrinkled her nose and stuck out her tongue.

Cord threw back his head and laughed, daring to hope the tension was over for the time being.

But he was prematurely optimistic, because Jaime suddenly asked, "What happens when we get to California?"

He hadn't expected such directness. "Well, I guess you go look for your father. That's why you're going there."

With a dogged shake of her head, Jaime pressed on. "That's not what I mean, and you know it. I want to know if we'll see each other there. I need your friendship. I need *you*," she emphasized boldly.

How in hell, Cord fiercely asked himself, could he be honest and tell her it could never be? No matter how bad it hurt both of them, he knew he was doing her a kindness to return to his own kind of woman, who accepted him for what he was with no thought or dream of a forever kind of love.

He drew a ragged breath, hoping the words would come out right. "I can't make plans. I may have to head back east. Maybe go by boat instead of waiting till the spring thaw," he lied.

Jaime felt a sinking sensation. Had she only imagined he was starting to care for her, all those times they had clung together so tenderly? Had she actually meant nothing more than the heat of the moment?

She watched with heavy heart as he got up and walked away. She had been leading up to asking for his help and confiding everything but realized with a sickening lurch that maybe she had been thinking with her heart and not her head. He was still holding a part of himself back, and therefore so should she.

During the day, he stayed busy hunting and fishing. He dried venison and trout for jerky, which would be welcome in the coming weeks. Jaime moved about as much as her ankle would allow, trying to regain her strength.

"If you'd been bit in the spring, you probably wouldn't have made it," he terrified her by explaining. "That snake hadn't been hibernating long, so his venom wasn't quite as potent after using it to paralyze prey all summer. In the spring, they're always more potent."

He told her he had once been bitten in Texas and showed her the scar on the back of his calf. "I know what you went through. I was only fourteen or fifteen, but I remember feeling like my whole leg was on fire."

She shuddered to see the faint mark, identical to the one on her ankle, where a knife had cut him open for drawing out the poison. "Well, it doesn't show. But what happened here?" They were standing close together, and she gingerly touched the scar on his cheek.

Cord drew back as though she had slapped him, eyes clouded with painful memories. "Don't."

He turned away.

Jaime was right behind him to apologize. "Wait, I didn't mean to pry. I was just curious."

He kept on going.

She stared after him in frustration, once more thinking how many shadows there were in Cord Austin's yesterdays. Only when she knew what they were could she ever hope to understand him.

That night, she sought his passion but had to be satisfied with a good-night kiss as he said "You need your strength for traveling" and turned his back.

She called on her pride to keep from crying with disappointment. If he did not want her, damned if she would beg.

But Jaime did not know his own desire for her was nagging like a toothache.

They set out again, and one morning she awoke to hear his soft curses at the sight of snow glinting on the high Sierra peaks above them. "There's a down-slope a day ahead, where we've got to ford the river, and then we'll be heading to the highest and most difficult point, Truckee Pass. It's the last major barrier between us and the Sacramento Valley, and we have to cross it before snows make it impossible."

Determined to keep their good humor and their spirits high, Jaime asked, with a wicked gleam in her eyes, "If we do get snowbound and starve, are you going to turn into a cannibal like those people in the Donner party and eat me?"

He looked at her and laughed. "You're awful. And that's not funny. And besides"—he also yielded to irreverent humor—"you wouldn't be first. The horses and mules would come first. I'd save the best for last."

When he looked at her like that, with tenderness and affection, Jaime dared hope she would find a way to break through that wall he placed around his heart by the time they reached their destination, and he would not want to say good-bye.

It was late afternoon, with dusky shadows falling, when Cord said they would make camp a bit early. "Tomorrow we ford the river. We passed some saplings blown down a little way back that I need to gather to twine up a raft. It'll be easier to get our supplies across that way and not have to weigh down the animals. They'll have enough trouble getting across if the water is up."

After unloading the mules, he took them and backtracked to gather the trees, while Jaime tried to get a fire going but strong winds prevented it. When he returned, he told her he'd discovered a small cave nearby where they could seek shelter.

"I searched it out to make sure there weren't any grizzlies hibernating," he assured her good-naturedly. "After all, you've tangled with Indians and rattle-snakes, so it wouldn't surprise me to see you stir up a bear."

Jaime was struck by the thought that *he* was the only thing she wanted to stir up—but seemed unable to do so, of late. Every night, he turned his back after a perfunctory kiss, saying it was too soon; she was still weak. Painfully, she wondered if he was telling the truth, or if he was actually tired of her.

Darkness enshrouded them early within the shelter of the mountains and thick firs. They gave up trying to build a fire and made a supper of jerky and cold beans, then bedded down early for warmth.

Jaime lay still and quiet, mustering the courage to show him how much she wanted him.

Beside her, Cord was tense, struggling within himself to keep from taking her in his arms. If they could go the rest of the way without making love, he told himself, it would be best, but damn it, he wanted her fiercely.

Suddenly, resolve blown to the wind, they each yielded at the same instant and rolled to face each other.

With a groan, Cord reached out to tear away the nightshirt she was wearing. Roughly, he pulled her against him, her soft breasts squeezed against his chest as his hands dove to cup her buttocks and pull her tighter still.

Jaime could feel his hardness pressed between her thighs as she lifted her face eagerly for his kiss. His mouth on hers was warm, hungry, and fierce with desire. Possessively, his tongue touched hers before moving to devour her face, her neck, finally lowering to lick her heated, thrusting breasts.

Sweet delight washed over her from head to toe, as she closed her eyes and opened her thighs to receive him. "Take me," she whispered shamelessly as passion soared through her.

He did so.

And together they reached once more to the stars.

Finally, arms about each other, they fell into a deep, peaceful sleep, while the cold night winds howled beyond.

Inside the cave, daylight did not penetrate early. They were both exhausted. Cord was sleeping later and deeper than usual, and his ability to awaken at the slightest sound failed him.

He did not hear the men creeping into the campsite.

They had seen the mules and the horse tethered nearby and knew there had to be people about. Stealthily, they began to look around.

It was only when the four of them stepped to the entrance of the cave, their guns pointed, that Cord flashed awake.

"What the hell—" He reached for his revolver, always close by.

"Don't do it, mister."

He stared up at the gun pointed at his face.

"We don't aim to kill you, but we ain't aiming to let you kill us, neither."

Jaime awoke at the sound of the voices and screamed when she saw the faces staring down at her. Cord murmured to her to be calm, then demanded of the intruders, "What the hell is this all about? Who are you?"

The one standing closest had a rifle and stepped even closer to warn with a snarl, "Shut up, mister. We'll do the asking—"

That was all he had time to say before Cord moved with lightning speed to grab the gun barrel and yank it forward before jamming it painfully backward into the man's gut. Whipping the weapon around to point, he lunged to shield Jaime with his body before challenging all of them, "Which one of you wants to die first?"

White-faced, eyes widening, the men threw down their guns. The one who'd had the rifle stock jammed in his stomach had fallen to his knees and was clutching himself and moaning in pain.

Cord sprang to his feet. "Now somebody better start talking and tell me what the hell this is all about." He was furious but also disgusted with himself for allowing them to sneak up on him as they had. He was becoming more and more careless lately, and he knew it was because of Jaime and the weakness caused by his feelings for her.

"We're settlers," one of the men said, Adam's apple bobbing nervously. "Part of a wagon train that's stuck down around the bend at the crossing.

My name's Lem Potter. This here's Tobias Dugan and Cuthbert Young, and that's Norman Bryson." He nodded to the one writhing on the ground.

Young spoke up, "We was out huntin' this morning and saw your animals and found your camp. Can't blame us for coming in with guns. How'd we know there weren't Injuns in here?"

Jaime was sitting up, clutching the buffalo robe to her chin. Still frightened, she met their curious, nervous stares with her own.

Cord decided they were on the level. He laid Bryson's gun aside to begin pulling on his clothes. "How long have you been there?"

"Near 'bout three weeks." Lem told him.

Dressed, Cord motioned them outside, giving Jaime her privacy.

Lem asked, "You gonna tell us who you are and what you and your missus are doin' out here by yourselves?"

Cord was not about to go into the details of his misadventures. "I was heading up a wagon train to California, but it disbanded at Salt Lake."

They were impressed, and Cuthbert Young marveled. "So you and your missus kept on going alone. That's real brave of you, mister. And you must know the trail good, too. Mind telling us your name?"

Cord sat down on a rock and bent to pull on his boots. He did not see the way they were exchanging glances, grinning with excitement. He introduced himself, then felt the need to make it clear, "Miss Chandler is not my wife. I'm helping her get to California, where she's meeting her father. She didn't want to stay back with the others. What has you stalled?" he went on to ask. "Why haven't you moved on by now?"

The others looked to Lem, who had more or less been in charge of late. He took a deep breath and endeavored to explain their plight. "Well, the fact is, we don't know what to do. We don't have nobody to lead us. Our wagon master dropped dead when we were getting ready to cross the river. Heart attack, best we figure. Since then, we ain't moved because, the truth is, we're just plain scared to try to ford that river without nobody telling us how to do it or what to do when we get on the other side."

Cord raised a skeptical eyebrow. "What about the sentinels? The men who worked for your wagon master?"

A pained shadow fell across Lem's face as he recounted their tale of woe. "It was a family thing, him and his sons. We left Council Bluffs, Iowa, last April. Fifty-two wagons. We got hit by cholera as we were coming across the Rocky Mountains and lost over half. Some of the others turned back. Wound up there was only nine families left. Everybody was pretty worn out and downhearted, and when Captain Humphries died, we figure his boys just couldn't go on. We buried him that day, and next morning when we woke up, they was gone and—"

Cuthbert broke in, "They took most of the food in the supply wagon too; that's another reason we figured we was better off to stay where we're at. There's plenty of game and water, and since there's not many of us left, we figured we'd just wait till a mail rider or

JOIN THE
TIMELESS ROMANCE READER SERVICE AND GET FOUR OF TODAY'S MOST EXCITING HISTORICAL ROMANCES FREE, WITHOUT OBLIGATION!

Imagine getting today's very best historical romances sent directly to your home — at a total savings of at least $2.00 a month. Now you can be among the first to be swept away by the latest from Candace Camp, Constance O'Banyon, Patricia Hagan, Parris Afton Bonds or Susan Wiggs. You get all that — and that's just the beginning.

PREVIEW AT HOME WITHOUT OBLIGATION AND SAVE.

Each month, you'll receive four new romances to preview without obligation for 10 days. You'll pay the low subscriber price of just $4.00 per title — a total savings of at least $2.00 a month!

Postage and handling is absolutely free and there is no minimum number of books you must buy. You may cancel your subscription at any time with no obligation.

GET YOUR FOUR FREE BOOKS TODAY ($20.49 VALUE)

FILL IN THE ORDER FORM BELOW NOW!

YES! *I want to join the Timeless Romance Reader Service. Please send me my 4 FREE HarperMonogram historical romances. Then each month send me 4 new historical romances to preview without obligation for 10 days. I'll pay the low subscription price of $4.00 for every book I choose to keep – a total savings of at least $2.00 each month – and home delivery is free! I understand that I may return any title within 10 days without obligation and I may cancel this subscription at any time without obligation. There is no minimum number of books to purchase.*

NAME_____

ADDRESS _____

CITY_____STATE_____ZIP_____

TELEPHONE_____

SIGNATURE _____

(If under 18 parent or guardian must sign. Program, price, terms, and conditions subject to cancellation and change. Orders subject to acceptance by HarperMonogram.)

GET 4 FREE BOOKS

(A $20.49 VALUE)

TIMELESS ROMANCE
READER SERVICE

120 Brighton Road
P.O. Box 5069
Clifton, NJ 07015-5069

another wagon train came through and follow along."

Hearing that, Cord exploded. "Didn't anyone tell you the mail riders don't come through here? They've got their own trail, narrow and accessible on horseback only. We would have taken that route ourselves, but we had a wagon I wanted to bring through as far as possible. The mail riders cut off way back on the trail.

"If we hadn't come through," he went on, staring at them incredulously to think they could be so uninformed, "you might not have seen anybody till next spring, because I doubt any more wagon trains will dare to come through this late. There's liable to be five or six hundred feet of snow in these passes by then. You'd either freeze to death or starve, because you sure as hell can't hunt with that much snow piled up. You took a hell of a chance," he finished in disgust.

"Yeah, I guess we did." Lem looked at his friends. "We was dumb, all right, 'cause nobody told us about the mail riders going another way. We figured all we had to do was wait."

"Well, you thought wrong," Cord snapped. "You were crazy. The best thing for you to do is get yourselves together and cross that river and follow the trail and get out of here."

Tobias Dugan spoke for the first time. "But if the snows catch us, we'll be stuck again, 'cause we'd never be able to find the trail. You see, we never had no guidebooks or maps, and when the Humphries boys left, they took all that with them."

"That's right." Cuthbert Young chimed in. "We're stuck right where we are unless we find somebody to take us the rest of the way."

Lem grinned and licked his lips in anticipation of being the one to make the happy declaration. "Well, boys, the heavens have smiled on us this day, because we've found him. Come on. Let's go tell our families we're moving out."

Cord had been about to go back inside the cave to tell Jaime to get ready to move on, but instead he looked at the men warily. Surely they didn't think he was going to be roped into becoming their leader.

"You come too," Lem urged, motioning him to follow. "The folks will want to meet you, *Captain* Austin."

14

When they topped a ridge, Cord could see their encampment. If he and Jaime had continued only a little farther the day before, they would have stumbled right on it.

He scanned the pitiful scene. The wagons did not look too bad, but some of the canvas was in dire need of patching. Trees had been cut down to build crude huts as shelter against the harsh weather, but he shook his head to think how the first big wind to come along would blow them right into the water.

The remaining men in the party had been fishing, but at the sight of Lem and the others returning with a stranger, they came running. The women, scattered about in the midst of various chores, gathered to watch apprehensively, small children clinging to their mothers' skirts.

Concerned that Cord had not said a word as they made their way back, Lem felt his confidence slipping. Maybe, he began to fear, Cord would not be willing to lead them. "We'll give you whatever we got to take us the rest of the way," he offered. "Nobody's got much money left, but I think I can speak for everybody when I say we'll gladly give you what we have."

Cord knew he really had no choice, because he wasn't about to go off and leave them stranded. And they were right to fear getting lost on the other side of the river. As green as they appeared to be, they wouldn't stand a chance if the snows did come. "Call your people together," he said with resignation. "If I agree to take you back, there's got to be some understandings."

A short while later, he again found himself standing on the back of a prairie schooner looking out over a sea of unfamiliar faces. However, it was different this time than back in Missouri. Instead of faces shining with excitement and hope, he saw weariness and broken dreams.

He had quickly inspected their wagons and teams, finding all in good shape to continue on. The men had obviously not spent the past weeks sitting idle; they had made needed repairs in the event a mail rider did come along. And, since everyone seemed healthy for the time being, there was no reason to doubt any of them would make it.

Now they waited to hear words of encouragement and optimism from their new leader, but Cord had no intentions of allowing them to be overly sanguine.

"I know it hasn't been easy since you left home," he began, "and now it's going to get worse. We've got another fifty miles to go into the deep hills, then, just beyond Truckee Lake, we've got to climb to the highest and most difficult point at Truckee Pass. It's the last major barrier between us and the Sacramento Valley.

"See that?" He pointed above them, where snow glinted on the high ridges. With a stern glance at random faces, he warned, "Any time, it could start snowing here. And you don't know trouble till you've been snowbound in the Sierras. So we've got to keep moving, no matter what happens, and I don't want any complaining.

"We move out at first light every day," he continued, wanting to make sure they all understood exactly how it was going to be. "We take no layover days. We go in the rain. We push every step of the way. No excuses. And my word is law. I give an order, and it's carried out. No compromise, no arguing.

"Remember." He narrowed his dark eyes for emphasis, pausing to allow his words to soak in. "I didn't ask for this job. And the day you forget I'm in charge is the day I do the same thing your sentinels did—ride on."

A low murmuring went through the crowd, as some thought him too arrogant and imperious, but Cord meant what he said. He was not about to let their stubbornness or stupidity jeopardize his life or Jaime's.

He scanned the crowd and saw her standing to one side. She was looking at him with a mixture of bewilderment and, yes, disappointment. He knew she did not want to join the wagon train, preferring for the two of them to be alone the rest of the way. Well, that would have been nice, he privately acknowledged, but maybe it was better this way. God knows, it was wrenching his gut, the way he felt about her, but the end was coming, and they had to get ready for it. It would make it easier for him to have responsibility, others to think about.

He went on to explain that they were immediately to start getting ready to ford the river. "Load the rafts you built earlier. Secure your wagons. We move out at first light. And one more thing," he advised. "Every one of you men can consider yourself a sentinel. I'll delegate duties, but you are all responsible.

"Now get busy." He dismissed them, stepping off the wagon. "You've had your rest. It's time to work."

He started in the direction he had seen Jaime, wanting to talk to her. Before leaving with Lem, he had gone back into the cave long enough to tell her about the wagon train they'd happened on, but he hadn't confided that it looked as if he was going to have to take it over. He had wanted to talk about that in private. But even though she had found her own way and was now aware of everything, he still felt the need for the two of them to discuss it.

"Austin, hold up."

He turned to see Norman Bryson walking toward him, scowling.

"You damn near broke me up inside," he accused angrily.

Cord regarded him coolly. "That should teach you a lesson about getting too close to a man when you've got a gun on him. Now what's your problem?" Cord had other things to do besides listen to him gripe about having been bested in front of his friends.

Norman's eyes narrowed. "I want to get something straight between me and you before we even cross that river. I'm not going to be your slave. I'll do my part, but don't push me hard, 'cause I ain't no cow heart like the others. It wasn't my idea to hole up here. I wanted to keep on going, but my wife wouldn't hear of it unless everybody else went along too. But I want you to know I wasn't scared. Maybe the rest think of you as an angel sent by God, but I don't, 'cause I can get my family to Sacramento without you, and don't you forget it."

Cord smiled thinly. "Fine. I'll keep that in mind, so if you can't follow orders you can strike out on your own."

Norman knew he was being scoffed at and didn't like it. Wanting the parting shot, he said, "Well, I got my own idea about the leadership qualities of a man I find naked in a cave with a woman he ain't married to. Seems to me a man like that would have other things on his mind besides getting decent folk to California."

Cord resisted the impulse to knock him on his butt. He wasn't worth it. Neither was he going to waste time bandying.

He left Norman staring angrily after him and went in search of Jaime.

When he didn't see her, he decided she had gone back to their camp to start getting their things together. He turned to go after her, but just then Lem Potter called to him.

Regretfully, he knew talking to her would have to wait a little while longer.

Jaime found herself surrounded by a group of women. Introductions were made, but she could not grasp all the names—only the one who had drawn her behind the wagon, Jerusha Potter, and the one who looked at her with unconcealed scorn, Thelma Bryson.

Softly, hesitantly, Jerusha got to the point of their confrontation by saying, "We understand you and Captain Austin have been traveling alone together, dear."

Jaime stiffened in defense. "Yes, that's right. I was the only one who wanted to continue on from Salt Lake, and he was kind enough to take me." Glancing about, she saw they were all staring at her with disdain, except for Jerusha, who seemed more concerned than condemning.

"Well, I'm pleased to tell you that's changed now, because you aren't alone any longer. I'll send my man, Lem, to get your things and you can settle in our wagon. It might be a mite crowded with us and our little ones, but we'll make room for you."

Only then did Jaime notice three little faces peering out from the back of the wagon, two girls and one boy. The boy stuck his tongue out and drew back inside.

No, she thought in panic, she would not share a wagon with three children and two adults, all strangers. She had been doing just fine sleeping outside with Cord. He made sure if the weather was bad they had shelter, and now that he had agreed to lead the caravan, surely there was a supply wagon she could use. She would not have to resort to moving in with the Potters or anyone else.

"Thank you," Jaime said, forcing a smile and stepping back, "but I'll be fine. Captain Austin will see I have a place, perhaps in the supply wagon. I won't need to trouble you."

Thelma snapped, "It would still be living in sin."

Jerusha shot Thelma a look that said she wished she would stay out of the discussion, then turned to Jaime once more. "She's right. Captain Austin will have to sleep there alone, and —"

"He'll sleep out in the open or find shelter like he's been doing," Jaime interjected. "That's what we've had to do since we abandoned our wagon."

"He'd sneak in at night," Thelma predicted. "Soon as you figured everybody was asleep."

Jaime shook her head. "I don't have to listen to this."

She started to leave, but Thelma swiftly moved to block her way. "Just a minute, missy. We're decent Christian folk here, and we'll not have you living in sin right under our noses. You aren't going to carry on like you been doing, not while you're traveling with us."

Jerusha hastened to intervene, "Now wait, Thelma. If they decide to go on without us, what will we do? We have to reach some kind of understanding here. I'm sure Miss Chandler will be the first to agree it's not proper for her to sleep with Captain Austin."

"I said"—Jaime spoke through clenched teeth—"he will sleep out in the open like he's been doing these past weeks."

"But you were sleeping with him when they found you this morning," Thelma declared, shrilly, triumphantly, hands on her hips and eyes glittering maliciously. "Naked as a jaybird, the two of you; that's what my man said. Is that what you expect us decent folk to put up with, you all ruttin' at night in front of us and God?"

One of the other women cried, "We'll not tolerate it!"

"No, we won't," another joined in. "You either move in with Jerusha or we'll keep waiting for somebody else to come along and save us."

Jaime was about to say maybe that would best anyway, since they obviously thought she was not worthy of their company, but Jerusha held up her hand for silence and scolded, "Stop it. All of you. We aren't here to condemn her. We want to help her, and ourselves, so we can be on our way before winter sets in, but we aren't going to be able to if we keep arguing.

"Miss Chandler." She focused on Jaime. "Please understand we don't mean to hurt your feelings. We just think it would be better for everyone, especially our children, if you don't continue bedding with Captain Austin outside the sacrament of marriage, at least while you're with us. So please, move into my wagon, and I promise you'll be treated like one of the family. When the trip is over, the two of you can certainly do as you please. But for the duration, we must ask that you conduct yourselves properly."

Jaime's head was spinning. A day ago, she was blissfully happy, weaving her way through the Sierras with Cord and savoring the time alone together in hopes he would come to care for her as deeply as she cared for him. Now she found herself the object of scorn, branded immoral, and any second she expected Thelma Bryson literally to cast the first stone and lop her on the side of the head with a rock.

What could she say? What could she do? While she certainly had sense enough to know it would be indecent for her to cavort with Cord as she had been doing when they were in private, she could not stomach the thought of being torn away from him altogether.

Suddenly he appeared, stepping around the end of the wagon. Sweeping them with stormy eyes, he asked suspiciously, "What's going on here, ladies?"

Jaime started to speak at the same time as Jerusha, but it was Thelma who raised her voice to drown them both out. "I'll tell you what's going on here," she cried, "We've just told your companion we won't put up with your immoral behavior, that's what. From here on out, you travel like decent folk, or we don't go with you."

At that, Jerusha wailed, "Oh, Thelma, will you please hush? You make it sound like we're doing him a favor to let him lead us, and that's not so." Her face etched with pleading, she turned to Cord. "Please understand, we aren't trying to be unkind. We just feel it would be best if Miss Chandler moved into my family's wagon."

"And I agree wholeheartedly."

The others gasped in surprise, and Jaime looked at him furiously. The silent message he was sending with his eyes said not to argue, it was the way it had to be.

He continued addressing himself to Jerusha. "Your husband already told me of your very kind offer, and I'm sure Jaime appreciates it as much as I do." The look he gave the women said it was best they make no comment as he added, "It's been hard on Jaime, traveling as we've had to do, but with none of the others in our group willing to continue on from Salt Lake, she had no choice if she wanted to keep heading for California. It's a blessing for her to have shelter and chaperones for the rest of the way. Believe me, we're both grateful."

Relieved it was all settled, Jerusha patted Jaime's arm and again told her she would be warmly welcomed into her family fold.

"Well, we'll be watching," Thelma warned with a haughty sniff. "You can be sure of that."

Cord bit back an angry retort. Taking Jaime's arm, which she stiffened at his touch, he led her to where they would not be overheard and rushed to explain, before she could unleash her fury. "It's the way it has to be. I don't like it anymore than you do, but it can't be helped. There is no way we can continue traveling together, sleeping together, among all these people. You would be treated like a whore. There would probably even be trouble with the young bucks, the boys in their teen years, who'd figure you were ripe for anybody's picking. The only thing we can do is move you in with the Potters."

"Indeed." Jaime faced him, hands on her hips, fingers of rage tapping up and down her spine. "Well, I've got something to say about this, and I don't want to move in with those people and their children. Why can't I sleep in the supply wagon?"

He shook his head. "It wouldn't work. You're an unmarried woman, Jaime. You should not be traveling alone. Everyone would think the worst. They'd figure I'd be slipping in at night—and I probably would," he added with a wink.

Jaime was not amused. "I don't care what people think."

"I do. If I'm to lead them, I need their respect."

"They need you more. Without you, they're helpless." He searched her eyes. "Would you have me abandon them?"

"You know I wouldn't." And it was so. Despite everything—the scathing words of Thelma Bryson and even having to crowd in with the bratty little boy who had made a face at her—Jaime knew in the final analysis she could never condone leaving these people in the wilderness.

He sighed. "Then it's settled."

Jaime nodded. "I guess I have no choice."

He gave her shoulder an awkward pat, fighting the impulse to draw her into his arms. "I'll go pack the mules and get the horse." He noticed she was carrying her satchel.

He turned away but had not gone far when Jaime called softly to ask, "Will we be able to find some time together in the next weeks? I . . ." She swallowed hard against the lump in her throat before admitting, "I've got so used to being around you."

And Lord knows, Cord thought silently, miserably, he had got used to being around her too and would miss her terribly. But maybe it was fate stepping in to make it easier to say good-bye. "Sure," he lied, knowing he had to use the time to drift away. "I'll see you every day on the trail."

"That's not what I meant."

He knew that but was not about to dwell on it, instead warning, "Those women are going to be watching us like hawks. I've got trouble enough getting us through the passes without stirring them up, so we can't take any chances."

"Maybe we'll see each other when it's over," she murmured hopefully, "and talk about your helping me find my father."

He saw the longing, the love, in her eyes and could not bring himself to tell her what had to be.

"Maybe," he lied, knowing all the while he would somehow have to find the courage at trail's end to leave her and never look back.

Living with the Potters was not as bad as Jaime had feared. Too unhappy over being separated from Cord to care much about anything, she wasn't really bothered by the cramped quarters, and the children weren't so bad. When ten-year old Thaddeus had stuck out his tongue at her for the second time, she had made a face back at him. He had burst into giggles, and the two became friends.

After she'd had time to think about it, Jaime had to

admit the present situation was best. There was no way she could have continued to sleep with Cord around these people. As it was, the women, with the exception of Jerusha, had regarded her with open scorn and contempt in the beginning. But after a time, and under Jerusha's influence, when they realized she was willing to work as hard as they were, they eventually softened and things became tolerable.

But if Jaime thought the road just traveled had been grueling, she quickly found, as did the others, it was nothing compared to the rough way ahead.

They climbed into a forest, dark with evergreens, where the branches of trees hanging above them were like tightly woven webs. Entering a stone-banked ravine with tall steep sides, they moved around the base of a snow-covered peak.

Days melted into each other as they followed dry watercourses twisting through stands of tall pines, maneuvering between precipitous hillsides, always casting wary eyes toward increasingly snowy peaks.

Cord had meant what he said about using every hour of daylight. When at last he would signal to make camp, everyone was exhausted. The men would muster enough energy to tend the animals and make any needed repairs by lantern light, while the women hurried as fast as their sore muscles would allow to get a meal together. Then everyone would bed down and fall asleep immediately.

Jaime was no exception. Though she missed Cord terribly and longed to be in his arms, there was no time to dwell on her misery. She saw him during the day, of course, but he was always busy, barking orders, pulling a stubborn team of oxen, quickly helping repair a broken axle or free a stuck wagon. When they did happen to see each other, he would nod or wave, but never did he stop to talk.

She knew he met with the men after supper, to talk about anything on their minds, and that he bedded down in the supply wagon to escape the brutally cold winds, when he was not taking his turn at sentinel duty. But she did not dare go to him, even though she desperately longed to.

Jaime had made up her mind: when they reached California, she would tell Cord everything about her father and the map. Till then, it was best they concern themselves only with the arduous situation at hand. She also hoped he missed her so much he would be as anxious as she to resolve everything between them.

The weeks passed in a wearied blur. Spirits were lagging. Except for those acting as teamsters, everyone walked, for the path was far too rugged to be comfortable inside a wagon.

One morning, lost in thought as she trudged along, Jaime did not at first notice the weather. Only when the wind abruptly slammed into her, thrusting her forward, did she look skyward to see a whirling gray fog rushing in from out of the west. Directly above, the sky was still blue but dark and lowering clouds were fast approaching. The wind screamed though the pine trees as it rose higher, sending the branches wildly swaying.

Staring straight ahead, her mouth dropped open in shock as she saw a mountain directly ahead completely disappear as the oncoming storm covered it in blinding snow.

"Pull into a tight circle!" Cord bellowed to those at the reins as he charged by the wagons on his horse, frantically waving his arms. "It's a big storm and a bad one. Get the animals inside the circle. Tie them down."

The men cracked whips and leather and hurried the teams to follow orders. The women screamed for their children to come running and quickly scrambled after them into the shelter of the wagons. By the time Jaime clambered in behind Jerusha and her brood, tiny flecks of ice were stinging her face as she looked into a wall of swirling snow.

They huddled together, the canvas cover whipping crazily in the assailing wind. They feared any moment it would be torn off and disappear into the frenzied blizzard.

Jaime saw the children shivering, despite the woolen coats they wore. She took off her heavy buffalo robe and spread it over them, and Jerusha smiled and whispered, "Bless you, dear, but please share our blankets."

And she did so, also sharing their prayers and softly offered hymns as the relentless storm screamed all around them.

By morning, it had passed. Mercifully, only a few inches of snow were on the ground. It was bitterly cold, and Jaime's fingers ached in her ragged gloves as she helped gather wood from broken tree limbs to get a huge campfire going.

Cord called them all together as they sipped hastily boiled coffee. As always, he avoided eye contact with

Jaime, lest his heart betray him in his gaze. "We were lucky," he told them. "The drifts on the trails aren't real deep, and even though we're probably six thousand feet up, the sun will melt off most of the snow by midday, so we can keep moving. I want everybody to get some food in their bellies, and then we roll."

No one wanted to ask how much farther they had to go, and Cord was not about to tell them. Survival depended on their focusing on the day at hand and not thinking about tomorrow.

As they set out, he could not resist reining his horse up alongside Jaime to remark, impressed, "I see you've parted with your robe."

She followed his gaze to where the three Potter children walked close together, the buffalo hide stretched across their backs in a wide cape. Making her voice light, she said, "Well, I just figured it was time to get rid of the smelly old thing."

With a soft chuckle and a tip of his hat in salute to her compassion, he continued on.

Jaime watched him go, chiding herself for experiencing a sudden thrilling rush.

Her mind silently screamed that if it was all ending for them, as she had begun to suspect during the past miserable weeks, she had to stop caring.

"So tell that to my heart," she whispered bitterly and kept on walking, head down so no one would notice the tears.

15

The storm fully abated, and once more the travelers were blessed with good weather. But while everyone else rejoiced over drawing closer to their destination, Jaime's hurt increased over the way Cord avoided her.

She walked with the women. At first, she had been a source of curiosity. They had fallen eagerly in step every day to ask questions. Some were friendly, while others were prying, but all she would reveal about herself was that she was going west to meet her father. Eventually they gave up, and conversations focused on the journey at hand.

One afternoon, when she was walking with Jerusha Potter, Cord reined in on Jerusha's side. It was his habit to make sure he took time to speak to each and every adult during the day to ensure all was well, and also, Jaime knew, to bolster spirits, if necessary—but never did he address her directly. He always made sure she was with someone else.

Jerusha, who never seemed to need cheering, greeted him warmly. "It's always good to have a chance to chat with you, captain. How about telling us what we'll find when we get to Sacramento? I can't wait. Crossing these mountains has been the worst part of the trip, I tell you."

Cord stole a look at Jaime from the corner of his eye. As always, when he was around her, he could tell she was worried about the way he was treating her. He felt a flash of regret but knew it was best for both of them.

Responding to Jerusha's question, he said, "You're going to find quite a boomtown there, that's for sure. John Sutter settled there first and built a huge fort, but he fell on hard times and sold out. His place is in ruins now, but for a time it was the first bit of civilization the earlier pioneers saw after leaving the East."

"Oh, dear, if it's expensive to find lodging there, we'll have to keep going. We don't have very much money with us."

Jaime grimaced to think how she didn't have any. She hadn't worried before, because Ruth and Martha had promised they would persuade their new husbands to help her when they got to California. Now she had no one and didn't know what in the world she was going to do when she reached San Francisco to keep from starving and have a roof over her head till she could locate her father. Still, she figured she was actually in no worse shape than she was the night she left home so long ago. She hadn't had a cent to her name then either.

Cord told Jerusha he was taking them to a place they would find clean, fairly comfortable, and most of all, cheap. "It's run by some Kanakas that Sutter brought from the Sandwich Islands, and they offer the same hospitality he used to give the earlier pioneers. It's at the edge of town, away from the gambling halls and saloons. I can promise you'll like it, because I know from firsthand experience." Kicking his horse into a trot, he called with a grin, "We'll be there before you know it."

Still not glancing at Jaime, he rode on to the next group of walkers.

Jaime stared after him with longing but told herself for probably the thousandth time that he had made no promises and owed her nothing. Theirs had been a melding of spirit and body sired of desperation and loneliness. The needs that had brought them together no longer existed; therefore, they had no further ties to each other.

With a determined lift of her chin, she knew she was stronger for the experience, no matter how deep the heartache. She had learned so very much. When it came right down to it, there was nobody she could depend on except herself. Everyone she depended on had let her down.

Yet from deep within, something reminded her that the trip wasn't over. She hated that niggling feeling which kept hope alive. Truly, she yearned to forget yesterday's passion, but her secret self was not ready to let go.

It started snowing again, and for two days they walked in the swirling flakes, grateful the temperature had not dropped sufficiently to allow accumulation. "Living on borrowed time," was how Cord put it when he spoke to them at night, as they huddled about the huge fire built within the ring of wagons. Any time, the skies could open and relentlessly cover them with several feet of frozen white, so they pushed ever onward, despite weariness and chill.

Finally, they came down a rocky slope and headed up a slight incline. Cord promised they were about to gaze on a landscape dotted with farms and houses leading into the bustling port city of Sacramento. At last, civilization loomed.

Thaddeus Potter ran ahead. "I see it!" he yelled, and pointed. "Sacramento. The river. Everything. It's a real city!"

The men broke into a run to join him, yelling so loudly that horses began to stamp about nervously. Women abandoned their children to run to their husbands in unbridled joy. Some wept with near hysteria, arms tightly about each other. The youngsters broke into cartwheels and dances.

Jaime stood to one side, relieved to have arrived but not wanting to intrude on family celebrations. She noted Cord was also hanging back from the others and wondered how it would have been had they not stumbled on the stalled wagon train. Would they have grown closer? Would they now be clinging together, dizzy with plans for a future they would share? Perhaps not, but at least they would not regard each other as strangers.

As promised, Cord led them to the lodge, situated on the grounds of what had once been Sutter's Fort.

A few buildings still remained but were in great disrepair.

The dark-skinned Kanakas greeted them warmly. The men helped unhitch the mules, oxen, and horses and took them to shelter. The women showed the weary travelers inside the warm lodge, where they reveled in the smell of their first good meal in too long to remember.

The menfolk drifted away to celebrate with whiskey, cider, and cigars, while the women began settling their children before offering help with supper.

Jaime found herself alone once more. It was a time for families, and she had no one.

One of the Kanaka women, a plump, motherly sort, noticed her standing to one side. Walking over, she offered a big smile, said her name was Tolah, and then asked, "Is anything wrong? You aren't joining the others to make merry."

Jaime was quick to assure her everything was fine, but she had neither appetite nor family to make merry with and would appreciate being shown to her quarters and told where she could take a real bath in a real tub.

Tolah pursed her lips thoughtfully. "By yourself, eh? Well, I just found out all the rooms will be taken by the families, but there's a place we use for storage. I'll find a cot while you get your bath. Then you'll feel like celebrating."

Jaime doubted it but said nothing.

She was led upstairs and down a wide hallway to a room no larger than a closet. It was cluttered, but Tolah began shoving around boxes and crates and remarked, "At least it's better than the back of a wagon."

Jaime was quick to agree.

After bathing, she put on her clean dress. They had camped two nights ago by the river, and, like the other women, she had done her laundry, wanting everything fresh for arriving in Sacramento. Now she realized she actually did feel better. She was also hungry, her appetite whetted by the delicious smells wafting up.

Hiding her satchel way under the narrow bed that Tolah had brought in, Jaime brushed her long gold hair, pinched her cheeks for rosiness, pasted on her brightest smile, and descended the stairs.

With so many crowded into the lodge, it was necessary to take turns at table. The men were served first, then the women, and finally the children, with whom Jaime found herself seated, since she was late.

By the time she finished, the men had disappeared once more with their cigars and whiskey, and the women were starting to bed down the children.

Because so many families needed shelter, they spilled over into cabins in the rear. Jerusha, assigned to one of them, had her brood in tow as she headed out the back door and paused to say to Jaime, "I'm glad you made it down in time to eat. I got worried when you didn't sit with the women, but one of the Kanakas—Tolah, I think her name is—said you wanted to settle in."

"I wanted a bath," Jaime explained, "and now I feel much better. I still can't believe we're here. Do you know how long before we continue on?"

"Lem and the others are talking with Captain Austin about that now." She frowned. "There seems to be some differing opinions as to how long we should stay. Some are so worn out they'd like to rest a week or longer and take in the sights of the town. Some, like me and Lem, want to keep on going after a day or two. I'm sure something will be decided tonight, though." Giving Thaddeus a little push, she continued on her way.

Jaime hoped those wanting to leave won out, for she was anxious to reach her destination.

Tolah set a huge bowl of apple dumplings in front of her. "I don't think I can." Jaime frowned, hand on her stomach to indicate she was full.

"Eat," Tolah said with mock sternness. "You're thin as a rail."

She took a bite. It was delicious, but she had eaten more at this meal than at any other in the past months and was stuffed. Tolah had returned to the kitchen, so she pushed back the dessert and quietly left the dining room.

The men had gone into the living room, but she discovered a small parlor at the end of the hall. No one was around, so she sank down on the couch in front of a cozy fire and began to mull over what she should do. There was no point in asking Lem or any of the others to help her look for her father. They all had families and their own business to tend to. They had no time to concern themselves with her problems. Maybe she should just get up her nerve and confront Cord, despite the way he'd been treating her, and offer him a strictly business proposition. She had no way of paying him now, but if he would wait for his money—

"Well, well, so this is where you ran off to. I been looking for you, little lady."

Jaime jumped, startled at the sight of the bearded man towering over her. He wore an outfit of deerskin, stained and worn, suede boots laced to his knees, and a wide-brimmed felt hat.

Without asking, he dropped to sit beside her. "You're one of Austin's women, aren't you?"

She inched away from him. "I came with Captain Austin's wagon train, yes," she said uneasily.

"Where's the rest?" He glanced about the room as though others might be obscured by the shadows.

Jaime asked thinly, "What are you talking about?"

"The women Austin told me he was going east to get last time he came through here. All the ones I seen so far look like they got husbands already. You're one of them, ain't you?" He licked his lips in anticipation like a dog about to happily devour a bone. "I was watching you through the dining room window, eatin' with the younguns. I didn't see no man around, so I figured you was on your way to San Francisco to meet up with one."

He did not give her time to protest, slinging a beefy arm about her shoulder to yank her close as he proudly declared, "Well, you ain't got to go there, 'cause here I am. I told Austin to bring me one, that I didn't care what she looked like, just so she was female, but I sure did luck up with you. You're real pretty."

"No. No, you've got it all wrong." Jaime pushed at

him, but he held tight. "I'm not one of the brides. They dropped out a long time ago—"

He chuckled. "Well, that don't matter. You got a husband?"

"No, and I don't want one. Now let me go." She pushed at his barrel-like chest with both hands but to no avail.

He ignored her protests. "I can take real good care of you. Give you a good home, lots of younguns too."

She stared at him, wide-eyed and incredulous.

"The name is Cotter. Link Cotter. I got my own place north of here. Got a cabin, too. Winnie, she was my first wife, died last year tryin' to birth our first youngun. It died too. I ain't been able to find nobody to take her place—till now." His lips spread in a snaggletoothed grin.

She saw it coming—the kiss he intended—and ducked in time for his mouth to strike her forehead instead. With a cackling laugh, he caught her chin in his burly hand and held her, viselike. "Aw, come on, little lady. You and me are gonna get along fine. Now give me a little kiss, and then we'll go find Austin and I'll pay him whatever he's askin' for bringing you to me."

His lips, thick and wet, mashed down on hers, and Jaime panicked and bit him. "Let me go!" she cried furiously.

With a delighted yelp, he drew away. "Well, I see I got me a real spirited filly, and that's fine, 'cause there's nothing I enjoy better than breaking a feisty colt." He silenced her protests with his mouth.

Suddenly, he was yanked away and roughly slung to the floor. "What the—" Looking up at Cord's fiery glare, he scrambled to his feet and began backing away.

Jaime stood, angry and indignant. "He thinks I'm one of the women you were taking to California and wants to marry me."

Cord was trying hard not to laugh. "Sorry," he said to Link, "but Miss Chandler is going to San Francisco to meet her father, not a husband."

Caterpillar brows knit together and dark eyes flashed as Link reminded angrily, "You was supposed to bring me a wife, Austin. I been waitin' long enough, and I ain't waitin' no more. When you get to San Francisco, you just tell her daddy she's found herself a husband. He can be our first guest." He shot another grin at Jaime, and she shuddered.

"Forget it, Link." Cord reached out and took Jaime's hand and headed for the door.

"Hey," Link roared, right behind them. "Hey, this ain't right. I want her, and I'll pay you plenty." He sucked in his huge belly so he could reach inside his belt and take out a small pouch, which he waved frantically. "Gold in here, pure gold. It's more'n what I planned to spend, but I figure she's worth it."

Cord kept on going, leading Jaime back to the kitchen and to the porch outside.

She was shivering, and not from the frigid temperature. He dropped her hand, and she stepped away from him.

"Are you all right?" He searched her face in the light spilling from the kitchen window.

She nodded. "He meant no harm."

"No, Link just wants a wife, that's all. Just stay away from him the rest of the time you're here."

"And how long will that be?"

"I've no idea. They're still arguing."

It was the first time they had been alone in weeks, and she seized the opportunity. "Cord, listen, we haven't talked lately, and—"

"And we've needed to," he interrupted, afraid of what she might be about to say.

He didn't want to hear it. If she loved him, he did not want her to put it into words, because once it was said, it would be harder to deal with.

Taking a step away from her, he was almost babbling in his haste to end the encounter. "I've meant to tell you how courageous I think you are. I've really come to respect you, like no other woman I've ever met. I was wrong to think you couldn't make it. You're going to be all right. I know you will."

She felt a rush of panic. It sounded as though he were saying good-bye, and she had to talk fast. "Cord, you have to listen. I need your help to find my father. I don't know a soul in San Francisco, and I've heard it's a huge place. I'll be lost."

"You've got friends from the wagon train. They'll help you."

"But I'd rather you did." She hated herself for begging but was convinced he was her only hope. "And my father will pay you when we find him. You see, he was investing in a gold mine owned by a man in San Francisco, and he was going to make lots of money. If you can help me find that man, he can tell us where to look for my father. His name is—"

"I can't help you." He cut her off. "I've been away quite a while. I've got business of my own to tend to.

I'm sorry. Besides, a lot of men have lost everything they had by investing in worthless gold mines. I hope your father isn't one of them."

Their eyes met and held, as they assessed one another. He longed to throw resolve to the wind and crush her in his arms, while she was fighting to keep from bursting into tears.

"I think," he said finally, "you'd better get inside before you freeze."

Jaime bit her lip. Later, she would hate herself for casting pride to the wind, but, dear Lord, she was desperate. Drawing a deep, ragged breath, she whispered shamelessly, "My room is upstairs, to the left, the back corner. If you'll help me, I'll give you advance payment the only way I can."

"Oh, Jaime."

He groaned and shook his head as he bit back the impulse to tell her money was not the reason he was refusing to help. Damn it, he was afraid if he didn't walk away, and fast, he would never be able to.

"I can't," he said finally. "Take care of yourself." He stepped from the porch to disappear into the night.

By the time she got to her room, she was crying. But, hoping against hope he would change his mind, she left her door unlatched. And if he did come, she vowed fervently, she would find a way, somehow, to convince him to stay.

Cord was halfway to the bunkhouse where he was bedding down when Lem Potter caught up with him.

"Here." Lem held out a handful of bills. "We took

up a collection after you left. It isn't much. Certainly not near what you deserve after all you did, but we hope you know we're grateful."

Cord had already told them he didn't want their money, and he shook his head.

"Two hundred and fifty." Lem pushed it at him again. "Take it, please. We'll feel better if you do."

Cord remembered how, when he had gone through Jaime's things, he had not found any money. He was sure she was penniless, and if he'd been able, he would have offered her financial assistance till she reunited with her father. But he'd had to spend more than what he had been advanced to buy what was needed for the whores and the brides. And he had lost it all, having to abandon wagons and teams along the way. He was broke himself.

He took Lem's offering.

"Bless you." Lem shook his hand. "We'll always be grateful for what you did."

Cord stuffed the money in his pocket.

When things quieted down and everyone was asleep, he would pay Jaime one last visit.

16

Jaime awoke to sunshine streaming across her face and the delicious aroma of hot coffee from downstairs.

For one drowsy instant, she could not remember where she was. But it all came quickly flooding back, along with painful awareness: Cord had not accepted her bold invitation.

She squeezed her eyes shut, commanding herself not to cry. It had been weeks since he'd held her and made her feel loved, cherished, in his wonderfully strong arms. He could have slipped in during the night. He'd always been adept at sneaking around without a sound. He could have come if he'd wanted to.

But he didn't, the torturing voice nagged from within. On the trail, he had no choice, but it's different now. He's probably thinking about the mistress he left behind. Maybe even a wife. You don't know anything about him, you know. He never told you one thing about his past: where he came from, family, nothing. He used you. You used him. It's over. Forget it, silly girl.

Wiping her eyes with the back of her hand, she dragged herself out of bed and dressed, then headed downstairs to join the others for breakfast.

As she descended the stairs, she could hear the excited babbling. No doubt, after a good night's sleep, spirits were even higher.

The long dining room table was crowded with the menfolk, but the children had been served and sat any and everywhere with their tin plates. The women stood with their food, and it was impossible to discern any topics of conversation, for everyone seemed to be talking at once.

Jerusha spotted her and came to take her hand, steering her to the back hallway. "I have wonderful news," she confided happily. "Lem met some folks who settled on Sutter's land ten years ago, and they kept on buying land and now they've got such a big spread they need help." She went on to explain how they had been offered a hundred acres and help in building a cabin, plus cows and chickens and pigs to get their livestock going.

"We can't turn it down," she said, giving Jaime an excited hug, "especially since we're almost out of money, so we're staying."

"That's wonderful. I'll miss you."

"Well, me and Lem don't have no family waiting, like Thelma. Her sister and her brood been out here fifteen years, she says. There's lots of others who've either got kin or know folks who plan to help them. Will you be able to find your daddy real easy, dear?"

"Oh, of course," Jaime lied.

Jerusha gave a girlish giggle and whispered, "What about Captain Austin? I should think, now the caravan is breaking up, he'd be coming around to get things started up between you two again."

Jaime laughed nervously, pretending to be shocked Jerusha could suggest such a thing. "Why, we were just traveling together."

"Oh, bosh." Jerusha waved her hands in protest. "I wasn't born yesterday, child. I got sense enough to know what happens sometimes between a man and woman when they're alone together, whether they mean for it to or not. That don't make it right, of course, but it happens sometimes, and it can't be helped. And I imagine if that's the way it was between you and him, the Lord will understand and forgive, especially if you join together in His name in marriage."

Jaime did not like the sudden turn the conversation had taken. Mustering an air of bravado, she said, "You were imagining things. We meant nothing to each other."

"That's right."

They both glanced up in surprise as Link Cotter stepped into the hallway from where he had been listening in the shadows by the stairs. He had seen Jaime come down but held back when Jerusha Potter squired her away, then decided he just couldn't wait any longer to talk to her and followed after them.

"If he cared anything about this little lady, he

wouldn't have ridden out and left her behind, now, would he?"

Jaime, stunned at the news, could only stare at him, but Jerusha was quick to protest, "I don't think that's true. Captain Austin would have told all of us good-bye." Good heavens, she wondered frantically, who was this rough-looking man and how much had he overheard?

"Well, he did just that." Link grinned. "Rode out just before day, he did. One of the stable boys told me they seen him, 'cause I was lookin' for him, to make sure he didn't interrupt me again while I'm proposing to Miss Chandler here. So if you'll excuse us"—he glowered at Jerusha—"we got private things to talk about."

Nervously, with a surrendering shake of her head, Jerusha shot a helpless glance at Jaime and retreated back down the hallway.

Jaime was too upset over Cord's abandoning her to be concerned about Link. In fact, she forgot all about him as she turned away, feeling more alone than ever.

"Miss Chandler." Link spoke gruffly. "We need to talk."

"No, we don't." She waved her hand in annoyance. "Now you must excuse me. I have things to do."

He clamped his hand on her shoulder. "Not till we talk."

Lordy, he thought dizzily, she was truly a prize, and there was no way he was going to let them randies in Frisco get a look at her. He was just a poor sodbuster, while some of them had struck it rich. They could afford to give her anything she wanted, and he wasn't about to lose her.

"Now listen," he began, "you ain't being fair to me. I may not be much to look at, but I swear I'll make you a good husband. Like I told you, I already got a cabin and a nice-sized farm. All I need is a wife and some younguns comin' along to help work it. What more do you want?"

"I am not interested. Now let me go." She tried to pry his hand from her shoulder, but he held fast.

The hot, quick temper Link was known for erupted. "Maybe you got another reason for turnin' me down," he said with a sneer of contempt. "Maybe what that woman was sayin' was so. Maybe there *was* something goin' on between you and that half-breed. And if there was, I damn sure don't want you for my wife. And no other decent white man will either."

Jaime stopped struggling. "What are you talking about?"

"Austin. I heard that woman saying she thought you two ought to get married to keep from sinnin'. And I saw the look on your face when you found out he rode off without a word. You better tell me, damn it. Have you two been to bed together?"

Ignoring his question, she fired back one of her own. "What did you call him?"

He spat the words. "Half-breed. That's what I call him, even though he really ain't got no Indian blood, I'm told. But that don't matter. It's said he was raised by Apaches, and that makes him one of 'em, as far as me and everybody else is concerned. Murderin' savages, that's what they are. And I don't want nothin' to do with no woman that would rut with one of 'em, of her own free will.

"But maybe it wasn't," he said suddenly, hopefully. "Maybe you couldn't help it. Maybe he raped you. Was that how it was? 'Cause if that's so, I'd understand, and—"

"Stop it!" she cried furiously, her mind spinning. If what this horrid man was saying was true, and if Cord had, indeed, been raised by Indians, it would explain so many things. Like how he could speak the languages of different tribes, how he knew native medicines and folklore. And she'd heard how Indians could move so quietly and stealthily.

She knew, also, it would explain his refusal to discuss his past, for there was terrible prejudice, even hatred by some, against Indians. A person with mixed blood was considered undesirable, a social outcast. Obviously, if Cord had been raised by Indians, it would be a stigma. No doubt, he had had painful experiences and therefore was determined to keep that part of his life a secret.

But it wouldn't have mattered to me, she acknowledged silently, wishing she had known back then, so she could have told him so.

Link gave her an impatient shake. "Hey, you listening to me? I asked you a question, woman, and I want an answer. Did you rut with that adopted Apache?"

Jaime slapped him. "I'm sick of your filthy mouth, and I'm sick of you pawing me. Now stay away from me, damn you."

He had released her when her hand cracked across his face, and he rubbed his cheek and fought the impulse to keep from slamming her with his fist. "Bitch," he hissed between clenched teeth. "He *did* have you, didn't he? And I don't want nothin' to do with you."

Jaime was almost to the end of the hallway when Jerusha came toward her, Lem right behind her. "Are you all right, dear?" they both asked at once.

Jaime assured them that everything was fine and said Link Cotter would never come near her again. Feeling the need to be alone, she thanked them quickly for their concern and started by, but Lem spoke up to say he thought it would be best if she continued on to San Francisco as soon as possible.

"A young woman has no business traveling alone. The sooner you meet your daddy, the better. I'm going to speak to Norman Bryson and arrange for him to take you with him and Thelma. I think they'll be leaving in a day or two."

Jaime shuddered at the thought. She didn't like the way Norman leered at her when no one else was looking. And once, when she had slipped away by herself to bathe in a creek and discovered someone spying, she'd been convinced it was Norman. She felt no less uncomfortable around Thelma, the only one among the women who had continued to regard her with contempt.

"I was thinking of going by steamer the rest of the way," she lied, for she had not made any plans, daring to believe Cord would have seen her to San Francisco, at least.

Lem and Jerusha looked at each other uneasily, then Lem asked, "You got the money, girl? It costs money to travel by steamer."

Jaime lied again. "Of course. Now don't you worry about me." She started up the stairs.

Jerusha called after her, "Aren't you going to eat breakfast, dear?"

"Later."

Jaime kept going, all the way to the sanctity of her room, feeling a frantic need to be alone and try to figure out what she was going to do.

Thinking she might find comfort in rereading her father's letters, she pulled the satchel from its hiding place. She took out the Bible and began to leaf through it.

And that's when she saw it—the money neatly tucked next to the dried and faded orchid.

With shaking fingers, she counted it. Two hundred and fifty dollars.

Fury began to creep over her.

Only Cord could have got in and out of her room without a sound, and who else would have put it there?

Had he seen the map? she wondered frantically. Or read the letters? No. She shook her head, told herself to calm down. It was dark. She had put the lantern out. But he could have come in the first light of dawn. He had managed to find where she'd hidden the bag and taken out the Bible, so why wouldn't he have seen the papers?

Everything seemed in place. Probably, he had just slipped the money inside. What difference did it make, anyway? Even if he had seen the map, he hadn't taken it.

She counted the money again, a bitter smile touching her lips. He had come to her in the night, but not to make love or say good-bye, only to pay for past services. After all, hadn't he once proposed that she could be either his doxy or his wife?

Perhaps, she told herself, she should be grateful. Now she could pay her way to San Francisco and have something left over.

Then with a jolt, she thought of something that really made her blood boil.

Francie.

The prostitute Cord had been expecting the first night they had met, sent to service him in exchange for his taking five hundred dollars off a gambling debt.

She stared at the money.

It was degrading enough to know he felt he owed her, but worse to contemplate he considered her worth only half of Francie's fee.

Never had she felt so degraded.

Had he been there, had he dared give it to her in person, she would have thrown it in his face. No doubt that was why he had sneaked in. It was his way of soothing his conscience for the way he'd used her and then dumped her, the bastard.

Tucking the bills back in the Bible where she'd found them, she took out the faded orchid.

For long agonized moments, she held it in her open palm. Then, as though she could destroy the memories of those nights in his arms, she began to crumble the crisp petals between her fingers.

As the brown bits and shreds fluttered to the floor, she watched them through a veil of tears.

Two days later, with less than a hundred dollars left after paying for the expensive passage from Sacramento, Jaime arrived in San Francisco and was instantly bedazzled by the teeming city.

She looked from the harbor, crowded with ships from everywhere in the world, to the tall buildings looming in the distance, and wondered dizzily what to do. She'd thought of nothing else, day or night, and still had no plan.

She saw the old man watching her from where he sat on the porch of a dilapidated-looking warehouse. He seemed harmless, and she was not about to approach any of the younger dock workers with their rude leers and suggestive remarks.

As she drew closer, she saw he was whittling something that was beginning to look like a ship. "Excuse me." She greeted him pleasantly, shading her eyes with her hand against the blazing late-afternoon sun.

A grin spread across the bearded, wrinkled face. Josh Becker could not recall ever seeing such a comely lass in all his sixty-nine years. Hair the color of the precious ore that had been his mistress till old age caught up with him, eyes the color of the Caribbean seas he'd once sailed as a lad. Truly, she was a sight to behold. "Well, now, what can I do for you, lassie?"

"My name is Jaime Chandler." She introduced herself.

"I'm Josh Becker."

"Pleased to meet you," she murmured politely before going on. "I'm afraid I don't know anyone in this town, and I was wondering if you could help me with some information."

"If I can, I'll be delighted." He patted the empty chair next to him. "Get out of that sun and tell me all about it."

And she did so.

He listened with interest to how she was trying to locate her father, who was living in Drytown the last she heard from him. "Well, now, your daddy must be a prospector. Can't think of no other reason he would have been in Drytown." He paused to snicker. "Never did figure out how it got its name. It sure won't due to a lack of neither water in the creeks or booze in the bars.

"It's over in Amador County," he went on, "about forty miles southeast of Sacramento, near Sutter's Creek."

"Named after the same man that built Sutter's Fort?"

"That's right, and after John Sutter stomped away mad when his empire fell apart after his workers ran off to the goldfields, things around the creek kept on growing. For a while, anyway. But I remember Drytown. I surely do. . . ."

Leaning back in his chair, the old man closed his eyes, as though by shutting out the present he could take himself back in time to younger days. Dreamily, he murmured, "I remember the dance hall at the Exchange Hotel. The floor was all slicked down by bales of hay shoved around, and the dancing always went on till three in the morning. They'd take up a collection to pay the orchestra. By four o'clock, the sun was startin' to rise. I was prospectin' then, myself, and it was all I could do to take pick and pan and head out to my diggings. But it was worth it. All that music and dancin' and lovely ladies. It was heaven to spend a night like that. It surely was."

His eyes flashed open as he returned from his golden days. "It ain't like that no more," he said sharply, almost angrily. "Placer diggin' wore out six or seven years ago, and then there was a big fire that about leveled the town. How long ago was it your daddy was supposed to be there?" he asked suspiciously.

"Going on two years."

"If he was still prospecting, he was wasting his time. But maybe you just thought he was diggin' there. Likely he was around Pokerville and Plymouth. They're still getting rich around them camps."

Jaime had a sinking feeling. What if her father's investment in Mr. Lavelle's mine had paid off, and he had been able to deep-pit mine but hadn't found the mother lode and just gave up? There was no telling where he would be now. All at once she knew her only chance was to talk to Mr. Lavelle, in hopes he could point her in the right direction.

Josh hoped she was not planning on going to Drytown and said as much. "It's a day and a night by stage from here to Sutter's Creek, and that's a long trip for a wild goose chase. Where'd you come from, anyhow?"

"Missouri."

He looked at her and shook his head in sympathy. "I hope you didn't come all that way for nothing, but if all you got to go on is knowing he was in Drytown two years ago, I'm afraid you did."

"There's something else. He was doing business with a man here in San Francisco named Stanton Lavelle." Her voice trailed away as she saw the strange look that came over his face. Warily, she asked, "What's wrong? Why are you looking like that?"

"Stanton Lavelle," he all but whispered, as though he did not dare speak the name out loud. Then, with a frown, he said brusquely, "You won't have no trouble findin' him."

He pointed toward the buildings beyond. "That was once the high-tide line. Now it's called Montgomery Street. You'll find a bunch of jerry-built banks and brokerage houses there. Keep on going till you get a block inland, where you'll come to a slope above the bay. That's called Portsmouth Square. That's where the finest hotels, the best restaurants, and the plushest saloons and billiard halls are located.

"And that, lassie"—he touched the tip of his knife to the brim of his hat in a gesture of finality—"is where you'll find Mr. Stanton Lavelle, or somebody that'll point you to him. He used to have an office in the Port Hotel building, but I don't know if he still does. Fact is, I hear he don't stay in the city like he used to. He built himself a mansion out of an old Spanish mission by the sea, farther north. Spends most of his time there since he got shot at a few times."

"Shot at?"

"He's got money and power, but he ain't exactly held in high esteem, Miss Chandler, for reasons I won't go into. Not fit conversation for a lady."

"Well, all right," she said finally. "I'll go into town and try to find him. But who do I ask?"

"Anybody." He laughed, as though enjoying a private joke. "You won't have a bit of trouble. All you gotta do is mention his name."

She thanked him, and he wished her well, and she hurried toward the rising buildings.

Finding her way to the Port Hotel, she paused outside the red-brick building to go over in her mind once more what she planned to say to Mr. Lavelle when she met him at last. She had considered the possibility his mine might not have paid off, and if that were the case, and her father had refused to turn the map over as pledged for his investment, there could very well be hard feelings.

Well, she decided, taking a deep breath and mustering all her courage, the time had come to find out exactly what the situation was.

There was no one else around, and she started toward the double brass-plated doors, excitement flowing.

Just then, a bedraggled man reeking of whiskey bumped into her and apologized. "Oh, lady, I'm sorry, so sorry. Didn't mean to hurt you, I truly didn't."

"I'm all right, really." She took a step backward, thinking what a pitiful wretch he was.

He looked at her with red-rimmed eyes and took

off his tattered hat to hold it in his hands. "Could you help a starvin' man, lady? That's why I fell into you like I did. I'm weak. Can't remember the last time I ate. About to pass out, I am. Just a pittance, anything, please."

Jaime really had nothing to spare herself but could not refuse him. She set her satchel down, opened it, and took out the lace handkerchief Jerusha had given her as a farewell gift. She had wrapped the rest of her money inside.

She took out a bill and was about to hand it to him when all of a sudden he snatched the handkerchief from her and took off running down the street.

"No," she screamed, waving frantically, picking up her satchel to chase after him. "Please, don't. It's all I've got, all I've got in this world. . . ."

Tears streamed down her cheeks as she ran, but by the time she reached the corner, which he had rounded only seconds before, he was out of sight.

17

The hotel manager made clucking noises of sympathy but scolded. "You never should have let him see your money, Miss Chandler. Sometimes the temptation is just too great. The safest thing to do with beggars is ignore them."

The policeman who had finally responded to her angry shouts had said the same thing, and Jaime repeated her earlier response. "I felt sorry for him."

"And now *I* feel sorry for *you*," the manager offered perfunctorily as he wondered what he was supposed to do with her. The police had brought her to the hotel, after she told them she was on her way inside when she was robbed. There was nothing they could do, they said, except make a report. There was little if any chance of catching the robber or getting her money back.

Jaime sat rigidly, staring out the window and thinking how she really should have known better, but at the time, had only wanted to help a starving stranger. Now, ironically, she might have to resort to begging herself.

The manager appraised her appearance and wrinkled his nose ever so slightly. Although she was quite pretty, she was obviously not of the upper classes. Her dress was clean but had seen better days. He suspected the robber had stolen what money she had, and the worn satchel she held on her lap contained all her belongings. Compassionately, he said, "I can arrange for you to stay here tonight as our guest, and tomorrow you can contact your family and make other arrangements."

"That's kind of you. Actually, I hadn't thought about where I'd stay."

He lifted his brows. "Then why were you coming to the hotel?"

"I was told I could find Stanton Lavelle."

The manager began to shuffle papers around on his desk, not looking at her as he said, "Mr. Lavelle vacated his offices here some time ago."

Was it her imagination, she wondered, or did she detect a sudden air of hostility? "Could you tell me where he moved?"

He waved his hand airily, "Who knows? The last I heard, he had sequestered himself in that fortresslike cliff house of his."

Her curiosity was whetted. "But why did he leave?"

"I'm really not at liberty to say. I don't think my superiors would want me discussing the personal problems of our business tenants. Let's just say there was an unfortunate incident, and the hotel thought it best he vacate." With eyes narrowed, he asked bluntly, "What did you want to see him about?"

She saw no reason not to explain that her father had entered into a venture with Lavelle a while back, and since he was the only contact she knew her father had in San Francisco—in all of California, actually— she felt Lavelle was her best hope of locating him.

The manager chose his words carefully, as he did not want to get too involved in any dealings concerning Lavelle. Taking pen and paper, he began to draw a crude map, explaining as he did so. "This will show you the way to his estate. It's not hard to find. The road runs right along the beach. You'll need to rent a horse and cart, though, since it's nearly five miles."

Handing her the map, he started to get up. "Would you like me to make the arrangements? If you hurry and leave right away, you can make it there before dark."

"No. But thank you."

With an inward groan, he sank down and waited for her to confirm his suspicion she was destitute.

She did so. "I'm afraid I don't have any money. That man took all I had. I'll have to take you up on your kind offer for lodging, and then I'll start walking first thing in the morning."

He was quick to protest. "I can't let you do that. Suppose the hotel pays for the cart and horse? It's about the same price as a room." Dear Lord, he just wanted to be rid of her. Strangers looking for Lavelle could mean trouble.

She did not hesitate to accept. "But only with the understanding that once I find my father I'll come back and repay you. I'm not the sort to take charity."

"Yes, yes, of course." He was already on his

way through the door to make arrangements to get her out of there.

The trail did wind close to the beach, and Jaime marveled at the breathtaking scenery. Once outside the city, she saw there was a constant succession of coves and crescents. A line of sand dunes, low and rolling and fringed with bushes and low-growing reeds, lined the sandy stretches. High bluffs rose abruptly from the water's edge.

It was a world of beach and bluffs, with green tufts of grass and wildflowers creeping. The blue-green waters glistened in the late-evening sun as the waves broke softly in snowy masses of foam.

She saw fishing boats drifting and passed a few huts along the way, but for the most part it was a long and lonely stretch. With a shiver, she commanded herself not to think of having to return alone, at night, if Mr. Lavelle did not take her to her father or offer her hospitality till morning. Her quest was not without risks, she knew, but there were no other options. Had she not lost the rest of her money, she could have used the hotel as her base and made day trips to search for her father. Now, she found herself truly desperate.

She also tried not to think of Cord and blame him for her plight. So what if he did consider her no better than a whore? She was not his responsibility and never had been. Yet to think of him provoked anger and bitterness, so she concentrated instead on the beauty of the moment at hand.

At last, the road trailed over a rocky headland projecting across the beach. Beyond, she could see a path leading from the sand. Bordered by a short stone wall on each side, it curved and disappeared into the rocky bluff. Gazing upward, she saw what could only be Stanton Lavelle's cliff house. It hung out and over the boiling sea, which at that point crashed wildly against the sharp, jutting cluster of rocks directly below.

The trail narrowed, but Jaime was able to maneuver the cart and horse between the walls. As she crested one point, she could see a wider road leading to the front of the house, for those traveling away from the beach at high tide.

But the massive structure could not really be called a house, she decided, staring in awe at the three-story structure reaching to the clouds above. Built by the Spanish for Franciscan fathers to convert the Indians, it did resemble a fort. And below, scattered about on the massive bluff, were adobelike structures with red-tiled roofs, constructed for other Spaniards to live in as they worked the lands around so long ago.

As she climbed yet higher, she could look eastward, away from the ocean, at rolling grasslands with cattle grazing. There also appeared to be acres of vineyards. Mr. Lavelle had obviously taken over the old farms the Indians had been taught to work.

With the lush valley on one side, the honeyed sea on the other, and the magnificent mission looming above, Jaime felt she had entered a world found only in storybooks.

But her feeling of enchantment ended abruptly when she rounded a curve to see a bearded man, with angry black eyes, standing in the middle of the path.

Jerking back on the reins to bring the horse to an abrupt halt, she met his challenging gaze uneasily.

He was holding a rifle but did not point it as he gruffly informed her, "Señor Lavelle did not tell me he was expecting a guest. Go back the way you came."

Fighting for composure, she responded, "I'll do nothing of the kind. It doesn't matter I'm not expected. If Mr. Lavelle is any kind of a gentleman at all, he'll not turn a lady from his door, especially with night approaching. And you go tell him that," she finished with a curt nod. "I'll wait here if you prefer, but I assure you I pose no threat to anyone."

He continued to stare at her insolently for a moment, then, with a grunt, he turned and disappeared around another bend in the trail.

He hadn't told her to wait, but Jaime decided it was best she did. He might be waiting to shoot her if she made a move and would swear later his warnings had been ignored.

After what seemed forever, he returned. "The guards at the house said he is eating dinner, and they don't dare disturb him, but if you go on up there, they will give you a lantern to help you see the way back to town."

"Oh, how kind," she muttered sarcastically, popping leather to start the horse moving onward. She had news for all of them, by God, because Stanton Lavelle could leave his precious dinner long enough to tell her if he knew her father's whereabouts. Surely that wasn't asking too much.

Darkness was rapidly descending, and as she drew closer, she could see lights coming from the massive stone building. In front, before two massive wooden doors, there was a courtyard. There, two other guards waited, as uncooperative and suspicious as the first man she had encountered.

"No one comes to Pointe Grande without invitation," the taller of the two declared without greeting. "You will leave."

"I will not leave."

As she got out of the cart, both men raised their rifles, eyes dark in warning.

"Now listen, you two," she began, hoping they couldn't hear how her knees were knocking together. Confronting angry faces and guns was frightening, but she'd be damned if she let them know it. "I didn't come out here hoping to be invited for dinner. I want less than five minutes of your boss's time, and that's what I'm going to have, or you're going to have to shoot me."

"We can do that, señorita," the short one assured her.

She liked him even less that his partner, because he grinned when he talked. A real cocky sort. "You probably could," she countered boldly. "You look like the sort who'd gun down a woman. But I'm not leaving here till I see him. So you can go tell him James Chandler's daughter has come all the way from Missouri and wants to know where he is. That's all I ask."

The guards exchanged wary looks. They did not really want to shoot her and finally decided to risk Lavelle's wrath and let him make the decision as to what to do with her.

After muttering to each other in Spanish, the short one went inside, while his cohort watched her suspiciously as she paced restlessly about the courtyard.

After what seemed forever, the guard returned. Grudgingly, he told her, "You can go inside. He will speak with you. Enolita will take you to him."

Enolita, a plump middle-aged Mexican woman, wore the same annoyed expression as the guards as she led Jaime through a twisting maze of corridors.

Stepping through another set of double doors, she found herself on a bridgelike structure, walled, with round open windows on either side. A brisk wind was blowing across, and Jaime dared to pause and look down in the gathering twilight, shuddering at the gaping crevice in the rocks below.

"Come, come," Enolita urged impatiently.

A little way farther, she lingered once more, this time as they passed a large room with shining floors of mosaic tile. Thick draperies of royal blue velvet hung at the huge windows, and French doors led out to a terrace overhanging the crashing waters below. "A ballroom." She had time to marvel, seeing a raised platform to seat an orchestra at one end.

Enolita tugged irritably at her arm.

Clutching her satchel, Jaime hurried after her.

Wondering how she would ever find her way back again, she was finally shown into what she supposed was Stanton Lavelle's study. It was the coziest spot she had seen so far. A leather sofa with matching chairs was positioned before a huge stone fireplace. Flames crackled in the grate. Rugs of bearskin and lamb's wool were scattered about the floor for warmth. In one corner was a huge desk, littered with papers. Lanterns bathed the room in a mellow, inviting light.

Enolita motioned her to sit down, indicated she should help herself to the liquor sitting on a bar to one side, and left.

Jaime looked at the crystal decanters, and her stomach gave a lurch. A drink of whiskey would surely knock her to her knees, as hungry as she was. How long had it been? Food had been plentiful on the steamer, but she had been trying to save her money and had eaten sparingly.

Save her money, she thought scornfully. She had saved it, all right—for the wily crook who had run off with it. Now she wished she had spent every bit of it on the boat, stuffing herself till she ached.

With a wave of delight, she saw a bowl of fruit, then realized she didn't know what it was. It looked like oranges but she was hesitant to eat one. But it *was* food, and she was starving. Still, it had not been offered to her, and she didn't want to be eating when Lavelle came in. Deciding a piece or two would not be missed and would be a blessing during the ride back to San Francisco, she quickly opened her satchel and dropped two of the oranges inside. She was about to close it but was unable to resist taking one more.

"That's a pomegranate."

Her hand froze in midair. She felt her face flame with embarrassment.

"It's quite delicious, but I'm afraid it contains a lot of seeds. I had the plants brought over from Africa, and it's been interesting to get them growing here." He crossed the room and held out his hand. "I'm

Stanton Lavelle, by the way. And you may help your-self," he added with a loose smile.

She was so ashamed to be caught stealing. "I . . . I'm sorry," she stammered awkwardly. "It's just that it was a long way out here, and I haven't eaten, and I know it was terribly rude of me, but—"

"Nonsense." He went to pull a cord hanging on the wall, and Enolita appeared almost at once. He instructed her to bring a tray of dinner. "Now then." He focused his attention on her once again. "You say James Chandler is your father?"

"That's right."

"And your name?"

She introduced herself past the lump of chagrin still lingering in her throat.

He gestured to the sofa. "I'm pleased to meet you, but frankly I'm astounded. James never told me he had a daughter. I was under the impression he had no family."

Settling before the fire, she appraised him as he seemed to be doing with her. He was of medium height and slender build. His dark hair was thinning on top, with silver creeping along the sides. He had a pencil-thin mustache, a firm set to his jaw, and Jaime thought she might have found him quite attractive if not for his eyes. Dark and piercing, they had a forbid-ding sheen, a coldness that was most disconcerting.

"Why did you come to me?" he asked bluntly.

"I was in hopes you could tell me where to find my father."

He leaned back in his chair, gazing at her through templed fingers. He found her truly lovely and was fascinated by her brilliant golden hair. "How did you know of my acquaintance with him, and what makes you think I know where he is?"

"The last letter I received, written nearly two years ago, said he was investing in your gold mine. Since yours was the only name he mentioned, and there's been no word from him since, I thought you might be able to tell me something."

With a short laugh, he confided, "To be perfectly honest, I'd like to know where he is myself."

Jaime gaped at him. "You mean you don't know? But what happened with your mine?" She didn't want to come right out and ask if her father's fears had come true, if it had, indeed, been a worthless venture.

His eyes grew even darker. "I'm afraid we weren't able to find the mother lode. Your father then reneged on his promise to back up his investment, and I lost a great deal of money."

Jaime shook her head from side to side in denial, a sinking feeling spreading throughout. "My father wouldn't do that without good reason."

Stanton gave a hollow chuckle. "And what reason is good enough to make a man not keep his word? He put up a map, with samples of ore, to a mine he'd been working himself but didn't have the money to dig any deeper. That's why he wanted to invest with me, to get the funds for hydraulic mining to search for his own mother lode. Only the map he gave me was bogus. No gold was ever brought out of that worthless pit. He swindled me. He never had any intentions of backing up his pledge with his own mine."

"I disagree." She refused to wither before his furious stare. "I think he put up a bogus map as protection against the possibility *you* might have been swindling *him*."

Just then Enolita came with the food, and a tense silence descended while she placed the tray on the table in front of the sofa. Pouring Jaime a glass of sangria and leaving the carafe, she hurried out.

As hungry as she was, Jaime was far too upset to eat. Instead, she sipped the wine.

Stanton drew a deep breath. "I did not swindle your father. He knew he was taking a chance that my mine would not produce, a chance every investor takes. But that does not give him or anyone else the right to go back on their word, their pledge."

"Did you say all this to him?"

"Of course, I did, but he ran away, disappeared. I tried to find him, but . . ." He spread his hands in a gesture of helplessness.

The spicy aroma of the food was starting to make Jaime feel nauseated. Her stomach gave a lurch, and she took another sip of the sangria, hoping to soothe it.

"I'm sure my father," she began, "would have given you the right map, or at least offered to buy back your interest in his mine, if he'd believed yours was an honest venture. He—" She broke off, swaying ever so slightly as he leaned forward, so close she could see the black specks on his irises and feel the anger emanating from him.

"Did he tell you that?" he demanded hoarsely. "Did he tell you he was giving me the wrong map because he didn't trust me?"

She was so weak and tired and hungry she could not think straight. Afraid of saying the wrong thing, she hedged. "I don't understand any of this, but I promise you my father is an honest man."

"Then why did he give me a bogus map, and why did he run away?"

She bit her lip and shook her head furiously. The food was making her sick to look at it. She pushed the tray away. "Is there anything you can tell me, Mr. Lavelle? Anything at all that might help me find my father? If there's been a misunderstanding, I assure you I'll straighten it out when I find him."

Stanton saw that she had turned pale. He went and yanked the cord to summon Enolita again, then sat beside Jaime on the sofa. She was leaning forward, her head resting wearily in her hands. "We'll talk tomorrow," he said gently. "I'm going to have Enolita show you to a room, help you into bed, and get you some warm milk. Maybe a bowl of soup. I suspect you haven't eaten lately, and you shouldn't have drunk the sangria on an empty stomach."

Jaime started to rise, but he held her back. "I can't stay here," she protested. "I don't know you, and I've no right to impose, especially after what happened between you and my father."

"But don't you see?" he asked, incredulous. "That's the reason I insist you accept my hospitality."

She turned to stare sharply. "But why? You think he's a crook."

"But there was a time when we were close, and I considered him a friend, and because of that I want to help his daughter."

Jaime was reluctant, although for the moment she had little choice but to accept. "Very well," she said finally, "but tomorrow we've got to have a long talk about all this."

The room Enolita took her to was on the top floor. A cool wind blew in from the ocean, stirring the white velvet draperies and billowing the canopy above the bed. There was a mahogany armoire, a washstand with pitcher and bowl, a mirrored dressing table, and a divan situated beneath the window.

Enolita turned back the blankets on the bed and, in broken English, said she would be back with the milk and soup.

Jaime changed into her nightshirt. She was exhausted and thought perhaps if she could sleep a little while, she would wake later and feel like eating.

She was about to lie down when she remembered the map and her father's letters. Maybe she was worrying needlessly, but hiding them would make her feel better.

Walking around, she noticed a thread hanging from the bottom of one of the draperies. Closer inspection revealed a loosening in the hem. The velvet was thick, with heavy folds. When she slipped the papers inside, they were not noticeable.

Satisfied, she crawled into bed, and as soon as her head hit the pillow, she was fast asleep.

She did not hear Enolita when she returned with the soup and milk, nor was she aware that Enolita searched her satchel.

18

Cord's mouth felt as if it were full of sand, and his head was pounding like an anvil. He lay on his side, watching miserably as the first light of dawn began to creep through the hole that was supposed to be a window.

The adobe was filthy and also cold from the ocean winds whipping through. Like all the ancient adobes dug out around the cliff, it had fallen to ruin. A miserable place for a rendezvous, he'd had no choice. Morena had heard he was back and sent a message by a trusted servant telling him to be there. He knew if he hadn't shown up, she'd probably have stormed right into the little guesthouse near the vineyards where he stayed, which would not have gone unnoticed by the vaqueros lodged not too far away.

She had brought a jug of wine, which they'd quickly consumed, and this morning he was paying the price.

He had told himself he only came back to explain what had happened so it couldn't be said he took Lavelle's money and ran off with it. But the real reason was Morena. He thought that being with her could make him forget Jaime.

It hadn't worked.

They had tried to make love, but it was Jaime's face he envisioned, her body he imagined he was caressing. Afterward, he had cursed himself for even making the effort.

That last night, when he had sneaked into Jaime's room to leave the money, he'd had to force himself to keep on going. It was all he could do not to crawl in bed with her, take her in his arms, and never let her go.

Only it wouldn't work.

Not with her.

Not with any woman.

He tensed as Morena began to stir. Stretching languorously, she slid an arm around him and began to stroke his chest.

He caught her wrist and held it. "You should have left a long time ago. It's almost light out."

She pressed her lips to his shoulder. "I couldn't leave you. It's been so long." Yanking free of his grip, she moved her hand boldly to his crotch. "Make love to me. Now. You know you want to."

He bolted from the bed and began yanking on his clothes.

Annoyed by his rebuff, Morena propped on her elbows and watched him. "What is wrong with you? You've been away for months. It was bad enough you didn't send word to me the minute you got back, but now you don't want me. What's wrong?"

Her blue-black hair was mussed and tangled about her face, which was puffy from too much to drink. Her chocolate eyes were watery and bloodshot. With her lips curved back in a furious snarl, she looked like some kind of demon.

His own ire rising, he told her. "This is the reason I had to get away from you in the first place. You don't know when to stop. You were about to get us both killed, and you're starting up all over again. Now put your clothes on and get out of here before he realizes you stayed out all night."

She fell back and yanked the covers up to her chin. "He doesn't care what I do."

"As much money as he spends on you? You damn well better believe he cares. He'd try to have my balls on a platter if he knew I'd been tapping what's his."

"If he cares so much, he should marry me. But no"—she slung her head from side to side—"he lets that shit-sack son of his run his life. He'll never marry me as long as Blake is around. And he promised. Even before she died. He said he'd kick her out and make me his wife."

"And you were dumb enough to believe him and tried to hurry things along by making sure his wife found out he had a mistress, which was a big mistake. That's why his son knows about you. But take heart." He reached to tweak her cheek with thumb and forefinger. "He did move you into the house before she was cold in her grave."

"I wanted more than that. And you know it. I wanted the respectability of marriage, not living with the servants."

"Men never marry their mistresses, and you know it."

"One day he will. You will see. But that has nothing to do with us. You will be my lover. I will never let you go."

"Stop talking nonsense and get out of here." He snatched the covers from her and flung them back. "Damn, it smells musty in here. You haven't been taking lovers and keeping this place up while I was gone, have you?" He flashed a teasing grin, hoping to get her out of her mood so she'd hurry up and leave.

It didn't work.

Wrapping the blanket about her as she got out of bed, she hissed, "*Bastardo!* I have been with no one except him, which is the same as having nothing. I was ready for you. Ripe for you. But you cannot say that, can you? How many whores did you take while I was here, living for the night I could be in your arms?"

"That's none of your business." He finished buttoning his shirt and reached for his holster. "Now you can stay here all morning if you want, but I've got things to do."

"No," she squealed, lunging to wrap her arms about his shoulders and press her head against his chest as she pleaded. "Don't go. Not yet. Not till you love me."

Gently, he disentangled himself and held her away from him but kept a good grip on her wrists, because she was plenty riled and he knew from experience what those long nails of hers could do. "Listen, damn it. We both knew when it started it couldn't last forever. You've got everything you want with him, and you're jeopardizing that by fooling around with me."

"He uses me," she wailed. "I mean nothing to him."

"And you use him, so it's a good arrangement, and you shouldn't ruin it. You aren't going to find a better deal, especially from me. I plan to hang around just long enough to raise the money to take me where I'm going, and right now I don't even know where that is."

"But you came back because of me," she accused hotly. "I don't care how many whores you had. It's always been better with me, and you know it, and that's why you're here. You care about me. I don't know who she is or what she did to take you from me, but I'll fight for you, I swear it."

"You never had me to lose. We had good sex. That was all. I told you way back then that you belong to him, and I'll never belong to any woman. That's the way it is, the way it has to be. When you stopped accepting it, I knew I had to back off. That's why I left you, and that's why I never should have come back."

"You made me fall in love with you, and now you treat me like your whore. Let me go, damn you!"

She dipped her head, intending to sink her teeth into his hand, but he saw what she was up to just in time to give her a shove that sent her sprawling backward across the bed. He finished strapping on his guns. "I'm sorry it had to end this way, but you can't say I wasn't honest from the start."

She leaped from the bed and caught him as he made it to the door, flinging herself against him. "You don't mean it. Tell me you don't. Tell me you will see me again, or I swear I'll come to your hut."

Cord turned and gave an exasperated sigh as she stood on tiptoe to shower his face with kisses, her hands all over him at once. Impassively, he stared down at her. "You're bound and determined to get us caught, aren't you? And what then? What are you going to do when he bounces your pretty little ass out and you've no place to go? You're sure as hell not going with me."

"That will not happen," she whispered huskily, stretching to lick and nibble his ear. "I am going to make him marry me, and then I will live like a queen. Till then, I want you for my lover."

"I told you I'd be riding on."

"Then love me as long as you're here. Say you'll meet me tonight."

"And what makes you think you can slip out again? I remember plenty of times I waited here for hours, and you didn't show because he called you to his bed."

Satisfied there would be a few more passionate encounters before Cord rode out of her life, Morena relaxed. "Don't worry about him. He's got other things to think about now."

"Like what?" he asked, not really caring.

She shrugged. "Some crazy woman who thinks he knows where her father is. He was one of the investors in Stanton's last mine, the one that left so many angry. He ran off instead of making good his pledge. She thinks Stanton knows where he is, but he doesn't."

Like a thunderbolt, it came back to him. Jaime had said her father was investing in a gold mine with a man in San Francisco. "What was his name?" he asked and held his breath.

"What do you want to know for?"

"Maybe I know him."

She laughed. "It happened before you came here, but since you're so curious, it's Chandler."

"No, I don't know him," he managed to mumble, every nerve in his body going tight.

"Don't forget," she called after him. "I will be here tonight."

She watched him go, wondering as he disappeared around a cut in the rocks why he was suddenly in such a big hurry.

Stanton smiled as Jaime devoured the platter of steak and eggs. "I'm glad you're eating this morning. Enolita said you were already asleep when she took your tray last night."

"Traveling all the way across the country and then finding my way here finally caught up with me, I suppose. I appreciate your letting me stay last night. I wasn't looking forward to the trip back to the city."

"I sent the cart and horse back by one of my vaqueros."

She looked up in surprise. "But why? I wanted to be on my way after we talked this morning."

"Where would you go, my dear? What would you

do? I want you to stay here. Maybe we can help each other."

She made no comment, waiting for him to continue.

He presented the plan he'd been up all night thinking about. "If I can find your father's mine, I'll work it and share the profits with you. Frankly, though, I'm at a loss as to where it's located. You see, I went to the claims office and had them look up the records, but your father never filed for a stake. Seems he didn't trust anybody. And that's sad, because if someone finds it in the meantime, he has no legal claim. All the more reason you and I should work together. I'll get back my investment, and you'll have money for your future. I'm still convinced his mine has a mother lode. It could be worth millions, but right now it's not doing anyone any good. So what do you say?" He held out his hand.

Jaime looked from it to him and shook her head. "No, I can't accept your offer."

"I'd like to know why not," he demanded, withdrawing his hand as his voice rose along with his ire.

Jaime did not mince words. "As I told you last night, my father gave you a bogus map because he didn't trust you. I intend to do some investigating on my own. If I find out he was justified, I don't owe you anything. If, on the other hand, I find he was wrong, then I'll see you get what's coming to you. I'll make good his pledge."

She jumped, startled, as he slammed his hands down on the table and roared, "That is unacceptable! I will not have you treat me as if I'm a crook."

She responded coolly, undaunted by his explosion.

"Finding my father is my first priority, but I'm also going to try and locate his mine, as well as discover whether yours was a legitimate investment."

His eyes narrowed. "Then you have the map, don't you?"

She forced the lie. "No. But my father wrote and told me approximately where it is. Maybe I can find it." She did not sound convincing even to her own ears.

Stanton leaned back in his chair, satisfied that she did, in fact, possess that map, but for the moment he would play along. "Your father is probably dead," he said then, wanting to unnerve her. "You're all alone."

Jaime closed her eyes, prayed he was wrong, then murmured, "I'll manage somehow. Right now, I suppose I'd better get my things and start walking to San Francisco. I've imposed enough on your hospitality."

She started to rise, but his hand snaked out to clutch her wrist. "No, please don't go yet. I've got another offer."

She sat back down, willing to hear him out to avoid an unpleasant scene but not about to relent.

"Regardless of what you think of me, I did, at one time, hold your father in high regard. We were good friends. So for the sake of what used to be, and because I have nothing to hide, nothing to be ashamed of, I'm willing to help you despite how you feel about me. Stay here. I'll finance your investigation, your search for the mine, and when you find it, when you come to realize my own was a legitimate operation, perhaps you will prove your honor by paying your father's debt to me."

She chewed her lip thoughtfully. His offer was tempting, but something made her leery.

"What's wrong?" He chuckled. "Does it bother you so much to think you might discover it's your father who's the swindler? Are you afraid to give me a chance to prove my own integrity? Are you scared of what you'll find out?"

"No, Mr. Lavelle." She looked him straight in the eye, deciding she really had nothing to lose and everything to gain. "After what I've been through the past months, there's not much that could scare me anymore. I'll accept your offer."

"Good. Then it's settled." He smiled, satisfied, and jangled a silver bell to bring Enolita with more coffee.

Jaime accepted another cup, as he changed the subject to brag about his empire, how he had turned a Franciscan mission into a magnificent estate.

She was only half listening, lost in thought as she wondered where to start. Perhaps she should go to Drytown, to the area where the mine was situated. If her father was hiding out there, maybe he'd hear she was around and come to her. Dismally, she realized it was a long shot but she had no other plan for the moment.

She didn't notice that anyone else had come into the room until Stanton bellowed to someone behind her, "What are you doing back? I told you to stay in the city and wait for the ship due in with my crystal chandelier from Austria."

Jaime looked around to see a boyishly handsome man with dark hair and warm blue eyes coming toward her. Ignoring Stanton, he graciously took her hand in his to press it to his lips before introducing himself. "I'm Blake Lavelle, and I know already I'm pleased to meet you." He drew out the chair beside her and sat down, devouring her with his eyes. "God, you're lovely. That hair!" He reached to touch a golden strand. "Tell me, who are you?"

Before she could respond, Stanton said in a bored tone, "Miss Jaime Chandler, meet my son, Blake." He went on to inform Blake. "Her father was one of my investors, and he's dropped out of sight. She's come all the way from the East to try and find him, and I've offered her our hospitality."

"That must have been quite a disappointment to find him missing," Blake murmured sympathetically, "but rest assured, we'll do everything we can to assist, as well as make you comfortable. Will you be staying long?"

"I'm not sure." She wished he would stop staring at her so adoringly.

Suddenly, Stanton decided to take over the conversation. "I think we should have a party to show off both Miss Chandler and the new chandelier," he suggested jovially. "We haven't had a big social in a long time. What do you think, Blake?"

"A splendid idea. We can't keep such a rare and precious treasure to ourselves—and I'm not talking about the chandelier," he added, with a wink for Jaime.

She laughed, relieved the mood had become lighter. "That's kind of you, but I've nothing to wear, and besides, I need to concentrate on searching for my father."

Stanton seized the opportunity to enlighten his son as to Jaime's financial plight. "Unfortunately, our guest is in dire straits. She apparently has no money and very few belongings, but we can take care of that, can't we?"

Jaime looked down self-consciously at the faded dress she was wearing.

Blake's eyes flicked over her, taking in her dimensions and shape. "Yes, you're about the same size my mother was. She had lovely clothes, and they're still hanging in her armoire. You can take your pick."

Jaime had been so absorbed in her own worries she'd not even thought about whether Stanton was married, and now she realized he was actually a widower. "Oh, no." She refused at once. "I couldn't—"

Blake cut in to declare, "You can and you shall. She was a generous person, and if she were alive she'd insist on it herself." He stood, taking her hands to pull her gently to her feet. "I'll start making out the guest list for the party while you go through her things. Be sure to pick out a riding outfit, and I'll take you on a tour of the estate when you're done. Not all of Pointe Grande is situated on a cliff hanging over the sea," he added cheerily.

Jaime found herself being whisked from the table and out of the room. Only moments after meeting Blake Lavelle for the first time, she was entranced by his warm and outgoing personality. His cheerfulness was a pleasant contrast to the gloomy mansion, and she found her spirits lifting.

He held her arm as he steered her through the narrow corridors, talking all the while. "I'm still wondering if you're real. I've been waiting for you my whole life, you know."

"Of course you have," she said playfully. "But I'm not real. I'm a figment of your imagination."

"You mean a ghost? Well, that's all right. A lovely lady ghost is nice after all those dismal Franciscan fathers I've seen floating around. I hope you'll stay awhile."

She become serious. "I'm afraid that would be imposing. Surely in a place as large as San Francisco I can find work and rent a room somewhere."

"I won't allow it," he declared breezily, pausing before a closed door and searching his pockets for a key. "Besides, I'm going to marry you and then you won't have to work."

She stared at him in wonder, not sure whether he was altogether teasing.

He unlocked the door and pushed it open, moving to one side for her to enter.

The furniture in the room, consisting of an ornately carved bed, tables, desk, and armoire, was all of dark wood. But everything else was done in shades of pink: the spread and canopy, the dressing-table skirt, the cascading curtains. Even the curving divan was upholstered in pink velvet, and a rug of soft rose covered the floor.

"It's lovely," Jaime said breathlessly, in awe. "Your mother had excellent taste."

"She was very dainty and feminine in everything she did. I like to think I inherited some of her charm."

"I'm sure you did." She bit her tongue to keep from saying he couldn't have got it from his father.

Blake went to the armoire and opened it. "Take your pick."

Never had she seen such an array of stunning gowns, but she still felt uncomfortable.

He sensed her reluctance and assured her, "You're welcome to it all. An hour should give you enough time. I'll be waiting in the dining room. Walk straight when you start back. Don't turn anywhere. The Franciscans intended for anyone wandering about to lose the way."

She gave him a grateful smile. "I'll be fine."

He started out, then paused to look at her quietly for an instant before proclaiming in a voice filled with emotion, "You look like her, you know."

Not knowing quite how to respond, she thanked him.

And then he was gone.

She began to go through the dresses, thinking how, even though Blake was attractive and nice, it would be a long time before her heart could open to any man. It still hurt deeply to think of the one who had left her without a backward glance.

Time slipped by, as, fascinated by such a vast collection, she could not make up her mind. Then, spying the one tucked way at the end of the rack, she gasped out loud with delight. It was fashioned of watered silk, shades of green and blue melded together in shadows of gold swirling throughout. It was off-the-shoulder, with a dipping bodice encrusted with tiny teardrops made of—what? She blinked in disbelief, drawing the creation closer to the window and the light, and lo and behold, saw her suspicions were correct. The teardrops actually appeared to be tiny gold nuggets.

She knew this was the dress she wanted to wear, knew she had to try it on.

Quickly changing, she stood before the full-length mirror, twisting and turning to marvel at the heavenly creation.

The door to the next room opened slowly, quietly.

Jaime was too absorbed in the exquisite gown to be aware of anything going on behind her.

Then she saw it, in the mirror: the maniacal face of a woman enraged.

And she was holding a knife.

19

Morena had been in Stanton's room when she heard the noises coming from the one adjoining. Investigating, she was terrified for one frozen moment to think she was looking at the ghost of Emily Lavelle.

Then it dawned on her.

The woman could only be James Chandler's daughter, and Morena had been momentarily taken aback because of her hair. It was like Emily's, a rare and brilliant color, almost like polished gold.

Indignity replaced fear, and she slipped the knife from the sheath strapped to her thigh and crept up on her to demand harshly, "What are you doing in here?"

Jaime stared with fear-widened eyes and began to back away as she stammered to explain. "Blake . . . Mr. Lavelle's son . . . told me I should come in here. Now put that away, please."

"Pah, he has no say." Morena swung the blade in an arc. "This is not his house. It belongs to his father, which means it also belongs to me, for I am soon to be his father's wife."

"Over my dead body."

They both turned as Blake walked in.

Jaime watched, relieved, as he crossed the room to grab Morena's wrist and squeeze until she dropped the weapon. Then he maneuvered her roughly to the door. "How dare you come in here and threaten a guest? You might sleep with my father, but so help me, if I ever catch you in my mother's room again, I'll give you the thrashing of your life."

He flung her into the hall, but before he could slam the door she shrieked, "Your father will kill you if you touch me, you shit sack—"

"I'm sorry." He whirled to face Jaime. "Pay no attention to her. She's my father's mistress, and I'm furious my father lets her live in the house. But she's not allowed in here, and I promise she won't bother you again. It's just a good thing I came to see why you hadn't finished yet."

Jaime was still upset but pulled away as he tried to put his arm about her shoulders to comfort her. "I really think," she said raggedly, "I should go back to San Francisco."

With a sweeping grin, he caught and squeezed her hands. "You'll do nothing of the kind. I won't allow it. God, you're magnificent in that color. And your resemblance to my mother is absolutely remarkable. No wonder Morena was so mad."

He dropped her hands and walked to the bed, where she had spread out several outfits.

"Did you find a riding costume? Ah, the garnet

velvet, a splendid choice. Now hurry and change. I'm anxious to show you about."

He breezed from the room, closing the door behind him. Jaime ran to lock it, as well as the one adjoining, then wondered dizzily what she had got herself into by being so desperate. But for the time being, she could only accept the Lavelles' hospitality and hope for the best.

Jaime was relieved that Stanton was nowhere around when she finally met Blake in the dining room. She declined his offer to have an early lunch, because she was anxious to see the rest of the estate.

The horse she was given was a mare, dark red in color, and promised to be quite gentle. Blake's was a large dapple-gray stallion. Its high spirits were evidenced in the way it pawed the ground, snorting impatiently to be on its way.

They rode first through the vineyards, as Blake explained how the Franciscans in Alta California began growing grapes early in the eighteenth century. "By 1800, the groves here had every kind of fruit you can imagine, and my father cultivated date palms and plantains. He has a huge greenhouse where he experiments with different exotic plants and flowers, such as orchids."

Jaime's memory was painfully jarred to think of her first orchid . . . her first love.

He went on to describe life in the 1700s, when more than seven thousand Indian converts lived in the various missions up and down the coast. Artisans were brought from Mexico—masons, millwrights, tanners, shoemakers, saddlers, and potters—to teach them.

"It was quite a place before the American conquest, and when my father was able to buy the mission here, he changed the name to Pointe Grande and built his own empire."

"It's more like a fort, with all the guards and walls and fences," Jaime ventured to remark.

"Yes—well, my father has some enemies, I'm afraid. I try to stay out of his business, and he never tells me anything. But I hear rumors now and then."

"Did you know your father claims my father reneged on a pledge to invest in one of his mines?"

She knew by the look on his face that he did, even before he began to hedge. "Well, a little something. That was a pretty big mine, and a lot of people got upset, but I really don't know any of the details."

She hesitated, then decided it had to be said. "My father gave yours a bogus map to his mine as a pledge, because he didn't trust him."

Blake raised an eyebrow. "You mean he thought my father salted his mine to lure people to invest in it?"

"I don't know what you mean by *salted*."

"Unscrupulous people do it to make hard-rock mines appear to have gold in them. It's done by shotgun or a large-caliber pistol. You load with fine gold dust instead of buckshot, and if the barrels have plenty of flare, and a man stands back far enough, he can blast the whole face of a barren drift with particles of gold."

She was fascinated and wanted to know. "So how can you tell if it's been done, salted, that is?"

"Because you can't blast just any kind of dust. You have to know what you're doing, because it has to be the kind that would have got there in the normal course of geological events. I heard of one instance where a man salted his mine with particles of free gold that were deeper and redder in color than usual under a microscope. A suspicious investor ran a bullion assay and proved there was a trace of copper, which is used by the Royal Mint in London to make gold hard enough for use in coinage. There's no way that dust could have come from that mine.

"Another way," he went on, "is to take a few bushels of ore from a good mine and scatter it at the bottom of a shaft or along the drift of a mine that's poor. But salting isn't as prevalent as it once was, because investors are getting smart enough and wary enough to hire the services of professionals to appraise the property."

"Why wasn't that done with your father's mine, the one that caused so much trouble?"

"It was," he said matter-of-factly, "but I heard he hired the appraiser himself, and that's why so much hell was raised when the mine played out. There were those who claimed the appraiser wasn't honest."

"And what do you think?"

"Nobody likes to think his father is capable of hornswoggling," he retorted lightly, then added with a frown, "I'd really rather talk about something else, if you don't mind. I'm not like my father. I don't worship gold. I'm like my mother. Money never meant that much to her. Land is the thing. And freedom. You could have moved her into one of those hovels carved out in the cliff and she'd have been happy. My father was always the greedy one. Not her. And I feel the same. That's why I'm interested in the vineyards, the gardens, and when I inherit this one day, I won't be living in that monstrosity of a palace he's created. I'll live simply and happily.

"With a wife who's just like my mother," he added with a caressing smile.

Jaime glanced away, not meeting his adoring eyes as she asked, "Was your mother happy with your father?"

"No. He was a tyrant, and it was bad enough even before he took Morena as his mistress, but after that my mother eventually couldn't take any more. Oh, she knew he had lovers, mistresses, from time to time, but Morena was different. Morena made up her mind she was going to get my father to divorce my mother and marry her so she could move into the mansion and have the status of wife instead of mistress. So she made sure my mother knew about her. That made my father mad, but he was too infatuated to get rid of her."

"But he didn't marry her when your mother died. How long has it been?"

"Two years. But that doesn't mean anything. I think he would have married her if not for me. He knows I blame her for Mother's death."

Jaime was curious but refrained from asking further questions. After all, they had only met that morning, and she felt somewhat disconcerted already at the way he had bared his soul to her.

Suddenly, he blurted, as though he had to share the pain, "My mother killed herself."

"Oh, Blake, I'm so sorry."

"I was the one who found her. She—"

Jaime reached to cover his hand with hers. "Really, you shouldn't be telling me all this. We're practically strangers."

His mouth curved in a mysterious smile. "You're wrong. You see, I've been waiting all my life for this, and when I walked into the dining room this morning and saw you, my heart almost stopped beating. No," he repeated fervently. "We can't be strangers, because I've known you always."

"Oh, Blake." She shook her head. "I wish you wouldn't talk this way. I'm glad we met, and I certainly appreciate your friendship, but I've only got one thing on my mind right now, and that's finding my father. I'm not looking for romance."

He took a deep breath, forced a bright smile, and yielded. "Very well. We'll let the future take care of itself, but meanwhile I want you to know I'm willing to do anything I can to help you with your search."

Jaime relaxed. They had wound up on the beach, directly below the highest point of the bluff. On one side the ocean glistened in the sun like gold flakes dusting the green waves beyond the frothy whitecaps. Bordering opposite were the cliffs, stretching skyward as though trying to touch the clouds.

They rode in silence. Jaime allowed her mind to drift.

Blake stared toward the outcroppings where ridges eventually met sand. Suddenly, with a low curse, he dug his heels into his horse's flanks, sending him at a gallop toward the rocks.

Jaime urged the mare to follow, curious over what had upset him.

"Devil worship." He pointed to a pile of flat stones, five or six feet high and covered with a weird collection of beads, feathers, shells, and what looked like bits of food. "It's an ancient Indian custom that goes back hundreds of years, one the Franciscans had to deal with when they were trying to convert them."

Jaime shivered instinctively to contemplate such a thing.

He went on. "Every once in a while, one will spring up. I've always suspected Morena has something to do with it. She's a half-breed. Her mother was full-blooded Yahi. For reasons nobody quite understands, their tribe was attacked by white settlers about four or five years ago and nearly wiped out. The few who survived scattered. By then, Morena was already being kept by my father. I think she gave some of them shelter in the caves, but I can't prove it.

"So I find these from time to time." He gestured with a disgusted grimace. "It's an altar to a god they're terrified of called Cooksuy. This homage you see, the beads and things, is called *pooish*."

"The missionaries didn't succeed in converting all of them, did they?"

"Hardly. It was disastrous. The Spanish came to find gold and tried to force the Indians into Christianity, but instead brought new diseases that wiped out entire villages, destroyed their culture, and made slaves out of them. The Indians eventually deserted the missions and fought back, waging their own war. So today they're hated and given the contemptible name of Digger Indians, because they eat a lot of roots and clams—digging for them, of course.

"And they sneak out of their hiding places to do this." He dismounted and began to scatter the rocks and offerings. "They build a big fire and dance around and go into some kind of trance and later swear they summoned Cooksuy up out of the flames in the form of a large white serpent or a bull with fiery eyes." He paused to laugh. "But it doesn't work, or I'd have been dead by now, because I have an idea Morena tries to call up her demon spirits to get me out of the way. One of these days, my father will wake up and run her off, and then the Diggers will come out of those rocks up there where they hide and we won't have to put up with this nonsense."

They rode on down the beach, and Jaime listened with interest as Blake talked on, about himself and his love of the land, about his mother and how much he had adored her. It was obvious, however, that he did not hold his father in high esteem, and not altogether due to his obsession with Morena. Jaime came to the conclusion that if Stanton Lavelle was, indeed, unscrupulous, Blake was not involved. In fact, she suspected he didn't like his father at all.

The sun began to bleed into the sea. Reluctantly, Blake said they had to be getting back but added happily, "This is like it used to be when Mother was alive. We rode together and forgot all about the time."

Jaime felt another uncomfortable wave.

"I want you to know something."

She tensed.

"I said I'd help you look for your father, and I will,

but you have to agree to stay here in the meantime."

She turned her head to stare at him in wonder. She could have told him she had little choice but instead asked why he was giving her such an ultimatum.

His face lit up in a grin. "Don't you know? Dear, dear Jaime, I'll give you all the time you need, but surely you know by now I'm falling in love with you."

Aghast, she cried, "Blake, I made it clear—"

He held up a hand against her protests. "I know, but all I'm asking is a chance. Fair enough?"

Jaime wondered again what she had got herself into. He was sweet and kind, but she did not love him and somehow knew she never could. Yet for the moment she could only agree to his offer. Managing a tight little smile, she murmured, "Fair enough."

Stanton Lavelle leaned back in his leather chair and took a deep draw from his cigar. He swirled the bourbon in his glass and stared across his desk at Cord. "You owe me something, Austin."

Cord had suspected when he got word Lavelle wanted to see him that it had something to do with money. "Sorry." He repeated his words from the day before. "I don't see it that way. I did the best I could."

"At least you had guts enough to come back and admit you failed. Most men wouldn't."

Cord was getting impatient. He had other things to think about, like figuring out a way to get to Jaime without anyone seeing him. He wanted to know what the hell was going on but did not think it wise to let it be known they were acquainted.

With an exasperated sigh, he reminded Lavelle, "You said all this yesterday. What's on your mind now?"

Stanton flushed with annoyance. He didn't like anyone questioning his motives, especially those he considered subordinates. For an instant, he considered telling Austin to get the hell out, but he knew Cord was best-qualified for what he had in mind. "I'm offering you a job."

"I've got one. Working with the vaqueros."

"I'm offering you something much better, with a future. It could lead to big things. Big money."

Cord shook his head. "My future is south of here. Mexico, maybe. As soon as I make enough to get me there." And as soon as I make sure Jaime is going to be all right, he promised himself.

"I'll make it worth your while to hang around a little longer."

Cord's interest was piqued. A little longer was all he needed. "I'm listening."

"I need a hired gun. It's said you're the best."

"True. But I don't believe in killing a man for money, so I'm not for hire."

Stanton's patience was wearing thin. He was not used to anyone turning him down. He slammed a fist on the desk. "You listen to me, damn it. I'm not asking you to kill anybody. I'm asking you to protect me. And like I said, you owe me. The least you could have done was sell the wagons and animals and brought me the money from that."

"True. But it would have held me up crossing the Sierras. I didn't want to chance it. Besides," he dared add with a crooked grin, "everyone knows you can afford the loss."

Stanton's eyes narrowed. "I'll be the judge of what I can afford to lose, and the fact is, since I backed off from hard-rock mining, I don't have the wealth I used to have. And I don't like that, Austin. I don't like it one little bit. I like being rich, and I intend to keep on being rich."

"So what's that got to do with you needing a hired gun?"

"I had to sequester myself here after a disgruntled investor took a shot at me at my office in San Francisco. He missed and I was lucky, because I didn't have a bodyguard then. But now that I'm going to be getting out more, getting back into hard-rock and hydraulic investments, I don't want to take any chances. You'll go with me and keep watch."

Cord thought about how very little he actually knew about Lavelle's business. When he had first drifted onto Pointe Grande, he'd been hired to work with the vaqueros. When he eventually got involved with Morena, she had filled him in on Lavelle's family—how his son refused to get involved in the War Between the States because he didn't want to leave his mother and how she eventually committed suicide.

When Cord did not say anything, Stanton tried another ploy. "You know, if you're as good with a gun as they say, you have nothing to worry about, so what's your problem?"

"Actually, I don't have one," Cord replied dryly. "But you do, since you're the one getting shot at."

"Look, Austin." Stanton crushed his cigar in a tray, biting back his temper. "I'm offering you a chance to make some real money, not the lousy pay of a vaquero. All you have to do is be close by when I'm around people, like the big party I'm having to introduce a lady guest who'll be staying here awhile. I want you to hang around in the shadows and keep your eyes open."

Cord felt a rush to realize the party would be a perfect place to run into Jaime without arousing suspicion. Still, he did not want Lavelle to think him too eager. "If the pay is right, I'll do it," he said finally, in a tone that hinted it didn't really matter one way or another.

Stanton grinned and held out his hand to seal the bargain.

"With one stipulation," Cord stated quietly.

Stanton's smile faded.

"It doesn't include being ordered to kill anybody. I'm a hired gun. Not a hired killer."

"But you'd shoot somebody to keep them from killing me, right?"

Cord shrugged. "There are ways of saving a life besides taking one."

"That's good enough for me." Stanton held out his hand once more.

This time, Cord took it.

As he maneuvered his way out through the maze of passageways, Cord was relieved not to run into Jaime. As anxious as he was to talk to her, he wanted first to do a little investigating on his own.

If he had known, back when they were together, that

Lavelle was the man she'd be looking for in San Francisco, things would damn sure have been different.

Now he found himself wishing he had yielded to his gut feeling as he left Sacramento and gone back to her. It had taken every shred of self-control he had to keep putting distance between them.

But he had done so, because he felt it was best— for both of them.

And now, with a pang of sadness, he knew when the time came, he would have to find a way to do it again.

Morena paced about angrily, restlessly, her curses bouncing back at her from the dirt and stone walls of the dugout. The scene with Stanton over her threatening Jaime Chandler with a knife had been ugly. Blake had wasted no time in telling her father, and Stanton had been furious. He had slapped her several times and threatened to kick her out of his mansion, out of his life, if she ever did anything like that again.

He didn't want the gold-haired bitch upset, because she could lead him to her father's gold mine. Morena knew all that, but she was still mad over his hitting her and also infuriated that Jaime had been allowed in Emily's room to help herself to her clothes.

Morena was staunch in believing no one had a right to Emily's room or Emily's clothes except herself, by God.

She had stormed out, planning to spend the rest of the night with Cord and take out her fury in a carnal way. Many times she had come to him in a frenzy and rode him all night long like a wild stallion. No other man she had ever bedded came near to matching her passion. Cord Austin miraculously surpassed it.

She wanted him fiercely this night.

"But where is he now?" she cried out loud, striking the air with her fists.

Gathering her shawl about her, she left the hut. She had threatened to go to his place, and now she would show him she meant it.

But he was not there.

She pounded on the door, then entered and fumbled in the darkness for a lantern. Lighting it, she glanced about but saw none of his belongings, no sign of him at all.

He had left.

A bowl and pitcher sat on the table by the stripped bed.

She sent both shattering against the wall.

Meanwhile, not too far away, in the hayloft of a barn with a good view of the cliffhouse above, Cord settled down for the night.

Maybe it was not the best of lodgings, with hay prickling and the odor of horses wafting from the stalls below, but he could keep an eye on the goings-on at Pointe Grande . . . and Morena would never think to look for him there.

20

In the days since her arrival, every time Cord had caught a glimpse of Jaime, Lavelle's son was always with her. He cursed himself for the way it needled him. What difference did it make? If not Blake, some other man would come along to try and win her hand. She was lovely. It was inevitable.

And it was none of his business.

Once he either found her father or got her settled somewhere, she would be out of his life. This time, for good.

But what was rankling in the short while he had been nosing around was why Chandler would have dropped out of sight without attempting to stay in touch with Jaime. It didn't make sense, especially since she had indicated that he had communicated with her right before all this happened. This made him suspect that Chandler might well be dead, murdered. Whatever the truth, Cord was sure Stanton Lavelle had had something to do with it.

Another thing that worried him was fear of what Lavelle might do if he thought Jaime knew where her father's mine was located, maybe even had possession of the right map.

Cord was not going to rest easy, would not even think of riding on, till he got to the bottom of the Chandler mystery.

At last it was the night of Lavelle's party, and some of the wealthiest and most prominent people in San Francisco and the surrounding areas were coming. Most, Cord knew, probably despised Lavelle, but they leaped at the chance to visit the famed cliff house.

Cord had positioned himself on the terrace where, from the shadows, he could observe everything.

Earlier in the day, workmen had installed a new crystal chandelier, and the expensive jewels of the women glittered and sparkled in its shimmering prisms.

An orchestra played while some of the guests danced. Others sipped champagne or gathered about tables laden with food.

Cord watched Lavelle as he mingled graciously, shaking hands and exchanging pleasantries with the men, complimenting the ladies. All the while, he kept an eye out for Jaime. The terrace was going to be a perfect place to attempt contact. He figured Blake would be unable to resist bringing her out to such a romantic spot. Light spilled from the ballroom onto baskets of flowers brought from Lavelle's greenhouse. The air was fragrant with the smell of the potted eucalyptus trees and honeysuckle vines trailing the mission walls. If they appeared, Cord hoped she would not give him away before he could signal to her to get rid of Blake so he could have a moment alone with her.

A ripple went through the crowd. Cord saw everyone looking toward the doors leading into the ballroom, and he moved closer to see what was going on.

It was Jaime.

In front of him, just inside the terrace doors and unaware of his presence, a woman clutched her throat in surprise, then turned to whisper frantically to her husband, "My God, for an instant I actually thought it was Emily come back to life. I've never seen anyone else with hair that color till now. And she's wearing her dress too. How could anyone forget it, with those solid gold teardrops sewn into the bodice? She wore it to our gala, remember?"

Cord wasn't looking at the expensive nugget decorations. He was thinking how the turquoise shades of the watered silk gown matched Jaime's eyes. Lost in her beauty, he felt a heated rush to remember all those wondrous nights together beneath the stars.

He gave his head a vicious shake, commanding himself to concentrate on the moment at hand and not the past.

Blake escorted her proudly to the center of the room. Stanton joined them to clap his hands for attention before loudly announcing, "Ladies and gentlemen, I would like to present to you our guest, Miss Jaime Chandler, who's just arrived from Missouri. I'm sure you will all make her welcome."

Cord did not miss the way Blake hovered beside her, beaming. He didn't know much about Stanton's son. Some of the vaqueros called him *cobarde*, a coward, because he had once fainted at the sight of all the blood at the *calaveras*—the cattle slaughter pens. He preferred, it was said, to spend his time in the vineyards or vegetable gardens and stay away from the rougher side of ranch life.

And he was not the only one who noticed Blake's obvious infatuation with Jaime. The woman who had spoken earlier nudged her husband and remarked, "Well, now we know why Blake hasn't taken a wife. I always did say he was a momma's boy, and now he's found someone who looks just like her, I think we'll be receiving a wedding invitation soon."

Cord melted back into the darkness.

The evening wore on. From time to time, guests wandered out to the terrace but did not notice Cord where he stood, concealed. He was starting to think Blake and Jaime would not appear, when suddenly they did.

He listened while Blake gushed to Jaime over the way everyone was astonished by her resemblance to his mother. "They say I shouldn't let you get away, because you're so lovely, and I certainly don't intend to."

Cord could not help smiling to see how she quickly turned her head so Blake's kiss would fall on her cheek and not her lips.

With a sigh over her rebuke, Blake moved to stand at the wall and gaze out toward the sea. "I said I'd give you time, and I will, but it's hard when I love you more each day."

In the light spilling from the ballroom, Cord could observe her face. She did not look at all pleased.

With a deep groan of misery, Blake whirled to try and take her in his arms again, but she held him off. "Please, don't. You promised you wouldn't."

"I know, I know. It's just so hard. I'm sorry."

He walked away from her then, going to the other side of the overhang, and that's when Cord knew he had to make his move. He stepped from the darkness and into the light, holding his breath for fear Jaime would scream at the sight of him.

Her eyes widened. Her hand flew to her mouth to stifle a gasp. Frantically, he shook his head from side to side, pressing a finger to his lips to signal for silence. Then he nodded toward the door, lifted his hand as though sipping from a glass, indicating she should get rid of Blake by sending him to get a drink.

She understood and called to Blake as Cord retreated.

"It's so nice out here. I'd like to stay awhile, but I'm thirsty. Would you get me some champagne, please?"

"Of course, darling. I'll be right back." He hurried to oblige.

As though wondering if her eyes had deceived her, Jaime approached the screen of eucalyptus cautiously, fearfully.

"It is you," she breathed in wonder.

"Hello, Sunshine."

She wondered if he could hear the wild pounding of her heart and put her hands behind her back so he wouldn't see how they were shaking. "What are you doing here?" she whispered thinly.

He knew there was no time for anything except

getting right to the point. "Stanton Lavelle is the man who hired me to bring back the women. I work for him now as his bodyguard."

She gasped.

He rushed on. "I had no idea he was the man you were planning to see in San Francisco. If I had, I wouldn't have left you like I did."

Jaime fell back a step at the anguished memory of that morning when she had felt so degraded. "Why did you? Did you really think me no better than a whore?"

It was Cord's turn to be astonished. "What gave you that idea?"

"The money you left in my Bible. Remember our deal?" She laughed shortly, bitterly. "I was to be either your wife or your whore. Well, I'm certainly not your wife, but you kept your end of the bargain by paying your whore, didn't you?"

"That's nonsense. That was money the pioneers collected to pay me, and I wanted you to have it. I figured you were broke."

"I was. I am." She confirmed bitterly. "I was robbed in San Francisco. That's why I'm now beholden to the Lavelles."

He frowned. "There's a reason for Lavelle's benevolence. I've heard your father gave him a bogus map to a gold mine and Lavelle wants the real one desperately. He probably thinks you can lead him to the mine. You can't trust him."

"If not for him, I'd have no place to stay."

"You will," he vowed. "I'm going to try and help you locate your father, and if I can't I'll see you're taken care of."

"Oh, I'll be taken care of." She lifted her chin a bit, starting to recover from the shock of seeing him. "According to Mr. Lavelle, my father's mine is full of gold. And all I have to do is give him the right map and let him mine it, and he promises to share it with me. But I'm not that naive. Not anymore," she added dryly.

"Then you have the real map?"

"That's none of your concern. You wouldn't help me when I asked, and now you want in on the gold. But I don't need you anymore, so leave me alone."

She had started to turn away, but he reached to grab her and yank her back. "You've got to listen. If Lavelle believes you've got that map, he'll stop at nothing to get it. And how do you know Blake isn't after it too?"

"He's not like his father. He can't stand him. Besides, he doesn't even want to talk about it."

"Well, do you have it?" he repeated impatiently.

"I'm not going to tell you."

"Damn it, Jaime, don't be so stubborn. What if your father is dead? What are you going to do then? You're at Lavelle's mercy unless you let me help you."

"I know what I'm doing, and believe me, I don't intend for Stanton Lavelle to get his hands on that mine. My father wrote me all about how he didn't trust him. That's why he gave him the bogus map in the first place. But if the investment had proved legitimate, he would have honored his pledge and paid his debt somehow."

"I think it's dangerous for you to keep staying here," Cord said tightly.

"I have nowhere else to go."

"Well, at least give me the map for safekeeping."

"No."

He had seen that look in her eyes before, the first night they met, when he'd told her he wouldn't take her to California. He knew her mind was made up now, as it was then.

"And why should I trust you anyway?" she challenged frostily.

He drew a deep breath and let it out slowly as he framed his answer carefully. "I can understand how you feel after things happened as they did, but believe me when I say it had to be that way."

She hated to ask but had to know. "Is there someone else?"

He laughed softly, tenderly. "No. You're special to me, Sunshine, and while I'm no good for you, you've got to let me help you out of this mess."

"I'm not sure." She wished her knees would stop knocking together.

"Blake is going to be back any time now. Make up your mind."

She bit down on her lower lip, desperate to believe him. Despite all the time she had spent with Blake since arriving, she did not feel he cared whether she was ever reunited with her father. Yet in only a few moments of being with Cord, her world suddenly seemed so much brighter.

"All right," she whispered finally. "Where do you want to start?"

"First, we need to talk. I've got to find out from you as much as I can about your father. I'd like to read his letters if you have them."

Sarcastically, she asked, "Didn't you see them when you left my pay in the Bible?"

He flinched at the barb.

She went on to say she would allow him to read them but added, "I won't give you the map. And when I can, I'll see that you're rewarded for your help."

He thought if he didn't get away from her then and there he was going to throw caution to the wind and kiss her till they were both out of breath, because being so close to her was getting to him, damn it.

"I'm not interested in a reward. I just feel responsible for your being in this mess."

They stood for long moments in tense silence.

Neither heard, or noticed, when Morena stepped out on the little balcony above. Seeing them, she stepped closer, straining to hear, her face twisted with rage.

"Go," Cord said finally. "But slip back out here when you get a chance. Wait till no one is around and then come over here. I'll be waiting."

He gave her a little push away from him, but it was too late.

Blake had spotted them.

"What's going on here?" He rushed forward, handing Jaime her glass of champagne to free his hand so he could pull her back into the light. He looked at Cord suspiciously and could tell by the way he was dressed he was not one of the guests. "Who are you?" Then it came to him. "I know. You're that hired gun of my father's, aren't you? What are you doing here, annoying Miss Chandler?"

"He . . . he's just doing his job," Jaime said uneasily.

"I saw him, and I was scared, and he was apologizing for frightening me, that's all."

Blake began leading her back toward the ballroom. "I'm going to speak to my father about this. I don't like his kind hanging around."

Cord settled back to wait for her to return whenever she could.

And while he waited, he would try his damnedest to stop thinking how good it would have been to have held her, kissed her. . . .

Morena knew every inch of the mission. By the time she was old enough to learn of the Franciscans and how they had tried to convert her people to Christianity and the ensuing problems, the war between America and Mexico was over. The mission, like so many others built by the Spaniards, was abandoned, and she and the other Indian children had played there.

When she grew older, she had used the old chambers as a place to take men who were willing to pay for her voluptuous body. The money helped keep her family from starving, for her mother had many children but no husband. The Yahi men would not have her after she had slept with a white. Morena would close her eyes and pretend it was not a stranger violating her body but her husband making tender love. She would envision herself as queen of the mission, and never was it falling to ruins but always a palace in her mind.

She had watched from a distance when Stanton Lavelle came with all his money and power to buy the ruin, rename it Pointe Grande, and turn it into a most magnificent estate. One day, she dared sneak inside for a firsthand look, and that was when he saw her and, at once, knew he had to have her.

But Morena had wanted more than money from Stanton. She wanted to be his wife. And now the only thing stopping her was Blake.

It was because of Blake that Stanton would not let her go to the party. They'd had a bitter fight, with Morena throwing her worst tantrum ever, but Stanton would not relent and told her to keep away. He was running things this time, he had said firmly. She was to stay out of it.

But determined to at least watch the festivities, she had sneaked into a room with a balcony affording a partial view of the ballroom and terrace. That was how she happened to see Cord and Jaime and heard them plan to meet on the terrace later.

She intended to be there when they did. Because of her vast knowledge of the mission, she knew about the gouged-out places in the wall leading downward to the ballroom terrace. The Franciscans had built it as an escape route. The way was slippery, but she knew it well, for she often prowled around, watching Stanton, when he had no idea she was anywhere near.

She stepped onto the terrace.

Cord whirled about, gun drawn, hammer cocked, then burst out in disgust. "Morena. What the hell are you doing here?"

"You don't come to me anymore," she whispered petulantly. "So I have to come to you."

He holstered his gun. "It's over. Now get out of here before somebody sees you."

She had timed her arrival perfectly, for she had waited to make her presence known till she saw Jaime finally weaving her way back toward the terrace after Blake had been persuaded to dance with one of the other ladies.

And just as Jaime appeared, pausing to allow her eyes to adjust to the dim light, Morena made her move.

She threw herself against Cord, crushing her mouth against his, arms twining about his neck as she clung to him.

Taken by surprise, he froze, only for an instant, but it was long enough for Jaime to arrive on the scene, and what she saw appeared to be a loving embrace between two very willing people.

At the precise instant Cord came alive to try and disentangle himself from Morena's frantic hold, he heard Jaime's soft cry of shock.

He whirled about, still trying to get Morena off him, but she was holding tight and babbling loudly about how he had to stop teasing her this way. He saw Jaime run back into the ballroom and caught a glimpse of her stricken face.

Finally, he managed to get a good grip on Morena's wrists and squeezed so painfully she had to let him go.

But Morena knew her scheme had worked. "You see?" she said gleefully. "If I can't have you, neither can any other woman."

21

"*I want you to know* I'm upset by all this," Blake said tensely as the stagecoach bumped and rattled its way toward San Francisco. "At first, I was just worried about how mad my father would be if he found out I'd taken you on this trip. He said to keep you away from the mining towns, because they're no place for a lady, but that's the least of my concerns now, because I'm afraid you might actually believe what that old coot said."

Jaime, lost in her musings, stared out the window without really seeing the barren land.

She had persuaded Blake to take her by private stage to Drytown, an almost deserted place. At first, none of the prospectors hanging around the dilapidated saloon had wanted to talk. But she had wheedled and begged and was finally directed to an old man who was willing to speak his mind, saying he was too old to worry about the consequences. And besides, he had wanted to make clear, James Chandler had been his friend.

"And he won't no cheat like the men said who come looking for him. He told me that mine he'd invested in was salted. Gold chloride had been poured into drill holes to raise the assay value when the assessments went up, only he couldn't prove it."

"I'm not sure I understand what you mean."

Blake had spoken up then to explain grudgingly how even though a man bought stock in a mine, his investment sometimes did not stop there. He was still obligated to meet demands for assessments for machinery or deeper exploration if needed.

The old man's Adam's apple had bobbed up and down as he said excitedly, "That's what happened, for sure. James told me new capital was demanded, and he was told to come up with cash this time, instead of pledging his own mine. That's when he got mad and did some digging on his own and found out the drill holes had been plugged. He told me he was going to turn the man responsible in to the law, and that's the last time we ever talked. He just dropped out of sight."

"And men came looking for the mine later?" Jaime had asked.

"Yep. But they couldn't find it. James swore nobody ever would without the right map. He said he was going to make sure he saved it for his girl," the old man had added with a warm smile and a wink.

"This makes me sick," Blake cried suddenly, bringing Jaime back to the present. He was pointing out the window as they passed an excavation site. The hillside was gouged out, destroyed by high-pressure monitors blasting away into the earth to wash the gold-bearing gravel down into the waiting sluices. "There has to be a better way to search for gold besides tearing the earth apart," he grumbled.

Jaime made no comment, not wanting to engage in conversation just then. She was disappointed not to have found even one clue as to where her father might have gone. And hearing from someone else that Stanton Lavelle was suspected of being a swindler filled her with anger.

For the moment, however, she was tired and found herself wishing she could fall asleep to escape the misery, if only for a little while.

It had been several days since she had witnessed Cord and Morena locked in a torrid kiss. She had not said anything about it to Blake for fear he might suspect she had once been involved with Cord. That was her humiliating secret to try and forget.

Persuading Blake to leave the very next day, she'd not seen Cord since and hoped she never would again. Obviously, he had been trying to trick her into turning the map over to him so he could give it to Stanton. So now she wanted nothing to do with him ever again.

They stopped overnight at a way station, where Blake rented them each a private room. Early the next morning, they continued on their way, arriving at Pointe Grande just before dark.

Despite Blake's urging to rest awhile and calm down, Jaime found her way to Stanton's office.

Dreading the scene sure to come, Blake went with her.

Stanton met Jaime's fury with his own. "Where the hell have you two been? How dare you leave without telling me where you're going?"

Jaime did not wither beneath his threatening glare. Ignoring Morena, who lounged on the sofa wearing a revealing dressing gown, she recklessly unleashed all the anger that had been boiling since Drytown. "You are a swindler, Stanton Lavelle. Maybe I can't prove it, but my father could, and I think that had something to do with his disappearance."

"Now you wait a minute." He looked at Blake. "What the hell is she talking about?"

"I took her to Drytown," Blake admitted hesitantly. "A prospector told her Chandler was getting ready to prove you plugged drill holes with gold chloride when he just dropped out of sight."

"You took her there?" he roared. "You took her there to try and prove your own father might be guilty of swindling, maybe even murder?"

"No, no—"

Jaime interrupted. "I want the truth. I want to know what happened to my father."

"All I know is that he obviously ran away to keep from paying his debt, and frankly I'm outraged by your insinuations. But I realize you're upset, and I'll make an allowance for that." Actually he was thinking how if Blake hadn't fallen for her, he would already have the map by now, and she would be out of there, dammit.

Blake gingerly slid his arm about Jaime's waist and urged, "Come on. This isn't accomplishing anything."

Jaime shrugged off his embrace, gaze still riveted on Stanton. She knew he was lying, could feel it in her bones and see it in his face, but what real proof did she have? "I'm going to find out," she vowed, fists clenched at her sides. "Believe me, I'm not going to stop till I do. If you're innocent, I'll apologize. But if you're guilty, if you did harm my father, so help me you'll pay."

Stanton looked at Blake and spread his hands in a helpless gesture. "She's obviously distraught. Traveling all this way to face such disappointment is a tragedy. I'm glad you're befriending her, but I must ask you not to cater to her despair. You're only doing her harm and making the situation worse."

Blake nodded reluctantly, but as Jaime shot him a withering glare, he knew he had to take a stand for her sake. Clearing his throat, he proceeded cautiously. "Well, the truth is, I seem to recall a lot of people felt something wasn't quite right with that last mine. Some of them were really mad. You even got shot at. So maybe Jaime is right in thinking you might not have a claim on her father's mine, and—"

Stanton bolted to his feet. Jaime jumped, startled, and Blake clamped his hands on her shoulders protectively.

"Don't you ever insinuate I swindled anybody, you hear me, boy?" He towered above them, shaking both his fists. "You don't know what you're talking about. You've *never* known what you were talking about when it came to my business. So you keep your mouth shut and tend to your gardens. And for now, get her out of here before I really get mad."

Jaime knew there was no point in arguing further and turned to leave. Stanton called after her, "I'm going to forget all this, little lady, for your father's sake. He'd want me to look after you."

When they were gone, Morena began to slowly clap her hands together. "Bravo. You can be proud of that performance."

"Shut up." He sat down and reached for the decanter on his desk and poured himself a stiff drink.

She went to perch on the corner of his desk. "You know what has to be done with her."

"I can't. Not yet. First, I'm going to try to buy her out, offer a lot of money she won't be able to turn down."

At that, Morena laughed shrilly. "You don't *have* a lot of money. That's why you've been desperate for Chandler's gold, remember? And now that we've found out he has a daughter, we're wasting time."

"I've *got* to try to do it my way, because if anything happens to her, Blake will hold me responsible."

"Pah." She spat. "I am sick of him running your life. If not for him, I would be your wife now. Like you promised."

Stanton snorted. "If you hadn't been so stupid as to let Emily find out about us, he wouldn't hate you like he does."

"That doesn't matter. He'd never have accepted your marrying a mestiza, and you know it, especially one with Yahi blood."

He'd never accept me marrying a whore, Stanton thought, cursing himself for having made such a fool promise in the first place. But it been a weak moment, when she was torturing him with her lips, her tongue, and he'd have said anything right then. "We're going to wait," he declared testily. "I intend to make him see she'll never marry him as long as she's obsessed with her father. Once he does, he'll persuade her to take what I'm willing to give her and be done with it."

Morena met his defiant eyes. "There are other ways."

His hand snaked out to grab her about the throat. "Stay out of this," he warned. "You took over last time, and where has it got me two years later?"

"Two years?" she hooted. "You gripe about two years? What about me? Look how long I have been waiting for you to keep your word to me. Besides, there was no other way but my way, and you know it. But soon it will be over."

He let her go, flinging her away from him. "This time I make the decisions."

She flounced from the room. Stanton poured himself another drink and tossed it down. He was angry to think how he had to put up with the bitch, because she had the upper hand. She could expose him, ruin him. He had to do something about that. And soon.

Jaime had been so infuriated she had told Blake she would not be joining him for dinner. She was far too overwrought to have an appetite anyway. She had proceeded to her room, unlocked the door, then gasped in shock to realize the room had been ransacked.

She immediately went to the drapes, where she had hidden the map and letters in the hem. With a sigh of relief, she found they were still there.

Sitting down on the divan, she pressed her hands to her throbbing temples and told herself to calm down. Her first impulse was to go tearing back to Stanton and curse him for daring do such a thing; then she decided to wait. Right then, she was exhausted and knew she needed sleep so she could think straight, decide what to do next.

She undressed and put on one of Emily Lavelle's filmy gowns, then lay down to brood. She wished she could leave. But where could she go? Blake was her only friend. Cord Austin, damn him, had proved once again he could not be trusted.

Finally, despite the emotions churning inside her, she fell asleep.

Cord had managed to bribe one of the servant girls into telling him which room was Jaime's. The girl hadn't been interested in his reason for knowing, only with the money he paid her and his promise never to reveal she had told him.

He figured her door would be locked, and he wasn't about to announce herself formally by knocking. So, shortly after midnight, when all was quiet, he lowered himself from the roof by rope to her window.

It was closed but not locked and opened with a soft click.

Jaime stirred. She was not sleeping well.

He struck a match, and, in its flare, saw her and

promptly blew it out. Without a sound, he went to her, placing a hand over her mouth.

Jaime instantly awoke in terror and tried to scream as she strained in the darkness to see her attacker.

"Don't scream."

She ceased her struggles as the familiar voice came to her through her panic.

He eased his hand up slowly.

"What are you doing here?" she whispered through clenched teeth, sitting up to push him away. She clutched the sheet beneath her chin. "Did you come back thinking I'd tell you where the map is since you couldn't find it?"

"What are you talking about?" he asked sharply.

"Stanton sent you, didn't he?"

"No. But you don't believe me, do you?"

"Why should I? You work for Stanton, and you were hoping you'd be able to convince me to turn the map over to you, but then when I saw you with that woman, you knew your plan was ruined. Now get out of here." Her voice rose menacingly.

He covered her mouth with his hand again, pressing her back against the headboard. "You're wrong. Morena had been spying and knew you were coming back. She chose just the right second to make sure you found us together. But that's not important now. I came here to tell you I've talked to some of Stanton's guards, and one of them let it slip, after I got him half drunk, that he and some of the others brought a man, an American, in here against his will. They left him with Stanton and never saw him again. Now that doesn't prove the man was your father, but it's something to go on, especially since I was able to get the guard to pinpoint the time: two years ago. He remembered because it was right after Emily Lavelle killed herself, and everybody was spooked over that."

As he spoke, Jaime had ceased to struggle, and he removed his hand. Lighting the lantern next to the bed, he could see how her room had been searched.

He turned back to her. "If you'll give me another chance, I'll do what I can for you."

She searched his face for some sign he was really telling the truth. "Do you swear Stanton didn't send you?"

"I swear it, Jaime. He doesn't even know we're acquainted. Morena may have told him we were talking at the ball, but if she did, he didn't think anything about it."

"All right," she said finally. "I'll give you another chance." She proceeded to tell him about her visit to Drytown and what the prospector had told her.

Cord listened quietly, then summarized. "Between what the two of us have learned, we've got reason to believe Lavelle had something to do with your father's disappearance but not enough to take to the law."

"But we can't give up," she said fiercely, blue-green eyes sparkling in the lantern's glow.

His laugh was soft, tender. "I think we've proved it's not our nature to do so."

Her face broke into a smile to remember how they had met and conquered the many challenges of the trail. And, in that poignant moment, Cord could resist her no longer.

He brought his mouth down to hers, hungrily covering it with his own.

Jaime could no more have stopped him than she could have turned back the tide that crashed recklessly on the rocks somewhere below her window. Her needs and wants thrummed in her pulses, shutting out everything but the welcome feel of his arms about her, the hot possession of his lips on hers.

From somewhere deep within, something warned she was opening herself for still more heartache, but she knew she had to risk that kind of pain for the exultation of the moment. Despite everything, she wanted him, loved him.

He had softened the pressure of his mouth, his tongue moving against hers in a sweet seduction she could not resist. Hesitantly at first, she reached for him, fingers pressing into the hard muscles of his back, a groan of need and want rising in her throat as he stretched out the length of him, drawing her down beside him.

She could feel evidence of his desire against her belly, and she strained yet closer to demonstrate her own.

He began to slide the gown from her shoulders, and she moaned softly, languorously, as he found her breasts. Lowering his head, his tongue grazed the sensitive nubs of her nipples, and she could feel them grow taut and swell. He took turns drawing them into his mouth.

She clutched at his hips, urging him closer. He maneuvered himself out of his trousers, while she caressed him. When he was naked, he claimed her mouth once more in a searing kiss. Her neck arched back as she gave herself up to the emotions he had created. In complete surrender, Jaime could feel the heat of her own body and reveled in it.

He raised his mouth slightly. She could feel his lips move, and she gloried in the sound of his deep and husky voice as he proclaimed, "I want you as I've never wanted another, Jaime."

He rolled to his back and took her with him, cupping her buttocks and pulling her tightly against him. She spread her thighs and allowed him to enter, a sigh of pleasure rocking from her very soul.

Over the grinding rolls and waves of ecstasy as he drove himself into her, Jaime rose from the exquisite sensation to torment herself with the reality of how he had only expressed his desire.

He had not, would not, speak the words she longed to hear, the same words she dared not utter to him.

Together they rode to the crescendo of their passion, and afterward he held her locked against him.

"I've missed you," he murmured finally, biting back the impulse to admit how he loved her.

"And I missed you," she whispered in return, squeezing her eyes tightly against the burning tears of frustration.

Morena stepped back, silently closing the door to the secret passage in the wall.

She returned the knife to the sheath strapped to her leg but did not immediately retreat, for she was too upset and knew she had to get hold of herself, lest she lose her way in the dark labyrinth that was the bowels of the mission.

Searching Jaime's room had been a waste of time, and Morena had returned to deal with her, despite Stanton's orders to let him handle it—but she had not counted on finding Cord in Jaime's bed, and now she was livid with rage.

Morena knew she could not tell Stanton, for she was not about to divulge the existence of the secret passage. Besides, she preferred to handle the situation in her own way.

But for the moment she could only wait.

There would be another time to send Jaime Chandler to meet her father—in hell.

22

Between making love and talking, Cord and Jaime slept little. Finally, he knew he had to leave before the servants began stirring about. With a last searing kiss, he told her to let him take over the investigation. "All I want you to do is avoid further confrontation with Lavelle. Let him believe you're losing hope, giving up. As long as he thinks you aren't about to stumble onto anything and figures sooner or later he'll get his hands on the map, you're safe."

He left her then, climbing out the window and up the rope that would take him to the roof.

The room was silent. Rosy fingers of dawn picked away at the darkness, shadows bleeding farther away.

Jaime was warmed by the memories of the night just past, her lips bruised by his kisses, body tingling from passion spent.

He had talked, and she had listened. He admitted

his involvement with Morena in the past, assuring her it was over.

Though nothing had been discussed about the two of them, no mention of anything beyond the moment, Jaime had silently resolved, with her head tucked on his muscular chest, his strong arms tight about her, that if this was all she could ever have of him, it would have to be enough. She would seize the present and dare not question the future.

When Enolita came to her door to announce that breakfast was served, Jaime was ready. She had dressed in a pink gingham dress—borrowed, of course, from Emily Lavelle's wardrobe. She had brushed her hair back and tied it with a ribbon. The finishing touch was to paste on a bright smile and swallow the anger that ever smoldered within to think how her father might have met his fate within these gloomy walls.

Suppressing a groan of disappointment to find Stanton sitting at the table, Jaime managed to murmur a pleasant "Good morning" and nod in his direction as Blake leaped to pull back her chair. She could not help wondering why Morena never appeared in the dining room. Probably Blake would not stand for it.

Waiting till her coffee was poured, Stanton declared jovially, "I hope you slept well and feel differently about things this morning, my dear."

Out of the corner of her eye, Jaime saw Blake draw up, as though anticipating another scene.

She stirred sugar into her coffee as she replied calmly, "Well, I must say it was disturbing to find my room ransacked." Turning to gauge his reaction, she was impressed by how he was able to appear genuinely surprised, even angry.

He looked from her to Blake with rage-widened eyes, his lips a thin white line. "I don't know anything about it, but you can rest assured I'll find out. Now listen to me." He faced Jaime once more, laying his hand, palm down, on the table in a beseeching gesture. "I want peace between us. As I said last night, I can understand your being upset, coming all this way to face such heartbreak and disappointment, but I swear to you I did not swindle your father, and I had nothing to do with his disappearance.

"Now we both know you have no money," he continued, "so the thing for you to do is accept my offer to buy your father's claim from you, because we both know you've either got the right map or you know the exact location. Now, frankly, I want you to know I'm taking a big risk. After all, if he would pledge with a bogus map, I wouldn't put it past him to pledge with ore that didn't really come from his mine. But for your sake, because I feel sorry for you, I'll buy you out.

"So just name your price," he finished magnanimously.

Blake was delighted. "That's wonderful, Jaime; it would solve all your problems. You can forget the past and get on with your life. And so can I," he added meaningfully, as he reached to take her hand.

Jaime was paying no attention to Blake, for she was fighting the urge to throw her coffee in Stanton Lavelle's lying face. If he hadn't ordered her room searched, who had? Certainly not Blake. Remembering Cord's instructions, however, she managed to sound apologetic as she declined. "I really don't want to make any decisions about anything for the time being. I've done a lot of thinking and reached the conclusion that I'm exhausted from the long journey out here and too tired to think right now about what I should do. Give me a few days."

Blake enthusiastically voiced his approval. "A wonderful idea. We can ride and walk on the beach. Maybe you'd like to spend a few days in the city—"

"Blake, be quiet," Stanton thundered, then reminded Jaime, "I said you could name your price. That shouldn't take a lot of thinking, for God's sake. Just tell me what you want. Turn the map over to me, and then you can rest all you want to." He wasn't worried about raising the money, figuring he could arrange a short-term loan for any amount. She wouldn't have it for long, anyway. He'd make sure of that.

"Not now," she said, and began to nibble at the eggs Enolita placed before her.

Blake saw the look on his father's face, sensed an explosion coming, and tried to head it off. "Jaime is probably right. It might be best if all of us just didn't talk about it for a while, and—"

"Will you stay out of this, goddammit?" Stanton screamed, banging his fist on the table so hard his coffee turned over and soaked into the lace cloth. "Last night she accused me of being a swindler and insinuated that I'd done away with her father. Today she doesn't want to talk about it. This is my house, and I want to get this mess settled once and for all."

He leaned closer to Jaime to warn her harshly. "You'd better take my offer, young lady, before I lose patience with you." He got up and quickly walked out of the room, afraid of what he might do if he stayed.

"Jaime," Blake began miserably, "I'm sorry—"

"You don't need to apologize for him. Sooner or later, he'll see I'm not giving in to him."

He squeezed her hand in comfort. "Let's spend the day riding. I'll have Enolita pack a picnic basket. You need to get your mind off things."

She accepted eagerly, anxious to escape, if only for a little while.

Stanton was walking into his office when Morena stepped from the shadows in the hall. "I was listening back there. She turned you down. Now there is only one thing left to do." Her voice was as cold as the echo in a tomb.

"Not yet, damn it. And why the hell did you ransack her room after I told you not to? It points suspicion to me, and I told you I had Enolita look through her bag the night she arrived, and she couldn't find anything."

"You know she has the map. She was just smart enough to hide it right away."

He blocked the doorway, not wanting her inside. "I told you to stay out of it. You're only making problems."

She gave her thick blue-black hair an arrogant toss. "No. You are *paying* someone to make problems."

"Now what are you talking about?" He glanced over his shoulder at the whiskey decanter on his desk.

So what if it was early in the day? The way things were going, he needed a drink.

She longed to be able to tell him about finding Cord in Jaime's bed. Instead, she shared something else she knew would alarm him. "You think you are paying the gringo, Austin, to be your bodyguard. Instead, you are paying him to ask the guards and vaqueros questions, the ones who were here two years ago, asking if they know anything about an American named Chandler."

The fury began deep in his toes and worked its way up, and by the time it swept completely over him, Stanton Lavelle could hear the enraged thudding of his own heart. "Find him." His words were barely audible, spoken between tightly clenched teeth. "I don't know what's going on here, but tell the guards to find him and bring him to me right away."

He closed the door, went to his desk, poured himself a drink, and gulped it down. It didn't slow his boiling blood, and he had another. And another.

The day wore on. By midafternoon, Stanton was very drunk. He sent Enolita, in a hail of curses, to find Morena and ask where in hell was Austin. She returned, pale with fright, to inform him apologetically that Morena could not be found.

He lay down on the sofa in his office and passed out. When he awoke, the room was dark. His head was pounding, and he tossed down another drink before summoning Enolita. She told him she'd tried to wake him for dinner but couldn't. He yelled at her that he wasn't hungry, and if she knew what was good for her she'd find Morena, by damn.

Carrying a bottle with him, he told her he was going to his greenhouse, then staggered out.

Blake and Jaime were sitting in the parlor, resting from their day's ride, when Enolita came looking for Morena. Curtly, Blake told her he didn't know where she was and didn't care.

Wringing her hands, Enolita said, "I know you don't care, but your father went to the greenhouse after screaming at me for hours to find her. I don't know what's wrong with him. He's been drinking all day, and he's like a madman."

Blake sighed and excused himself to Jaime. "I'd better go see about him. Sometimes he gets violent when he's had too much to drink."

Jaime tried not to sound too eager as she told him to go ahead. "I'm tired. I think I'll go to bed." Actually, she had been waiting for an excuse to retire early, so she could go to her room and wait for Cord.

"Then I'll see you at breakfast." He kissed her hand and left.

The greenhouse was situated near the highest peak of the cliff but sheltered from the wind by a sloping ridge. Stepping inside the glass structure, Blake drank in the rich, loamy smell he loved. It was his favorite place, a tropical garden lush with the fragrance of the myriad of plants his father cultivated.

Blake liked the orchids best, with their purple and pink and lavender petals that looked as though they'd been sprinkled with sugar. He moved past their regal beauty, guided by the sounds of his father's ranting and raving.

Stanton took one look at his son and roared, "What

the hell are you doing here? I've got other things on my mind besides your whining and sniveling."

Blake blanched. Never would he get used to his father's abrasive nature. "I was worried about you. Enolita said you were . . . upset." He didn't want to say drunk.

"Damn right I am." His words were slurred. He turned the bottle up to his lips, no longer bothering with a glass. Then he looked at his son with red-rimmed eyes and commanded harshly, "But you can get out. All the way out." He raged on, waving his arms wildly, the liquor spilling. "I'm sick of you. Just like your mother. Weak. Cowardly. Good-for-nothing. I shouldn't have married her. Shouldn't have had you. Morena is right. I ought to marry her and have strong sons."

Blake tried to hold back but could not. Tearing him to pieces was one thing, but he would not tolerate such disrespect and ridicule of his mother. "You have already dishonored my mother's memory by moving that half-breed whore into this house, but if you marry her and give more breeds your name, you can forget I'm your son, because I'll change mine, by God."

Stanton moved so fast Blake never saw it coming. All he knew was that he was slammed in the face and went sprawling to the dirt.

"Now get out." Stanton towered over him, swaying from side to side. He punctuated his words with a hard kick to Blake's ribs.

With a grunt of pain, Blake curled into a fetal position, clutching his stomach.

Stanton kicked him again, this time in his buttocks. "I said to get out, damn you. You're worthless. Just like your mother. Damn her too. I hope she rots in hell."

Blake tasted blood from the cut on his lip. Though he was swept by anguish, he managed to raise his head to whisper, "I'll kill you for that—"

Stanton lifted him by the nape of his neck and the seat of his pants and flung him between the tables. "Get out of here, before I kill *you*, you good-for-nothing coward."

Blake could hardly focus his eyes through the descending sea of pain. He crawled on his hands and knees, past the orchids, oblivious to the rich smell of the earth, onward and out into the night.

Morena saw him as she made her way to the greenhouse. "So. You grovel like the worm you are."

He struggled to his feet, still clutching his side, and moved away from her as fast as his agonized body would allow.

Morena entered the greenhouse, undaunted.

The instant Stanton saw her, he shouted, "Damn you, where have you been all day? And where's Austin? I guess you've been rutting with him like the whore you are."

At that, Morena paled but was only momentarily taken aback as her own ire erupted. "You pompous son of a bitch, how dare you speak to me that way?"

He slapped her and sent her reeling against one of the tables. "Don't curse me, damn you. Now answer me. Where's Austin?"

"I don't know. I looked all over." She looked at

him in loathing. "You will pay for this. You know what I can do to you."

"Threaten me, will you?" He started toward her, drunk and incensed beyond all reason. No longer did he fear the consequences of ridding himself of her for good, as he'd longed to do for the past two years after discovering just how evil she was. "I'll break your neck if you even think about it. Now get out of here and find Austin. And when I'm finished with him, I'll take care of the rest of the mess around here, which includes you. I'm going to kick you out of here and send you back to your worthless people."

"Don't be a fool, Stanton."

He struck her again, with the back of his hand, knocking her to her knees. Reaching down, he yanked her up by her hair, and she screamed and fought, but he silenced her with his fist.

As she lay at his feet, fighting to stay conscious, his words came to her through the great ringing in her ears.

"Stupid Yahi squaw. Did you really think I'd ever marry trash like you? Get out of here before I kill you."

Fearing for her life, Morena could only retreat.

Sometime later, Cord entered the greenhouse. He saw a lamp burning at the opposite end and headed that way. He found Lavelle slumped in a chair, taking small sips from the near-empty bottle he held. Lavelle blinked as he looked up, as though trying to focus his eyes amid the drunken fog that enshrouded him.

Cord was expressionless. "You want to see me?"

Stanton sat up straight, anger making his head clear a bit. "Damn right I do. Where have you been all day?"

Cord shrugged. "Riding around. Helping the vaqueros. You didn't say you needed me for anything else."

"You're lying. You've been nosing around, asking questions about things that don't concern you. Are you working for Jaime Chandler now? She doesn't have any money, so I can only guess how you're getting paid." He gave a nasty snicker.

Cord was not rankled. Words of fools never bothered him. He was, however, concerned with just how much Lavelle knew and asked calmly, "Mind telling me where you heard all this?"

"Don't worry about that. Just get your things and ride out of here. Tonight. After dawn tomorrow, my guards will have orders to shoot you on sight. You're a traitor." Stanton's hands tightened around the bottle, which he ached to bring crashing down on Austin's head. But he knew he didn't stand a chance in his condition. In fact, Stanton didn't like the way Austin was looking at him, anyway, his eyes smoldering like burning coals and his fingers twitching at his sides near his low-slung guns.

Cord smiled in a way that didn't change his expression at all. "I'll be back, Lavelle. I can't prove anything yet, but I've managed to find out enough to know I'm on the right trail."

"Wait a minute, come back here." Stanton started after him but could not walk as fast, because his head was spinning like crazy. "What are you talking about? What have you found out? I've nothing to hide. And if you come back, you're a dead man."

The greenhouse door closed behind him.

Stanton let out a string of curses in the stillness and stumbled back to the chair.

Tomorrow, he swore through the fuzziness wrapping about him, he was going to end the frustration once and for all. To hell with Blake and his infatuation with Jaime Chandler. She was here, and he intended to use her and would have done so two years ago if he had known of her existence. Then he would deal with Morena, make her do what should have already been done. Then he'd run her off, kill her if he had to. He didn't want her anymore. With Chandler's gold, Stanton knew he could find a real lady to become the next Mrs. Lavelle. One with class and background, one who would appreciate being the queen of his kingdom, by God.

His head lolled, falling backward as he finally passed out.

The position made his neck quite vulnerable for the shears that later pierced his throat.

23

Cord dropped to the ledge. Jaime had left the window open. She ran to meet him, and without a word they fell into each other's arms.

For long, tense moments they clung together. Finally, she drew back to search his face and felt a stab of apprehension. His expression was grave. "What's wrong? Did you find out my father is dead?" Her voice cracked.

"No." He gripped her shoulders, pressed his lips against her forehead. "But thanks to a banker steering me in the right direction, I was able to find one of the men who was also an investor in that last mine. He told me he lost a great deal of money and also suspected salting but—like everybody else except your father, it seems—lacked proof. He didn't know your father, by the way, but heard about someone pledging a bogus map.

"He says he wishes now *he'd* been smart enough

to pledge with bogus money," he added with an amused smile.

"So we're right back where we started from." Jaime turned from him with a sigh and went to sit on the divan, eyes downcast. "We can't prove anything, and even if we could, that's not going to tell us what happened to my father. But I have to keep believing he's still alive."

"Of course you do." He sat down beside her. He could see she was depressed and dreaded telling her of the scene in the greenhouse.

She related the conversation with Stanton at breakfast and said, "He was very angry and tore out of the room, and I haven't seen him since."

With a deep breath of resolve, Cord decided to get it over with. "I just did. In the greenhouse. It seems someone told him I've been asking questions. He accused me of working for you and ordered me off the estate, unless I want to be shot on sight."

She looked at him in horror. "Oh, Cord, no. Then you have to leave, but what about me?" Realizing how panicked she sounded, she added, "I mean, I can't do much snooping when Blake is always around."

"Don't worry. I intend to keep on till I've run out of ideas, but I can't risk coming here to see you anymore." He thought a moment. "There are steps below the greenhouse, leading down to the beach. Nobody ever uses them, and some of them have crumbled badly, but they're safe enough if you're careful. That part of the beach will be a good place for us to meet, because the guards avoid it. The Yahi Indians build altars there, supposedly to summon their gods."

"I know. Blake showed me one when we were riding. It was creepy."

"They do it to scare the guards into not going any farther. Some of them live in caves in the cliffs just north of there. Anyway, meet me there at midnight. You'll have to grope your way in the dark. You can't risk using a lantern, because the guards might see the light. But with luck, all this will be over soon."

"I don't see how." She shook her head dismally. "Just when we think we know something, we run into a stone wall and can't find out anything else. I'm beginning to think it's hopeless. If Stanton did do away with my father, he covered his tracks well. We aren't going to be able to prove anything. I think I should just get out of here and try to find a way to work my father's mine. If he is alive, surely, sooner or later, he'll come out of hiding."

"Don't do anything impulsive. Give me a few more days."

She looked at him sharply. "Are you on to something you aren't telling me about?"

"I'm not sure." He did not want to get her hopes up, only to let her down if his suspicion proved wrong.

"You're always keeping something from me," she accused, but gently.

His smile was wistful. "I suppose it's always best to keep a part of yourself private."

Jaime took a deep breath. It was time she let him know his past did not matter, for she had decided perhaps that was why he held so much of himself back. "Maybe you do so because you've known prejudice, but that wouldn't be the case with me. It doesn't matter to me you were raised by Apaches."

His face turned to stone. "Where'd you hear that?"

"Link Cotter told me, back in Sacramento, the morning you left." She plunged on, figuring she'd gone this far, she might as well say it all. "Frankly, I wouldn't care if you did have Indian blood, or even if you were *all* Indian. You saved my life once, and I'll always be grateful."

"Some people feel if a man lives with Indians, it's the same as being one, which makes him a savage, socially unacceptable and not to be trusted. That's why I keep it to myself, but unfortunately some of the soldiers at the fort in Texas where I once worked spread the word, and it keeps following me."

"I'd like to hear about it, if you care to tell me."

He nodded. "Maybe it'll take your mind off your own troubles."

And so he told her of those years with the Apaches, how they came to be and the circumstances that finally, mercifully, brought them to an end. "I learned a lot. I've no doubt it saved my life a few times during the war. But it was a miserable existence, one I'd never want to endure again. I'd like to forget it, but I knew the day that preacher swore he was going to beat the savage out of me that it would always be with me, like a brand."

She touched his hands, which were clenched on his knees. "Maybe not. Maybe one day you'll settle down and live a normal life. Have a wife. A family." She tried to keep her voice light, so he would not detect the longing she fought to conceal.

In that crystalized moment, when their eyes could not deny becoming the mirror of their souls, Cord looked at her and knew, beyond all doubt, she loved him. Just as he loved her. But what could he do? His father's blood flowed in his veins, and he could not cast aside the image of his father clinging to his mother's cold, stiff body for days, beating off the swooping vultures as he refused to let her go.

It was one thing to love someone, Cord, reasoned miserably, but another to let that love gnaw away and destroy a man's spirit, his will to live. No, by God, he resolved fiercely, he'd not be so weak. He would live his life with commitment to no one except himself.

Jaime shivered, but not with cold. She detected something in Cord, something mysterious and disturbing, but knew it would do no good to probe. For a moment, she had almost felt as though she had touched that part of him he kept locked deep inside, but a shadow had crossed his face. He had withdrawn behind the invisible barrier once again.

Reminding herself that she had made a personal vow to savor the moment and not think of the future, she moved to twine her arms about his neck and kissed him deeply.

Cord's blood became a heated river of desire racing through his veins. His hands gently cradled her face, holding her captive as he reveled in the delicious touch of her tongue.

He drew his mouth from hers to trail hot wet kisses down her throat, feeling her tremble at his touch and melt against him. Her robe fell open, her naked breasts spilling to welcome his touch. He raised hungry eyes to feast upon her, sweeping her tiny waist, her rounded hips, and her slender legs.

With a husky groan, he lifted her in his arms and carried her swiftly to the bed and laid her down. He unfastened his holster, pausing to ask, "Is the door locked?" She nodded. He tossed the guns aside recklessly, then peeled quickly out of his clothes.

The spark that had so easily ignited erupted into raging, hot, licking flames of passion that would not, could not be denied. He stretched out beside her to pull her almost roughly into his arms. "Tonight," he avowed raggedly, "I'll be a savage, my dearest, because I want you as I've never wanted a woman before."

But want me forever, my darling, Jaime cried within, not for this moment, not for this night, but always and ever!

Unable to speak the longing of her heart, she could only show him with her body how much she cared.

Enolita ran screaming toward the house, feet slipping on stones wet from the ocean spray as she struggled to keep from falling.

In Jaime's room, the sound was barely heard, for the greenhouse was situated on the northernmost point, at the opposite end of the mission. Cord stirred, but only slightly. Jaime's head was on his shoulder, and her arm about him tightened as something tried to needle her awake. Yet they slept on, exhausted from their frenzied passion.

Blake was downstairs, brooding in the parlor. He was still aching in body and spirit from the ugly confrontation with his father. Startled to hear Enolita yelling, he painfully pulled himself from the chair and went to see what was going on.

She shoved open the door leading into the rear hallway, still shrieking at the top of her lungs. He grabbed her shoulders and gave her a vicious shake. "Get hold of yourself and tell me what's happened," he ordered tersely.

For a moment she could not speak as she struggled to breathe past the sobs choking in her throat. Finally, she managed to whisper raggedly, "Oh, Señor Blake. I'm so sorry. So sorry. It's your father. I found him in the greenhouse. He's dead. Murdered. Oh, *mi Dios, mi Dios.*" She lapsed into her native tongue.

He pushed by her and, despite the sharp stabs of pain in his side from his father's brutal kicks, rushed to the greenhouse. Enolita followed close behind, fighting hysteria.

He saw the shears sticking from his father's throat and froze. Then, with a roll of nausea, he whirled about dizzily to clutch the edge of a table.

Enolita whimpered, "Who would do such a thing?"

"Get the guards," he managed to croak. "Now."

She fled to obey.

With great effort, Blake forced himself to turn around and go to his father, blanching to see how his eyes were frozen in the horror of the final seconds of his life.

Later, Blake would wonder why he reached out for the weapon and supposed it was because he found it grossly offensive to leave it stuck there, blades swallowed by the curdling blood.

His hands closed about the handle.

"Oh, God, no."

Startled, he yanked the shears out, and blood that had not yet coagulated spurted on his hands, his clothing, as he whipped about to see Morena coming toward him.

"What have you done?" She saw the scissors and threw up her arms to fend him off. "No, don't hurt me. Dear God, why did you kill him?"

With a cry of indignant denial, Blake flung the shears away from him. "I didn't do it. He was already dead." He pressed his fingers against his temple, smearing blood on his skin. "You've got to believe me. I didn't. I couldn't."

Suddenly he fell silent, washed with disgust to realize he was groveling to the woman he despised.

He swung his head from side to side. "Damn you, no. I don't have to defend myself to you." His eyes narrowed. "But it was *you,* wasn't it? You killed him. The two of you were always fighting, and lately it was getting worse. You killed him because he finally told you to leave, didn't you?"

She ran by him to fling herself at Stanton's feet, wrapping her arms about his legs as she wailed. "No. Never. I loved him. I could never do such a thing, I swear it. But I know who did. It could only have been him."

The sounds of shouting came from outside as the guards rallied to Enolita's alarm.

Blake jerked Morena away from his father's body,

unable to bear the sight of her clinging to him. "What are you talking about? Tell me what you know about this, damn you."

Her words tumbled out in a frenzy. "Austin. The bodyguard your father hired. He had me spread the word this morning he wanted to see him. He was furious because someone had told him Austin was enamored with Jaime, and he knew you were courting her, and he was going to run him off. And I saw him come in here right after I left to go to bed. I had tried to get your father to come with me, but he was determined to wait and have it out with Austin.

"Now look what he's done." Her voice rose shrilly once more. "He's killed the man I love, all because of your whore." She looked up at him accusingly with angry, tear-filled eyes.

Blake grabbed her. Resisting, she threw herself to the side, against a table, knocking over plants as he shouted, "You're lying. Jaime can't be involved with anyone else. She's with me every day. And don't you call her a whore," he warned.

Some of Morena's bravado was returning, and she taunted him. "Every *day,* did you say? What about the nights? It is Austin who sleeps with her. Not you."

Two of the guards came running in. Enolita was right behind them.

Incensed beyond reason, Blake had raised his hand to strike Morena, but she caught his wrist. "I can prove what I say."

The guards were staring, momentarily paralyzed, at Stanton's body. Then one of them came alive to grab Morena and twist her arms painfully behind her back. "What do you want us to do with her?"

Enolita pushed her way forward. "No, no. It couldn't have been her. I heard her come in and go to the cellar, and he was alive then. I know, because he called me to bring him more whiskey. Then later, when I started out here to ask if he needed anything else because I wanted to go to bed, I saw that man, Austin, coming in. I went back to wait, and I fell asleep. When I came back, this is what I found." She pointed to the body and shuddered.

"You see?" Morena shrieked as she struggled with the guard. "Austin was the last one here. It could only have been him." She watched anxiously as Blake silently debated whether to believe her. When she had found Cord in bed with Jaime, she had made up her mind to get rid of him, one way or another. And now the time had come.

"I can prove it, damn you," she yelled impatiently. "They are together right now." And she knew that to be so, for she had crept through the secret passage to make sure.

She continued to taunt. "Are you man enough to face it? Or are you so hellbent to punish me because your father loved me that you're willing to let them laugh at you behind your back over how blind and stupid you are? Or maybe you're just such a coward you can't stand for these men to see what a fool you are for your whore."

Blake saw the way the guards exchanged uneasy glances. He did not believe for one minute that Jaime was involved with Cord Austin, sexually or otherwise, but was aware, if he did not accept Morena's challenge, that his credibility, his very manhood, would be in doubt forevermore. The story would spread, first among the guards, then the vaqueros, and, ultimately, beyond Pointe Grande and all the way to San Francisco. Everyone who heard would think him weak, spineless.

"Let her go," he said to the guard, "but if she's lying, she'll hang."

Morena did not like revealing the existence of the hidden passage, but she knew Jaime's door would be locked from the inside. By the time the guards broke in, Cord would either kill them or go out the window. She wasn't taking any chances. Besides, she'd not be needing the secret way again. With Cord out of the way, Jaime would be helpless, which meant Morena would soon have the map, the mine, and, ultimately, all the gold she needed to build her own palace. Blake Lavelle and Pointe Grande could go to hell, along with everyone else who had dared cross swords with her.

Enolita was sent to get blankets to cover the body, then wait for further orders. Blake did not want the other guards or vaqueros awakened, nor the word of his father's death to spread, till he had settled with Morena.

She led them down in the cellar to a far corner edged in cobwebs and smelling of dampness and mold. Standing before a dust-caked wine rack, she instructed, "You must be very quiet, or they will hear us coming through the wall. I will go first, but stay close behind me. When we get there, I will push open a hidden door in the room, that looks like a molded panel on the other side. And I will prove once and for all I speak the truth," she added, with a vengeful glare at Blake.

"How did you know about this passage?" he asked coldly.

She told him how the secret had been handed down through her family, concluding with a smirk, "So you see, having Yahi blood has its advantages. Even your father did not discover it when he bought the mission and remodeled. It was too well hidden."

With a soft grating sound, she pulled the wine rack forward, revealing the black abyss within. "We go in darkness," she said, motioning to one of the guards to set aside his lantern. Reluctantly, after a nod from Blake, he did so.

They wound their way upwards, weaving around and around on a tiny narrow stairway.

Blake felt as though he were going to smother in the enveloping darkness and began to wonder if it were all a trick and Morena planned, at some point, to turn and shove them all backward and make her escape. Or perhaps she had a gun, or still possessed the knife she'd threatened Jaime with. He told himself to be ready, lagging behind a few feet, dragging his hands against the cold, clammy rock wall on either side, ready to support himself should she attack. Behind him, he could hear the heavy breathing of the guards.

Morena stopped.

Blake braced himself and held his breath, straining to hear as she whispered, "You must stoop down to enter a hole that will take you inside the wall. Be very careful."

Blake bent down, and reached to jerk at the arm of the man behind, indicating he should do the same.

It was narrow. His chest and buttocks brushed against the stone molding of the wall, and it was necessary to walk sideways. Soon, however, the way widened, and he watched anxiously as soft light began to spread within the passage as Morena slowly, soundlessly, opened the panel.

She stepped back in triumph so he could see into the room.

Blake took one look and felt a sharp pain as his heart shattered.

There, bathed in the glow of the bedside lantern, he could see them, locked in each other's arms . . . naked.

With a bellow of rage, he burst into the room, the guards spilling out behind him, guns drawn. One of them spotted Cord's holster on the floor and kicked it out of reach.

Jaime screamed at the same instant Cord came alive to realize they were trapped.

"Bastard," Blake hissed, towering over them. Cord tried to get up, but one of the guards pushed him back down as Blake warned, "Don't move, or I'll have you shot here and now."

Reaching to draw Jaime away from him, Blake urged tenderly, "Get your robe. Cover yourself. I know this isn't your fault."

Morena laughed.

Blake whirled on her angrily. "Get out of here."

She refused. "I intend to see him pay for what he did. You killed him, damn you. And you'll die for it."

It was all starting to come together for Cord. He could see the open panel in the wall revealing a hidden passage within. Morena had been spying, had led them to him. And now it appeared Lavelle had been murdered, and the finger was pointing at him. "I didn't do it," he said calmly.

"The hell you didn't," Blake yelped.

Behind him, Jaime scrambled for her robe, trying to think amid the madness surrounding her.

Blake raged on. "You killed him because he found out you've been forcing yourself on Jaime, preying on her vulnerability, her grief over her father, and he was going to see you were punished."

Cord shook his head. "You've got it all wrong. It wasn't like that. I saw him. We talked. He was mad over me nosing around asking about Chandler and told me to get out, but that's it. He was alive when I left him. And Jaime had nothing to do with it."

"You're lying. Now get your clothes on, unless you want to go naked to your execution."

Cord sat up and reached for his pants. "Ever hear of a trial?"

"I'm not wasting time. You're going to hang, Austin. Tonight."

"But not because you think I murdered your father, right? It's your way of revenge because of me and Jaime."

Blake hit him with his fist. Cord's head snapped back, but only slightly. Rage emanated from his every pore. "Hitting a man with two guns pointed at him is real brave, mister."

"Was it braver for you to stab my father with garden shears, you son of a bitch?"

Jaime threw herself at Blake. "No, don't do this. I know you're upset over your father, but Cord didn't kill him. He's been here with me, all evening," she lied.

Blake grabbed her by her arms and gave her a gentle shake. "Listen. I'm not angry with you about any of this. I love you, and I'm going to take care of you. It's you and me now. Forget your father. He's probably dead, just like mine. We're all alone, but we don't need anybody else."

Focusing on Jaime, Blake had turned his back on Cord. Morena was listening, amused. The guards stood on either side of Cord but were not watching his face. Jaime, however, could see him. She was standing between him and the window, and with only a slight flick of his eyes, he let her know he wanted her to get out of the way.

Slowly, she inched her way to the side, trying to keep attention on her. "No, I won't listen to you," she babbled nervously. "And you can't do this. It's wrong. Cord is innocent, I tell you—"

He made his move.

Racing to the window, he lunged out and reached up to grab the rope he had left hanging from the roof. Jaime threw herself between him and the guards. Blake yelled at them not to shoot.

Morena, enraged to realize Cord was escaping, bolted forward to try and shove Jaime to one side, but Jaime had grasped the window's frame and was holding on with all her might.

The guards rushed to pry her fingers loose, finally succeeding and slinging her into Blake's waiting arms, but it was too late. Leaning out the window they stared up into the moonlight just as Cord disappeared onto the roof.

Trying to maintain his hold on Jaime as she struggled against him, Blake thundered his orders. "Get downstairs. Alert everyone. Ring the big bell in the tower. Surround the house. Be ready when he climbs down. Hurry. Go."

They charged out of the room in a loud clatter. Morena was right behind them.

"Let me go, damn you." Jaime fought against him, as he tried to wrestle her down to the bed in an attempt to calm her. "You can't shoot him down like a dog. He didn't kill your father, I tell you. Why won't you listen? Why are you so determined to see him die? Because of me? You've no right. I never promised you anything."

"But he violated you," Blake said, choking on a sob to think of them together. "He raped you. It had to be that way. You'd never give in. I know you wouldn't. Now stay here, please. He has to pay for what he did to you, to my father."

He rushed out of the room then, following after the others. Jaime bounded from the bed in quick pursuit.

At ground level, the other guards were responding to the sharp pealing of the bell. They were shouting, yelling, and Jaime watched in horror as the night came alive with the hysterical voices of men running in all directions.

Then came the cry she had prayed she would not hear, the words that chilled her bones to the marrow.

"He's trapped. On the cliff behind the greenhouse. He tried to go down the steps to the beach, but we headed him off. We've got him now."

Jaime forced her trembling legs to run in that direction, all the while praying for a miracle. Dear God, they couldn't kill him. They couldn't. . . .

She slowed, terror choking the very life from her as she struggled to breathe despite the painful quickening in her chest.

She could see him. Standing at the dangerous apex for which Pointe Grande took its name, Cord faced the angry advancing mob, his back to the boiling sea below.

"Take him alive," Blake yelled. "I want to watch him hang for what he did."

They moved closer, dozens of determined, enraged faces. Jaime froze, but only for an instant, then began to run once more, screaming Cord's name over and over.

Blake seemed to appear from out of nowhere to wrap his arms about her waist and hold her back. "Stay out of this, Jaime. He's a murderer. And you're only making a fool of yourself. Listen to me. I want to help you. We'll forget all this. I want to marry you anyway. You'll never want for anything ever again. It doesn't matter what he did to you. I love you—" His voice broke, and he burrowed his face in the thick softness of her hair and let the tears flow unashamedly.

Jaime felt his body convulsing with sobs as he continued to hold her tightly. She could not escape him and could only watch helplessly as the men advanced on Cord.

She threw her head back and screamed long and loud, and he looked to her. Their eyes locked in the eerie light of the flickering torches the men carried.

Cord knew he had only one chance—the sea. But only if he was able to propel himself far enough out to miss the rocks when he landed. Beyond, he knew the water was deep, and the tide was brutal, and death was almost certain—but at least it would be by his own hand.

With one last glance of longing at the woman he loved, he turned and hurled himself off the cliff.

24

Jaime locked herself in her room and cried till there were no tears left.

It had all happened so fast. Cord was dead, and her heart, her life, was shattered.

They could not find his body. They had searched the beach, the rocks, and said it had to have been washed out to sea. So now it was over, all of it, and she had nothing left but broken dreams and precious memories.

It was midmorning when Enolita came to knock on her door and call sorrowfully, "Señor Blake, he is so upset. He begs you to join him and help make the arrangements for his father."

Jaime did not respond. She was trying not to think, to close herself within a meaningless void to try and hide from the grief that burned and smothered to the very core of her being.

A little while later, she watched impassively as the

panel in the wall opened quietly. She was lying on the bed, on her side, thinking it really made no difference who it was or what they wanted. Maybe it was Morena, come to kill her. So what? Jaime could think of no reason left to live anyway.

Blake stepped out of the passage. He hesitated, unsure of what her reaction would be at his unexpected appearance, but when he saw her lying there so docile, he rushed to kneel beside her. "Are you ill, Jaime?"

She looked at him blandly. "What difference does it make?"

"Because I love you"—his voice cracked and tears welled in his eyes—"and because I need you. We need each other."

"Leave me alone."

"Hear me out, please. I've sent for the law, to report everything, and now I have to make arrangements for my father's funeral. I need you to help me."

She sat up, gathering her robe about her tightly as she faced him, hostility boiling. "Why would I help you do anything after what you've done? And by the way," she asked contemptuously, "are you going to admit to the law how you drove a man to his death? I hate you for that, Blake. I always will."

"You're just upset," he said softly. "All this has been a terrible shock for both of us, but we have to go on and try to forget."

"I'm leaving here. I won't stay in this evil place."

"I can't allow that. Not now."

Her eyes widened. "You can't keep me here."

"No. Not indefinitely. But the next few days are going to be difficult for me. I want you beside me.

Then I'll give you money to make your own life some-where else if that's what you want. Don't you see I'm hurting too? It was like a knife to my heart to see you here with Austin last night, but I can make myself forget it, and we can go on from here, into the future together, because I love you so much I'm willing to do anything to have you."

"I never led you to believe I cared about you beyond friendship. You've no right to expect more from me now. Especially after last night. You killed Cord as surely as though you put a gun to his head and pulled the trigger."

For the first time, Blake did not try to hold his temper back, voice rising shrilly as he lashed out. "He murdered my father, whether you're willing to believe it or not. He was the last one seen going into the greenhouse."

She matched his fury with her own and cried vehe-mently, "You don't know that."

"He had a motive."

"So did Morena."

"Why would she kill him? With him dead, she has nothing. She's lost everything, because she knows I despise her and won't allow her on the premises. She's already gone. She took off last night. No." He shook his head from side to side in dogged resolution. "Morena didn't do it. She'd never destroy the only security she had."

Jaime raised an eyebrow. "Maybe your father ordered her to leave, and she killed him in a fit of rage."

"He would never have done that, no matter what she did. They might have fought a lot, but he was bewitched by her. He didn't even cast her aside when she went to my mother and told her she was sleeping with him. And he didn't turn her away when she drove my mother to blow her brains out," he added raggedly, biting his lip to hold back the sobs choking in his throat as the memory of how he had found her came thundering down.

Jaime felt a slight stirring of pity but lashed out. "The least you could have done was give Cord a chance to try to prove his innocence."

To her surprise, he nodded contritely.

"You're right. I should have. And I probably would have if he hadn't chosen to kill himself instead. I was mad right then and wasn't thinking straight. Seeing my father dead, then the woman I love naked in the arms of another man—it was all too much."

"That doesn't excuse what you did," she snapped. "Now get out of here. I'll stay till after the funeral because I need the money, but I'll see you get it back."

Despite how he felt about her, Blake was still embittered by what he considered her betrayal and retorted, "That won't be necessary. Just think of it as payment for a favor."

Jaime, not about to be scorned, retorted stiffly, "I don't take payments for favors, but I will accept your offer of a loan."

"Whatever makes you happy," he conceded. He got up to leave but first closed the panel. "You won't have to worry about anyone sneaking in on you again. I'm having the opening in the cellar sealed today."

Jaime lay back down and closed her eyes. She didn't care if a dragon came out of the wall. Cord was dead, and so was her heart, and beyond escaping from Pointe Grande, she didn't care about anything.

The investigation of Stanton Lavelle's death was routine. Cord Austin had, in the eyes of the law and everyone else, confirmed his guilt by diving off the cliff.

The night before the funeral, Blake instructed the servants to open up the ballroom and receive the visitors in there, owing to the large number expected. Dreading it all, he invited Jaime to join him in his father's study for a drink to fortify himself.

She accepted, thinking how he had not seemed particularly distraught once the initial shock of his father's death subsided but was surprised, nonetheless, at his cryptic comment about so many people coming to call.

"Hypocrites. All of them. They hated his guts. Yet they come in droves."

"Some of them came to the ball he gave for me. They didn't seem to feel that way then."

"They wanted to see the inside of the house. It's quite a novelty, you know, building a magnificent place like this out of an old mission. They leaped at the chance to see it."

"So why do they come now?" She really didn't care; she was merely making conversation to pass the miserable time.

"Maybe they think you and I will be getting married and having more socials, and they'll be invited. It could be like that, you know," he added plaintively.

Jaime gave him a cold look.

With a sigh, he poured another drink. "Actually, I think they want to see his body. No doubt, it spread like wildfire how he was stabbed with garden shears. Maybe they thought they could see the wound. Ghouls." He spat the word in contempt.

"But you ordered the coffin closed."

"Damn right I did." He downed his drink, then looked at her over the rim and asked suddenly, "Do you really hate me so?"

She saw no reason to be less than honest. If it angered him and he refused to keep his part of the bargain, she would leave anyway. "You killed a man I loved with all my heart. I realize you had no way of knowing that at the time, but it doesn't change the fact he's dead."

"But how?" He slammed the glass down on the desk and looked her straight in the eye, searching for some meaning to the insanity of his world. "How could you fall in love with a man you only slept with? How could you know what he was really like? You and I, we had days, weeks together. We knew each other. We were friends. I shared your despair over your father, whether you thought so or not, but there was nothing I could do. I had my suspicions, but I suppose"—he went on to dare admit—"I just wasn't man enough to stand up to my father and do anything about them. I regret that now, because we'll never know the truth, and I can't undo what's been done. But I'd like to know, I *have* to know, how you could have fallen in love with Cord Austin so easily. I don't mean to hurt you, Jaime, God knows, but the fact is, I thought you were more moral than that. I put you on a pedestal with my mother."

Jaime was unmoved. "People have to take responsibility for those they place on pedestals, Blake. They put them there because of what they think they see in that person and what they choose to believe about them. As for my falling in love with Cord, there's no reason not to tell you now. The fact is, we knew each other before."

Blake sank into his father's chair and listened in awe as Jaime recounted the tale of the wagon train.

"So you see," she finished, with a smile from her very soul, "I was already in love with him before we became involved intimately. Right or wrong, it happened."

"I'm glad you told me this," he said quietly, honestly, "but it doesn't change the way I feel about you. I still want to marry you."

"When Cord went off that cliff, he took my heart with him. I'll never be able to love anyone ever again."

"You could try."

"It wouldn't work."

"Well, regardless of how you felt about him when he was alive, how can you grieve for a murderer?"

"Because I don't believe he did it. I don't know who killed your father, but it wasn't Cord."

"Perhaps you'll feel different when you're over your shock." He sighed with resignation. "For now, let's go and greet the ghouls, shall we?"

The evening wore on. Jaime felt terribly uncomfortable, knowing her presence was giving the impression that she was actually more than a mere houseguest who happened to have the misfortune to be present at a time of tragedy. Standing beside

Blake, she was well aware everyone thought they were betrothed, which, she suspected, was his motive in wanting her there. He hoped she would be pressured to change her mind.

At last, the crowd began to thin. Everyone promised to return for the funeral the following afternoon, when Stanton Lavelle was to be buried next to his wife in the mission cemetery.

When they were alone, Blake invited Jaime to have another drink, but she declined, saying she was tired. Instead of going to her room, however, she began to wander through the house. She had learned her way around and wound up in the kitchen, where Enolita was cleaning up after having served the guests.

Slipping behind her, unnoticed, Jaime made her way outside. It was a beautiful night. A full moon was shining down from a clear sky, dripping a path of liquid silver across the tranquil sea. All seemed peaceful, a balmy breeze whispering across the land.

She skirted the greenhouse. She had not been there since the murder and did not intend to go there now. Instead, she was drawn beyond to the place where Cord had met his destiny.

For a long time, perhaps half an hour or more, she stood in the same place where Blake had restrained her that night. Plaintively, she gazed toward the spot where Cord had been trapped. Never would she forget the way he had looked at her in his final moment. He had never said he loved her, but in that last second she had seen it in his face. And though he was gone forever, that precious memory was something no one could ever take away from her.

Finally, she gathered the nerve to proceed to where he had taken that fateful plunge to his death. Had he thought by some miracle he might survive? she wondered, then decided he had. Cord was no coward. He would have taken the chance.

Only he hadn't made it.

She stared down at the waves crashing among the rocks amid swirling chunks of foam. That was the view straight down. A short distance beyond, the water gleamed dark and ominous in the moonlight, for it was deeper there. If Cord had been so fortunate as to land there, he might have been able to swim to safety, but it was not likely. Probably an undertow had caught him and held him under till he drowned.

What had he been thinking in those last moments? She tortured herself. Did he blame her? After all, if not for her problems, he would not have had any of his own because he would not have been involved.

She also recalled how she'd had a feeling he was keeping something from her, had stumbled on a clue he was not yet ready to share. Now she would never know.

She began to tremble. Then great, clutching shudders began to rock her from head to toe. Dear God, would it never end? Was she doomed to forever feel that a part of her had died?

She covered her face with her hands and wept, then finally swiped furiously at her eyes—and that was when she saw it.

With petals like silver sugar sprinkled on lavender and purple satin, an orchid lay nearby, anchored against the wind by small rocks.

With trembling fingers, she retrieved it.

Who would leave it there? she wondered with a chill touching the marrow of her bones. No one knew about her affinity for the rare and special flower except Cord, and she did not believe in ghosts.

Blake knocked on her door early the next morning, carrying a tray with coffee and one of his mother's gowns folded over his arm.

Sleepily, Jaime put on a robe and admitted him. She'd stayed up most of the night, unable to rest as she continued to wonder about the orchid and how it had got there.

He saw it lying on the table as he went to put the tray down. He frowned. "How did you get in the greenhouse? I had it locked."

"I haven't been there."

"Then where did you get this orchid?" he asked suspiciously.

"I found it."

"But where? I still don't see. . . ." He decided it didn't matter. Probably some of the vaqueros had gone in through windows that had been broken when he'd flung Morena into them. Wanting to view the gory scene, they may have been tempted to steal some of the unusual blossoms and had dropped a few.

He held up the dress, a gray taffeta with simple lines. "It will be perfect for the funeral. My mother wore it when the last of my father's relatives died about five years ago. It's still nice, don't you think?"

Jaime shrugged. "If you want me to wear it, I will."

With a sigh of exasperation, he threw the gown across the end of the bed. "It doesn't have to be like this, you know. We could be friends again. You could act as if you care a little."

"I do care," she said, then added dryly, "about the money, that is. That's the only reason I'm still here, and you know it."

He turned on his heel and left, shoulders slumped.

Jaime did not care he was hurt. His feelings were of no importance to her, regardless of how he had helped her in the past. He had caused Cord's death, and she would never forgive him.

The service was held in the ballroom, which again had to be used for the large crowd attending. Afterward, only a few joined the procession on the rugged path to the old mission cemetery. The rest remained to enjoy the refreshments Enolita had prepared with the help of a dozen other servants.

The minister led the way, as six of Stanton's guards carried the flower-bedecked casket. Jaime stiffened as Blake took her arm and drew her next to him to walk behind it.

At last it was over. The minister offered a prayer. The wooden box was lowered into the grave and covered with dirt and rocks. Everyone wandered away, but Blake held tight to Jaime and refused to budge. She knew grief for his father was not the reason, for she could see how his eyes were fixed on his mother's grave.

It was getting dark. Jaime squirmed uncomfortably

and tried to pull from his grasp. "I'm ready to go back now. Stay if you want, but let me go."

He held tight. "Surely you can stand my company a little longer."

"It's not yours I mind," she said with a shiver and waved with her free arm at the graves around them. "It's theirs. I don't like being here."

With a somber nod at his mother's resting place, he murmured, "She doesn't either," and then, reluctantly, led Jaime away.

Despite Jaime's protests, as soon as everyone had left, Blake ordered Enolita to prepare and serve a sumptuous dinner for the two of them. Afterward, Jaime thanked him politely. "It was thoughtful of you to want to have a nice meal for me my last night here, but it really wasn't necessary."

"It's just something I wanted to do for you." He held up his glass of wine in toast to her, took a sip, then added somberly, "But it isn't your last night here."

Jaime's brows raised sharply. "Yes, it is. I agreed to stay till after the funeral."

"Our agreement," he corrected frostily, "was that you would stay till it was all over. It isn't. Not yet. I want you to stay a few more days. I'm making arrangements to move out, and until I do, I don't want to be alone."

She bit out the reminder. "You've got servants."

"It's not the same. You're my friend." He smiled almost petulantly. "Besides, it won't look good for you to leave the day after the funeral. Where do you have to go, anyway?"

Jaime looked him straight in the eye. "I will stay two more days, and then I am leaving, with or without your financial help. I will walk to San Francisco if I have to. I will stand on street corners and beg like the man who robbed me, if necessary, but so help me I mean to go."

She excused herself and fled to her room. He might be able to make her stay two more days, but that didn't mean she had to spend her time with him.

It was dark. Moonlight spilled in through the open window. She started to light a lantern, then decided she liked the mysterious silver shadows and opted for the darkness.

Sitting on the divan, she stared at the bed and thought of that last night in Cord's arms when he had held her, kissed her. Never would she forget those enraptured moments. She would always hold them in her heart to take out and savor on a moonswept night. She could hold an orchid to her lips, and think back, and—

Where was the orchid?

She remembered she had left it on the table near the window, but as she got up to get it she was startled to see it lying on her pillow. Enolita had probably put it here when she made the bed, and she was touched. The grumpy Mexican had never acted as though she liked her well enough to do anything beyond what was expected.

Jaime picked up the flower and pressed it to her cheek. Walking to the window, she gazed out at the ocean, glimmering with specks of silver. She stood there for long moments, sorrow coming in great shuddering waves to think of Cord and how deeply she loved him.

Finally, she told herself she had to go to bed and try to sleep, even though her dreams were haunted by the glorious memories of the happiness, the passion, they had shared.

She laid the orchid on the table, then froze as she saw there was another right beside it.

Two orchids in the moonlight.

She gripped the edge of the table to steady herself as every nerve screamed raw and ragged.

It had to be.

There was no other explanation.

Moving as fast as she dared on her shaking legs, Jaime managed to make her way downstairs and out of the house.

Where would he be waiting?

Picking her way among the rocks in the silvered night, she returned to where she had found the first orchid. She was not surprised to find another there and felt a thrilling rush as she grabbed it up and clutched it to her bosom.

Then it came to her: the beach. He had said it would be safe there.

She forced herself to go slowly down the crumbling stairs, despite the urging of her heart to hurry, lest it be a dream that would end any second.

At last, she reached the bottom safely and stepped into the sand.

Whirling around and around in the whipping wind and mist from the crashing waves in the distance, she dared call out, "Cord, are you here?"

He came from out of the darkness to silence her with his lips, and they clung together for long poignant moments that left both of them shaken.

"You're alive," she whispered in awe when she could at last speak. "I can't believe it." She ran her fingers over his face, his neck, his shoulders, wanting to be sure he was real.

Anxiously, he told her how he had feared she would leave before he could let her know he had survived.

"But how did you?" she asked, laughing and crying all at once.

"I managed to lunge out far enough that I missed the rocks and hit the deep water. I stayed offshore while they searched. God, Jaime." He drew a deep breath of incredulity as he gazed down at her moon-bathed face. "I wasn't sure you'd understand the signal with the orchids. I left the first one where I jumped off, hoping you'd go back there, but when you didn't come last night, I had to take a chance and go in through the window and leave another on your pillow."

"That's when I realized it had to be you." She threw herself against him once more, wanting to touch and feel and savor the miracle of it all.

"Jaime, there's something I have to tell you."

She drew back, hearing the tension in his voice. Then, through a sudden fog of hope wrapped in fear, his words penetrated.

"I found your father. He's alive. I haven't spoken to him, but it could only be him."

She would have fallen had he not been holding her so tightly. He went on to explain how he had spent the last few days confirming his suspicions. "I had a feeling all along he didn't just disappear. Lavelle had nothing to gain by his death and everything to lose, and I figured he'd been holding him captive somewhere, determined sooner or later he'd give him the location of his mine.

"What puzzled me, however," he continued, "was why he didn't use you to make your father talk as soon as he had you in his clutches. Then the pieces started to fit together. Blake falling for you complicated things. Lavelle couldn't whisk you away without Blake getting suspicious, and he didn't want to risk that. It was easier to try and get the map away from you. But, the most important thing is, I don't think he ever knew where your father was."

Jaime blinked, confused. "I'm not following you."

"It was Morena, don't you see? She knew Lavelle was desperate for that mine, because he firmly believed it had a mother lode. The man I talked to in San Francisco told me Lavelle had got an assayer's report on the ore your father put up as proof of the worth of his mine, and the assayer assured Lavelle it came from the area where it was supposed to.

"Anyway"—he rushed on—"as long as Morena had your father, she had control over Lavelle, but all that changed when you came along. I believe that's why she murdered him. He probably got fed up and told her to go to hell, because he had you and didn't need her or your father anymore. So her plan now, of course, with Lavelle dead, is to get to you and use you the way she planned all along."

"But where is my father?" She cried anxiously. "Take me to him, please."

He hated to tell her it was not possible right then. "He's being held in a cave about a mile north of here. Some of Morena's Yahi friends watch over it. That's how I pinpointed where he was; I saw them taking food in. But we can't risk getting him out unless their attention is diverted, which I'll do tomorrow night. We've got to wait till then. But tell me," he asked anxiously. "Have you seen Morena?"

"Not since the night of the murder. Blake says she knows better than to come back."

"But she will. She's just been waiting till after the funeral, when there won't be so many people around. Now here's what I want you to do. Go back to the house, but don't sleep in your room."

"But Blake had the opening to the passage sealed. She can't get in if I bolt the door from the inside."

"It doesn't matter. I won't feel safe with you there. Sleep somewhere else, so she won't know where to find you."

"I could go to Blake's mother's room."

"Fine. And tomorrow night, be ready to leave." He outlined his plan to build an altar and light a fire to make the Yahi think their dreaded god, Cooksuy, was miraculously appearing without being called. "They're superstitious, and they'll come running and forget all about the cave. After all this time, they aren't very diligent about keeping an eye on it anyway, or I never would have been able to get as close as I did. Still, I spotted two of them sleeping near the entrance, so I've got to lure them away, even it means waking all of them up, but they'll head to the beach to see what's going on."

He told her exactly how to find the cave and said she should go there at twelve. As soon as he made sure the Indians were concentrating on the fire, he would meet her up there.

Worried, she asked, "What if somebody sees us? We'll be trapped between them and Blake's men."

He took yet another orchid from inside his shirt and, though it was mashed, tucked it in her golden hair and smiled. "I've already taken care of that, Sunshine. You can swim, can't you?"

She swallowed and nodded nervously, wondering what he had in mind.

"I know of a calm little cove not too far away. There's a path leading to it opposite from where the Indians will gather. I'll steal one of their boats and hide it. We'll make our way there to escape and head for San Francisco and the law so we can make sure Morena pays for what she's done."

He pulled her close for one last kiss.

"Go now. I've got to go back in hiding in case she's sneaking around. It would ruin everything if she finds out I'm alive, and you need to make yourself safe for the night."

He started to melt back into the shadows, but Jaime did not—could not—move. She called to him, and he turned. "Cord, I—" She faltered, drew a sharp breath, and then spoke from her heart. "I thank God you're alive."

He blew her a kiss and hurried away, afraid if he stayed one more second he would never be able to leave her.

25

Jaime could not bear to lie in the bed where Emily Lavelle had killed herself. Instead, she settled on the sofa in her room but was far too excited to sleep. Dear Lord, she was still dizzy to think how this night she had learned Cord was not only miraculously alive but had also managed to discover her father's whereabouts.

Cord had held her and kissed her, and it was no dream or fantasy brought about by either sorrow or misty moonlight. It had been real. *He* had been real.

And tomorrow night she would see her father for the first time in ten years. It grieved her to think how he had suffered, but she shuddered to imagine what his fate would have been if Cord had not discovered the truth.

For hours, Jaime's mind whirled, but eventually weariness overcame her anxiety and she slept. When she awoke, sunlight was streaming through the window and Blake was shaking her as he demanded in a near frenzy, "What are you doing in here? You've had everyone scared to death."

Jaime looked from him to Enolita, both staring at her with wide, anxious eyes. She offered the only explanation she could think of on short notice. "All of a sudden, I couldn't bear to be in that room after what happened the other night. I didn't think you'd mind if I came in here."

Relieved she was safe, he told her he didn't care which room she took but repeated that she had given them quite a scare. "Enolita couldn't get you to come to the door, and when she found it unlocked, she went in and panicked to see you weren't there. We've been searching high and low. I thought you had run away."

"Nothing like that," Jaime denied tonelessly.

"Well, at least you've learned your way around and didn't wind up lost." He motioned to Enolita that she could leave. When they were alone, he shook his head in mock scolding. "Look at you. You didn't undress and you fell asleep here on the sofa. You can't be comfortable." His brows raised as he saw the orchids that had fallen to the floor. He picked them up. "Now where did these come from?"

Jaime managed to keep her voice steady. "I found some more when I was out walking."

He crushed them with an almost vengeance. "I'd like to know who broke in the greenhouse, damn them."

"If you don't mind," she said uncomfortably, "I'd like to go back to sleep. I have a headache."

"Are you sure you aren't just trying to avoid me?"

Telling herself it would soon be over, Jaime managed to deny pleasantly, "Of course not. I really and truly don't feel well."

He softened at once. "Forgive me. I'm just upset because, unless I can have time to convince you to change your mind, you're going to be leaving me."

And sooner than you think, she thought happily, gloriously.

The day passed with agonizing slowness. Jaime forced herself to join Blake for dinner, afraid, if she didn't, he would insist on having trays brought to his mother's room so they could dine there. She would have a time getting rid of him then. But she was too nervous to eat. Darkness had fallen. In a few hours it would be time to go, and she was on fire inside.

Blake watched her with concern and finally asked, "Are you all right? There's something wrong. I can tell."

"I still don't feel well, and I didn't want to come down here, but I knew you'd insist." She avoided eye contact.

He pushed his own plate away. "It's me. I know it's me. You can't stand the sight of me, because you blame me for your lover's death. Oh, Jaime, Jaime." He reached out to her to plead, "Tell me what I have to do to make you see how much I love you. I'll do anything. Just don't leave me. Give me a chance to show you how happy I can make you."

Suddenly, Jaime lost all patience and told him with an exasperated sigh, "You don't love me. You only think you do. I remind you of your mother, and you adored her, and you miss her, but that's all it is. You don't build a future with someone based on that kind of love, Blake. It would never work.

"Now you're going to have to excuse me." She stood. "Nothing I say makes any difference to you anyway. I'm going to bed now." She hurried out before he could protest.

Blake stared after her with longing. She was wrong. He did love her. And he always would.

He got up and went to his father's study and headed straight to the whiskey decanter on the table behind the desk. He had never been much of a drinker, but after the nightmare of the past few days, bourbon had become a good friend.

He was on his second glass when there was a frenzied knock on the door. "Who is it?" he yelled irritably, then froze to hear the report.

"That woman. Morena. We have her."

Blake raced to fling the door open and found himself staring down at Morena's glittering black eyes. A guard stood on either side of her, gripping her arms.

One of the men explained how she had boldly come to the front of the house, demanding to see Blake. They did not turn her away, he said, because Blake had issued orders he was to be told if she appeared.

Grabbing her and slinging her into the room, Blake slammed the door in the guards' faces after telling them to get back to their posts.

"I was going to pay you a surprise visit, but your guards had all the entrances blocked," Morena informed him mockingly.

"Maybe that's because I've been expecting you. Now tell me what you want." He sat down behind the desk again.

She laughed, a gloating sound that grated. "If you were expecting me, then you should know."

"I want to see if you've got nerve enough to ask."

"For money?" She began to walk aimlessly about the room, glancing at Stanton's things as though she had never seen them before. "That takes no nerve. I'm entitled to a share of your father's estate. He took care of me when he was alive. He would want me cared for after his death. Give me what is rightfully mine, and you will never see me again."

"I'm never going to see you again anyway. I only told the guards to bring you to me if you showed up so I could tell you to your face I'll have you shot if you ever come around here again. You didn't mean a damn thing to my father. You were just a whore. Obviously a very good whore, because he kept you around longer than the others he had through the years. If he had wanted you to have anything, he'd have left it to you in his will. I've read it. Your name wasn't mentioned. Only mine. Pointe Grande belongs to me now, and you've got five minutes to get off of it."

She wandered lazily to stand near him. "Maybe I have no legal claim, but you owe me something anyway."

He turned his back on her in a gesture of scornful dismissal. "You're crazy. And you seem to forget I hate you for driving my mother to her death."

Morena took a step closer to the whiskey decanter, which he could not see. "I've always regretted your blaming me for that," she lied, proud of how she was able to make her voice so simpering. "I only wanted her to leave him. I never thought she would do something so desperate."

"My mother was unhappy," he said, more to himself than to her as he templed his fingers and leaned back in the chair to gaze through them thoughtfully. "But I don't want to discuss her with you."

She moved quickly, slipping a tiny vial from the bodice of her dress and emptying the contents into the nearly empty bottle. The juice of the Mexican poppy would quickly put him to sleep. When he awoke later, she would be gone and so would Jaime, and no one would ever know how she had managed to spirit her away right under the guards' noses.

She moved back quickly as he whirled around. "Remember, if it wasn't for me, you'd never have found out the truth about Austin," she said.

Blake poured himself another drink. "You should be grateful I gave you a chance to prove it. Otherwise, you'd have been hanged that night, and you know it."

"And that would have made you a murderer." She stepped away from the desk and sat down on the sofa. "Where is your lady love, by the way? Still grieving for her lover?" Morena still felt a sad little jolt to think of Cord's having to die. She had enjoyed him immensely and doubted she would ever be able to find anyone else like him. But he had betrayed her and had to pay the price.

"It's none of your business, but she went to bed early. She's not feeling well." He watched her suspiciously as he gulped down the bourbon, then said, "I'm not going to give you anything, Morena, except a warning to get out of here."

She nodded, blinking her eyes as though trying to hold back tears. "I should have known you'd have no sympathy for me. I have nowhere to go. No money. Nothing. And now you tell me you will kill me if I dare come back to the only home I have ever known. I played here as a child. I know every inch of this mission." She rambled on, stalling for time, waiting for the narcotic to work.

It did not take long.

Soon, Blake's eyelids began to flutter, and his head started bobbing ever so slightly. He yawned, interrupted her to tell her to leave, he was tired of her whining, but it was an effort to raise his hand to point to the door. A great dark cloud was descending. He swallowed against it, tried to open his eyes wide to see past, but then the fog wrapped him in a paralyzing cocoon and he slumped in the chair, unconscious.

"Fool," she whispered with a small gurgle of delight. "Did you really think there was only one opening to the passage?"

She had tried the one in the cellar earlier in the evening and found it sealed. But she had anticipated that it would be and was ready with her other plan, which was to surrender at the front door, saying she could find no other way in, then pretend she had come to beg Blake for money. The only opening to the passage on this floor was in Stanton's study, and she had to find a way to get into it without arousing suspicion. Figuring that was where Blake would be, she had been ready with the poppy juice. If he hadn't been drinking and there was no way to drug him, she had been prepared to turn to drastic means as a last resort—like the knife strapped to her leg.

The secret opening in the study, like the one in the room where Jaime slept, was concealed behind a thick panel. No one would ever suspect it existed unless they knew the mission as she did. Touching the pressure point, it slid open easily. All she had to do then was make her way upstairs. If, for some reason, the panel in Jaime's room was blocked, she could enter through any room up there. Morena smiled to think how she had not given away all her secrets.

With a deep sense of relief, she stepped into the darkness. Soon she would have everything that was rightfully hers. Jaime would turn over the map, unable to bear the sight of her father's torture, and Morena would kill them both.

She had not waited two years for nothing, she thought, as she made her way silently. And if Stanton had not turned on her, if he had kept his word to marry her, he would be here to share the victory— instead of feeding the worms.

Finally, she reached Jaime's room. The panel opened effortlessly, but a quick glance about in the moonlight evoked a sharp curse as she saw it was empty.

She clenched her fists and frantically tried to think where Jaime might be. Blake would not sleep long. In a milder dose, the Yahis used the poppy juice to relieve toothaches, so it was not terribly potent. She had given

Blake a strong dose, but only enough to keep him unconscious till she could disappear with Jaime. Of course, she could have poisoned him with something else but had wanted to avoid killing him if possible. After all, with untold riches waiting in the future, Morena was not about to be hanged for murder.

There were secret doors in many of the other rooms, but Morena doubted Jaime would be in any of them. Probably she had gone for a walk. There was nothing to do but wait and hope she returned soon.

Jaime also waited.

The room seemed almost hallowed, eerily aglow from the milky white light pouring through the windows. A little earlier, she had gone out in the hall to listen and make sure all was quiet. Her plan was to go down the back stairway and leave by the rear door toward the greenhouse. She was confident she would not encounter any guards there, because everyone avoided that area since the murder.

Finally, it was time.

Jaime grabbed her satchel, started for the door, and then, with a loud groan, slapped her forehead and uttered an oath. In her excitement, she had forgotten the map and the letters. They were still hidden inside the drape in the other room, but she knew she could not leave without them.

Opening the door slowly, quietly, she let herself out and proceeded to tiptoe down the hall. Reaching the room she had abandoned, she slipped inside without making a sound.

She was halfway across the floor, heading for the window, when the cold steel of the knife pressed against her throat.

She froze, paralyzed by terror as the familiar voice whispered against her ear. "Scream and you die."

The blade pricked her flesh, and she felt a stinging sensation.

"I want the map," Morena said harshly. "I know you have it."

Jaime was afraid to speak with the knife against her vocal cords but managed to choke out the lie. "I don't have it."

"I know you do, but there's no time to argue. You'll tell me where it is later. For now, if you want to live to see your father, you will do as I say and come with me quietly. Make one sound, and the knife will be fresh with your blood when it enters his heart."

Jaime was not about to protest. It was past time for her to leave. Soon Cord would be lighting the fire. As soon as he did, he would head for the cave. Probably, he would get there ahead of them and be waiting.

Everything was going to be all right, she told herself as Morena pushed her inside the secret passage. All she had to do was cooperate with Morena and not let on she was walking into a trap.

Blake lifted his head, which seemed to be weighted down with bricks. His eyes felt as though they were full of sand, and he strained to focus amid the dizziness engulfing. He had not had that much to drink, remembered only being on his third when everything went black, so what had happened?

Morena!

His feet hit the floor with a thud, rocking him with a wave of nausea. The bitch had drugged him.

He glanced about wildly. Where the hell was she and what was she up to? God, it was hard to think, because his brain felt caught in an ever-tightening vise.

Deciding she was probably stealing everything she could get her hands on, he started to reach for the cord to summon Enolita and the guards but then, with a start, noticed something strange about the wall beside him. It looked as though part of the wood had been pulled loose, but closer scrutiny revealed it was actually a sliding panel. "By damn," he breathed aloud, spellbound. "There are secret doors all over the place."

He hesitated only long enough to take the gun from the bottom drawer where his father had always kept it. Then he entered the darkness. He still felt sick, but the fierce desire for revenge fueled him onward. He relished the thought of taking Morena by surprise, and when he got through with her, she would never dare come back, by God.

Groping along, he found a stairway and was about to go up, when, from somewhere below, he heard the sound of footsteps. He headed in that direction, confident he was on her trail.

The stairs wound deeper and deeper into the bowels of the mission. Blake calculated he was below the cellar. Suddenly, he heard a door opening and closing, and, in between, the unmistakable sound of the ocean's roar.

Quickening his step, he bumped into a wall and bounced backward. He turned in all directions, but there was nowhere to go. His hand brushed against a handle, and when he pulled it a door opened. He stepped outside, and it closed with a bang behind him. When he tried to open it, he discovered it had locked from inside.

Just then, water suddenly washed over his feet. He realized with a jolt he was standing inside a pile of rocks, which explained why no one had ever spotted that opening into the mission. Pushing forward, he squeezed himself through the narrow tunnel, fearing any second a giant wave would come rushing in to bury him beneath a wall of salty water.

His trousers were soaked to his waist by the time he waded out and onto the beach. Ahead, in the moonlight, he could see the churning water. The tide was coming in and soon the rocks would be completely submerged. If he had arrived much later, he would not have been able to exit by that door. Morena would have escaped.

But where the hell was she? he wondered desperately as he stomped about in the foam.

At last, he spotted her but gasped in horror to see Jaime was with her. They were leaving the beach, winding their way up the side of the cliff.

He raised the gun to fire it and demand they stop, but held back as he realized Morena had to have a reason for abducting Jaime—and he intended to find out what it was.

He started after them but had not gone far when he saw flames leaping skyward from somewhere on the beach. The Yahis were trying to call up their devils again. He'd had enough of Morena and her people, and once he'd settled with her about Jaime, he'd order the guards to clear out those cliffs once and for all, no matter what it took. But he did not have time to worry about them now.

Morena slowed at the sight of the fire, but only momentarily. She had not known the Indians were planning an altar for Cooksuy this night. She could see them running to gather and shook her head in scorn. She fed their superstitions to control them but never believed in nonsense like a large white serpent rising from the ground, as some swore to have seen.

Ahead of her, Jaime stumbled, and Morena gave her long hair a yank and ordered, "Be careful. The way gets steeper." She pressed the tip of the knife into her back to let her know she was right behind her and still had the weapon.

Jaime had started to worry when they did not see the fire after leaving the mission but was relieved when the flames finally leaped skyward. If Cord was not there ahead of them, he would be there soon.

At last they reached the cave. A torch burned just inside the entrance, and Morena lit another from it to hold aloft as they proceeded within.

The path was wide enough so they could walk side by side. Jaime shivered as invisible fingers of damp and cold wrapped about her. She felt like crying to think her father had been imprisoned in such a miserable place for so long.

They rounded a sharp curve. Morena caught Jaime's arm and gave her a jerk to the side. "Want to see the way to hell?" she asked, grinning. Without waiting for a response, she held up the light so Jaime could see a yawning hole in the floor of the cave. "It drops to an underground pool inside the cliff. There is no escaping. Death is certain. And this is where both you and your father are going if you don't cooperate with me."

"And if we do, you'll let us live, right?" Jaime could not keep the sarcasm from her voice. "We'll walk out of here free as birds, while you go sailing off to dig my father's gold mine."

Morena gave her a shove to set her walking again. "I will let you live in the cage with your father till I have all the gold I need. Then you can go free, because I will be in Mexico living like a queen."

Jaime did not believe a word of what she was saying but decided not to goad her further. It was best to cooperate, say as little as possible, and wait for Cord to arrive.

They had only gone a few more steps when a man called from around the next curve in the hollow voice of someone who has lost all hope. "Who's there? You got food for me? Please, I'm so hungry. . . ."

Jaime did not have time to wonder whether it could really be her father, because Morena cackled shrilly and grabbed her to push her around the bend and cry, "You've got a visitor, Chandler."

Jaime went sprawling to the rock floor, scraping her knees but oblivious to the pain as she raised up on her hands to look into a face she could not recognize.

In the eerie light of the flickering torch, she saw his eyes were sunken back in his head. The rest of his face was covered by a beard that trailed halfway down his naked, emaciated chest. His matted hair was almost completely white and hung down his back. He wore only trousers, tattered and torn. His feet were bare.

Bony fingers wrapped around the bars of the cage that held him prisoner. He stared at her, bewildered and confused.

At first, Jaime could not get the words out, and when she could finally speak she did not recognize her own voice as she croaked, "Poppa. It's me. Jaime."

He broke down crying. "Oh, Jaime, girl. It can't be you. But it is. Lordy. I should've known. That hair. Spun gold like your mother's. Oh, Lord, child." His head banged against the bars as sobs racked his wasted body. "I never meant for them to get hold of you."

With an agonized cry, Jaime lunged for him, arms outstretched, but Morena's hand snaked out to grab a handful of her hair and give a painful yank. "Wait. You'll have plenty of time to slobber over each other later. Right now, you've got five minutes to decide to tell me where the map is. Otherwise, we're going to have a little party. We'll start by inviting some of the young Yahi bucks to come and have some fun with you." She gave Jaime a vicious shake, then bared red lips in a gloating smile as she looked at James Chandler. "And you can watch.

"You *will* give it to me," she said confidently, releasing Jaime so she could throw herself against the bars and attempt to embrace her father.

James mustered what strength he had to roar, "You'll kill us anyway, you bitch!"

Morena had started to leave but paused. Lips twitching in a humorless smile, she responded, "That depends on how long you keep me waiting. But remember. There is a difference between dying and begging to die."

After igniting a torch stuck in the wall near the cell to leave them light, Morena made her way farther into the cave. There was a bottle of wine stashed back there, and she badly needed a drink.

As soon as they were alone, James exploded. "Oh, God, girl, why did you come?"

Jaime pressed her fingertips to his face in a loving caress. "I had to. I missed you so. But don't worry. It's going to be all right. Someone is coming to help us."

Hope flared. "Who? Tell me."

"A friend. That's all I have time to tell you now, but he'll be here any minute." She fell silent at the sound of footsteps coming from the cave's entrance and turned to see light approaching. A soft cry of joy escaped her lips as Cord rounded the bend.

He set his torch aside and reached for Jaime as she cried, "Morena is here. I forgot the map and went back to get it, and she was there waiting for me and made me come with her. She doesn't know you're coming."

He released her, did not waste time asking questions. Drawing his gun, he aimed it at the lock on the cage and told Chandler to stand back. "We'll blast you out of here and take off."

He raised his gun to fire, but with a singing swish, a knife shot through the air to strike his hand. With a grunt of pain, he dropped the gun.

Morena dove to retrieve it and motioned him to back against the wall. Jaime rushed to his side, wincing in horror to see the gash the blade had made.

Morena's expression was calm as she mused aloud. "What a pity for you to survive such a fall, only to wind up being killed by your own gun. You really should have stayed out of all this, Cord. Your meddling has cost you your life." With an ominous click, she pulled back the hammer.

Blake had heard voices as he made his way through the cave. He went forward slowly, able to see by the flames of the torch at the entrance, and headed for the light in the distance. Coming around the curving rock, he had but a second to appraise the situation before aiming his gun and firing. He was not an expert shot. In fact, he had little experience at all with guns. He missed, and the bullet ricocheted off the rocks to disappear in echoes of fading whines.

But his effort had not been wasted, for Morena had been caught off guard just long enough when the shot rang out for Cord to make his move. Lunging, he hit her with his shoulder to knock her off the feet, as Jaime scrambled to grab the gun from Morena's hand.

Blake looked on, astonished. Things were happening too fast. He'd not yet had time to grasp the fact that Cord was alive. "H-how did you—" he stammered.

"Don't worry. I'm no ghost. I managed to hit the deep water." Grateful that he could shoot with either hand, Cord used his left one to draw his second gun and fire at the lock, shattering it. He drew Chandler out and into Jaime's waiting arms.

Blake shook his head to clear it, trying to figure it all out. "And that's Jaime's father?"

Cord nodded. "Morena kept him here with the help of the Yahis. I don't think she let your father know exactly where he was, but he knew she had him." He looked at Jaime. "You'd better get going. I'm right behind you. We've got to be headed in the opposite direction before the Yahis get up enough nerve to come see what all the shooting is about."

He looked at Blake. "You coming?"

Blake shook his head. "They won't bother me. They're scared of white men. But make sure they don't see you leaving with Morena's prisoner."

Jaime's lips moved wordlessly. She did not know what to say but felt the need to offer something. If Cord had not survived the fall, Blake would have been responsible for his death, but the fact he was now alive was due to Blake's intervention. "Blake, I—" she began, then faltered.

He sensed what she was feeling. "It's all right. I'm glad I followed you. Maybe it makes up, somehow, for all the misery I caused."

"Thank you," she whispered chokily.

He forced a smile. "At least if you can't think of me with thoughts of love, you won't think of me with regret."

"Never. You'll always be my friend." With her arm about her father, she led him away.

Cord ripped off part of his shirt to wrap around the wound in his hand. He then started after Jaime but paused to turn around and face Blake. "I didn't kill your father." He nodded to Morena, who was crouched on the floor, glaring up at him with hate-filled eyes. "She did."

When they were out of sight, Blake ordered Morena to get to her feet. "He was right," he said tonelessly. "You murdered my father."

She lifted her head with a proud motion. "Of course I did. I wasn't about to be kicked out like garbage. He beat me and cursed me one time too many."

"You will hang," he promised, waving the gun to motion her to start walking. "Only this time, I'm going to let the law do it the right way."

"Will you be there to watch?" she surprised him by asking.

"I wouldn't miss it for the world."

They walked on for a few moments in silence, then Blake could not resist unleashing some of the pain welling inside by tormenting her. "It hurts to hang, you know. Not as bad as garden shears being rammed in your throat, but it hurts. I saw a man hang once. His face turned red, then blue, and his eyes bugged out of his head; then his tongue came out, all black and swollen. People were laughing."

"And with my dying breath, I will laugh at *you.*" They had reached the part of the trail that passed the great gaping hole, but Morena forgot about it as she let her own fury loose. "And others will laugh when I tell how you were so stupid you believed your mother had the guts to kill herself."

Blake felt his blood rushing to his head. "Shut up about my mother. I'm warning you. You're the reason she did it."

"She didn't kill herself, you shit sack." Morena was delighted to tell him at last. "There's a hidden door from the secret passage into her room too. I slipped inside and left a cup of tea by her bed, tea made with mistletoe berries. I poisoned her. And after she was dead, I blew her brains out and put the gun in her hand so everyone would think it was suicide. I was hiding in the wall, trying to keep you from hearing me laughing when you found her."

Incensed beyond reason and completely out of control, Blake hurled himself at her, intending to choke her till she could laugh no more.

Morena was ready for his attack and leaped backward, planning to dart around him and make her escape, for that was why she had goaded him into exploding. It was only when her feet slipped and she felt herself falling that she remembered the danger. Grabbing hold of the edge, she hung precariously by her hands as she begged in panic, "Help me. Please! Don't let me fall."

"I ought to," Blake snarled, reaching out, "but I want you to live to hang, damn you."

He froze, astonished, as she suddenly let go and disappeared down the hole.

It was a long time before the screaming stopped.

And he never did hear the splash when she hit the water.

But then Blake figured it must be a real long drop all the way to hell.

He would have helped her, pulled her out, but for some strange reason, she had decided to end it all. Maybe it was his telling her about how awful it was to hang. He didn't know. He didn't care. All he wanted now was to let the past go and get on with his life.

He turned to go.

The large white serpent Morena had seen rising up from behind him was no longer there.

Epilogue

Jaime sat beside her father's hospital bed, holding his hand and smiling gratefully as the doctor assured them he was going to be all right. "He needs rest. Good food. Lots of care and love."

With a glance at Jaime as he left the room, the doctor knew James Chandler would lack for nothing.

James motioned for Cord to step closer, for he had been standing in the background, not wanting to intrude. "I can't thank you enough. You saved me. Saved my girl."

Cord shook his head. "I couldn't have done it if she hadn't been strong enough to do her part. Like on the wagon train." He felt a warm rush as his eyes met Jaime's.

"Well, it's over." James was beaming. "And as soon as I've got my strength back, I'm going to work my mine, and we'll be rich, darlin'." He squeezed Jaime's hand.

She seized the opportunity to ask something that had needled her all along. "I never wanted to mention it to Stanton, but what I never understood was why he was willing to believe the ore samples you gave him were actually from your mine. I mean, it looked as if you gave him a bogus map, because you didn't really have a mine worth anything. So why was he so convinced you did?"

James stared from her to Cord incredulously. "You mean he told you that's all he ever got from me? A bogus map and a few ore samples?"

"That's right."

He shook his head in disgust. "That liar. I gave him the wrong map, I admit. But having a map, even if he *didn't* know at the time it wasn't worth anything, wasn't enough for him. He wanted more gold. I wound up giving him several thousand dollars in ore. He knew I had to be getting it from my mine. That was proof enough for him, and also partial payment on my debt, but I wasn't worried, 'cause I knew if he hit the mother lode in his mine, and my investment paid off, I'd be well staked to go for my own.

"Only it didn't turn out that way," he said bitterly. "When I started suspecting he'd salted, I told him I wasn't giving him any more. And when I discovered he'd plugged drill holes, I was about to turn him in. Only he got wind of what I was planning.

"And we all know what happened next," he concluded grimly.

Jaime got up, patted his hand, and tucked the sheet beneath his chin. "There's no need to bring back the pain. Besides, the doctor said you should rest. I'll be back later, and we'll talk about where we'll live when you get out of here."

Enthusiastically, he told her, "I've got a shack near my mine. It's not much, but it's good enough till we can do better. And that won't be long, I promise. With his help"—he nodded happily in Cord's direction—"we'll find a way to finance hydraulic mining, and then we'll all be rich."

Jaime kissed the top of his head, feeling uneasy over his optimism that Cord would be around to help. In the three days since they had reached San Francisco, things had been hectic. Cord had gone to the law, and officers had gone with him to Pointe Grande to arrest Morena. They had learned of her death, questioned Blake, and decided the case was closed. Staying at her father's side constantly, she'd had no time alone with Cord, and through it all she had not allowed herself to think about the future.

Now she knew the time had come.

As Cord took her hand and led her from the room, she could tell he had something on his mind by the tight-set expression on his face.

The hospital was situated on a pleasant knoll overlooking San Francisco Bay. They walked out onto the grassy lawn, neither speaking. Jaime wondered if he could hear her heart pounding. She had wondered the same thing so many times in the past when he was near.

They stopped walking.

Cord started to speak, but suddenly Jaime knew

she could not bear to hear him say what would surely break her heart forevermore. Foolish though it was, she had clung to some hope he might love her too, and now she dreaded his pity. Her words tumbled out in a torrent. "Don't pay any attention to my father. Goodness knows, nobody expects you to hang around and work after all you've done. I'll see you're rewarded handsomely when we do make a strike, I promise. But you've had to deal with my problems enough, and I know you've got your own life to live, and—"

"Sunshine," he said with a chuckle, the corners of his mouth turning up in a smile, "you talk too much."

He silenced her with his lips.

They clung together, there on the windswept knoll. And when he could finally tear himself from the kiss, he continued to hold her tightly as he made his confession, "I was afraid to love you, Jaime. I was afraid loving a woman made a man weak. Someday I'll tell you how I came to feel that way, but it's not important now. The important thing is for me to tell you that I love you. I found that out when I jumped off that cliff and thought I was going to die.

"Loving you saved me," he went on to explain, in a voice thick with emotion. "It made me strong, not weak. It enabled me to survive, to propel myself out far enough to reach deep water. And when I finally hit, and the waves closed over me, and my lungs were filling up, and I thought I was surely drowning, it was your face I saw. I knew I had to survive. For you. For the love I feel for you and always will."

"And I love you," she said solemnly, looking up at him through misty, happy tears. "I always have. I always will."

And from that day forward, Jaime and Cord knew they could face and conquer anything that dared stand in the way of their deep and abiding love.

ORCHIDS IN MOONLIGHT by Patricia Hagan

Bestselling author Patricia Hagan weaves a mesmerizing tale set in the untamed West. Determined to leave Kansas and join her father in San Francisco, vivacious Jaime Chandler stowed away on the wagon train led by handsome Cord Austin—a man who didn't want any company. Cord was furious when he discovered her, but by then it was too late to turn back. It was also too late to turn back the passion between them.

TEARS OF JADE by Leigh Riker

Twenty years after Jay Barron was classified as MIA in Vietnam, Quinn Tyler is still haunted by the feeling that he is still alive. When a twist of fate brings her face-to-face with businessman Welles Blackburn, a man who looks like Jay, Quinn is consumed by her need for answers that could put her life back together again, or tear it apart forever.

FIREBRAND by Kathy Lynn Emerson

Her power to see into the past could have cost Ellen Allyn her life if she had not fled London and its superstitious inhabitants in 1632. Only handsome Jamie Mainwaring accepted Ellen's strange ability and appreciated her for herself. But was his love true, or did he simply intend to use her powers to help him find fortune in the New World?

CHARADE by Christina Hamlett

Obsessed with her father's mysterious death, Maggie Price investigates her father's last employer, Derek Channing. From the first day she arrives at Derek's private island fortress in the Puget Sound, Maggie can't deny her powerful attraction to the handsome millionaire. But she is troubled by questions he won't answer, and fears that he has buried something more sinister than she can imagine.

THE TRYSTING MOON by Deborah Satinwood

She was an Irish patriot whose heart beat for justice during the reign of George III. Never did Lark Ballinter dream that it would beat even faster for an enemy to her cause—the golden-haired aristocratic Lord Glassmeade. A powerfully moving tale of love and loyalty.

CONQUERED BY HIS KISS by Donna Valentino

Norman Lady Maria de Courson had to strike a bargain with Saxon warrior Rothgar of Langwald in order to save her brother's newly granted manor from the rebellious villagers. But when their agreement was sweetened by their firelit passion in the frozen forest, they faced a love that held danger for them both.

COMING NEXT MONTH

A SEASON OF ANGELS by Debbie Macomber

From bestselling author Debbie Macomber comes a heartwarming and joyful story of three angels named Mercy, Goodness, and Shirley who must grant three prayers before Christmas. *"A Season of Angels is charming and touching in turns. It would take a real Scrooge not to enjoy this story of three ditsy angels and answered prayers."*—Elizabeth Lowell, bestselling author of *Untamed*.

MY FIRST DUCHESS by Susan Sizemore

Jamie Scott was an impoverished nobleman by day and a masked highwayman by night. With four sisters, a grandmother, and one dowager mother to support, Jamie seized the chance to marry a headstrong duchess with a full purse. Their marriage was one of convenience, until Jamie realized that he had fallen hopelessly in love with his wife. A delightful romp from the author of the award-winning *Wings of the Storm*.

PROMISE ME TOMORROW by Catriona Flynt

Norah Kelly was determined to make a new life for herself as a seamstress in Arizona Territory. When persistent cowboys came courting, Norah's five feet of copper-haired spunk and charm needed some protection. Sheriff Morgan Treyhan offered to marry her, if only to give them both some peace . . . until love stole upon them.

A BAD GIRL'S MONEY by Paula Paul

Alexis Runnels, the black sheep of a wealthy Texas family, joins forces with her father's business rival and finds a passion she doesn't bargain for. A heartrending tale from award-winning author Paula Paul that continues the saga begun in *Sweet Ivy's Gold*.

THE HEART REMEMBERS by Lenore Carroll

The first time Jess and Kip meet is in the 1960s at an Indian reservation in New Mexico. The chemistry is right, but the timing is wrong. Not until twenty-five years later do they realize what their hearts have known all along. A moving story of friendships, memories, and love.

TO LOVE AND TO CHERISH by Anne Hodgson

Dr. John Fauxley, the Earl of Manseth, vowed to protect Brianda Breedon at all costs. She didn't want a protector, but a man who would love and cherish her forever. From the rolling hills of the English countryside, to the glamorous drawing rooms of London, to the tranquil Scottish lochs, a sweeping historical romance that will send hearts soaring.

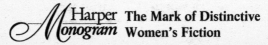

Harper Monogram The Mark of Distinctive Women's Fiction